"Things go terribly wrong for these engrossing charac[...]
Catherine McKenzie's latest tour de force . . . Truly ri[...]"
—MARY KUBICA, *NEW YORK TIMES* BESTSELLING AUTHOR OF
THE GOOD GIRL AND *PRETTY BABY*

FRACTURED

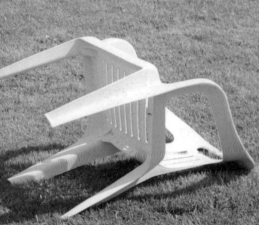

Catherine McKenzie

INTERNATIONAL BESTSELLING AUTHOR OF *HIDDEN*

PRAISE FOR *FRACTURED*

"A contentious past leads a young couple to move thousands of miles from home to an exemplary family community when things go terribly wrong in Catherine McKenzie's latest tour de force, *Fractured*. When tragedy strikes, everyone is a suspect, as McKenzie masterfully weaves together the stories of Julie and John: strangers who become friends, neighbors who become enemies. A tightly drawn narrative that begs the question: How much can we really know about those living closest to us? Truly riveting!"

—Mary Kubica, *New York Times* bestselling author of
The Good Girl and *Pretty Baby*

"After page-turners *Smoke* and *Hidden*, McKenzie is back with another gripping work that explores the limits of trust and the startling intersections of our lives. Tautly written and intricately plotted, *Fractured* will keep readers guessing until the final page."

—Paula Treick DeBoard, author of *The Mourning Hours* and
The Drowning Girls

"Chilling and tense, *Fractured* is one hell of a twisty ride through the hearts and deeds of people who just might feel familiar enough to make us wonder about ourselves. And the punch at the end is everything it should be. A great read!"

—Jamie Mason, author of *Three Graves Full* and *Monday's Lie*

"Suspenseful, insightful, and cleverly structured, Catherine McKenzie's *Fractured* is a page-turning pleasure. I couldn't wait to find out what would happen next."

—Leah Stewart, author of *The Myth of You and Me* and
The New Neighbor

"*Fractured* is a well-crafted, extremely addictive story that kept me turning page after page, eager to put all of the pieces together. When the secrets of Pine Street all click into place, you are left with a highly satisfying conclusion that I promise you'll find yourself pondering long after you read the last page. This is definitely another masterful piece of fiction from one of my favorite authors, Catherine McKenzie."

—Emily Bleeker, bestselling author of *Wreckage*

"Beautifully plotted. Breathlessly paced. *Fractured* is a difficult book to put down. But its insights into love, marriage, and obsession ensure that you'll be thinking about it long after you do. This is Catherine McKenzie at her best."

—Matthew Norman, author of *We're All Damaged* and *Domestic Violets*

"Catherine McKenzie has crafted a tightly wound tale of complex relationships and engrossing psychological suspense. A finely wrought novel of human strength and frailty, cracked marriages and torn friendships, love and jealousy, *Fractured* kept me guessing until the very end."

—A. J. Banner, bestselling author of *The Good Neighbor*

"*Fractured* shatters the cheery facade of a Cincinnati community to expose the dark side of picket fences, block parties, and speed bumps. Think of it as a welcome basket with a ticking bomb inside. This page-turner of a mystery also features a novelist who may or may not be the neighborhood's bad apple. A thrilling achievement!"

—Neil Smith, award-winning author of *Bang Crunch* and *Boo*

FRACTURED

Other Books by Catherine McKenzie

Smoke
Hidden
Spun
Forgotten
Arranged
Spin

FRACTURED

Catherine McKenzie

Published by Lake Union Publishing, Seattle

www.apub.com

Amazon, the Amazon logo, and Lake Union Publishing are trademarks of Amazon.com, Inc., or its affiliates.

ISBN-13: 9781477817940 (hardcover)
ISBN-13: 9781503937826 (paperback)
ISBN-10: 1477817948 (hardcover)
ISBN-10: 1503937828 (paperback)

Cover design by Rex Bonomelli

Printed in the United States of America

For Abigail Koons

Today

John

6:00 a.m.

I'm still not certain what it was that made me begin my daily morning vigil at the front windows.

Something innocuous, I'm sure. That's what I'll say later today, surely, when I'm asked. Whatever the cause, the effect is that it feels like my days have always begun this way. Me in my boxers, coffee mug in hand, staring out the window at the neighbor's house. And that my days always will begin this way, although I know neither is possible.

The coffee in my mug is strong and bitter. A plume of steam rises from it, circling the rim. We haven't turned the heat on yet, so the hardwood floor is cold beneath my bare feet. As I catch a draft from the window that needs caulking and the skin on my arms turns to gooseflesh, I think about how important these moments of silence are to me. The time it takes for me to make a cup of coffee and drink it.

These are the moments I have to consider. To watch. To plan.

A shadow appears to rise and fall across our narrow street. I move the lace curtain aside to get a better look. I've always hated these curtains. Their femininity. The way they don't actually provide the privacy they promise. A wedding gift from my wife's parents. Impossible to say no to. Impossible to tuck away.

The slip of glass I've uncovered reveals only the cracked black pavement beyond my front stoop. It's fall. The few stunted trees that line our street are tinged with red, orange, and gold. Soon, the multicolored leaves will be just another chore for me to complete. Tumbling across the road. Wedging themselves into the gutters. Clogging the street drain. But for now, they dance merrily in the first light, casting an innocent glow over the breaking day.

Innocent.

This day seems innocent; the house across the street does too. I'd never thought a house could be anything but. I still don't, really; only with everything that's happened, it's easier to blame something.

Something inanimate.

Something improbable.

Certainly not myself.

So I blame the narrow house with the dark-yellow clapboards and white trim. The one I watch every morning. I blame its red door and double-hung windows that look back at me, unblinking.

It's easier than blaming myself.

That day—two months ago—began this way too. Me at the window. The coffee in my mug still too hot to drink. Then, later, the awful squeal of tires. The scrunch of metal on bone. The shouts. The tears. The professions of innocence.

There's that word again. One I'd never thought much about before, but is central to my life now.

There's a shuffling noise above me. One of the curtains across the street twitches.

I drop the flimsy fabric from my hand.

Today, of all days, it wouldn't do to be caught looking.

Welcome, Neighbor!

On behalf of the Pine Street Neighborhood Association ("PSNA"), I'd like to welcome you and your family to the neighborhood. We're excited to have you join us and hope you'll love living here as much as we do! Fair warning: we take being good neighbors seriously, but don't be alarmed! It's all in good fun.

I'm tucking this note into one of our custom Welcome Baskets. You'll find the following items enclosed**:

- Our PSNA Welcome Packet, full of information about things to see and do around Cincinnati
- Our PSNA Restaurant Guide, full of peanut-free and gluten-friendly suggestions vetted by our very own residents
- Some healthy snacks to tide you over until you make it to the grocery store
- A contact list for everyone in the PSNA

Please e-mail me (cindyandpaulsutton@ gmail.com) with your contact information as soon as possible. I'll sign you up for our mailing list, so you will start getting our newsletter right away and don't miss any of our amazing social events. If I do say so myself, we know how to rock the party in Mount Adams.

Speaking of social events, our monthly block party is at our house next month. Please join us at Pinehurst (that's #12 Pine Street) on November 1st at 6:00 p.m. sharp! More information about the block parties (including our alcohol policy) can be found in the Welcome Packet.

Again, welcome. We can't wait to get to know you.

Best,

Cindy Sutton, PSNA Chair and Founder, 2009–Present

**Please let me know if you didn't receive *all* of these items.

Eden Park

Julie

Twelve months ago

My first morning in the new house, I rose at the crack of dawn, slipped into the running clothes I'd left at the end of the bed, and let myself out the front door with our German shepherd, Sandy, as quietly as I could.

It was early October. The morning had a fall crispness about it. I pulled at the zipper on my running fleece, bringing the hood up over my head and pushing my bangs out of my eyes. Sandy panted next to me, her breath clouding around her black muzzle.

The houses on our new street were a riot of color. It was why I picked this neighborhood. Its hilly streets and close-together houses reminded me of San Francisco with a touch of Cape Cod thrown in. Set on the slopes of Mount Adams—one of Cincinnati's seven hills— the buildings are tall and narrow, with painted siding or weathered shingles. Below them flows the Ohio River, a happy mix of green and blue. There's a big stone church at the top of the street, hidden treed paths, and a small commercial strip full of pretty red brick shops and restaurants a few blocks away.

I'd never been to Cincinnati before we moved there, which was, I admit, part of its appeal. Moving to an entirely new place, where I had no history, seemed like the right solution to the mess my life had become. I spent weeks studying maps of the area before we moved so I'd know my way around and could start my new life with as few hurdles as possible.

I recited the directions to Eden Park in my head as I ran down the hill. I'd kept the route simple: Parkside to Martin Drive, which would eventually lead me into the Authors Grove.

Or so I hoped.

Those words—"the Authors Grove"—jumped out at me the first time I explored the area online, and I knew immediately I'd make it one of my first stops. I hadn't yet found an adequate explanation of its name, but I imagined a peaceful place, full of inspired light. Or perhaps it contained benches dedicated to Cincinnati authors who wrote about the Ohio River, the seven hills, the city's history. When summer came around again, it might be the right place to sit and think. Or it might be an anomaly on the map, more enticing in the imagination than in reality.

Too many things had turned out like that for me.

There wasn't any formal entrance to the park, just the sudden growth of large, leafy trees, and a sign indicating that's where I was—a plaque on a stone pillar with a gargoyle sitting on top of it. I stopped for a moment to do my warm-up stretches and stave off the edge of fear that had crept into my gut. I reached for the disk that hung from a lanyard around my neck. Both a tracker and a panic button, I wore it as constantly as the step tracker around my wrist. It relayed a signal to a base station in my house and an alarm company in an undisclosed location. Trying to calm my nerves, I went over the commands Sandy and I learned together in training school. *Stay, growl, attack.*

Nobody knows you're here, I told myself as I leaned down into a starter's position, my hands on the cold ground. *Stop making excuses. Get ready to move in three . . . two . . . one . . .*

Go!

I never found the Authors Grove that day, only more hills than I imagined, and the limits of my fitness. Five miles later, I slowed as I reached the beginning of my new street.

We'd come to Cincinnati because it was the first place Daniel got offered a job. I'd insisted we move after Heather Stanhope discovered our address in Tacoma and started visiting it on a regular basis.

Who knows how many times she'd been there before she was found out? Sitting in her car watching me put out the garbage, or eyeing Daniel as he mowed the lawn. Or making it all the way to our front door without knocking, stopping to riffle through our mailbox. What need did a view of the outside of my house fill in her? Why did she keep junk mail with my name on it? Because it was something I *might* touch? All those hours she'd spent, slouched low, trying to be inconspicuous, was she working up the courage to confront me? And if so, for what? Or was she just hoping her mere presence would work its way into my consciousness? And what had led her to finally start leaving traces of herself behind—a series of things she called "presents," but only gave the gift of fear?

There was no way of knowing any of it without asking.

I shuddered and banished the thought.

Heather Stanhope will not ruin my life.

That sentence had become a daily affirmation, said as often as my OCD-inclined husband washed his hands. It left me feeling as raw as his winter skin.

I heard footfalls behind me. A tall man in running clothes. I saw no more of him with my quick glance. My brick-red front door was five, four, three, two, one driveway away. When I stopped, Sandy was looking at me, waiting for my signal, a snarl in her throat. I stood by the large black-and-green garbage and recycling bins that got picked up weekly on a day I had yet to learn. The man behind me turned right onto his own stoop. His house was similar to mine—a turn-of-the-century-size building with several modern additions built over the garage and out the back. It had light-blue siding, black paint around the windows, and a shiny black front door.

He gave me a small wave. "You one of the Prentices?" he asked. "Julie, I'm guessing?"

My shoulders tensed. *Growl*, I thought, flexing my hand to get ready to give Sandy the sign that would send her bounding toward his throat.

"You guys were in the last neighborhood-association newsletter," he said, as if he could sense my unease. "I'm not stalking you or anything."

I forced a laugh and tried not to flinch at the word "stalking." "Of course not."

We left our front stoops and met in the middle of the street. I signaled Sandy to stay where she was. Despite the run, I was too jumpy. The last thing I needed was to draw attention to myself on my first day by having my dog attack a total stranger.

"I'm John Dunbar," he said in a pleasant voice, a bit drawn out. I didn't know enough yet to determine whether this was the local accent or something particular to him. He started to reach out his hand, then stopped. "Four miles makes for a pretty sweaty handshake."

"Five miles for me," I said, with some pride. Two years before, still carrying the weight I'd gained while pregnant with the twins, I hadn't been able to run around the block. "Or at least I think it was. With all those twists and turns in the park, it's hard to tell. Anyway, I can take it."

His grip was warm and steady, and I tried to match its strength with my own. I focused on his face. Brown eyes, graying blond hair—from what I could see of it under his running cap—the kind of skin that would burn if left too long in the sun. Rugged.

"I like a strong shake in a woman," he said.

"So do I."

"Ha. Well. Another thing we have in common."

"We have things in common?"

"There's the running, obviously."

"Oh, right." I felt flustered and looked down at the pavement. We were wearing his-and-her versions of the same Asics running shoe. "Look," I said, wiggling my toes so my shoes moved up and down. "We match."

"Weird."

"I'll say. These are my husband's running shoes."

"Funny."

"You think I'm joking."

He frowned. "I—"

"I was. I was joking."

"Ah. Not completely in sync, then."

"I guess not."

A creaking bike rounded the corner onto our street. A teenage boy was struggling up the hill with a heavy bag slung over his shoulder. He reached in and tossed a paper at the first house.

I turned toward my driveway. "Stay, Sandy," I said in my best command voice.

"Should I warn him?"

"He'll be fine. But, wow, a newspaper boy. I haven't seen one of those in years. Do people still read the paper?"

"They do. How else would we know whose cat got stuck in what tree?"

"Local paper?"

"Local paper," he agreed.

The bike squeaked closer. I could hear the *thump* of newsprint landing against the house one door over.

We watched the boy pedal toward us. He was tall and thin and had that straw-colored hair you usually only see on young children.

He applied his brakes and stopped inches from John, who didn't flinch.

"Aw, man. Thought I'd get you that time."

John ruffled the top of his head.

"Julie, this is my son, Chris. Chris, this is one of our new neighbors, Mrs. Prentice."

"Hey."

"Forgive him. That's teenager for 'Nice to meet you, Mrs. Prentice.'"

"Don't worry about it. I've got two of my own who think they're already teenagers. And nobody calls me Mrs. Prentice. It's just Julie, or, if you insist on formality, Ms. Apple."

"Apple like the fruit?" Chris asked.

I felt a nervous prickle at the back of my neck. I hadn't meant to use my maiden name. It was another thing I was supposed to have left behind in Tacoma, along with the horrible weather.

"Chris!"

I forced out a laugh. "You think that's the first time I've gotten a raised eyebrow with that last name? They still doing that 'Banana Fana Fo Fana' thing in school these days, Chris?"

"Apple, Apple, bo-bapple, Banana-fana fo-fapple—"

"That'll do, young man." John fake-covered Chris's mouth. His voice wasn't quite as deep as his father's, but seemed midway to getting there. I guessed that he was about fourteen or fifteen years old.

He ducked away. "Da-ad."

Chris wheeled his bike to the side of the house and dropped it in front of the garage.

"He never puts that thing away," John said. "I keep telling him someone's going to run over it someday."

"Isn't that how things have been for time immemorial? Nothing changes."

"Except for the Tinder thing."

"I should know what that is, right?"

"Please. I don't even know what that is. I look words up on the Internet and throw them into conversations randomly so my kids think I know what they're up to."

"How's that working for you?"

He crossed the fingers on both hands and raised them to shoulder height. "No pregnant girlfriends yet."

"Nice."

The church bells went off—a deep, booming gong. I looked at my watch. It was 7:00 a.m.

"Hell," I said. "I should scatter."

"Right. Me, too. It was nice meeting you."

"You, too."

We stood there a moment even though we'd said good-bye.

No, you hang up, I thought, and turned to leave before he could see me blush.

I trotted the few steps to my front door and placed my thumb on the keypad to unlock it. I'd made a special trip out a few weeks before to make sure the locksmith had installed it properly. He clearly thought I was insane, but security wasn't something I fooled around with.

"I really enjoyed your book, by the way," John called after me as I eased the door open.

My shoulders rose to meet my ears.

Please don't ask if it's based on me, please don't ask if it's based on—

"You must have quite an imagination."

I turned and smiled. "Why, thank you, neighbor."

Sam and Melissa were waiting for me inside the door, still in their footy pajamas. They were six years old that fall, identical as two children of the opposite sex could be: dark-brown hair, big brown eyes fringed with long lashes, and creamy skin that tanned, even though I lathered them in SPF 75 and made them wear sun shirts whenever they were outside for more than ten minutes.

Melissa leaped into my arms with her usual cry of "Momsy!" before I was fully through the door. Sam clambered onto Sandy, saying "Giddy up!" Sandy gave me a pitiful look.

"Dan! Daniel?"

"In here," he called from the kitchen.

I slung Melly onto my back and walked down the hall. The previous owners had spent a fortune knocking down walls to turn a web of small rooms into an airy sequence of spaces that flowed one into the other: living, dining, kitchen. The walls were painted in a watery palette, blues and grays that combined with the light-oak floors to make it feel like a beach house. Though we'd done the extravagant thing and had the movers pack and unpack us, the house was nowhere near organized. Paintings leaned against the walls, there were empty boxes everywhere, and I was pretty certain most of the furniture would end up in a different place from where the movers had left it, even though they'd followed the plan I'd left for them to a *T*.

The kitchen was what sold me on the house. It had a mix of white and dark cabinets, and the entire back wall was made up of windows that overlooked a large deck with a fantastic view of the Ohio River. It was going to be a "bitch to heat," as Daniel said, but for someone who spent most of her waking hours indoors, good light was everything to me. Especially after living in the Pacific Northwest for ten years. Tacoma has more than two hundred cloudy days on average, enough to make anyone reach for a sunlamp. Or an SSRI.

"Are we really going to be late on the first day?" I asked Daniel, who was looping his tie through his shirt collar as he watched himself in the reflection of the microwave. He'd had a haircut, which came out a tad too short. His red hair was starting to thin at the crown, but I hadn't worked up the courage to ask him if he'd noticed. Daniel was that rare exception: a good-looking redheaded man. His skin tanned where it should've burned. A smattering of freckles set off his gray eyes. His beard was just the right length between scruff and in need of a trim. I'd hoped at least one of the twins would take after him, but instead they were carbon copies of me.

"Why would today be any different?" He finished the knot on his tie, securing it in place.

"One can always hope."

"Well, if you hadn't been outside flirting for so long . . ."

"What? I—"

He grinned and planted a kiss on my forehead. "Relax, honey. A little harmless flirting is what keeps life interesting."

Quiet descended on the house an hour later as the church bell sounded out once again. I watched Daniel drive away with the kids securely in the backseat of our sedan—no SUVs or minivans for us because we'd both had a lifelong hatred of the things—and took a cleansing breath.

I walked through the first floor, picking up the evidence of the daily struggle it was to get the twins out of the house. A pair of Superman Underoos; the infinite pieces of LEGO I was always stepping on; the Pokémon cards Sam announced he wanted two days into kindergarten, which he guarded jealously from his sister, but wasn't responsible enough to put into the plastic sleeves in the binder he'd gotten on their birthday. I could spend my days picking up after them, ferrying them to and fro, tending to their every need.

I had done just that for the first half of their lives, and I might still be doing it if not for The Idea that led to The Book that led to . . . well, it was hard to encapsulate my life after that in two capitalized words.

But all that had happened, and now I was on deadline for Book Two. That one was easy to capitalize, though it didn't quite capture my certain knowledge that it would never measure up to The Book. The Deadline (really, this was such a cheap writer's trick, but one that appealed to me too much, I feared) was a hard-won twelve months away. That meant I had to write 274 words (rounding up) a day to reach the 100,000 words that would make up the manuscript. Which sounded totally doable, ridiculous even, given the fever dream in which I'd written the first one. But with everything, with *life*, it meant I actually had to write 1,000 words a day between the hours of nine and three Monday to Friday, when the twins reappeared and robbed the house of the silence I needed to go to the dark places required to write . . . I didn't know what yet, exactly, which was a large part of the problem.

Everyone's life has its complications.

Sometimes you get to choose them, and sometimes they're thrust upon you.

The trick is knowing which is which.

Birthday Boy
John
Twelve months ago

I woke on the morning of my forty-fifth birthday with a thud.

That's what it felt like, though I was safe in my bed. Like falling in a dream.

My eyes snapped open. I couldn't tell where I was. I felt a moment of panic, then forced myself to think. My life came back to me in bite-size chunks. Home. Bed. Wife. Birthday. Forty-five.

How the fuck did that happen?

I waited for my heart to slow, then checked the time: 5:35 a.m.

Fantastic. I was already waking up at the old-man hour my father always kept.

I knew myself well enough to know there wouldn't be any point in trying to go back to sleep. Instead, I lay there, listening to Hanna breathe. She's always been a perfect sleeper. Lights out minutes after her head hits the pillow. Waking precisely one minute before her alarm. I teased her about it, but I was simply jealous. I was well acquainted with all the hours of the night.

Eventually, I got up. Might as well take advantage of the early hour to do . . . what, exactly? I had no hobbies I could do at that hour. I felt too restless to read. I went to the bathroom to empty my bladder. Did this also come along with forty-five? A shrinking bladder and less and less sleep? I caught sight of myself in the full-length mirror. I'd always prided myself on being fit for my age. But could I still say that?

The mirror told me no.

I went into our closet and looked for my running stuff. I'd had all these plans in the spring to train for a half marathon. Best-laid plans. Set aside.

It was time to take them up again. That, or succumb to the inevitable.

So I suited up, wrote a note for Hanna, and ran into the dawn.

I got back to the house in under an hour. My legs felt rubbery and my shoulders ached. I was as out of shape as I feared. But all that disappeared in the minutes I stood speaking to our new neighbor, Julie. After our conversation, I waited on our front stoop and watched until she disappeared into her house. *A celebrity in our midst,* I thought. Nothing that exciting had happened in Mount Adams since I didn't know when.

Inside, Hanna and the kids were standing in a half circle with we've-planned-something grins on their faces. Hanna was holding a plate. It was covered with the top of our wok.

"Happy birthday, Dad!" Becky and Chris said loudly before breaking into an off-key version of "Happy Birthday."

Hanna lifted the lid. Two sparklers lit up the numbers they were sitting on, above a gooey chocolate cake. Forty-five. Or fifty-four, the way she was holding it. I longed to reach out and turn it around. Instead, I plastered a big grin on my face.

"Cake for breakfast!" Becky said. "Isn't it awesome?"

"It is. Very awesome."

"Can we have it now?"

"Of course," Hanna said.

We trooped to the kitchen. Hanna handed me a knife. Becky and Chris broke into another round of "Happy Birthday," changing the "Happy birthday, dear Da-ad" to "Happy birthday, old ma-an."

Hanna shushed them. "Be nice, kids. Now, John, remember, no talking until you've taken the first bite and made a wish."

I made a zipping sign across my lips. This was one of Hanna's cardinal rules. The Magical Birthday Cake Wish. Apparently, total silence between blowing out the candles (or, in this case, removing the sparklers), cutting a piece, and eating a bite was essential for the wish to work.

I cut a piece and ate a large bite off the fork she handed me.

A long run, and cake for breakfast.

I'd had worse starts to a year.

The kids wolfed down their pieces, then followed Hanna's instructions to get themselves ready for school. We needed to push the day into overdrive. It was already seven thirty. We were all going to be late if we didn't get a move on.

"What's she like?" Hanna asked me in our bathroom a few minutes later. "The new neighbor? Chris said you were talking outside."

She was brushing out her hair and applying makeup simultaneously. I was toweling off from the world's fastest shower. I could already feel my muscles protesting the fact that I hadn't stretched. I didn't know if magic birthday wishes worked, but I made a birthday resolution: regular runs. At least four miles a day.

"She's famous," I said.

"Oh? That wasn't in the newsletter."

A few years ago, our down-the-street neighbor, Cindy Sutton, elected herself head of our neighborhood association and started a weekly newsletter with a few of the other stay-at-home moms. Cindy's heart was in the right place, and she was popular on the street because she was generous with her time, particularly to new mothers. But the first time I'd gotten the newsletter, I'd hit "Unsubscribe" immediately. Unfortunately, Cindy was on to that game. She policed the mailing list like the Neighborhood Watch she soon had going. Within days, Hanna strongly suggested I resubscribe to keep the peace. I caved and read it haphazardly so I could make conversation when I ran into her. Accordingly, I'd read all about the Prentices before they arrived. Daniel was in advertising. Julie stayed at home. Two kids. A dog. From Washington State.

"Don't tell Cindy," I said. "I got the impression Julie wanted it kept to herself."

"Why tell you, then?"

"She didn't. I recognized her."

"Who is it?"

"Julie Apple."

Hanna looked puzzled. My wife is not a fiction reader.

"She wrote that book. *The Murder Game*? You know, the one everyone was talking about a couple of years ago?"

She tapped the side of her head. "I got nothing."

I kissed her. She tasted like a mix of toothpaste and chocolate frosting. She didn't look twenty anymore, her age when we'd started dating, but I actually preferred this version. She was strong, sure, capable, beautiful. I was a lucky man.

"I've always found it amazing how you can remember every detail of your cases, and yet where popular culture is concerned, it might as well have taken place on Mars."

"We haven't landed on Mars yet, have we?"

"Funny."

"I've only got so much RAM up in here," she said, tapping the side of her head again. "I need to save it for the important things."

"Such as?"

"Such as things I should remember to do more often." She was eyeing the towel I was barely holding up. "Not bad for forty-five."

"Oh, yeah?"

"Yeah." She turned her head. "Kids! You better hurry or you're going to miss the bus."

Becky shouted up the stairs. "I thought you were driving us?"

"Not today. Get a move on!"

Hanna took a step toward me, placing her hands on my hips. The towel fell to the ground. We stood silently as we listened to the kids grumbling and shuffling around. The front door opened and closed.

"I have a meeting at nine thirty," I said.

"I guess you're going to be late. Okay?"

"Are you kidding? It's a birthday wish come true."

She started to unbutton her blouse. "See, I told you. Those wishes work."

"I'll never doubt you again."

What's the difference between Googling and stalking? Julie had written in an article a year before she moved across the street. *When do you cross the line from curious to obsessed? From fan to fanatic? Compliment to threat?*

That article propelled Julie from having written a book everyone was talking about to being someone everyone was talking about. I read it that afternoon at work in a down moment. It chilled me. It was a cry for help from someone who was baffled. Who was scared. Who was hoping that by making her struggle public, the woman who was making her life miserable would stop.

She didn't.

Later, as I stood in a line of parents who were shouting encouragement from the sidelines of the Hyde Park soccer field, her words stayed with me. Nothing good had come of that article. Her stalker seemed to receive more sympathy than Julie. The vitriol aimed at Julie in the comments section was the worst kind of misogyny. Calls for rape and dismemberment. Suggestions of book burnings.

I tried to concentrate on Becky's match. The air smelled of wet earth and dying grass. My feet were cold in my leather work shoes. I made a mental note to make sure I had boots in the trunk of my car for the rest of the soccer season.

"Have you signed the online petition yet?" someone next to me asked.

It was Cindy. Behind her stood two of the other moms she usually hung around with, Leslie and Stacey. I waved to them, but they were engrossed in the game. Cindy was wearing a red anorak and a whistle around her neck. She'd been warned that if she blew the whistle one more time she wasn't going to be allowed to attend games. I was fairly certain that wouldn't stop her if anyone came near her fifteen-year-old daughter, Ashley. She and Becky played on the same team despite their two-year age difference. Becky was tall and precocious and loved the sport. Ashley was a halfhearted player forced onto the field by her mother.

"What?" I said.

"The petition," Cindy said. "The one I circulated last week? About installing speed bumps on our block?"

I stared at her blankly. Of all the things I couldn't give a crap about, speed bumps had to be at the top of the list. In fact, I was opposed to them, but I knew better than to voice that opinion.

"I haven't had a chance to look at it yet. Is there, uh, a deadline?"

"Well, no, not per se, but—"

The ref blew his whistle sharply and threw a red flag, then signaled to stop the play. Someone yelled that there was an "injury."

"I think someone's hurt," I said to Cindy.

"What? Oh, is it Ashley? I can't see her . . ."

I tuned her out as I scanned the field. Girls from Becky's team were circled around someone lying on the ground. One of her legs was twisted at a terrible angle, covered in mud to the knee. I couldn't see her head, but bile rose in my throat as I checked the other girls. Not Becky. Not Becky. Not. Becky.

I started running, my shoes sticking in the mud. In the seconds it took to reach her, panic washed through me. I flew to the ground, almost twisting one of my own stiff legs. Becky's face was pale, her blonde pigtails caked with mud.

"Honey, are you okay?"

"Dad?"

I cradled her head in my lap. The damp earth soaked through my pants. "It's going to okay. It'll be okay."

One of the other dads—an EMT who volunteered at games—was examining her leg gently. Our eyes met. He shook his head and pulled out his cell phone. I felt sick to my stomach.

"Dad? What's happening?"

"Nothing, honey. We're going to have to go to the hospital."

"My leg hurts. It really, really hurts."

Her blue eyes were brimming with tears. Her freckles stood out on her pallid skin.

"I know, sweetheart. You're being really brave."

She closed her eyes. She became paler. I took off my jacket and laid it over her torso.

"Is she in shock?" I asked the EMT.

"Likely. The ambulance is two minutes out. They'll stabilize her."

"You hear that, Becks? Two minutes, okay? Just hold on for two minutes."

Her eyelids fluttered. "I'm sorry."

"What are you sorry about?"

"Your birthday surprise."

"I thought that was this morning?"

She shook her head, then winced.

"Hold still. Don't move till the ambulance gets here."

"We had this whole thing planned."

I kissed her forehead. There were beads of sweat on it. My heart was racing. I was having trouble breathing.

Control yourself, I thought. *Control yourself for Becky.*

"I don't need a whole thing."

"Cake," she said. "More cake."

"We'll eat it when we get you home."

She nodded, keeping her eyes shut tight. I held her as tightly as I could until the ambulance arrived. The EMTs moved swiftly across the grass, carrying a spinal board. They lifted her gently onto it after making sure she didn't have a neck injury. We flew across the field to the ambulance. She grimaced as they started the IV, but her features soon relaxed as the siren wailed overhead. I tapped out a text to Hanna, asking her to meet us at the children's hospital on Burnet. Telling her that Becky had broken her leg but that she was okay.

Hanna met us in Emergency, her face stained with tears. Once she saw that Becky was okay, she leaned into my shoulder and wept. Becky was amazing while they set her leg—less badly broken than I thought. She was young, and going to heal quickly, the doctor said. Hanna and I were allowed to stay with her through most of it. We were even the first ones to sign her cast.

When we got home, Chris had added a layer of frosting to my second birthday cake, fashioning a pretty realistic-looking cast. He was being gentle with Becky, too. It was nice to see them getting along, something that hadn't occurred often since they'd become teenagers. I remembered how protective Chris always was of Becky when she was little. "Sister," he used to call her, for years after he could say her name easily.

In bed later that night, Hanna and I marveled at how you never knew, in life, what might happen in a day. We counted ourselves lucky that this was the worst thing that had ever happened to Becky. We'd had friends who'd faced cancer. One who'd lost a child to SIDS. Chris and Becky were healthy and well. If we could survive the next couple years, we could let go of the worst of our fears.

I closed my eyes on the day, feeling both relieved and happy.

The first day of my forty-sixth year. And hopefully the worst.

Best-laid plans.

I woke early again the next morning. I dressed in my running clothes and took my coffee to the window. I drank it as I looked out over the street. At six on the dot, Julie left her house and began her morning run.

I put my coffee down, exited quietly, and ran after her.

Thinking what a difference a day makes.

Today
John
7:00 a.m.

By the time Hanna, Chris, and Becky come downstairs, I'm standing at the stove making pancakes.

"Will you make me a giraffe, Dad?" Becky asks.

At fourteen, she's taller than Hanna now, taking after my side of the family. My sister's five eleven, but "I'm not going to be *that* tall," Becky says on a regular basis. As if saying it enough times will get her bones to stop growing.

She tucks her arms around my middle, pressing her soft cheek into the space between my shoulder blades. Making pancakes is usually my Sunday job. But everything is turned upside down now. Sunday has become Monday. Right down to the syrup waiting to be heated up in the microwave, and the starchy smell of cooking pancakes.

"Course I will, muffin."

I pour the complicated shape into the sizzling pan. It's taken years of practice, but I can now make reasonable facsimiles of most of the animal kingdom out of pancake batter.

"What about you, Han?" I ask. "A nice bumpety rabbit sound good?"

"Ugh," my wife says, rubbing her flat belly like she used to when she was pregnant. "I can't eat."

"Who knows when we'll get lunch, though?"

I think of how testy Hanna can get when she doesn't eat. Combative. The opposite of what we all need her to be today.

What I need her to be.

"Twelve thirty," Chris says.

He's sitting at the glass kitchen table, reading the newspaper he used to deliver, before.

Before.

After.

Our life is split down the middle now. The Dunbar Family Fault Line.

"What's that?"

"They break for lunch at twelve thirty."

I look at my son. At just-turned-sixteen, his hair is as blond as when he was a baby. Sitting there in the first suit he's ever owned, he reminds me of myself when I was interviewing for jobs after college. When I put on my own suit, someone will say, the way they always do, how much we look alike. How easily it could be to get us confused, from a distance.

Up close, the differences are more noticeable. The scar across his left cheek. Our weight. Chris has always been slim. But in the last few months he's lost the ground he gained training for baseball last summer. Undressed, he looks like one of those skinny men in the comic books my father saved from his childhood. The ones getting sand kicked in their faces.

God knows what will happen if we aren't around to look after him.

"We should all definitely eat, then," I say as lightly as I can.

He shrugs. Hanna watches him with that same mix of love and apprehension she's been wearing for two months. As if Chris might act unexpectedly. She's also dressed formally, her light-blonde hair pulled back from her face. She's wearing a black shift dress and a blazer she usually wears for court. Which is, I guess, appropriate, given where we'll be spending our day.

"Watch out, Dad. It's going to burn," Becky says, peering around my side. Her straw-colored hair is a tangled mess. Has it been like that for days and we haven't noticed?

I turn back to the pan and flip Becky's giraffe over just in time.

It breaks in half at the neck.

I try not to see that as a sign.

Close Neighbors Make Good Neighbors

Julie

Eleven months ago

November 1 was a rainy fall day. It was still dark when I woke, and it felt like we might never see the sun again. The house smelled damp, and I wrote a note to remind myself to speak to Daniel about it.

A month after we'd moved in, I was well settled into my routine. When you have an entire day alone in front of you, routine is important.

Every weekday looked something like this: run with Sandy at six, make breakfast by seven thirty, argue the twins into their school clothes by eight, negotiate with Daniel over who was going to do what on the chalkboard schedule I'd painted on the back of the kitchen pantry door by eight thirty. By nine fifteen, I'd be showered and at my desk, positioned in front of the sun-facing windows on the large second-floor landing I'd claimed as my writing space. Then I'd check the little calendar I'd set up, the one that told me what my word count was for the day, with the total goal—100,000—and the number of words already written noted at the top. *That* total wasn't moving upward as fast as it should be; eleven months till my deadline and I only had 7,500 words, 833 short of my goal for October. I had to step it up, and I was counting on my routine to help me get there.

For reasons that still aren't entirely clear to me, part of my routine was that I never talked to our across-the-street-neighbor, John, not after the first morning, no matter how often our paths crossed, and they crossed often. Perhaps it was Daniel's comment about us flirting, but the most I ever did was nod at him when we passed each other on our daily runs. He didn't try to strike up a conversation, either, and after a few weeks, I formed the impression he was actively avoiding me. If I looped right around the park, I'd pass him running in the other direction. We'd acknowledge each other the way all runners do, but neither of us made a move to change course. I could've made the first move, but somehow I never did.

Running used to be a joint activity for me. Back in Tacoma, I ran with my friend Leah, our paces well matched, and our goal—losing the twenty pounds we'd never shed from our pregnancies—the same. We'd talk kids and neighborhood gossip, and in the worst of what happened after The Book came out, she'd listen to me vent with endless patience. All the time alone with my thoughts was new, but not entirely unwelcome. After a mile or two, a steady thrum would begin in my head, one that usually blocked out everything, which was a good thing, on the whole.

It was coming on toward eleven, and I'd written 789 words, which made me happy, though my fingers were feeling numb against the keyboard. We still hadn't figured out the heating—our house was over a hundred years old, and its Victorian builders must've been freezing or sweltering at all times, depending on the season. The previous owners' renovation had revealed prized Rookwood tiles around the fireplace, but hadn't extended to replacing the original cast-iron radiators. Their sighs and creaks often set my heart thumping. I'd heard radiators needed to be bled to work effectively, but there was something so gruesome about the sound of that, I'd left off investigating any further. Instead, I sat in front of my large, silver-rimmed computer screen with a blanket draped across my lap, rubbing my hands together.

I glanced at the timer that sat in the right-hand corner of the screen. In five minutes, the block I'd placed on the Internet would be lifted, and I'd have fifteen minutes to browse.

Fifteen minutes only.

That was what I allowed myself once every two hours, whether it was for research or the abyss that was Facebook.

When the alarm chimed, that's exactly where I went, checking my personal and fan pages for the first time that day. Another limit I'd imposed: I could look at information about myself twice a day, and twice a day only. That sounds so narcissistic, put down in black type like that, but the vanity of it had long been replaced by compulsion. The Internet is the world's biggest cocktail party, anonymity replacing alcohol in the alchemy of gossip, and who doesn't stop to listen if someone uses their name? Only someone a lot stronger than I am.

Working quickly, I posted *Happy Birthdays!* for the eight "friends" whose birthday it was that day. (Why do people take pleasure from someone they don't know wishing them "Happy Birthday" when reminded to? Another one of life's unanswered questions.) Then I checked my fan wall for new posts.

Oh my God, I just finished reading The Murder Game and I can't believe I didn't see that coming! You're my favorite author, ever!

I liked the post and wrote a short *Thank you!* beneath it before perusing the comments.

Your an idiot, some charmer had written. *The ending was obvious. Women don't know how to right.*

My pulse beat in my ears as my eyes ran down the page.

Don't listen to him, Julie! He can't even spell!
If you don't have anything positive to say, why say anything at all?
What's your problem, bitch? Freedom of expression, yo.
Julie, you've got to block this guy!
What kind of misogynistic asshole are you? Go away.

It went on and on, seventy-nine comments in all, all written in the twenty-three minutes since the original post was made.

A knot grew in my stomach. I could smell my own sweat. A while back, I'd read something that described reading negative reviews as a form of cutting. I've never understood what drives people to slice their own flesh, but the analogy struck a chord. I'd built some defenses against this sort of thing in the last couple of years—I'd had to—but I always felt raw and cut open when I came up against the worst of it.

I still couldn't understand what it was about The Book that brought out the vitriol. (Or the positive passion, for that matter, but that was another failing.) I wasn't the only one to suffer such abuse, but it felt personal, nonetheless.

And yet I read the rest of the comments, every single one of them.

I was about to go in search of a cute video about puppies to erase the lingering ache in my heart when a name stopped me cold.

Heather Stanhope was back, and this is what she'd written four minutes earlier.

Julie Apple helped murder my best friend. Fun game, right?

My hand flew to my mouse to delete the post, but before I could get there, the browser shut.

I clicked to open it again, and a red message flashed across my screen.

YOUR BROWSER HAS BEEN CLOSED AS A RESULT OF YOUR MYSANITY SETTINGS. ACCESS WILL BECOME AVAILABLE AGAIN IN TWO HOURS. THANKS FOR USING OUR SERVICE!

I slammed my frozen hand on my desk in frustration, slicing it open on the sharp edge.

Cutting, indeed.

"But how can she be commenting on my page?" I asked my lawyer, Lee Williams, as I paced around my living room with my cell phone pressed to my ear. At $650 an hour, he was supposed to be the best there was in Doxxing Law, a new and expanding area fighting against people who published personal information about others online. The word "doxxing" was one of many I'd had to learn, along with "catfishing" (pretending to be someone online in order to trick them into a relationship), "doxbin" (a sketchy document-sharing website that lets people share personal info, kind of like WikiLeaks for scuzzy ex-boyfriends), and more legal terminology than I'd ever be able to use in fiction.

"We've been through this, Julie." Lee had a surprisingly high voice for someone as tall and wide as he was. The first time I met him, it had been hard not to giggle, but that might also have been the result of the vodka I'd taken to mixing into my morning orange juice at that point in time. "If she creates new e-mail addresses and online profiles, there isn't much we can do other than report her once she writes something and get them blocked."

"Isn't she violating the court order? Can't they put her in jail, or at least cut off her Internet access like they do for pedophiles?"

"The law isn't there yet, I'm sorry to say."

"Well, what about suing her, then?"

"You know my feelings on that matter."

I'd paid enough for him to tell me. *The only day someone's happy they took a defamation suit is the day they file the proceedings,* he'd said with a practiced cadence. Every day afterward would be depositions and investigations and insinuations: everything I'd been trying to avoid in the first place. Plus, the added publicity, all of which I'd stated a million times I was sick of.

And there was also this: truth was a defense.

"You need to find a way to move past this," he said. "Have you given any more thought to canceling your Facebook account?"

I looked out my window and sucked at the cut on my hand, the raw taste of my own blood on my tongue. I was always doing stuff like that—banging into things, grazing myself on sharp edges. A clumsy klutz, Daniel called me, because the redundancy made sense in my case.

John was up on a ladder, his hands in his gutter. The rain was beating down, and he looked soaked to the skin. Water was flowing over the gutter and down the side of his house. There must be a blockage somewhere. What else would bring him outside in a tempest?

"Then she wins," I said.

"There are no winners or losers here."

"Easy for you to say."

He made that clucking sound of disapproval he used when I'd tried his patience. It was a sound that made me feel less than nothing, like my feelings were the product of mass hysteria.

Were these really my only options? Leave social media entirely or learn to put up with being harassed without being able to do anything about it?

I'd already moved across the country; must I disappear completely from view?

"How's the book coming?" he asked.

"It'd be going a lot faster if I didn't have to deal with this shit."

"I'm sure. Shall we leave it at that, then?"

"There's nowhere else to leave it, is there?"

"No, I'm afraid not."

We hung up. I watched John as he fished around in his gutter, then finally came up with a large clot of leaves. Water started gushing from the drain spout. John gave out a whoop I could hear through the rain.

If only my own life could be unclogged so easily.

"Why are we going to this again?" Daniel asked as we walked down our street at the end of the day with the twins running ahead of us.

The rain had finally stopped. Water was still coursing down the street, flowing like a young stream. We were on our way to the monthly block party at the Suttons'. Once a month, our Welcome Packet had advised us, one of the forty houses on our two-block street took a turn hosting the others for a "fun-filled Friday night." *Close neighbors make good neighbors!* was the motto footnoted across all fourteen pages of "Helpful numbers" and "Little-known facts."

I'd met Cindy Sutton a few days after we'd moved in. She'd interrupted me in the middle of rewriting a tense scene that was crucial to setting up Book Two to bring me a large welcome package, including a basket full of "healthy snacks for your kids because *I'm sure* you haven't had time to figure out where the organic section is in Kroger's yet."

I'd taken it from her in semistunned silence, and gotten rid of her by mumbling something about needing to pick my kids up from school. I realized how unsubtle her comment was a few days later when I finally made my way to the grocery store; only someone actively seeking to avoid the organic section could miss it. Later, as I wiped down the twins' orange fingers with heavy-duty wipes—they'd consumed an entire bag of Cheetos—I'd felt guilty. But everything's okay in moderation, I told myself, and made them eat an extra serving of vegetables at dinner.

"Because we're trying to blend in?" I said to Daniel. I'd been the one to suggest we attend, which would not normally have been my thing. But I needed new friends, I'd realized that afternoon after my fruitless conversation with Lee. I needed someone I could vent to when the Heather Stanhopes of the world turned up, without it costing me $650 an hour.

"Did you tell that to them?" Daniel nodded at the twins, who'd insisted on wearing their Halloween costumes to the party. Sam was in full pirate regalia as Jake from *Jake and the Neverland Pirates*. Melly was Merida from *Brave*, her bright-red, curly wig giving her several extra inches in height. They hadn't taken them off since they'd put them on yesterday afternoon to—as admonished by the Welcome Packet—do our trick-or-treating while it was still light out.

Smart neighbors make safe neighbors!

"You know they're going to wear those costumes until Christmas," I said.

We were dressed more casually than the twins, me in a pair of dark skinny jeans with a gray cashmere sweater I'd bought when The Book hit #1, Daniel in jeans and a pullover that made his eyes look a startling shade of blue.

"Likely."

"And blending in has never really been our strong suit."

"That's a fact."

"Am I the only person in the world who hates Halloween?"

"Pretty much."

I swatted Daniel's arm. "Well, why'd you marry me, then?"

"Because you were smoking hot. That sloppy ponytail and those librarian glasses . . ."

We'd met during finals my last year of law school when he'd snuck into the law library to study. He was leaving out the sexy sweatpants I was also wearing, ones I hadn't changed out of in three days.

"Where'd those glasses get to, anyway?" Daniel asked.

"They got lost two moves ago."

"Pity."

He leaned in for a kiss, his beard tickling my face.

"Mommy, Mommy, do it, do it!" Melly stopped us before the kiss began, tugging on my hand. Sam wedged in and made a bridge between her and Daniel.

Daniel and I smiled at each other across their costumed heads.

We spoke together. "Ready to swing, kids?"

"Yes!"

We pulled our arms back, and they readied themselves with glee.

"Oh, thank you," Cindy Sutton said, taking the bottle of Malbec from Daniel with a note of apprehension. Her house was one of two Cape Codders on the street, finished in bleached cedar shingles. Pretty in a faded-cheerleader kind of way, Cindy probably weighed ten pounds more than she was comfortable with, extra weight only a woman would notice. She lowered her voice. "You know this is a *nondrinking event,* right?"

"Of course, of course," Daniel said, using his boardroom charm. "This is for after everyone leaves."

He smiled broadly and gave her a slight nudge, a combination that almost never failed to bring out a flutter in any woman between eighteen and eighty.

Cindy was no exception.

"I'll just beetle this off to the kitchen, then," she said, a flush on her cheeks. "Wouldn't want anyone to get the wrong idea!"

"How could anyone get the wrong idea?" Daniel asked me after she'd left and the twins had scampered off in the direction of the squeals issuing from the basement. "I thought the whole purpose of a block party was that you could walk home safely after drinking one too many?"

"Apparently not."

"Was this nondrinking aspect in that packet thingy?"

"Maybe?"

"We are *never* coming to one of these again."

"Come on, babe."

"Okay, then, next time I'm bringing a flask."

"That's the spirit."

I searched the room for a familiar face, feeling that same anxiety I always did in a room full of strangers. Daniel was a born salesman; alcohol or no, he would make three lifelong friends by the time the cling film was taken off the crudité platter. But me? Before the twins stole me away from the world, I was a failed lawyer who hadn't found anything to replace what I always thought would be my career. I drifted from job to job, never settling at one thing for more than six months. When I'd gotten pregnant, I was actually working for a temp agency, and that's how my life felt—temporary.

"Julie?"

I blinked a few times and hoped I hadn't been talking out loud. I did that occasionally when I was thinking out a scene. When you live up in your head all day, sometimes it's hard to distinguish what's real from what's imagined.

"Oh, hi, John," I said. He was wearing a dark-blue V-necked sweater and a pair of comfortable-looking cords. He looked different out of his running clothes. Older, perhaps, though not in a bad way. Distinguished. There were laugh lines around his eyes, and a five o'clock shadow across his chin.

I felt a prickle on the back of my neck. No wonder I was running in the other direction.

"You look like you could use this," he said, handing me a blue Solo cup full of pink punch.

"Thanks. It is dry in here."

"This might help with that."

I took a sip and nearly started choking. The punch was heavily spiked with something.

"Am I tasting rum?" I asked.

"Spiced vodka."

"Ah."

"I should've asked first. You do drink, don't you?"

I wondered, briefly, if he'd been reading up on me. My supposed stint in rehab was one of the many rumors circulating about me, even though I'd stopped adding vodka to my orange juice before it became public or a real problem. Though I had to monitor myself, I felt safe enough having a drink or two at a party.

"God, yes," I said to John. "Sorry, I'm feeling spacey today. It's been a weird one."

"Cindy and her no-drinking policy probably don't help."

"How did that happen?"

"It may have had something to do with someone—I'm not saying who, mind you—ending up in a kiddie pool a few years ago at one of these shindigs."

"Oh, well, then."

I caught Daniel's eye across the room and waved him over. I introduced him to John, and Daniel cast me an amused look. He's notoriously unjealous, which is mostly a good thing, but sometimes provokes me.

"Take this," I said to Daniel, handing him my cup. "You and John are of one mind."

Daniel took a healthy swallow.

"Ah, my good man." He took another. "My good man."

"Apparently, John's the reason these parties are nonalcoholic."

"Who, me?"

"It was totally him," a woman said, joining us. She was either a young-looking forty-five or an old-looking thirty-five, which might have made her forty, but I doubted it somehow. "I'm Hanna. This miscreant's wife."

She had the same nearly white-blonde hair and pale-blue eyes as her son, Chris, and that tall, athletic look I'd never achieve, even if I ran a marathon every week. I felt a spark of envy, then dismissed it.

We said our *How-do-you-dos* while Daniel drained the remainder of my drink.

"Hey," I said, when he handed my cup back empty, "that was mine."

"Oops," Hanna said, laughing. "Don't worry. John's got more where that came from."

John stole a glance over his shoulder, then started to pull a flask from his pocket. He was stopped by a bloodcurdling scream emanating from the basement.

"Melly," Daniel and I said together, and started to run.

Good Neighbors Make Safe Neighbors

John

Eleven months ago

Right up until the screaming started, the November block party was the usual dull affair.

When the parties started years ago, they'd taken place in summer. Humid nights laced with beer and barbecue. The air thick with the smell of charcoal and meat. The men would gather in the backyard, slapping at the mosquitoes nibbling on our necks. Our wives would shoo the kids inside to add a layer of "safe" bug repellant to the inch-thick sunscreen they already wore. Steaks would be charred. Vegetable skewers would be blackened. The ice in the cooler would melt the labels off the twelve-packs of beers we'd lugged down the street on our shoulders.

I don't recall when the block parties became monthly. Hanna would. But I do recall when they became deadly—boring, that is.

Two summers ago. Brad Thurgood and I had drunk a few too many. It was inhumanely hot. Work had been a constant press of stress. I didn't know Brad had promised his wife, Susan, that he'd stop drinking. Or that she'd threatened to leave him if he didn't. Sure, Brad drank hard on social occasions. But he was a jovial drunk. As I'd learn later, that was a public facade. Behind closed doors, his joviality turned to nastiness.

We all wear masks. The challenge is keeping them in place.

After dinner and dessert, Brad and I retreated to two lounge chairs around the inflatable kiddie pool with a six-pack. Susan had charged out of the house an hour earlier, her lips white with fury. He'd shrugged and cracked a beer. Told an off-color joke. I admit, I was enjoying the evening despite the drama. Hanna had also left with the kids, tired from a long day in court. She'd encouraged me to stay. But after I'd tripped over a loose paving stone and tumbled into the kiddie pool, even I was ready to acknowledge it was time to call it a night.

I'd sloshed up the street in my still sodden clothes, passing Susan and Brad's house. She was stacking his dresser drawers on the sidewalk. Things didn't look good for Brad. I should've escorted him home, but he'd waved me off. Feeling the anger emanating from Susan, I was glad I'd stayed out of it.

The hangover the next day was painful. I was swearing to myself that I'd take it easier next time when Hanna bounced on the end of the bed—deliberately—to tell me an e-mail had already gone around informing the street of the policy change.

"Our block parties have policies now?" I said, wishing she'd stop acting like the mattress was a rocking chair.

"You can't really be surprised. You've met Cindy, right?"

"Why do we put up with her?"

"Oh, come on. She means well. Besides, she does a lot of good for the neighborhood. You know she does."

"I guess." I turned over. I felt as if I was at sea. "Why don't they just ban me—us—from attending?"

"No way you're getting off that easy."

"I'll have to try harder next time, I guess."

"Not too much harder, I hope. Brad's out for good, I hear."

I told her about the drawers I'd seen Susan placing outside.

"That'll never be us, right?" she asked, frowning. She was dressed in her yoga clothes, an outfit that should've been asexual, but wasn't on Hanna. She took staying in shape as seriously as she did everything else. I admired the results.

"No way," I said. "Why don't you come over here?"

"And do what? Punish you for your transgressions?"

"You could torture me a little."

She laughed, but I knew that laugh. That laugh said *yes*.

"I have to take Becky to soccer in forty minutes."

"Better lock that door quick, then."

Two years later, standing in Cindy's living room, I smiled to myself, caught in the sense memory of that morning with Hanna. Then my smile dropped as I thought about the conversation Hanna and I were going to have to have when the party was over. When I was going to have to tell her I'd been laid off from the IT department at Procter & Gamble after nearly eleven years.

It wasn't personal, they'd said the day before. They were doing another round of cuts. Six hundred jobs this time. Some calculus of time and age and level of responsibility had spat out my name. I was a good employee, not an amazing one.

In some sense I wasn't surprised. That didn't help the goddamn sting, though.

I should've told Hanna straight away, but I couldn't bring myself to. I needed to sit with the information for a bit. And then, earlier that day, I'd meant to tell her when she got home. But she'd had a good day in court, and was keyed up the way she is when she's put a witness in their place. She was chattering around the house, trying to work out her excess energy. Collecting the glasses that seemed to multiply across our house. Stowing them in the dishwasher. She'd given me a kiss, her tongue darting in and out of my mouth quickly. She made a face as she reminded me about the block party. I raised the possibility of skipping it, but Hanna said she wanted to go.

That's when I went in search of the flask.

It was a relic from the days when I was attending a bachelor party every other month. But getting fired when you're forty-five seemed like as good an excuse as any to put it back into use.

Hanna laughed *that* laugh when she saw me filling it.

Yes.

We'd had a few pulls from it on the short walk over. Becky was spending the night at a friend's house—her first sleepover since she'd broken her leg the month before. She was getting the cast off in a few weeks. In the meantime, it had so many overlapping drawings on it that it reminded me of a sleeve of tattoos. We'd have to find a way to keep it for her.

Chris had uncharacteristically darted ahead of us on the way to the Suttons'. He'd quickly disappeared into the basement. I'd given a generous pour from the flask into our punch when Cindy's back was turned. And I was happy to have an excuse to talk to Julie again in a way no one could reproach. Nothing to see here, folks. Just two new neighbors getting to know each other.

Wasn't that the whole purpose of these parties?

Daniel seemed like a good guy. A man after my own mind, as Julie said. This was the person I *should* be getting to know, I told myself.

43

Maybe tomorrow, after I confessed to Hanna, I'd cross the street and ask Daniel if he could come out and play.

So, a standard evening, all in all.

But secret alcohol or no, the party was straight-up dull till the screaming started.

Hanna and I followed Julie and Daniel down the stairs to the basement. The kids were supposed to be under the supervision of Cindy and Paul's oldest daughter, Ashley. I hoped she was more attentive to babysitting than she was on the soccer field.

We found a frozen tableau. Toys scattered everywhere. More kids than I could count. The cushions pulled from the couch to form some kind of fort. The air felt sticky and smelled of buttery popcorn. Ashley was standing next to Julie, looking stricken. They were surprisingly alike. Both petite and curved. Long brown hair that fell in a wave past their shoulders. Julie was holding her wailing daughter to her chest. The bright-red wig of her Halloween costume was clenched tightly in the little girl's pudgy hands.

The other twin, the boy, was standing with his fists at the ready. There were a couple of boys surrounding him. Another girl was lying on the floor, crying.

"What's going on down here?" Cindy asked a bit breathlessly, landing with a *thunk* behind me.

Julie's son took a swipe at one of the boys, making light contact.

"You, you stop that immediately!" Cindy said.

"Sam!" Julie said.

Cindy put her hand on Sam's shoulder. He swung around, looking ready to take her on as well.

"Sam!" Daniel said. "Hands by your sides."

Sam dropped his hands as two red spots formed on his cheeks. Daniel picked him up. He clung to Daniel's neck as he stood next to Julie. They were each holding a child on the opposite side like two parentheses.

"Theys was hurting Melly!" Sam said, then starting sobbing, his fists shaking against Daniel's chest. "She didn't do nothing."

The other children reacted like an angry mob.

"Not true!"

"She did!"

"Her fault!"

The children's voices tumbled over one another's. As the volume increased, I could feel the headache starting right behind my eyes. The flask felt like an unfortunate weight in my pocket.

Cindy spent the next several minutes trying to find out what had happened, but it was virtually impossible. All that seemed clear was that Melly had been in the middle of it. Child after child turned and pointed their finger at her like they were identifying an accused on the stand.

"Daniel," Julie said, after the third girl had done this, loudly enough to be heard over the din.

He must have understood something in her tone. They made their way in unison to the stairs.

"You can't just leave like this," Cindy said. "Not until we know what happened."

Julie turned on her heel at the bottom of the steps. "My daughter's upset and I'm taking her home. You want to play detective to a bunch of unreliable witnesses, you go right ahead."

"She's quite something, isn't she?" Hanna said as we walked home later. Once again, Chris had gone on ahead of us. He was slouching up the street with his hands in his pockets. It turned out he'd been downstairs with Ashley. They'd been tangled together on the couch watching television, keeping half an eye on the kids. I hadn't known anything was going on with them, but Hanna didn't seem surprised.

"Who, Ashley?"

"I meant Julie."

I looked up at the moon. It was big and full, a flashlight beaming onto our street. I thought there was something about Julie, too. But I was 100 percent certain Hanna didn't want to know about my morning bouts at the window. How I waited with my coffee for Julie to leave. Or how I timed my runs to catch a glimpse of her. I'd been asking myself for a month what I was about, but I wasn't waiting long enough to listen to the answers. Something about the whole situation had a power over me. Part of it was her, but there was more to it than that.

Regardless, I was enjoying the feeling too much to unpack it or put it away.

"Why do you say that?" I asked.

Chris reached our front door. He stood there, patting himself down, looking for the keys I knew he'd forgotten because he was always doing that.

"Just how intense she is, I guess."

"Are you forgetting the Peanut Butter Cookie Incident?"

"Are you suggesting *I'm* that intense?"

"I would never be that stupid."

"Uh-huh. I mean, who makes peanut butter cookies these days? Honestly?"

When Chris was ten, someone brought peanut butter cookies to the school's bake sale and didn't identify them properly. Two kids ended up in the hospital with anaphylactic reactions, including Chris. We knew he was allergic, but we'd been told it was mild. Hanna had insisted on carrying an EpiPen at all times just the same. Something I was immensely grateful for as I stabbed it into Chris's thigh while I told him to breathe, breathe, *breathe*! When we knew Chris was going to be okay, Hanna's anger knew no bounds. She and Cindy even launched an "investigation" to try to find the culprit. It was unsuccessful. The only way she was able to calm herself down was to write a detailed Statement of Claim with the "Defendant" left blank. It was tacked to the corkboard in our kitchen until the edges began to curl. As far as I knew, it was still sitting in Hanna's desk drawer, ready to be served the moment the perpetrator was identified.

We stopped in front of our house.

"I'm just saying, if someone was hurting her kid, it stands to reason she'd get protective."

"That Melly kid was the bad one, though," Chris said.

"How would you know?" Hanna asked in a teasing tone. "I thought you were too busy sucking face to notice anything."

"Yuck, Mom. Sucking face? What does that even mean?"

"Is that not what it's called these days?" I asked. "Hooking up, right? Or is it hanging out?"

"Whatever. Anyway, that little girl is evil."

"Christopher!"

"She is, Mom. She was totally goading the other kids to do crap. Ashley had already given her, like, two time-outs."

"So what happened?"

"They were just roughhousing, throwing pillows, stuff like that. But that girl, Melly, she kept making the other girls cry. So Ashley put her in a time-out, and then she'd be let out, and she'd apologize in this sweet way. They'd start playing together again, you know the way little kids do, and then that other girl was yelling, and Melly's brother was there, and then everyone was coming down the stairs."

"Remind me not to hire you as a babysitter," I said, putting the key in the lock and opening the door. Chris scooted into the house, his phone already out of his back pocket.

I hadn't wanted to give him that phone. But he'd saved up the money from his paper route, and Hanna preferred to be able to contact him when she worried. I gave in. You didn't stay married for twenty years without knowing when to do that.

I turned to close the door. Hanna was still on the front step.

"Han? You coming in? It's cold out there."

She was looking across the street at Julie's house.

"What kind of person writes something like that?"

"Like what? *The Murder Game*?"

"Yeah. I read it the other day."

"You did?"

"I had a slow day at work. Anyway, that main character, Meredith, she seemed so passive, and then . . . and she's totally based on Julie, right? They look alike, anyway."

"What the hell are you saying?"

Hanna shivered. "I'm not sure. But something's not right."

Sent: November 1, at 11:28 p.m.

From: Cindy Sutton

To: PSNA mailing list <undisclosed recipients>

Re: Block Party rule amendment

Pine Street Friends!

Effective immediately, all children under 10 who attend our monthly block parties must be accompanied by one—if not both—of their parents at all times. Group babysitting will no longer be provided.

See you all soon!

Cindy Sutton

PSNA Chair and Founder, 2009–present

Today

John

8:00 a.m.

The short drive down to 9th Street is a tense affair.

Hanna, Chris, and I are in my car, a Prius we bought a couple years ago when we had enough optimism to care about our impact on the environment. We'd ended up ordering it in a bluish teal, not the color any of us imagined it would be from the brochure. We'd had a good laugh when we went to pick it up. Becky called it our "ocean car."

Life tip: when a car dealer tries to talk you *out* of a car color, you should take that advice.

Becky wanted to take a ride in the ocean today. Our "no" was emphatic. Instead, she's spending the day at home. Sending her to school seemed a cruel addition to everything we had gone through in the last two months.

We're in the thick of rush hour, crawling along the twisty side streets. A route I picked out years ago to avoid the worst of the traffic.

My hands are tight on the wheel. The seat is too close, though I don't bother adjusting it. Chris was the last one to drive the car. A short drive around the block to see if he could do it. A step I'd both encouraged and dreaded. I'd been happy when it was over.

So, adjusting the seat feels like it would be a slight. A reminder of something he should've done differently.

He's had more than enough of that.

The sky is a slate gray, thick with the rain that's predicted for later. The air around us feels dense. Full of thoughts we don't express. Sighs we expel. Like that fug that frosts the windows in the winter. Like we're covered in it too.

My mind is a junkyard of thoughts. The turns are automatic enough that I don't have to concentrate. I wish I could. I wish we could be making jokes like we used to make in the car. Playing "Do You Want To . . . ," our own brand of family fun.

Do you want to be a long-distance truck driver? (Said after passing a transport truck.)

Do you want to be a bank robber? (Said after a top-of-the-hour news story about a bank robbery.)

Do you want to be a . . . whatever mundane topic crossed our paths.

But what's the point? I'd never said yes to one of those questions, not once.

Forty-six years old and I still don't know what I want to be.

There's only an infinite list of what I don't.

Right when I can't stand the silence anymore, I find a parking space in front of the building. I have a momentary wish to yell "Costanza!"—another joke between Hanna and me, based on that *Seinfeld* episode where George gets the perfect parking place. A completely inappropriate thought for today. Crowding in with all the others.

The Cincinnati City Prosecutor's Office is located in an older building on East 9th Street made of chiseled gray stones accented by brick-colored ones. If it was designed to be imposing, it succeeds with me. I can only imagine what Hanna and Chris are feeling.

We sit in the car for a moment after I turn off the engine. Our lawyer, Alicia Garson, is standing a few feet away on the sidewalk next to a trolley stacked with banker's boxes. She's fiddling with the bungee cord that holds the boxes in place. Even from here she looks nervous. I count the boxes again. How has this case gotten so much paper associated with it, so fast? And given that she's not allowed in the grand jury room with us, why has she brought it all with her?

"I've never been in there, you know," Hanna says. Her chin is trembling. She has the dark circles under her eyes she gets when she hasn't been sleeping. Somehow, I didn't notice them till now.

"In the building?"

"All these years, I've never done a criminal case. I don't even know how to get someone out of jail. If they hadn't let us surrender voluntarily, I wouldn't have known what to do."

She starts to cry.

I thought the time for tears was over. That's what she told me when we learned they were taking the case to a grand jury. That at the end of it there could be an indictment.

We had to get serious, she said. We had to be resolute. As if it was the waiting for the next step that was the thing to mourn. Not the loss itself.

But here she is crying, and I'm not sure what to do. Chris is in the backseat, his suit already rumpled by the ten-minute drive. If things were normal, I'd take her in my arms and hold her until the tears went away. But my seat belt's in the way, and our lawyer's looking at us expectantly. There are journalists gathered by the front doors. Waiting for us, most likely. One of them could snap a photograph that will end up on the front cover of the *Cincinnati Enquirer*.

Family in Crisis.
Tears Come Too Late.

Guilty Tears?

Julie would do a better job at captioning our crisis.

I unclip my seat belt and reach across the bucket seat as it zings into place.

"The problem with the Costanza," I say, "is that it sometimes gets you to your location sooner than you accounted for."

Hanna looks right into me, the way only she has ever done.

"Is *that* the problem?"

"It is," I say. "It really is."

Christmas Cake
Julie

Ten months ago

Sometimes a cake is just a cake.

That's what Daniel told me that snowy night at the beginning of December. I'd complained to him about the rock-hard Christmas cake I'd found on our front porch that afternoon when I'd taken Sandy out for her walk.

"It's probably one of those 'Good neighbors make good friends' kind of things, Jules," he said to me in the kitchen. We were making stir-fried rice with everything in the fridge that was about to reach the end of its life. We did this once a week. It was how most of the vegetables in our house got eaten. "What about this broccoli? Do you remember when you bought it?"

"It's fine," I said. "Toss it over. And I don't think so—remember that terrible snack basket Cindy left us? I tried to give the twins one of the granola bars, and Sam almost broke a tooth. Anyway, we've been here for two months. The Welcome Wagon's done. Thank God."

He lobbed me the broccoli and I started cutting it up.

Daniel shook a carrot to check its limpness. It flopped easily. He tossed it in the trash. "Are you sure? Have you checked the fine print in the rule book?"

Daniel was teasing me, I knew, but he also should've known how I'd react when something unexpected turned up on our doorstep.

Heather used to leave things for me. Notes. Photographs. Even a stray sock once—laundered, but still, who does that?—but also, baked goods. The twins had plowed their way through two chocolate cupcakes each before I realized Daniel hadn't brought them home as a treat. I called poison control, but the woman on the phone told me, in a reproachful voice, that no, they could *not* pump the stomachs of two five-year-olds, not unless I was 100 percent certain they'd ingested poison. She said to watch them carefully and, if they showed signs of anything, to bring them to the ER.

Sam threw up in the middle of the night, but then he also admitted that he'd eaten three cupcakes, leaving only one for his sister. I spent a sleepless night composing vitriolic e-mails to Heather, which I knew I'd never send, and talking myself into finally bringing proceedings. But when Sam sprang from bed in the morning asking for pancakes, I knew he was fine. And I didn't have any actual proof she'd left the cupcakes. The police didn't find any fingerprints but the kids' on the packaging. She'd grown smart since the sock incident, which had landed her a few hours in jail and a tightening of her restraining order because a passerby had seen her, but nothing more. But that's when I'd first brought up moving to Daniel. A fresh start, I'd called it, excited by the possibility. A new life without any Heather in it.

"All Christmas cakes must be left between the hours of ten and two," I said in a monotone, "wrapped in clear cellophane and clearly identified as nut-free, gluten-free, and dairy-free."

"No way. It doesn't actually . . . oh, ha. Ha, ha, ha."

"I just think it's weird, that's all."

Daniel closed the fridge door and walked over to me. He wrapped his arms around my waist. He smelled freshly laundered, even though it was the end of the day. "Are you worried? You haven't heard anything from her lately, have you?"

"Not since that one Facebook post a month ago."

"Maybe she's moved on to other targets?"

"Do you think that's possibly true?"

I felt guilty about how happy the thought made me.

"One can hope, honey." He rubbed his thumb across a bruise on my forearm. "What happened here?"

I looked down. The bruise was green around the edges. "Not sure. You know I'm always bumping into things."

"My clumsy klutz." His hands moved to my face, winding into my hair.

"No kissing!" Melly yelled from the floor, where she was working on a massive LEGO complex. She'd been saying that off and on since she was three. Mommy and Daddy were not allowed to kiss, never ever. We mostly ignored her.

"How do you think you're going to get a baby brother or sister?" Daniel asked her, releasing me. He bounced over to her, grabbed her by the ankles, and dangled her in the air as she squealed in delight.

"Stop it, Daddy, stop it!"

He put her down, and she immediately requested that he "Do it again! Do it again."

This went on for a few minutes. Her squawks were so loud I didn't notice Sam enter the room until he tugged at the belt loop on my jeans.

"Someone's at the door, Mommy."

"You didn't open it?"

"Course not. *Stranger danger! Stranger danger!*" He started running around Daniel and Melly, the noise now reaching epic proportions.

I left the kitchen and walked to the front door, wondering if someone really was there, and what they must think of the sounds coming from within.

I pressed my thumb to the lock panel. It beeped to let me know it was releasing. When I opened the door, Hanna was standing there in a dark-blue coat. Our front walk was lit up by the motion-sensor perimeter lights, a bright barrage that was intentionally dazzling. The snow swayed down slowly around her. With her blonde hair in a ponytail, no makeup, and a nose red from the cold, she looked only a few years older than her daughter, Becky.

"Hi, Julie. Sorry for dropping by unannounced."

"No, that's fine." We both flinched as one of the twins let out a particularly high-pitched shriek. "You can see why I didn't hear the door."

"You know, sometimes I actually miss those days."

"You don't expect me to believe that, do you?"

"Only if you're really gullible."

We grinned. The common bond of motherhood.

"So, what's up?" I asked.

"I was such a scatterbrain this morning. I realized I didn't leave a card with the cake and—"

"*You* left the Christmas cake?"

"Yes, and . . . I know this sounds stupid, but Cindy's particular about leaving a note with them to let people know they're nut-free, and I have a kid with allergies myself. You were probably wondering who left it. I know I would be."

As happened too often, I wondered whether she'd been checking up on me, if she knew about Heather and all the things she'd left on my doorstep. I told myself I was being paranoid.

Only, what does paranoid mean when everyone *is* talking about you?

"I was wondering, to be honest," I said.

"See, I knew it. Plus, Christmas cake. Who actually likes that stuff, right?"

I laughed. "You want to come in for a second?"

She glanced over her shoulder. All the lights were on in her house. It looked like a miniature home caught in a snow globe.

"I probably shouldn't. Big drama going on at home."

"Oh?"

"Our son, Chris. Have you met?"

"Yes, briefly. He delivers the newspapers in the morning?"

"That's the one. Anyway, he broke up with Ashley, the one who was supposed to be watching the kids at last month's block—"

"Party?" I finished for her. "Aren't kids just awful to one another sometimes?"

I gave Hanna my public-persona smile.

When we'd asked Melly and Sam what had happened that night, Melly broke down in tears and admitted she was saying mean things to the other girls because they didn't want to play with her. But she hadn't shoved anyone, she swore up and down; the girl had tripped on a toy. We'd given them both a stern talking-to and then put it out of our minds.

This wasn't the case for the rest of the neighborhood. At the December block party a few days earlier, which we'd attended in spite of Cindy's e-mail about unaccompanied minors because Daniel insisted we not be cowed, it was clear that what should've been an unremarkable event—a bunch of six-year-olds fighting, good grief—had taken on a life of its own. Cindy had cornered me to ask whether I was "getting help for Melly," and I interrupted not one, but two, conversations that were clearly about me, the room going silent when I entered, the words "that child" quickly hushed.

When I'd told him, Daniel was even more pissed than I was. He was fiercely protective of the twins, and me, too, for that matter.

"And adults," Hanna said. "Adults can be very cruel."

"Agreed."

I felt a moment of kinship with her that I hadn't felt since Leah and I had said good-bye after our last run together. Leah and I had only talked once since I'd left, and exchanged a few errant texts. How had I not felt the loss of that friendship more keenly? We used to talk every day. She knew everything about my life. I was lonely, I realized. I needed to reach out.

"Anyway," Hanna said, "he's kind of heartbroken, poor puppy. I should go."

"Thanks so much for the cake."

"You can toss it in the trash if you want to."

She turned to walk away. I spoke from instinct.

"We should get a coffee sometime. Or a drink?"

She turned back, her scarf wiping across her face. "I'd like that."

Ten days before Christmas, I stood with half-frozen feet at the children's playground in Eden Park. It was next to a lookout over the Ohio River, a sunken circle lined with cedar chips and containing a row of swings and a rock-retaining wall Sam liked to climb. On a clear day, I could see far into Kentucky as I kept half an eye on the twins.

The twins, oblivious to the cold, were swinging on the creaky swings in a way that always made me nervous. They pumped their legs hard and swung so high, heedless of the danger.

That's how you go through life when you're six.

Fearless.

I often wished I could be that way, that I didn't see the dangers hovering around me, my children, my family, that I could throw away the lanyard around my neck and leave my front door unlocked.

A normal life, I thought. *That's what a normal life would look like.*

It was coming up on Christmas break, which would arrive at an unwelcome moment. I'd finally found some momentum in Book Two—23,298 words written, yeah!—and my deadline felt like it might be obtainable. The characters were so clear in my mind that I had to stop writing half an hour early each day so I could be sure I was present enough to focus on the circuitous drive to the twins' school. Two and a half months in Cincinnati and I was still getting lost on the way to Walnut Hills, where their Catholic private school was located.

I'd also learned the hard way when I was writing The Book that if I didn't leave myself some time to transition between the real world and the one in my head, bad things could happen. A seat belt left undone or a failure to check a blind spot. Nothing had ever come of these lapses, thank God, but each time I'd caught myself committing one of them, I was left shaken and sick.

The truth was, I hadn't wanted to be a mother, not when it happened, maybe not ever.

I know that sounds awful, but I had a whole other life planned for myself with Daniel.

After too many aimless years in Tacoma, I'd finally found something like a purpose. We were saving up. When we had enough put aside, we were going to buy a boat and sail the Great Lakes in preparation for doing something more adventurous like the Caribbean or the Med. On the weekends, we'd take out a boat at the Tacoma Yacht Club—Daniel's parents were members—and sail around Point Defiance Park looking for orcas. We'd eat seafood caught off the boat, slathered in garlic and butter, and then we'd make love below deck, moving in time to the sway.

I've made it sound better than it probably was. Memory does that—brightens some things and washes out others. But we had a plan, and that plan changed the day a plus sign appeared on the stick after two minutes of anxious pacing. A plus sign—an unsubtle symbol that meant I was supposed to think something was going to be added to my life, but it didn't feel like that, not at first, and certainly not when I found out I was having twins.

That began to change the moment they started kicking. And when I held them in my arms for the first time and they suckled my breasts and looked up at me with wonder, I pushed the doubt aside and never thought of it again.

They were an addition to my life, the best addition, and this life wasn't better or worse than what I'd imagined, it was just different. It was bigger and smaller and brighter and darker, and I certainly got way less sleep.

But on the days I caught myself behaving erratically, recklessly, putting their lives in danger, I couldn't help but question myself.

Was some subconscious part of me trying to *make* something happen?

Spin my life onto some other track?

"You quit it! You quit it right now or you're going to get a smack!"

My head snapped around in time to catch a hand rising, flashing through the air and landing on the backside of a kid about the twins' age. The sound reached me a moment later, muted because it landed against the boy's hands, already protecting his rear end from what he knew was coming.

I was shocked—not because I hadn't wanted to give the twins a smack now and then when no amount of time-outs would achieve acceptable behavior—but because it was in the park, in public, where anyone could see.

The child was wailing at the woman's feet, yelling, "Mom, you hurt me!"

I had one of those moments where I pull out of myself like I'm watching a movie.

I knew what happened in that movie. One of the shocked and chattering mothers on the other side of the swing set would pull out their phone and make a call. The cops would show up. They would arrest this mother. She would spend the next two years fighting for custody of her children.

I'd seen a whole thing about it on the *Today* show.

But instead, she took three quick, deep breaths and looked up at me as if she knew I was there all along.

"Please tell me you're a bad mother, too," she said.

"I'm the worst."

I convinced the woman—her name was Susan Thurgood, and she lived down the block from us—to wait for me to collect the twins and follow me to the Bow Tie Cafe. I got the kids hot chocolates piled high with whipped cream, and pumpkin-spice chai lattes for us, a concoction I'd discovered a couple of weeks before when I'd needed to get out of the house to clear my head, and ended up stopping at the café because I was freezing. I'd been so delighted with it, I'd actually taken out my phone and posted a picture to Facebook with the caption BEST. DRINK. EVER., thinking, *My publicist will be so pleased.* (And when I checked, hours later, I was pleased, too; 485 Likes and no nasty comments. A miracle.)

The twins and Susan's seven-year-old son, Nicholas, consumed their drinks in relative silence. They were in that lull before the sugar high sets in, a glazed look in their eyes I used to call "crack baby" when the twins were breast-feeding. (Yes, it *is* a miracle my children weren't taken away from me by Children's Services.) Susan, on the other hand, who'd been so composed at the park when I would've been a mess, started crying two sips into her chai.

"I'm so ashamed," she said, dabbing at her eyes with a napkin. She had shoulder-length auburn hair—darker at the roots—and green-gray eyes. I liked how she kept her hair longer than most moms I knew. I hated how often women cut off their hair as soon as they had children, as if it were required to enter the priesthood. Or sisterhood. Or whatever.

"You didn't do anything wrong," I said.

"I did. You know I did. And it isn't the first time . . . ever since I kicked Brad out"—her voice shuddered—"I haven't been able to stop myself from giving Nicholas a spanking when he acts up."

"It's not illegal."

"I know, but I don't believe in it."

"Look, maybe it's not ideal, but . . . how many kids do you have?"

"Three," she said as if she couldn't quite believe it.

"Where are the others?" I was worried we might've left them at the park. It was something I could imagine myself doing.

"At a friend's house."

"Three is a lot to handle on your own." I stole a glance at Nicholas, who was eating the leftover whipped cream in his cup with an index finger. Sam started to reach for Nicholas's cup. I stopped his hand and took a coloring packet out of my bag.

"You can share this," I said sternly to Melly and Sam. "But if you start fighting, we are leaving immediately."

They muttered their *Yes, Mom*s and slipped to the floor.

"It's awful dirty down there," Susan said. "Says the woman who just slapped her kid in public."

"Spanked. Slapped sounds so . . ."

"Criminal?"

"Serious, is what I was going to say." I looked down at the kids. "I told you, I *am* a bad mother. I do not believe in Purell, and the five-second rule in my house is more like ten."

"Five-second rule?"

"You know, if someone drops something on the floor, it's okay to eat it if it's only been there for . . ."

Her face was blank. I started to think this was all a terrible idea.

Then she burst out laughing. "Oh, God, sorry, I couldn't resist. I don't know what's wrong with me today."

"Rough week?"

"Things have been rough ever since . . . do you speak French, by any chance?"

"I do, actually. I went to law school in Montreal. Why?"

"Nicholas's father," she said slowly in perfectly clear French, "is an alcoholic. He wouldn't go to treatment, so that's why I asked him to leave."

"Mon dieu."

"Indeed. But his son doesn't need to know that."

"We're learning French in school," Nicholas said. *"Un, deux, trois, quatre, cinq."*

"That's very good, honey," Susan said, not looking pleased. "Why don't you color on the floor with the twins?"

His face lit up. He looked like he was about to question his good fortune, then thought better of it and slid from his chair.

I told the twins to share. They nodded. Melly gave him a crayon.

"Quelle horreur," Susan said. "I'm going to have to learn a new language so I can speak without being understood."

"Are you saying you actually learned French for that purpose?"

"Pretty much. I knew a bit from high school, but when his older sister was a baby and I was up late at night, I had these language tapes—you know, Berlitz?—and that's how I really learned."

"That's genius."

"You think so? My husband—ex—, Brad, thought it was weird. He doesn't speak French, so all it meant was that I could speak to myself without being understood. And that might be our whole marriage right there, in a nutshell."

"I'm not sure what to say to that."

"Nothing to say, really. Hey, did that girl just take your picture?"

My head whipped around. A woman with her hair tucked up in a baseball cap was hurrying through the exit. Bile rose in my throat.

"Did you see what she looked like?"

"No, sorry, I . . ."

"Can you watch the twins for a second?"

"Sure."

I leaped up, grabbing my phone. I ran out of the coffee shop, looking left then right. I couldn't see her. The street was filled with lunchtime traffic. A gap opened up in the crowd. I thought I saw a baseball cap and started running up the hill.

"Heather! Stop."

People turned to stare as I pushed through the crowd. The woman in the baseball cap was running, too, but I was faster, more determined. I caught her at the crest of the hill and slapped my hand down on her shoulder.

"Hey!" she said, and even before she turned, I knew it wasn't her. Heather's voice was much deeper.

"What the hell, lady?"

She was younger than Heather, too. A teenager who looked nothing like her. Nothing.

"I thought you were someone else."

"Hey, wait. Aren't you that kid's mom? That Melly kid?"

"What, I . . ." It was Ashley. The girl who was supposed to be babysitting at the November block party. The girl who apparently broke John's son's heart. How could I possibly confuse her with Heather? "Were you taking a picture of me back in that coffee shop?"

"Of you? No. The coffee shop."

"Why?"

"It's for an art project. What do you care?"

"Forget it. Sorry."

"What's wrong with you?"

"I said I was sorry."

I turned to walk back down the hill. I heard her mutter, *"Crazy bitch."*

And what could I say?

Because that about summed *me* up right there, in a nutshell.

Password Protected

John

Ten months ago

I've heard that men are supposed to feel emasculated when they lose their jobs.

Breadwinner.

Man of the house.

Blah, blah, blah.

Me? When I got over the sting of being singled out in the first place, I felt joy.

I'd hated my job at P&G for as long as I held it. Basic IT work, adding levels of security to our network. Making sure people weren't downloading porn or trading sexy texts with their office phones. Some of the guys in the department got off on that stuff, acting like they were NSA agents when they were really just gossips and snoops. Things only got interesting the couple times we'd been hacked by competitors looking for new product-development information. But even that had its limits.

How excited can one get about the latest formulation for earth-friendly shampoo?

Hanna was the one who loved her job. Who was anxious to get to work on Mondays. Who didn't mind having to work nights and weekends when she was in trial. She loved puzzles, and that's what her cases were to her. A large puzzle to put together, a piece at a time, until the picture looked like she thought it should. We were lucky, too, that as a partner she made good money and had great health insurance. So the fact that I was unlikely to find another job immediately didn't mean financial ruin.

Once I got past the sticky moment of telling Hanna about it the morning after the block party, I spent the next couple of weeks doing all the shit around the house I'd let accumulate. Cleaning windows and tightening doorknobs. Replacing the burned-out lights in the kitchen that were difficult to reach. I brought Becky to get the cast off her leg, taking her to Graeter's for ice cream after, even though it wasn't ice cream weather. I raked all the leaves, cleaned out the gutters, and gave the lawn one last mow. Before the ground froze, I planted tulip and daffodil bulbs in the garden, something we'd talked about doing for years. Then I scraped the peeling paint off our front door. Sanded it down and repainted it a matte black that set off the shiny new address numbers I screwed into it.

Chris helped me with some of it on weekends and after school. By the time the third week of December rolled around, we'd strung Christmas lights on the front-door frame and wound them through the railing. He helped me pick out a wreath and a tree. The whole family spent an evening placing Christmas ornaments and tinsel on it, while Hanna's favorite Christmas-carol CD played in the background.

But then a funny thing happened. When the tree was done and we stood back to look at it in all its tinseled glory, Hanna said, "I don't think the house has looked this good since we inherited it from Aunt Wilma. There isn't a thing left to do."

She said that, and I felt the joy seep out of my body. Because she was right. There wasn't anything left to do. And now, a whole lot of life stretched out in front of me.

A blank space I had no idea how to fill.

I spent the next two days glued to the Internet. Trying to come up with some kind of job possibility to rid myself of the panic. How did women stay at home with their kids all day? How had Hanna?

I remembered the wild-eyed look she sometimes had when I came home when she was on maternity leave. Especially after Becky was born and she had both of them all day. I thought it was because the kids were running her ragged. She told me, years later, that it was the lack of adult interaction that was really driving her nuts. All those hours with nursery rhymes, and Barney, and primary-colored blocks. She wasn't built for it. She had a sneaking suspicion no woman really was, only no one ever wanted to admit it.

Now I knew how she felt. Yet, on the last day before the Christmas school holidays began, when the kids would be tumbling about the house all day, it felt like the last day of something for me, too. I both hated and craved the solitude being at home afforded me. Like those minutes at the window in the morning: me and my coffee and the view. The solitude was something that belonged only to me. Something rare in a shared life.

Regardless, I kept telling myself, it wasn't going to last for long.

I was in the middle of filling out a job application for a position at another personal-care company when our Wi-Fi went on the fritz. It had been doing that frequently, and I couldn't source the problem. I turned the router off and on, then clicked to connect to a Wi-Fi network. My own wasn't there, but there was one I hadn't seen before, an unsecured one called "50/50." I clicked on it out of curiosity, and it let me access it. I realized pretty quickly it was the Prentices'. A few more keystrokes brought me to their shared hard drive and an unorganized list of documents. The usual mishmash of stuff was there but also, tantalizingly, something called *Book Two*.

Without thinking about what I was doing, I opened it. I got an alert from Word that it was read-only because someone else on the network had it open, but I started reading anyway.

Whoever else had it open would be none the wiser.

"Did you want to come in?" Julie asked me, twenty minutes later. After my conscience kicked in and I closed the document, I'd slung on my coat and loped across the street to tell her that her network wasn't secure. She should do something about it before someone saw something they shouldn't.

Ahem.

"Sure." I stepped across the threshold and put my coat into her waiting hand. Our fingers brushed momentarily. "Your hands are freezing."

"Oh, I've been typing. That always happens. Closing in on thirty thousand words."

"What's that?"

"In the new book. Only seventy thousand to go!"

She rubbed her hands together. She was wearing black yoga pants, a white T-shirt, and a gray cardigan that belted at the waist. Her hair was pulled into a sloppy ponytail. She looked tired, like she'd just woken up from a bad nap.

"So, what's wrong with my network?"

I explained in a bit more detail, leaving out the snooping I'd been doing. Her eyes, which were unfocused since she opened the door, sharpened and then widened in alarm.

"You mean anyone can get into my documents?"

"Yes."

"How is that possible?"

"There's no password on your network, for one, but there are other protections we could put in place."

"But I put a password on it, I'm sure of—damn it."

"What?"

"The twins."

"They took the password off?"

"It must've been one of them."

"That's kind of sophisticated for a six-year-old."

"That's what I'm always thinking, too, but then they do these things . . . I think they're born with that information implanted in them now. At the park the other day I'm sure I heard a kid who was too young to talk say 'Netflix.'"

"Did you want me to fix the problem?"

"Could you? That would be fantastic."

She led me to the stairs and up to the landing. It widened out into an alcove where she'd set up her writing desk so that it looked out on the muddied waters of the Ohio River. It looked black that day, like it might frost over.

"This is a great space," I said. "I've never been upstairs in this house."

The walls were painted a sunny yellow. An herb garden grew in a long, rectangular planter on the window ledge. The air smelled of rosemary. It felt like being outside on a sunny day.

"Yeah, it's worked out." She indicated that I should sit in her desk chair. I did, and then she leaned over me to start to type in her password. "Wait, close your eyes."

"Uh—" Her hand covered my eyes. I could hear her typing a long word, one character at a time. Her hair brushed my cheek. She smelled salty, as if she hadn't quite washed off her morning run.

She took her hand away. "How do you know how to fix this, anyway?"

"I'm an IT guy. Was, I should say. I was laid off recently."

"Oh, no, that's terrible. Or is it? Did you hate your job?"

"I sort of did, yeah. But it also kind of sucks being home all day. The job market isn't great."

She leaned away from me. "I hated my first job."

"You haven't always been a writer?"

"God, no. I worked as a prosecutor for a year after I finished law school. In Montreal."

"Oh, like Meredith in *The Murder Game*."

She flinched. "Well, not exactly like that."

"I didn't mean—"

"No, I know. I'm overly sensitive."

"How'd you end up in Montreal?"

"My mom's Canadian, which meant I could go to a good law school like McGill and pay way less tuition."

"What about Ohio?"

"By way of Tacoma. Daniel's from there. We met at McGill when he was doing his master's. He was supposed to do his PhD after, but he decided he didn't want to be an academic, and I hated practicing law, so we moved to Tacoma." She looked down at the floor. "His parents helped us get on our feet."

"That was nice of them."

"It was. Anyway, should we get on with it?"

I went into her network settings and added a password, a series of letters and numbers that meant nothing to me. I picked up a pen and wrote them down on a scrap of paper.

"You can change this, but I won't remember it."

"Neither will I."

"That's kind of the point. Just keep this paper somewhere safe, but nowhere near your computer."

"That sounds like a recipe for disaster."

"How so?"

"There are no places in this house safe from the twins. In fact, I'm fairly certain that if I deliberately hide something, they find it faster."

"I remember what that's like. Okay, then use a phrase that would only make sense to you. Can you think of something?"

She scrunched up her face. "Got it."

I tapped on the keys again to bring up the change password screen. "Okay," I said. "I'm closing my eyes."

Her hand snaked around my face again. That salty smell. Tap, tap, tap. I could feel myself start to get hard like I used to when I was fourteen. Unbidden.

Before I could remember what I used to do to control myself, she leaned away. I blinked at the screen. A placid view of the ocean stared back at me. I was glad I was wearing a stiff new pair of jeans; they hopefully hid the obvious.

I cleared my throat. "I can put on some extra firewalls if you'd like?"

"Please."

"I'd need to download some software."

"Isn't that what you're not supposed to do? Download stuff from the Internet?"

"This is okay, promise."

"Go ahead, then."

I opened Safari, and her Facebook page loaded. I thought about mentioning the fact that she should sign out of her account every time if she was concerned about security. But I knew how easy it was to get lazy about that kind of stuff. Besides, I, uh, knew from some browsing of her page that she didn't tend to post personal things.

As I typed in the web address for some software I liked, I started talking as a way to try to distract my penis.

"Facebook is a bad privacy risk."

"I know, but I don't post anything I care about, or about where I am or anything."

"They keep changing their privacy settings, though. Like geolocating pictures, for instance. You can turn it off, but then a couple weeks later, you'll find it's back on."

"Geolocating? You mean something that says where a picture was taken?"

"That's right. It's getting pretty specific. The picture you posted from the Bow Tie Cafe last month said you were in Mount Adams."

"The picture I posted from the Bow Tie Cafe?"

What was wrong with me? I was babbling like a fourteen-year-old, too. Only fourteen-year-old me didn't talk to girls. He just stood in the corner giving them intense looks because he thought that was how you got girls interested in you.

"Sorry," I said. "Is that weird? The etiquette of all this online crap is so fucking complicated these days."

"I know. Are you supposed to pretend you didn't see that awkward photo online or . . ." She laughed. "Anyway, that photo was geolocated?"

"It was. Here, look."

I brought us back to Facebook and scrolled down her page to the pumpkin-chai latte picture. Her location was clearly showing next to her name.

"That's not good."

"It's not that big a deal, is it?"

"Well, kind of. I have a stalker."

"Oh, right, I read about . . . ugh, sorry, is that weird?"

She bit her lip. "You read the article I wrote in *Vogue*?"

"I did."

"That was just the tip of the iceberg. Honestly, you wouldn't believe it if I told you. Ha. I used to think it was flattering to have someone stalk you. What was I thinking?"

"Is *that* why you moved here?"

"Partly. Plus, I couldn't take the weather anymore. Anyway, I thought I saw her the other day, but it was only Ashley."

She described what had happened with Ashley on the street.

"Did you really think she'd followed you across the country?"

"Honestly, I wouldn't put anything past her."

I turned back to her screen as the browser closed. A message popped up.

YOUR NEXT WINDOW WILL OPEN IN TWO HOURS. YOUR MYSANITY TEAM.

"What the hell?"

She looked embarrassed. "It's this program I use to keep me from getting lost in the Internet."

"I've heard about those. So, is it saving your sanity?"

"Not as far as I can tell."

Today

John

9:00 a.m.

Alicia—Ms. Garson, to Chris—finds us a table at the nearest coffee shop, takes our orders, and acts more like she's our personal assistant than our chest-tightening, expensive lawyer. It was her suggestion to come here, away from the prying lenses and the hard sidewalk. It's a typical chain. A line of people in suits checking their phones. The tables crowded with young men and women on their laptops. It smells like French roast and heated-up breakfast sandwiches.

I hate these kinds of places.

Hanna's the one who picked Alicia to represent us. She asked around and was told Alicia was the one we wanted. She has a reputation as a wizard who gets things done that no one thought possible.

We could use some magic right about now.

My jury's still out on whether Alicia's magical. But the one time I saw her in court, at the bail hearing, she snapped into focus, stared down the prosecuting attorney, and intimidated the judge into getting what she'd promised us, a bonded release.

I've wondered more than once if the flutter is an act, but I guess it doesn't matter. I'll take flutter if it means this nightmare will end today.

When we're all seated and be-coffeed, Alicia launches into a rapid-fire reminder of how the grand jury system works. Nine citizens are chosen every couple of weeks from registered voters. They hear an outline of the evidence from the principal witnesses, led by the prosecutor. The accused doesn't usually testify. So, based on one side of the story, they decide whether there's sufficient evidence to charge someone with a crime. The standard of proof is low. Their deliberations are secret. No lawyer but the prosecutor is allowed in the room. The jury doesn't even need to be unanimous. If a majority thinks there's probable cause, the result is an indictment. It all sounds like more than what nine strangers should be able to decide on a regular Monday.

"The First Assistant Prosecutor will lay out his case this morning. He'll tell the grand jury what he thinks happened and what he thinks the charges should be. They've asked eight witnesses besides yourselves to be available to testify—"

"So many?" I ask.

"It's not typical. But because of our strategy—because you'll all be testifying today—they aren't taking any chances." She checks them off on her fingers. "The medical examiner, the first officer on the scene, the lead detective, Heather Stanhope—"

"Her?" I can't help interjecting. "What the hell?"

"Who is she?" Chris asks. His tie is loose around his throat, his shirt collar pulling away from his skin. I hear my father's voice telling me to *Straighten up and fly right*. A military man, the way we presented ourselves was his priority.

"She was stalking Julie . . . Mrs. Prentice," I say.

Alicia shakes her head.

Need-to-know basis, she'd told us once. There were certain things we didn't need to be told if we didn't know them already. She said that at our first meeting: if she didn't think it was helpful for us to be aware of something, she reserved the right not to tell us. We could take her condition or leave it. She, on the other hand, needed to know everything. Whether we thought it was relevant or not. All of our secrets, that's what she asked for. No surprises. Surprises, apparently, are what topple plans.

And some ridiculous part of me couldn't help but think: *And all the king's horses and all the king's men couldn't put Humpty together again.*

"John?"

"Yes?"

"Alicia asked you a question twice," Hanna says. She looks disappointed. A look I'm too familiar with, these days.

"Did you remember something?" Alicia asks. "Something important?"

"I don't think so."

"Then what, John?" Hanna says. "Pull yourself together. You've been in dream town all week."

I feel a twinge of anger. Hanna's the one, after all, who was crying in the car not half an hour ago. But she's right. I've been in dream town for a lot longer than that. And look where it's brought us.

It's just that sometimes you can't shake a dream. It clings to you like film.

"What are they doing here together?" Hanna says.

I turn to look. Susan and Brad Thurgood walk past the coffee shop, their eyes cast down, holding on to each other as if waves are trying to rock them out of a lifeboat.

"They were friends," Chris says. "Mrs. Thurgood and Mrs. Prentice. But they had some kind of fight, I think."

Three pairs of adult eyes travel to Chris. We wait for him to say something more.

"What?" he says, shrugging his shoulders. "You're the only ones allowed to know things?"

Pine Street Neighborhood Association Monthly Newsletter

January Edition

Hello Neighbors!

Brrr. It's cold out there! I hope everyone had a wonderful holiday season. Paul, Ashley, Tanner, and I certainly did!

If I may be allowed a humble brag [blushes!], our own Ashley just won a local photography contest! And with her camera phone, too. So, if you see Ashley trying to take your picture, say cheese!

A reminder that our campaign to have TWO speed bumps added to our street is still ongoing! You can sign the petition on our website: www.pinestreet-neighbors.com. In the meantime, please SLOW DOWN! Someone—name available upon request—drove by my house so quickly the other day, their tires were squealing!

Susan Thurgood will be hosting the February block party. If you haven't taken a look at the rules, please pop on over to the website, as there have been further amendments.

For those of you in the book club, this month's read will be *Eligible* by Curtis Sittenfeld (that's the new *Pride & Prejudice*—I am so excited!) But oh my goodness, what did I find when I was book browsing at Joseph-Beth? It turns out we have a famous author hiding among us! Julie (Apple) Prentice is definitely one for keeping secrets!

Stay warm.

Cindy Sutton,

PSNA Chair and Founder, 2009–present

Another Day in Paradise

Julie

Nine months ago

We skipped the January block party—the New Year's Holiday Countdown Extravaganza!—preferring instead to have a quiet evening at home, reminiscing about the crazy times we used to have in Seattle every year when we were young and foolish. We had a good laugh telling each other "Christie Brown" stories about our old friend who always seemed to get lost late at night whenever we spent any time in the city together.

The twins passed out at about ten, exhausted from the *Harry Potter* marathon we'd let them watch—*I want to see the bas-lisk, Mommy,* Sam kept saying, *make him come back!*—and Daniel and I made love illicitly on the couch as the ball dropped on the television, the first time we'd had sex outside of a locked bedroom door in years. I had one too many glasses of champagne and was feeling sexy and restless. A dangerous combination that had, in the past, led to Christie Brown–like trouble. But what could happen there, in safe Ohio, in our fortified house while our neighbors partied sans alcohol down the street?

A loud *smack!* against our window half an hour later disrupted our postcoital slumber, setting off the sensor alarm and bringing the terrified children tumbling down the stairs as I failed once, then twice, to enter the right code into the shrieking keypad. Sam started imitating the noise; Melly had her hands clasped over her ears. Daniel yanked open the front door and rushed outside with his shoes half on, letting the midnight air stream in. When I finally got the alarm to stop, he was standing in the middle of the road, watching the backs of a couple of teenagers as they pelted down the street, their hoots of laughter echoing into the night.

I looked at our front window. There was a large snowball stuck to it. Gummy snow was falling from the dark sky.

"Daniel?"

"It was just a bunch of kids playing a prank."

"What's a prank?" Melly asked, clinging to my leg. Sam was trying to put on his rain boots and do up his coat at the same time.

"A kind of joke," I said. "Sam, stop that. You have to go back to bed. It's really late."

"But I wanna have a snowball fight."

"Good idea, buddy," Daniel said, stooping to scoop up a handful of snow with his bare hands. He was in boxers and a T-shirt, and he was wearing his tennis shoes like they were slippers. He lobbed the snowball at me slowly. It splattered at my feet.

Melly laughed.

"Do it again, Daddy! Do it again!"

"Can we, Mom?" Sam asked. "Please?"

"Please, Momsy?"

"Come on, babe," Daniel said. "It's beautiful out here."

"You guys are crazy."

The twins knew that meant yes, and they vocalized their happiness as I bent down to help Sam finish suiting up, then threw a coat and boots on Melly. I put on my own coat and grabbed Daniel's from its hook. His whole body was shivering so hard I could hear his teeth clacking.

Sam ran to stand by Daniel, handing him his coat.

"Girls against boys!"

"How about Mommy and Daddy against the twins?"

"Grown-ups can't be on the same team!" Sam said.

Melly and I walked into the street. There was only one light on in John and Hanna's house, casting Sam's and Daniel's shadows toward us on the half-covered pavement. I thought I saw one of their curtains flutter. I blinked the heavy snow out of my eyes. The curtains were steady. Daniel beckoned me to him, then nudged Sam toward his sister.

"Unh-uh, no way, no fair," Sam said.

"Haven't you learned yet, kiddo?" Daniel said, aiming a large, soft snowball at Melly. "Life isn't fair."

Of all the things that are strange about having your book published, let alone read, the strangest is happening upon someone who's actually reading it. I'd been told this by other authors, but I didn't quite believe it until it happened to me. And, oddly, given how well The Book had done and how long it had been out, the first time it happened to me was when we were on our way to Mexico, three months after we'd moved to Ohio.

It was a few days after New Year's. We had a layover in LA on the way to Puerto Vallarta. In that big, anonymous airport is where I saw it: a woman intently reading a copy of *The Murder Game* while curled into her seat in the waiting area at our gate. I'd recognize that cover anywhere.

"Oh," I said to Daniel. "Look."

He followed my finger, then smirked at me. We'd been up since four in the morning. Melly had thrown up in the car on the way to the airport, and Sam had been particularly hyper on the flight to LA, but was now looking green.

"Someone's reading The Book," Daniel said. "Oh, my."

I whacked him on the arm. He'd forgotten to get a haircut before we left, and his hair was standing straight up, like a stop sign. "Quit it. I've never seen that before."

"Seriously?"

"Nope."

"Well, all righty, then. Oh, good, four seats together."

He walked toward the seats as the twins followed him. They were each wearing a small backpack full of their books and toys for the plane. Their shoulders were drooping under the weight of their inability to narrow their choices down to reasonable proportions.

I should've followed them. A good mother would have, but instead I stood there, watching the woman for a while longer. She was intent on the page, a slow reader. The copy she was holding looked like it had been read before.

I edged closer, wondering what the etiquette was. Should I ask her what she thought of it? Suggest she might want my autograph? What was I thinking? I didn't like that kind of attention, or so I was always saying. But yet, I would've paid to have been able to crawl inside her brain and watch the words I'd written unfurl through her synapses.

She adjusted the book in her hands. The back-cover copy was angled toward me. I read the words from afar.

Ten years working as a prosecutor has left Meredith Delay jaded and unsure of what she wants out of life. She's good at her job, but it haunts her. Her boyfriend wants her to commit, but she keeps him at arm's length. When she gets assigned to a high-profile prosecution involving the violent murder of a fallen hockey star, it appears at first to be just another case to work. But when her estranged law-school friend, Julian, gets accused of the murder, it takes on a whole new dimension.

Meredith, Julian, Jonathan, and Lily were a tight-knit group in law school. But now, Jonathan's defending Julian, and Lily's loyalties aren't clear. And when Julian invokes a rare—and risky—defense, Meredith is forced to confront their past.

Has something they played at as students finally been brought to death?

I took a few more steps. I was close enough to see that she was in the middle of the chapter where Meredith, Julian, Jonathan, and Lily meet after the verdict is released.

It's the chapter where the reader finds out if a murder occurred.

"I loved that book," I found myself saying.

The woman looked up, puzzled. Was I really talking to her?

"Oh, sorry. I just saw what you were reading and . . ."

She was young, midtwenties. Clear skin, bright-eyed, unbowed, and unlined by anything life had to dish out yet.

"I'm still not sure about it yet," she said in a Midwestern twang. *Su-ur.*

"How come?"

"It's kind of twisted, ain't it? Like, turning murder into a game?"

"It's a thought experiment. You know, to see if they can do it."

"Spoiler alert!"

"Sorry."

She shrugged. "No biggie. Besides, with the movie coming out and everything, it's kind of hard *not* to know what happened."

"Oh, no, the book's much different than the movie."

"How'd you know that?"

"I work in the business," I said, the lie slipping easily through my teeth. "I got to read the script."

That part was true. The Book had been optioned for film, and then greenlit. Someone—not me, though I'd kind of wanted to—had written a script and gotten stars attached. One day last summer before we moved to Cincinnati, I'd spent a day on set. A surreal experience, if ever there was one, like stepping into your imagination and having everyone follow you in. I just hoped, when the movie was finally cut and set loose in the world—we were getting a release date any day now, my agent kept telling me—that they hadn't murdered my book.

"Cool."

"It is cool. Say, what do you think of Meredith?" I asked.

Meredith, the protagonist. The one everyone assumed I'd based on myself, a charge I vehemently denied. But yet, for all my protests, she was the one I felt closest to.

"She's a bit off, isn't she?"

"In what way?"

"Julie," Daniel called. "I could use some help here."

We made eye contact. Sam was crawling on his back. Melly was silently crying.

"I have to go. Nice chatting with you."

"Sure . . ."

I hurried over to my family and spent the next few minutes calming Melly down while Daniel took Sam to the men's room for a bathroom break and a stern talking-to. Given the circumstances, we were probably going to have to break our screen ban and hook them into the iPads for the next flight.

When Melly finally calmed down, I felt a pair of eyes on me. I looked up from where I'd buried my face in her soft hair to find the girl I'd been talking to earlier watching me. She had my book closed on her lap, turned over to the author photo on the back. She glanced down at it deliberately, then back at me, raising her shoulders in a question.

I raised my own to her in response.

That's me, I wanted to say. *But it also isn't.*

Once we'd made it through the gauntlets of immigration, security, and time-share salesmen, the warm air and greenery greeted us like a balm. I closed my eyes and took a deep yoga breath, exhaling slowly.

The resort had sent a private car to pick us up, and just that alone—not having to struggle with luggage and the kids and making sure we weren't being ripped off by the taxi driver—was almost worth the price of admission.

The resort itself was even nicer than the brochure, and the brochure—found in my e-mail one day soon after we'd moved—was what had sold me on the place. As the twins pointed to palm trees and colorful birds, I told myself to be grateful for my life. The Idea, The Book, had changed it completely from one of struggle to one where I could see something I wanted and have it. So much of that change was good—the money, the recognition, the satisfaction I got in those moments when the words flowed out of me in what felt like an effortless stream—that it had to outweigh the bad. There was only one Heather Stanhope, and she was in another country. I'd been wanting to move for a while, and Heather was the perfect excuse. I'd spun a tale to suit my own whims, and not for the first time.

And then there was the simple fact that no one knew where we were. We hadn't even told our families precisely where we were going, mostly out of embarrassment at the cost. I'd actually hidden the total from Daniel, paying more than half of it out of an account he didn't know I had, so it would seem more reasonable.

What was the point of having money if you couldn't enjoy yourself once in a while? I'd said to Daniel time and again over the last two years.

"It's so green," Sam said, before nestling into my chest and plugging his thumb into his mouth.

"Okay, you were right," Daniel said. We were halfway to the semi-private villa we were staying in, on the edge of the massive complex that housed three thousand people at capacity. We were being driven in an oversize golf cart, a child on each of our laps. They'd been numbed into silence from all the travel and the lushness around them.

"Is that just a general statement, or are there particulars attached to it?"

"This," he said, waving his arm around. "This is incredible."

"Right?"

"I just wish . . ."

His thought trailed off, but I could follow it.

He just wished he was the one who could afford to pay for it.

I never thought Daniel would have such traditional thoughts; he didn't, either. But with my lack of drive after I quit the law, and then the twins, we'd fallen into an old pattern where he paid most of the bills. It was hard for me, for a long time, to reconcile his assuming that responsibility with my instincts to pay my own way in the world, but we both got used to it, I guess.

Then my book came out, and that all changed. Suddenly, I had more money than I knew what to do with. Paying-off-the-mortgage money. No-more-student-loan money. Setting-up-the-twins'-college-fund money. Sold in a bidding war. Sold in twenty-five countries. Sold to the movies. Another large sum for Book Two. "Fuck-you money," we called it, because it was easier than discussing the amount. In truth, I'd never even told Daniel how much it was, how much it still was every month. I'd even stopped checking that closely when royalty money from some part of the world arrived in my bank account, or what the amount was, and only vaguely absorbed how much they paid for Book Two, the book I was starting to suspect I might never finish.

The day I got that deal was the day I opened the other bank account, the one he didn't know about—not because I didn't want to share with him, but because I could tell it was all too much. It was too much for anyone, certainly for a penny-pinching DIY couple—we used to make our own pizza and Halloween costumes, for Christ's sake, and even, for a while, cleaning products. So many things can throw off the balance in a marriage, and money was doing that to us. It was easier to deny its existence most of the time than flaunt it or acknowledge its power.

All that being said, I'd wanted this vacation from the first moment the evil airline club I belonged to e-mailed me about it. I needed this vacation: its seclusion, its warmth, its color. And the fact that it was more than the price of the car I drove didn't faze me. I clicked to book it and told Daniel about it afterward.

"You'll get the next one," I said as we pulled up to the white adobe villa. Flowers whose scent I couldn't identify perfumed the air. I couldn't see the ocean yet, but I could sense it, the pull of the tide, the distant echo of waves hitting the shore.

"Run-down cabin by the ocean?" Daniel said.

"Wherever you want."

He smiled and leaned over the heads of our zoned-out children.

"I want you," he said quietly in my ear.

"No kissing!"

Despite the luxurious surroundings—there was actually a personalized butler service available, and a masseuse on call twenty-four hours a day—it took me two full days to relax. Two full days to shake off the lingering feeling I often had when I was away from my laptop that I should be working, putting down words, curating my social media profile, or at least thinking about these things at all times. It was worse than when I was a student. At least then, during summer or at Christmas break, there wasn't anything I could or should be doing. But writing was a job that followed you around everywhere. Bits of dialogue popped into my head at odd moments. A thorny knot of plot unraveled when I should've been listening to Daniel. A weird detachment could overtake me during a real-life moment, a feeling that I had to mentally capture it so I could use it later.

But I had a stack of easy novels to read and enough sunscreen to cover every inch of me. The twins spent their days in Kids' Club, happy as browning clams with their newfound friends. Daniel was content to float on a blow-up bed, reading one of the lengthy histories of England he loved. Our semiprivate infinity pool was quiet and peaceful and close enough to the ocean that the crash of its salty waves acted as a sort of white noise in my brain.

That and the margaritas. I limited myself to two a day (okay, maybe three, it was vacation, after all) and switched to wine at dinner. All this worked its magic on me so that by lunchtime on day three—the bar would start serving alcohol in eight minutes, but who was counting?—I felt a deep sense of peace I hadn't achieved since I didn't know when.

Which is why I felt perfectly safe taking out my laptop, connecting to the resort's Wi-Fi, and opening my author e-mail. As I scanned my in-box, adrenaline slammed the calm out of me. Along with the hundreds of unanswered fan letters (I'd long since given up feeling guilty about not getting to them all), requests for blurbs, and writing advice, there were several flashing red alerts; someone had tried to access my e-mail account from an unusual IP address and location. If it was me, I could ignore the message, but if it wasn't, then I should change my password immediately. I'd received the first message when we were in the air—impossible for it to have been me logging in from Mexico or anywhere else. When I checked, the IP address location was somewhere in British Columbia, but I knew enough from the last time this happened (Heather, who else?) that anyone with simple skills could make it appear as if they were logging in from nearly anywhere.

I couldn't believe this was happening again. Why couldn't she leave me alone? Why couldn't she just disappear?

Why couldn't she just *die*?

And right at the moment when the panic was crashing against my heart like the waves against the shore, the sun was blocked by someone standing above me, and a voice said, "Funny meeting you here."

Trouble in Paradise
John

Nine months ago

Hanna's family is into family vacations. Every couple years, her mother starts sounding the gong. *Wouldn't it be nice to spend some time in . . .* wherever it is that's caught her fancy that year. We're all expected to heed the call. Hanna pretends to hate these trips in solidarity with me. But I know she actually loves them.

In fact, when I told Hanna I'd lost my job, it seemed like the only thing that really bothered her was the possibility that we might not go on the trip.

"It's already paid for," she'd said, and it took me a minute to realize what she was referring to.

"You mean the vacation? Not really. Not entirely."

We'd put down a deposit and bought our tickets during a seat sale the month before. But the real expense, we both knew, would be the meals and drinks and tips during the week itself.

"Don't worry about it," Hanna said. "We can afford it."

And I knew the subject was closed.

It was one of the unwritten rules of our marriage. She had jurisdiction over things to do with her family. I had it over mine. The fact that my own family sought ways to *avoid* being together was my bad luck. All bargains have a losing side.

I put it aside. But in the space between Christmas and New Year's, I worked up my courage and brought it up again. Perhaps we could . . .

"No. Absolutely not," Hanna said. "And no mentioning the fact that you're out of work to my parents while we're there. Mom will be too stressed out. And she'll offer to loan us money."

"Would that be such a bad thing?"

She shot me a look. "You're seriously asking me that?"

She was right. At the beginning of our marriage, we'd borrowed money from her parents to do renovations to the house we'd inherited from my aunt. Although we had a payment schedule and easy terms, we got a reminder phone call from her mother five days before payment was due.

Every single month.

"Hi, kids! Just thinking of you! Oh, and if you were going to be late with the payment this month, let me know, okay? Love you!"

We'd never been late, not once. She always called when she knew we'd be at work and would get our machine. Seeing that blinking red light when I got home on the twenty-fifth of every month was enough to drive anyone crazy. I actually went to a bank to see whether we could take out a mortgage to pay her off immediately. The bank said no, and that was probably a good thing. A better thing happened when I "accidentally" dropped our answering machine and convinced Hanna not to replace it. We made a plan, adjusted our payment schedule to the most we could afford, and paid off the loan as soon as we could. Then we vowed we'd never borrow money from them again.

"Okay," I said. "Okay. We can't borrow money from your parents. But we really shouldn't be going on this vacation."

"I know. But we'll manage. And you'll find something soon, right? Another job."

"Of course I will."

We went.

And as I stood drinking my morning coffee in early January with a view of the ocean, it sunk in that I had no right to complain. We had our own condo. One room for Hanna and me, and one for the kids. The rooms were far enough apart that we could lock the door and make love quietly, something we'd done the previous two nights. The condo even had its own kitchen, which meant we could cook most of our meals and even bring in our own beer. That made the whole thing more manageable financially. The only thing that brought me down was how I was thinking about every dollar, every *peso*, that was going out the door.

I was really going to have to step up my job-search efforts when I got home.

"Hon, can you locate Becky?" Hanna called to me from our balcony, where she was sitting in what was not so charmingly called the "cuddle puddle." Basically a hot tub that was six inches deep, warmed daily by the sun. "I can't see her down there."

Becky had gone down to the pool an hour before with strict promises that she'd stay in view. Chris was off God knows where. But at fifteen, and a boy, different rules applied.

"I'm sure she's fine," I said. "Maybe she went down to the beach."

Hanna lowered her aviators. Her nose was bright red from too much sun on our first day. She was wearing a teal bikini that made me want to untie the knot around her neck.

"Yeah, okay, I'll go."

I grabbed a visor and my room key and went in search of Becky. She'd probably moved to a deck chair out of the sun. Or maybe she was in the bathroom. Hanna wasn't usually overprotective, not compared to the other moms. But she'd been reading about some kidnappings in the area before we left. She always researched wherever we went for a couple weeks beforehand. Usually, it was a blessing. But every once in a while, she'd fall into a wormhole of abstract facts, and we all felt the consequences.

It was nearing noon. The air outside our perfectly air-conditioned condo felt hot and heavy. I was glad I had my swimming trunks on. When I found Becky, I'd throw her in the pool and jump in after her. That always made her laugh.

I spotted her in a shady corner, lying under two towels. The only thing visible was the hand holding her book.

"Becks, your mom was worried."

The girl lowered her book. It wasn't Becky.

"Oh, sorry, I thought you were my daughter."

She raised her book, but not before she gave me a look that made me feel like I was a perv.

I walked among the deck chairs, a hint of alarm working its way into my bloodstream. Not Becky, not Becky, not Becky. How many times was I going to have to take that kind of inventory? Where was that girl?

When I'd checked every deck chair twice, I followed the concrete path down to the ocean. A group of teenagers were playing volleyball on the beach. Chris was among them, his shirt off, his shoulders red under the white film of sunscreen Hanna had applied before he left.

But no Becky.

"Hey, Chris!"

He caught my eye, then threw a look at the girl standing next to him. She was wearing a bright-red bikini that was more revealing than anything we'd ever let Becky wear. Her strawberry hair was a straight curtain down her back. Ashley and Chris had seemed to reconcile at the New Year's Eve block party, but maybe not.

"Chris!"

He jogged over. "What's up?"

"Have you seen Becky?"

"She was playing with us."

"Was? When?"

He shrugged. "Dunno."

"Well, do you know where she's gone?"

"Down the beach, I think."

"Alone?"

"Maybe she was with that Parker guy?"

My hands formed into fists. "What Parker guy?"

He shrugged again. I felt an uncharacteristic wish to throttle him.

"When did she go off with this guy? And do not shrug again, Chris. I swear to God."

"Man, sorry, Dad. It wasn't that long ago. Like ten minutes, maybe?"

"Which direction?"

He pointed down the beach.

I squinted into the sun. I could see two figures walking. It looked like they were holding hands.

I took off at a run. Despite the shape I was in, I found my breath laboring almost immediately. Maybe it was the humidity. Or maybe it was the vision of some oaf, some *boy*, laying his hands on my daughter. After a minute, I was close enough to confirm it was Becky. She was wearing a blue rash shirt we'd bought so she could learn to surf, and white shorts. I stopped a hundred yards from them to catch my breath, resting my hands on my knees. They stopped walking. The boy, fourteen or fifteen—Parker, presumably—took her hand in his. Then he reached up and tucked a lock of her hair behind her ear. He leaned in for a kiss. I stood up quickly.

My movement must've caught her eye, because she turned away from him right before his lips hit hers.

"Dad! What the—"

"You were missing," I said, trying to keep my voice even. The primal urge I had to pound this guy into the ground was hard to keep at bay. "Your mom was worried."

"Oh, jeez. I just went for a walk on the beach."

"Well, let's go back and tell her you're okay, all right?"

Parker stood there, not saying anything. His brown hair was shaggy. His board shorts looked like they might fall off his skinny frame. He hadn't even dropped her hand.

I was so not ready for this.

"Come on, Becks. Let's go."

She followed me reluctantly back to the pool, Parker trailing behind us. He stopped to play with the volleyball crew when we got to the stairs. She watched him for a minute, the red on the tip of her ears having nothing to do with the sun. When he didn't acknowledge her, she turned and stormed ahead of me. If this boy made my daughter cry, he was going to regret it.

Back at the pool, Becky sat in her deck chair and drew her knees up to her chin. She waved up at Hanna, who was standing at the railing on our deck.

"Happy now?" Becky said.

"Please don't go all teenager on me, okay? I'm not strong enough."

"It was bound to happen sometime, Dad. Deal with it."

She pulled her book out of her bag and disappeared behind it. I watched her for a moment, my heart still pumping too much blood.

"You're blocking my sun," Becky said.

"Right, sorry. Come up for lunch soon, all right?"

She grunted and I went searching for a free deck chair. I needed to jump in the pool. Maybe that would wash away the desire to commit a homicide.

I spotted an empty chair next to a woman who was frowning at her laptop under a wide straw hat. I stripped off my shirt as an oath escaped her. Then my heart was racing for a different reason.

I looked at her more carefully. Her skin was brown in an even way no one in my family ever achieved. Her breasts, encased in a light-blue top, were slightly larger than I'd imagined.

"Funny meeting you here," I heard myself say.

Sometimes I'm such a fucking asshole.

The four of us had dinner together that night. Me, Hanna, Julie, and Daniel. Hanna's parents were all too happy to watch the twins along with our kids. Shooing us out the door, telling us to go have fun in Puerto Vallarta.

Hanna gave me a look when I'd brought Julie up to our room to solve her latest tech crisis. But Julie played it smart. She'd tucked her arm through Hanna's and told her how relieved she was to see someone she knew. How she was sorry they hadn't had the coffee they'd promised yet.

It was all obvious lies to me. But I'd long observed that Hanna had difficulty discerning when someone wasn't telling her the truth.

Whether by choice or by crook, after a few minutes, Hanna's suspicions drained away. Julie and Hanna worked in the kitchen making lunch for everyone while I added yet another set of firewalls to Julie's laptop, and changed her e-mail password to a phrase Julie wrote on a scrap of paper. *You know it's all a gamble when it's just a game.* A lyric from a Guns N' Roses song, I discovered later when I searched for it on the Internet. I crumpled the paper and threw it in the trash, wondering at the meaning. If there was any to catch. She promised she'd change it again later to something no one but she knew.

Right before Daniel joined us with the twins, worn out from their morning in the sun at the Kids' Club, Julie was saying how amazing the place was. Hanna remarked how *odd* it was, really, that we'd both ended up at the same resort.

"You must've gotten the same e-mail I did," Julie said.

I turned around in my chair. Hanna's arms were folded across her chest, her hands tucked under her armpits as if she was holding herself together.

Julie continued. "I had no idea you'd be here at the same time."

I turned back to the laptop. I'd had to disable Julie's MySanity settings so I could make the necessary changes.

"It's fine," Hanna said, her voice tight. "Forget it."

Let it go, Hanna, I thought. *You're making things weird.*

Daniel and the twins tumbled into the room. Their noisy clatter put an end to the conversation. At lunch, over homemade quesadillas, it was Daniel who'd brought up us all going to dinner, saying he'd heard about this Cuban place he wanted to check out. Good food, good jazz, a menu full of mojitos.

Hanna's mother said they'd be happy to look after everyone, and we agreed to go. We left strict instructions with Hanna's parents that neither of our kids was allowed out that evening. I'd told Hanna about Parker, and the girl Chris had been eyeing.

"Maybe this will be the end of Ashley," Hanna said as we were getting changed. She didn't like Ashley. She reminded Hanna too much of the suburban mean girls who'd ruled our high school in Anderson Township. She hoped for better for our son.

"It's not like they're going to get married or anything," I said. "I can't believe you're not more freaked out by our daughter almost getting kissed."

"She's going to get kissed sometime," Hanna said, applying a coat of mascara to her lashes. "And more."

"Not on my watch."

She looped her hands around my neck. "Okay, caveman."

I kissed her. She ran her tongue along my teeth.

"We don't have to go to this dinner," I said.

"What? No way, I'm not missing out on a chance to spend a night with grown-ups."

The taxi ride to Puerto Vallarta was uneventful. The restaurant was as advertised, a gentrified piece of Cuba brought to Mexico. We were seated at a table on the second level overlooking the dance floor. The band blasted loud notes of Cuban jazz. The walls and tables were covered with graffiti signatures. Ernest Hemingway's famous scrawl dominated the wall behind the bar.

We started with the house mojitos, strong and fresh. I drank mine quickly. And the one that came after that. Daniel and Hanna were talking about some mutual business acquaintance. Hanna represented the company Daniel worked for. She laughed loudly at his impression of their in-house counsel. We all did, though Julie's laugh had a tinge of I've-heard-this-one-before.

"You've got something in your teeth," Julie said after I'd taken a sip from a fresh glass. I couldn't taste the alcohol anymore, always a bad sign.

"What?"

"Here," she said tapping her front teeth. "I always think it's better to tell someone rather than let them walk around like that. Sorry."

"It's fine. Really."

I plied a piece of mint out of my front teeth. Julie looked particularly lovely that night, in a coral-colored dress that flattered her curves. The humidity had curled her hair. She glowed with a kiss of sun. What was it about this woman? Two hours ago I'd been ready to ditch the evening to tumble into bed with my wife. But now I couldn't keep other thoughts from my mind.

"Maybe I'll stick to beer from now on," I said.

"Sounds like a plan," Daniel said loudly, his head snapping around for our waiter.

I picked up the menu, concentrating on the list of beers. I put myself on an internal clock. No more talking directly to Julie for the next hour.

Instead, as we ate the mix of Mexican and Cuban food, I focused on Daniel. We traded corporate hell stories as we matched each other beer for beer, then went down to the level below so we could be closer to the band. We watched them finish their set in companionable silence, then turned to the bar to get another round. I wasn't quite sure how many that made. I was past caring.

We clicked bottles.

"Thanks for helping Julie out, by the way," Daniel said.

"It's nothing."

"Nah, I know it's more than that. You did it before, too, with that password thing. Julie can be . . . a bit paranoid sometimes."

"Oh?"

"I'm not saying Heather The Stalker wasn't scary, but it's kind of like she was expecting something like that to happen. It's hard to explain."

"Was it weird for you, reading that book?"

"You mean Julie's book?" He was slurring his words, but then again, so was I. "A little, I'll be honest. I mean, she'd told me about some of that stuff before, but seeing it all written down like that . . ."

"What are you saying?"

Guilt crept across Daniel's face. "Nothing, man. I've had too much to drink. Here come the girls."

He swayed away from me toward Julie and Hanna as the band resumed their places. They began a rich salsa beat, and we all started dancing. Daniel and I were twirling the girls, passing them off between us like we were swing dancing. A few twirls in, Julie tripped against me, laying her hands flat on my chest. Her scent hit my nostrils—a mix of citrus and sweat with a hint of sunscreen this time. She leaned back and laughed, holding out her hands to me.

"My hero," she said.

"An IT hero. That's hot, I'm sure."

"Ah, but it is."

I stopped and stepped back. "We're all pretty drunk."

"Aw, don't ruin it."

She gave me a quick pout and turned to Daniel. He passed Hanna back to me, and we had an awkward moment where she went left and I went right.

"I'm so drunk," she said.

"I think we all are."

We left soon after that. Caught in the nighttime crowd, it took us thirty minutes to find a cab that would take us back to our hotel for a reasonable fee. The car that agreed to do it was so beat up it would've fit right in in Cuba. The seat belts didn't work, and the driver drove without regard for speed limits or basic safety. Hanna sat in the front seat with her hands covering her eyes most of the way.

Julie was on the hump between Daniel and me. We zoomed through a yellow-turning-to-red light and skirted a dump truck by half an inch. Julie and I made eye contact. She flashed me an enormous smile. It didn't take an insightful person to tell she was having fun. She was enjoying the danger even, getting off on it in a way.

Daniel was probably going to be a lucky man later.

I thought about what Daniel had said about Julie's book. *Seeing it all written down like that.*

And then I got a flash of one of the scenes in it. How the murder occurred in the dead of night. How the murderer crept through the house, then stood over the victim and sliced a knife into him so many times it rendered his heart beyond recognition.

Only, as I saw it in that moment, it was Julie standing there, the same dangerous grin on her face as her arm rose and fell.

Then we hit a bump in the road.

And when I looked over at Julie, her smile was gone.

Today
John
10:00 a.m.

We're sitting on a hard bench in the lobby of the prosecutor's building. The grand jury meets on the fourth floor, but we won't be allowed up there until it's our turn to testify.

Our testifying was Alicia's idea. An unusual step meant to stop this case at the grand jury stage, which is usually just a pass-through to a real trial. It's what she's known for. Ending things early, before they get past stopping. And most of me trusts her. But the part that doesn't is convinced this will all go horribly wrong.

The space is crowded with security guards and a metal detector. A prisoner in a white-and-black-striped jumpsuit and shackles is led through and into an elevator by two police officers. Harried clerks and lawyers rush past holding case files, nodding at one another. Rush, rush, rush.

The minutes tick by slowly. The air is stale, full of worry. I already have a bad headache forming behind my eyes.

The hardest thing about today, Alicia told us, was going to be the waiting. There wasn't a set schedule for when we'd be called to testify. Or even any guarantee that all the witnesses put down for our case would be called. That depended on what others said. What strategy the prosecutor was following. Whether he thought he'd done enough to convince the men and women who held our future in their hands to indict.

Chris is sitting next to me, absorbed in his phone. Despite all the media attention, we hadn't taken it away. I'd wanted to, but Hanna thought keeping things as normal as possible was the right way to go. And since none of us had any relevant experience, I gave in.

I watch Brad and Susan Thurgood work their way through security, their faces anxious. Brad is checking his watch as if he's late. I don't know where they've spent the last hour. Maybe at a coffee shop, like us. The elevator doors clang open. A court clerk emerges, her face pale under the fluorescent lighting. She has a rash of freckles across her face, like the footprints a small bird might leave in the sand. She looks at me, then shakes her head as Susan's name is called over the intercom.

Susan emits a small cry—"Oh!"—then puts a hand on Brad's shoulder. He stands with her, holding her elbow, leading her to the elevator to deliver her to the clerk. She walks into the small space like a child on the way to the principal's office. She looks much thinner than the last time I saw her. Brad watches the doors close, then shoves his hands in his pockets and walks toward the exit.

I look around. Alicia and Hanna are on the other side of the elevators in a close huddle. Who knows what they're talking about. We've been over the details so many times it all seems rehearsed now. A script we've had to learn, rather than something real that carved its way through our life.

I'm not sure what to do. Tell them Brad left and looks like he's never coming back? Is that even a real read of the situation, or just wishful thinking on my part? I'm not thinking rationally, I know. Brad's probably just getting some air.

He isn't the one who has anything to hide.

Yet something propels me to stand and follow him. Maybe I can get him to talk to me like he used to. Back before Brad and Susan broke up. When Brad had a few in him, he'd confide all kinds of things about their marriage. How Susan could only come if Brad said filthy things while they fucked. How he pissed away some of the kids' college fund—not everything, mind you, but *enough*—on Internet poker. How he thought about getting in his car sometimes and driving away without looking back.

I'd always clapped Brad on the back in those days and passed him another beer. Some of it I didn't want to know. To be honest, the thought of Brad and Susan having sex was like thinking about my parents doing it. The rest of it wasn't that different from the thoughts that flew through my own mind, some days. But after he and Susan split, I felt like I should've done better by him. Should've noticed it wasn't just the beer talking. Brad was reaching out. And the drinks I passed him weren't the help he needed.

I walk outside and look left, then right. I catch sight of Brad halfway down the block. His balding head is bobbing up and down as he walks briskly. This is not some casual stroll. He's making a break for it. I pick up my pace, the need to catch him accelerating in my chest.

Brad slows down when he gets to the end of the block. He looks around, maybe searching for somewhere to sit. His legs are shaking as he pats himself down.

"You need a smoke?" I ask, trying to sound friendly. But I'm standing half a foot closer to him than I should be.

He starts at the sound of my voice. When he turns to face me, he looks frightened, as if I might hurt him.

"I can't talk to you," he says, his voice wheezing. "They said."

"It's okay, Brad. I don't want to talk."

"You should have stayed inside, then."

"I'm not up for a while," I say. "I needed some air."

His eyes dart left and right. There are dark circles under them. Beads of sweat on his forehead.

"It's okay. There's no one watching us. It's just me. John. We were friends, I thought. Aren't we friends?"

"You don't know what it's been like . . ."

"I don't know?"

"No, I mean, I can't imagine . . ."

"It's fine, Brad. It's fine."

His hands flap at his chest again. His suit is too loose on him, bought at a time when he was twenty pounds heavier. There's a grease stain on his right pant leg. It doesn't seem right, somehow, the disparity between us. I should be the one too broken to dress properly. Too distracted to comb my hair.

"Fine?" Brad says. "It's fine?"

"I'm not sure why I said that. This has been . . . it's all so—what happened?"

"We can't talk about it."

"I know, you said. Let's just . . ."

I reach into my jacket and pull out my flask. I put it there last night, not entirely sure why at the time. I needed to be 100 percent on my game today, not nipping at the clear vodka I chose because it was the safest bet at going undetected.

"Remember this?" I say, tipping the flask back and forth. Its contents slosh against the sides.

Brad looks terrified. A shot of pure self-loathing courses through me.

"Oh, no, I can't. I don't drink anymore. I don't."

"But you were drunk that morning." I can hear the clank of the garbage cans like we're back there. Brad was stumbling around, talking to himself, trying to line them up like soldiers. "What were you doing there that morning, anyway?"

"I was just trying to help out my family."

"And what about today? What about *my* family?"

"I don't have a choice. They sent a subpoena. You *know* that."

Brad's eyes scan the area around us again. I'm blocking the way back to the building. Running away is not an option.

"I can't fucking do this," Brad says. "Please."

"Sure you can. Come on."

I take him by the elbow like he did Susan. There's a cement structure down the block the smokers use as a bench. I deposit him on it and offer him the flask. This time he doesn't protest, just takes it from me like it's inevitable. He screws off the top and swallows down more than I ever could.

"You do have a choice, Brad. You do."

"Oh, yeah," he says, his voice already slightly blurred. He takes another pull, an even longer one this time, which ends with a shudder. "What do you want from me, John?"

"Just tell them about the sun," I say. "And how it made it impossible to see."

The Curious Incident of the Dog Poop in the Night-Time

Julie

Eight months ago

John and I didn't keep up the pretense of running separately when we got back from Mexico. That first frozen morning as I laced up my shoes and made sure my hair was well tucked into my running beanie with the fleece on the inside, I knew he was doing the same thing across the street, checking his watch to make sure he timed his exit so that we'd start this day together.

I'd had these moments of precognition on and off throughout my life, knowing what other people were going to say before they did, even if it was an unusual word like "cacophony" or "salubrious." I'd hear the word in my head moments before they said it. Occasionally, it would be instructions. *Go to this coffee shop. Turn left.* It was usually something innocuous, but it had kept me alive once when the driver in front of me—drunk and two nights' sleepless, I learned later—applied his brakes for no reason at all, and I stopped mere inches from his bumper because I'd "seen" him apply his brakes ten seconds before he had.

To the extent I discussed it all, even with myself, I always made fun of it. *Not that I believe in this stuff,* I was fond of saying at dinner parties if the subject of coincidences came up. *But listen to this . . .* I'd hold everyone's attention—I did know how to tell a story—and when I explained how I'd twice in one day guessed where someone was from before they told me, they'd shake their heads and someone, usually a man, would call me a "witch," and everyone would laugh, and the conversation would move on. If I caught Daniel's eye, he'd roll his own, knowing, as I had said to him more than once, that I was a bit ashamed of myself when I told these stories. That they were an easy card to play in a social setting, and I was only ever telling half the truth of it.

Because it wasn't reliable, and there were so many other things that could explain it, and seriously, what was I saying, anyway? That I *was* a witch? That magic was real? That I was magic?

But then there was this: when I met Heather Stanhope for the first time, my mind clanged like a bell. It gave me a warning, but I befriended her anyway.

Because I didn't believe in that stuff.

Because magic wasn't real.

A warning sounded within me that morning, too, when I opened my front door and closed it firmly behind me, making sure it was locked. John was standing across the street in his winter running gear, a thin plume of his breath visible above his lips.

"Shall we?" he said, smiling in welcome.

I returned his smile and shook the warning away.

◆ ◆ ◆

How's this for irony?

The first time Heather Stanhope showed up at one of my book events, I was *glad* to see her.

I was on a book tour. Nothing grand or fancy, the tour involved me driving to a bookstore a couple of times a week, leaving the twins with Daniel or a sitter, putting on my "adult clothes," and applying a coat of mascara. That event was in the first month after the book came out. The Book was selling steadily, but it hadn't yet attained that strange velocity that occurred after it made it onto a couple of "Best of" lists and got downloaded thirty thousand times in one day when my publishers did a flash price drop of the e-book.

Sometimes no one showed up to these readings; sometimes twenty people did. I'd already found out that it was completely unpredictable, had enough store clerks tell me stories about [insert name of famous author] and how *no one* showed up for his signing at all.

It was one of those medium-size events at a Barnes & Noble in Seattle. I'd been snarled in traffic on the way there, feeling late, though I wasn't quite. When I got set up at my table, I realized I'd forgotten to bring pens again. It still hadn't sunk in that I was the one signing the books stacked neatly on the table.

It was a perfect Saturday afternoon for a trip to the bookstore. Not a sunny day—those never worked—and not too rainy, either. Just a gray haze that made you think you were safe leaving the house for a few hours and browsing. The store was crowded. A few women stopped by to chat, and then a line formed behind them. Not a long line, but enough so I was starting to feel good about the day, instead of feeling like the store had gone to a lot of trouble just for me, and all for nothing.

The line cleared out. The stack of books next to me was shorter, but still high. I'd managed to get black Sharpie on my fingers, and the fumes were giving me a headache.

"Is that really you?"

A tall woman with brown hair was standing in front of me. She had her hair cut short, almost boyish, and she'd put on a few pounds since law school, but in a way that suited her. She looked capable and strong.

"Heather?"

"Julie?"

I'd smiled and risen up from my seat to hug her across the table. She smelled, surprisingly, of marijuana.

"What are you doing here?" I asked.

"I could ask you the same thing. Wow. Did you write that?"

"I did!"

We caught each other up. I told her how Daniel and I had moved from Montreal to Tacoma after I'd quit the prosecutor's office, how I'd left the law behind, all about the twins. She told me how she'd spent almost ten years in New York, grinding, eating most meals at the firm, and when they'd finally offered her partnership, realizing she didn't want it. She'd moved to Seattle for a different life six months earlier.

"Did you make it back to McGill for the tenth reunion?" she asked.

"I skipped it. I guess you did, too?"

"Yeah. Too many memories. If they were going to do something for Kathryn, I would've gone."

She meant Kathryn Simpson, a classmate of ours who'd died during our third year.

I shivered. Someone walking over my grave.

"You still in touch with the others?" Heather asked.

"Booth e-mails me sometimes. I haven't heard from Kevin in years."

Booth was my law-school boyfriend; Kevin was Kathryn's. We all spent an inordinate amount of time together, and then Kathryn died, and the investigation happened. We started unraveling then. Booth and I broke up, and I met Daniel in the aftermath.

"I dedicated the book to her," I said. "I think about her often."

Something flickered behind Heather's eyes. "I didn't know you wrote."

"I didn't really until recently. I still kind of can't believe I wrote a whole book."

"What's it about?"

I tripped over my words. Though I was used to explaining it to strangers, I felt nervous telling her. "Four law students plan the perfect murder. Then, ten years later, one of them has committed it, and one of them has to prosecute them for it. Only it's not told like that."

Some of the color fled her face. She picked up the book and focused on the title. "*The Murder Game*? But . . . isn't that what you guys used to play at law school?"

By then, the warning gong in my head was so loud I was sure others could hear it.

Daniel and I had a deal. Once a week, he'd come home early from work and do the nightly routine with the kids. We'd had this agreement ever since he found me curled in a ball on the floor near the television when the twins were two and a half and up way past their bedtime. They'd been running laps in the living room, refusing to go to bed. Even the temptation of the iPad and unlimited Netflix had only started working after I repeated it three times *and* let them have sugar cereal. They were sitting on the couch with a large bowl of it in front of them, eating it like popcorn, when Daniel came home from a late business dinner. He said my name twice before I responded, and we had an awful fight about why I hadn't called him or someone else to come help.

It all came pouring out then: how I'd been writing in secret, and how I couldn't stand being at home all day without any adults to talk to other than the CrossFit moms who always made me feel like I was doing everything wrong. How the pregnancy weight I couldn't lose made me feel like I was back in high school, with clothes that didn't fit and the disapproving looks of my peers. How I couldn't take the weather any-more, and I thought I might be going crazy.

Daniel put me to bed and dealt with the kids. After a visit to my doctor resulted in an increase of my Wellbutrin and vitamin D doses, Daniel suggested two things: that I take a night off once a week to join a book club or hang with my girlfriends—whatever I wanted—and that we institute our own "date night" (as tacky as we both felt that was) on Saturdays. His mother would be all too happy to be our standing sitter, and we could explore some of the restaurants that had sprung up around Tacoma while we were being held captive by our kids.

We hadn't been keeping either of those nights up since the move. We hadn't found a reliable sitter (we certainly weren't going to use Ashley), and I didn't have any friends to hang out with yet. But as February rolled in, with its monochrome skies and its damp cold that was too reminiscent of a Tacoma winter, I broached the subject to Daniel. And even though I kept the note of panic out of my voice, I thought, he agreed immediately, then began Googling bonded babysit-ting services in the area.

I'd texted Susan casually that afternoon, wondering if she might want to go for a walk after dinner. I knew from the few brief text exchanges we'd had since that day in the park that Wednesday was Brad's night for taking the kids out. He took them for a dinner a week and every other weekend, Susan told me, if she was lucky. Father of the Year was his for the taking.

She'd written back enthusiastically, the number of exclamations marks in her text suggesting that she, too, was in serious need of a break. Who wouldn't be, in her situation?

I ate dinner with Daniel and the kids, sipping a nice glass of red while I sat back and watched Daniel cajole first Sam, then Melly, into eating their broccoli. While he did the dishes, I suited up for the cold and put Sandy on her leash. Despite my complaints and the tug of the winter blahs, Ohio cold was better than the old cold, Pacific Northwest cold, which seeped into your bones like the washed-up, sodden logs scattered across the beach.

Susan lived halfway down the street in a tall, narrow brick house. It was one of the things I was coming to love about Cincinnati: the variety in the real estate. In complete contrast to the housing development we'd lived in before, no two houses on Pine Street looked the same. Each was built to the original owner's whim, it seemed, with an errant turret here, a dormer window there. The only consistency, I knew, from my house search before we moved, was the panel of windows at the back of any house with a river view.

Susan was waiting on her front porch. She was dressed like me—long puffy coat, boots over her jeans, hat over her ears. When I thought back to how I'd wandered around with an open coat and no hat in my youth in upstate New York, I marveled. Was I thicker-skinned back then, or simply stupid?

"He doesn't bite, does he?" Susan asked, eyeing Sandy, who was sitting obediently on her heels next to me.

"He's a she. And no, not unless I tell her to."

"I've always been afraid of dogs."

"Do you want me to take her back? She hasn't had her second walk today and . . ."

"No, it's fine. I'm all about facing my fears these days."

"That sounds like a good precept."

She shoved her hands in her pockets. "You'd think, right? But, no."

We started walking down the street. It had snowed earlier, and it was safer to walk in the middle of the street than on the slippery sidewalks. We were getting an unusual amount of snow that winter, I'd heard on the radio that morning, but to me there couldn't be too much. It was one of the things I'd insisted on when Daniel and I were looking for a new place to live: there had to at least be the possibility of snow.

Susan and I hadn't agreed on any particular path, only that we'd walk for an hour at least. Sandy trotted along companionably next to us, stopping to pee on the small tree in front of Cindy's house, which always seemed to call the dog in like a homing beacon on my morning runs.

Susan looked around. "Don't let Cindy catch her doing that."

"I always clean up after."

"I'm sure. But you've met Cindy, right?"

"She can't control everything."

"She can try."

Though it was only eight o'clock, most of the lights in Cindy's house were off. A flickering glow from a television could be seen through the basement windows.

"I think we're safe," I said. "What's up with her, anyway? She seems to have a strange hold over everyone."

Susan laughed. "I can see how it would seem that way, but, well . . . her daughter, Ashley, had leukemia when she was a kid, and she came pretty close to dying. Cindy was so amazing. She quit her job and basically moved into the hospital, and I swear, she willed Ashley to live. When Ashley got better, Cindy never went back to work. I guess all that energy had to go somewhere."

"I can't imagine going through that."

"Yeah, it was awful. She can be over the top sometimes, but mostly she's this really generous person. She's helped out a lot since Brad left."

We wended our way through the neighboring streets. The clouds that had closed in around Mount Adams earlier in the day, making it feel as if we lived in a tree house, had finally dissipated, and Venus was shining bright in the sky next to a crescent moon. The cold air felt like a carbon scrubber in my system, washing out the impurities and taking them away with each frosty breath.

"Brad's in AA," Susan said suddenly when we crested the hill, as if she'd been gearing herself up to do it.

"Is that a good thing?"

"I think so. I asked him to. A million times before the end, I asked him to try it."

"Better late than never?"

"Ha. Yes. I guess. Who knows if it will stick."

"I almost did that," I said, surprising myself. I hadn't even told Daniel about the vodka-in-the-morning period of my life, though I'm sure he suspected something. There had been a few pointed remarks about skipping wine with dinner. Confrontation was never Daniel's strong suit.

"AA?" Susan said.

"A while back, after . . . I was in a bad place, and I was drinking way too much."

"But not now?"

"I imposed this rule on myself, to see if I could do it without help, and it worked. That, and better meds."

She glanced at me like she wasn't sure if I was joking.

"I suffer from depression. It's . . . it's fine. It's under control."

"You can't control everything," Susan said.

"Right. Funny. I . . ." Tears I couldn't explain sprang to my eyes, bringing with them a sense of panic. Unexplained tears were always how the depression started, and what made it so scary. "I don't know what's gotten into me. It's this stupid book deadline, I think."

"When's it due?"

"Eight months from now."

"That seems like a long time."

"I know, right?"

It was a long time. Only I didn't seem to be getting anywhere, day in and day out. I wrote my words—I had almost 40,000 of them. I advanced the players down the outline I'd written so many months before, in the heady days of The Book's success, when my publishers would have bought anything, my agent assured me—but make it good, anyway.

Rearranging the deck chairs on the Titanic, I'd taken to calling what I was doing on a daily basis. About as effective as playing the violin while it sank.

Susan patted me on the back with a practiced hand. Not too firm, not too soft. Just right.

"I thought this walk was about cheering each other up?" she asked.

"It was. It really was."

"Do you want to talk about it?"

"Not really."

"So let's go do something, then? What about one of those spiced-pumpkin thingies?"

"With whipped cream?" I said hopefully.

"I am definitely pro whipped cream."

We went to the Bow Tie Cafe. They let us bring Sandy in, and we unwrapped ourselves in the brightly lit space. The windows were steamed up from the nighttime crowd. Spiced pumpkin was, unfortunately, out of season, so we indulged in caramel macchiatos, and the tears were forgotten. Sometimes comfort food really does comfort.

On the way back home, Sandy ran at her favorite tree again, only this time, she took a long, decidedly human-looking poop. I sighed as I reached into my pocket for a plastic bag.

"Shit."

"That she did," Susan said.

"I forgot my poop bags."

"I can wait here while you go get one." She eyed Sandy. "Or maybe you could . . ."

"Right, I probably should—" I stopped and motioned for Susan to be quiet. Something had caught my attention and set my heart sprinting. We weren't alone. I put my hand above my eyes to shade out the street lamp and scanned the night. There. A white flash of something was hovering near Cindy's basement window.

"Sandy!" I said in my best command voice. "Attack!"

I let go of the leash, and Sandy bounded over the low snowbank toward what I was now certain was a man crouching by the window.

"Hey! Oww! Hey!"

A light flashed on in the basement, illuminating Sandy pawing at a man lying on the ground, his jacket in her teeth. His hands flailed, trying to push himself up and away.

The front porch light turned on, and out came Cindy's husband, Paul. He was wearing pajama bottoms, his feet stuffed into his running shoes. It was 9:45 p.m.

"What the hell?"

The man on the ground stopped struggling, lying still while Sandy half stood on his chest, growling.

"There's a man," I said, pointing. "He was trying to get into your basement through the window."

Paul came out onto the stoop, squinting.

"Did you call the police?"

"I did," Susan said, waving her phone in her hand.

"It's just Chris!"

Cindy and Paul's daughter, Ashley, streaked out of the house in jeans and a T-shirt.

"Chris! Are you okay?"

She stopped a few feet away from him as Sandy bared her teeth.

"I can't get up! He bit me."

"Call him off!" Ashley said to me.

I didn't bother correcting her pronoun. "Sandy! Release. Come."

Sandy looked at me like she wasn't sure I was serious.

"Release, Sandy. Release."

She reluctantly let go of Chris's coat. Down feathers flew through the air like snow. Ashley ran to him, dropping to her knees, trying to cradle his head in her lap.

"Chris. Are you okay?"

118

He sat up. There was a long, deep scratch across the left side of his face. Blood was seeping out of it onto his jacket. Now that he wasn't crouching like a thief, he looked young, vulnerable, scared.

"I'm fine."

"You're bleeding!"

"Ashley, you get back here this minute!"

Cindy appeared in the doorway, a bathrobe tied tightly around her waist.

Chris brought his hand up to his face. He pulled it away and looked at the blood as if it was an alien substance.

I handed Sandy's leash to Susan and moved toward him.

"Stop," Cindy said. "Stop right there."

I froze in my tracks. "I want to make sure he's all right."

"I'll do that," Cindy said, pushing past me. "I think you've done enough damage here tonight."

New Rules

John

Eight months ago

Hanna was waiting for me when I got back from my run, the morning after Julie's dog attacked Chris.

"Are you kidding me?" she asked as I kicked off my sodden shoes.

Big, sticky flakes were falling thickly outside. But for the company, I wouldn't have made it out at all. I pulled off my Windbreaker and wiped my face with the inside of my fleece.

"What's going on? Chris okay?"

I'd checked on him before I left. He was sleeping on his back, his arms sprawled out above his head. The bandage across his cheek was white against his red face.

"I think he's going to have a permanent scar. Don't you care about that at all?"

Hanna gave me one of her persecution stares, as I always called them.

"Of course I do. Why would you even ask that?"

"Because you were running with *her*."

She pointed toward the door. Directly through it and across the street was Julie's house.

"We ran into each other. No pun intended."

"Ha. Right. Don't treat me like I'm an idiot."

I felt nervous, although I hadn't been doing anything wrong. So Julie and I had taken to running together most mornings. I was sure I'd mentioned it to Hanna. At least once. I might've picked my moment. A moment when she was absorbed in the morning paper. But I had told her.

"I'm not," I said. "I mean, yeah, we run together sometimes. I told you that. Our schedules are similar. What's the big deal?"

"Whatever."

I hate it when she says that. Which she knows. An affectation she picked up from the kids years ago.

"Hanna, come on." I stepped toward her. I was wet to the core, but I took her in my arms anyway.

She squirmed. "You're ruining my suit."

"Forget the suit. What's going on?"

"I don't like you hanging out with her. And that dog of hers . . ."

"That was an accident. Chris shouldn't have been sneaking out of a window in the dead of night."

When Chris was frog-marched up the street by Cindy the night before, Hanna's anger had been directed at Chris. Once she'd made sure he was okay. Sneaking out of the house was not allowed. If he wanted to hang out with Ashley, it didn't have to be a secret. And if her parents didn't want them to be together, then we could talk about that. Maybe we could have a sit-down with Cindy and Paul and discuss it.

"No, Mom. No way," Chris had said, looking horrified. He was holding a damp cloth to his face. There was blood flecked across his shirt. Several spots the size of dimes marred his jeans. Hanna had the first-aid kit out, readying the Bactine and bandages.

"Well, we're probably going to have to have a conversation with them, anyway, given what happened."

"Nothing happened."

"Why were you sneaking out, then?"

"We were studying and we fell asleep on the couch. Her parents go to bed early, and I was supposed to have left at nine. They put the alarm on."

"So you sneaked out through a window?"

She pulled his hand aside and applied some Bactine to the cut. He winced.

"The sensor doesn't work on that window."

"And you know this, how?"

"Aw, Mom, come on. Stop cross-examining me."

Hanna softened. She always worried that she was too hard on the kids. Chris knew how to push her buttons.

She pressed a white bandage over the cut, affixing it with tape. We'd taken a first-aid class together when she was pregnant with Chris. CPR. What to do if your child was choking. Minor cuts and abrasions. We'd both come away terrified, but were happy to have the information when Chris turned out to be allergic to peanuts.

"Are you sure you're okay?" I asked.

"It's only a scratch."

"We should have the doctor take a look at it," Hanna said. "It's pretty deep."

"Can we do that tomorrow?" Chris said. "I'm tired."

Hanna acquiesced. She told Chris we'd discuss his punishment and let him know what it would be in the morning. Hanna encouraged him to find a replacement for his paper route, but he said he could do it. He and I had made a deal when he turned fourteen that if he saved up enough, we'd get him a car when he turned sixteen. Every day of tossing papers was a step toward his freedom.

When we'd climbed into bed, Hanna rolled toward me and said, "Do you think they were having sex?"

"Probably."

She punched me in the arm. "I'm being serious here."

"So am I. They're fifteen. They've been dating for . . . how long now?"

"Since summer."

I peered at her over the rim of my reading glasses. "Summer. I see. So, seven, eight months now, including breakups? Yes. They are definitely having sex."

"That doesn't bother you?"

"Becky getting kissed by some boy in Mexico was no big deal, but our son having sex is?"

"He's our baby."

"He's as tall as I am."

"And your first time was at . . ." She scrunched up her nose as if she couldn't remember.

"You know how old I was."

Fifteen and a half. Stupid in lust with Sara Henderson. Who'd go on to break my heart two months later. Even now, on the rare occasions when I ran into her, my stomach lurched. Back then, Sara was into mind games and manipulation. At fifteen years old, I was easy prey.

"I know how old you were, too," I added, teasing.

"I was *sixteen*."

"Which Chris will be before we know it."

"I know, I know. God, I felt so grown up back then. Like I knew exactly what I was doing and why I was doing it. Chris doesn't even know how to do his own laundry, and thinks milk magically appears in the fridge."

"Whose fault is that?"

"Both of ours, I think."

"You're right. How about, first thing tomorrow, we introduce him to the washer/dryer, and then send him out for groceries?"

"That sounds like a sensible plan."

She snuggled up against my side.

"Chris is a good boy," I said. "We've told him enough times to be responsible, and I think he will be. But I can talk to him if you want."

"Give him some pointers, maybe?" she said.

"Now that's probably going too far."

"Chris was trying not to wake Cindy and Paul," Hanna said to me the next morning, in response to my comment that Chris had gotten himself into this mess.

I released her, shivering in my running things. "So we're believing that story now?"

"Maybe, but you should see his face. It looks bad. I'm taking him to the doctor. And if he needs surgery . . ."

"What?"

"Well, you know people are responsible for the actions of their dogs, right? Legally responsible. It's called the one-bite rule, and—"

"You want to sue her?"

"Not her, exactly. Her insurance company."

"What's the difference?"

"She won't be out of pocket. If she's properly insured, this should be covered. Though, maybe not because it didn't happen on her property. Or if this wasn't the first time her dog has done something like this. I bet it isn't. We should look into that."

Hanna had this faraway look in her eyes. One I'd seen before when she was caught up in figuring out an angle she should take on a case. Or with me.

"Isn't it going to be covered by *our* insurance?"

"That's not the point. If Chris is permanently disfigured—"

"Hanna, come on. Permanently disfigured? It was a scratch. Are you seriously telling me that if a dog jumps on you when you're acting like a prowler, it's the owner's fault?"

"Well, yes, actually. That's what strict liability is all about. You're responsible regardless of whether you did anything wrong. But she did do something wrong. She told the dog to attack. Chris told me."

I felt a moment of unease. Julie hadn't mentioned that on our run. She'd felt bad, though, asking twice how Chris was. If I thought he'd need stitches. He was a handsome boy, she said. And she felt sick about it.

"Attack? She used that word?"

"You can ask Susan if you don't believe him. She was there, remember?"

"Of course I believe him. Let me process this for a minute."

I peeled my shirt from my body. I tossed it in the empty laundry bin that was sitting at the base of the stairs.

"You give Chris his laundry lesson?" I said.

"What?" Hanna said. She'd pulled her smartphone out and was scanning through her e-mails.

"Forget it."

I pulled a towel out of the linen closet and rubbed my hair. It was 7:20, and this day was already turning into a shit show. Whatever peace I'd gathered on my run was dripping away like the water I was trailing across the floor.

"Where's Chris? Is he back from his paper route yet?"

"Upstairs."

I went to find him. He was in his room, already locked into his laptop. I studied him from the doorway. He'd taken off the bandage Hanna placed over his cut. It did look worse than the night before, red and angry.

"You okay, Chris?"

"Yeah."

"Your mom's pretty worried about your face."

"It's fine."

I sat on the edge of his bed. His room had a faint musky smell to it. I couldn't help wondering if he and Ashley really had had sex. Maybe right there in his bed.

"Chris, can you turn around?"

His fingers dropped from the keyboard as he faced me.

"What is it?"

"What's going on with you and Ashley?"

"Nothing, Dad, I told you. I fell asleep."

"You're being careful, right?"

"Oh, man."

"I have to ask these things, kiddo. You know that."

"I don't want to talk about it."

"Me, either, to be honest. But when you're a grown-up, you often have to talk about things you don't want to."

Chris rubbed at his eyes, like sleep was still caught there. "Her parents are never going to let me see her again."

"Probably. Especially once we tell them you're sleeping together."

"What? I . . . what?"

"Relax, kid, relax. I'm just messing with you."

"Not funny."

"Probably not."

"You're not going to say anything to her parents, right? Please, Dad. Promise me."

"Don't worry."

His shoulders fell in relief.

"Everything will be okay," I said. "Let me get changed and we'll go to the doctor."

"Am I going to need stitches?"

He'd always hated needles. When he said things like that, he reverted back to little-boy status right before my eyes. Like an optical illusion.

"Hopefully not."

I patted him on the head and went to our bedroom. Hanna was there, still looking at her phone. She did this sometimes. Came upstairs for something, then got distracted by that goddamn device.

"I'll take Chris to the doctor," I said.

"Oh, for fuck's sake."

"You don't want him to go?"

"It's not that; it's this."

She handed me her phone. There was an e-mail from the neighborhood association, i.e. Cindy.

"New Rules," it was called. And as I read it, I was filled with disbelief.

Today

John

11:00 a.m.

There's a certain level of disorientation that comes with being thrust into someone else's world. I'm thinking about that now as I follow Brad back into the building, the illicit flask back in place, almost empty. There's nothing remarkable about the building; we could be in any number of government buildings, the state seal on the wall. Yet, everyone but me seems to know where to go. Where to sit. How to stand. What they can and will say.

But no matter how many times I rehearse it in my mind, I can't seem to make the pieces fit together. There's always something missing. Some part of the puzzle just out of view.

I'd first experienced this feeling when I was sitting in Alicia's office a week after the accident.

We'd already been through the first rounds of questioning on the day of, and the day after, the accident. Two homicide detectives, one of them very young, clearly on his first case. They went house to house like they were canvassing for the Mormon Church. Dark suits, dark ties, white shirts. Little notebooks that soaked up our words. Well-placed questions that encouraged us to speak openly. To hold nothing back.

They were all sympathy in those first conversations. As if they knew exactly what we were going through. Had been through something similar themselves. Had spent the same sleepless nights. The same endless loop of images tracking through their minds, wondering if there was anything, *anything*, they could've done differently.

They had a job to do, Detective Grey said, the seasoned pro. We could understand that. Someone was dead. A life cut short. She deserved their full attention.

Our full attention.

She had that already. She was all we could think about. It was all we were ever going to think about from now on, because how could we think of anything else?

And even as I thought that, I knew it was a lie. Whatever happened, thoughts of that day, of *her*, of all of it, would fade as memories do. Life would intrude, and other things, smaller things, would take precedence. Knowing that made me feel incomparably sad. But there was also a glint of hope. Because the stasis we were in already felt unbearable. The possibility that it would lift sometime, someday, was all that was keeping me going.

The first hint the police thought it was something other than an accident came that Labor Day weekend, accident plus three. If I'd taken a census, I'm sure I would've found everyone home that day on Pine Street. Forty houses, fully occupied. Normally, they would've fled to parts unknown. A long weekend, the last gasp of summer. Time to take advantage of the country club. Or a lazy few days on their boat on Lake Cumberland.

But there was too much holding our attention, keeping us from leaving. Even if the police hadn't asked us to stay put, we'd have been rooted to the spot. By the crush of media vans held back by police tape. Watching those black-suited men going from house to house. Our small stoops became our new living rooms. Meals were taken alfresco. Drinks consumed in sweating glasses.

Then the tech van arrived. Men in jumpsuits who stared at our street's cracked surface. Measured the rise and fall of the speed bumps Cindy finally convinced the city to install. Using lasers from the spot in front of Cindy's house to the corner where the church sat to get a precise distance. Placing small yellow markers in a pattern of numbers I couldn't decipher. Snapping away with their cameras like they were putting together a wedding album.

I watched all this from my usual place at the window, one of our lace curtains in my hand. None of us dared leave the house. Necessities were delivered by nervous-looking delivery boys and Hanna's assistant.

As the tech van drove away, Hanna came to join me at the window. She watched the activity for a while as I filled her in on what I'd seen the technicians doing.

"We need to get a lawyer," was all she said before walking away.

I hadn't protested. Hadn't even asked a question. This was her jurisdiction.

I'd already done too much.

Alicia agreed to see us the next day. When we got there, she'd been on the phone to her contacts in the police department. Had heard more than we guessed.

Hanna wrote her a big check, and she'd gotten down to brass tacks.

"There's a problem with the physical evidence," she said.

The boardroom she'd placed us in was like a fishbowl, glass on both sides. Behind us was a view of the baseball stadium and the river. The bridge to Kentucky glinted in the sun. Hanna and I had our backs to the view, facing an office of muted grays and blues and dark hardwood floors. Expensive art on the walls. Every time someone passed, I couldn't help but follow them with my eyes. A young woman in clacking high heels. A senior partner whose white hair shimmered under the bright pot lights. A harassed-looking clerk, his fist full of documents hot off the photocopier.

"John," Hanna said, her hand on my arm. "Did you hear that?"

"No, sorry. I'm . . . it's been hard to concentrate."

"I understand," Alicia said. "It's the shock."

She had a yellow legal pad in front of her, and she was on her second page of notes. Had Hanna already said so much? How long had I been staring off into space?

"She was saying that the physical evidence doesn't seem to support the fact that it was an accident," Hanna said.

They had my full attention now.

"It's the tire tracks," Alicia said. "Or the absence of them, I should say."

"I don't follow."

"If the car braked," Hanna said. "If it was braking at the moment of impact, then there should be tire tracks on the pavement. Tire tracks *before* . . . before where she was."

I tried to cast my mind back. Squealing tires was one of the sounds that had stayed with me. Even now, I can hear it like a song heard too many times on the radio. Each note imprinted in my long-term memory.

That, and the screams.

My hands gripped the edge of the conference table like they did the steering wheel. "And there aren't? There are *no* tracks?"

"Not before. No. *After*, yes."

"Which means that . . ."

"The car wasn't slowing down when it hit her. Not suddenly enough to leave tracks, anyway. The brakes were likely applied after the moment of impact."

"Is that the only explanation?" I asked. "Couldn't . . . couldn't there have been a delay between when the brakes were applied and the . . . impact. It all happened so fast, and the sun . . . it gets in your eyes when you turn that corner. You can't see anything. Anyone."

"Yes, that's what I understand. And that's what we'll argue."

"Argue?"

"If they decide to lay charges."

The world swayed. Hanna and I held on to each other, fingers gripping forearms. So hard, in her case, that I'd find bruises on my arms when I got undressed that night.

"What does that mean?" I asked.

"If they don't think it was an accident, then they'll seek an indictment."

"Indictment for what?"

Alicia reached across the table, placing a hand on each of us so that we formed a triad of connection.

"My source says they'll be asking for a charge of second-degree murder."

Check-In

Julie

Seven months ago

Dear Neighbors!

I've been privileged to serve as your leader since 2009. And as your leader, I've become concerned by some SERIOUS EVENTS that have occurred in our wonderful neighborhood recently. While I KNOW we all strive to make our little corner of the world as safe as possible, it has become clear that this is, unfortunately, not everyone's priority. Since we do not (yet!) have the ability to prescreen who moves into our area (for more on this please go to www.mystreetpetitions.com) we have to STRONGLY ENCOURAGE everyone who does to abide by our policies.

In case you missed my last few e-mails (spam folders can be tricky!), I thought I'd send this reminder about some of our newest, and most important, rules:

- As previously advised, all dogs will be required to be both LEASHED AND MUZZLED at all times while on the street if they weigh more than five pounds;
- All dogs should also be registered with the PSNA. That way, should there be any further incidents, we'll know precisely who's responsible;
- Curfew for all those under the age of 17 is 9:00 p.m. While we cannot force you to keep your child indoors after that time, any child not accompanied by an adult *will be assumed to be breaking curfew*, and parents will be advised accordingly.

Remember, all of the rules can be viewed at www.pinestreetneighborhood.com. Or stop by and ask for a laminated copy for your fridge. I have plenty!

Additionally, our neighborhood watch is now circulating TWICE NIGHTLY. If you see anything suspicious, please let the watch know. They're the ones wearing the yellow safety vests!

Finally, I'm excited to announce that our street is now enrolled in iNeighbor. This is a FUN, PRIVATE social network only for those who live on this street! You can learn more about it at www. ineighborhood.com, but I, for one, know that I'm most excited by the CHECK-IN function. When you get home from work, go to the site (there's a handy app for your smartphone, too) and "check-in." Ditto if you go to someone else's house. And if you leave for work, or to walk your (muzzled and leashed) dog, whatever you're doing, *everyone will know.*

And hey, if you see one of us "forgetting" to participate, don't fret. We can check one another in, too! You're all preregistered. Simply go to www. ineighborhood.com and type in—

"Oh my God, stop. Stop. My stomach hurts," I said to John.

We'd just gotten back from a run. March had roared in like a lion, and we'd skipped our usual time because the rain was pouring down like it was coming out of a fire hose. But when the sky broke open after lunch, my phone dinged with a text from John, asking, Is now a good time? I'd readily agreed; 42,634 words in, I'd discovered a huge, gaping hole in Book Two's plot, and was counting on the run to find a way out of the labyrinth.

Instead, we'd spent the run discussing Cindy's ridiculous e-mail from the day before. She'd been sending weekly updates to the "rules" since the day after the "dog incident," as she was now referring to it. New dog-leash laws. Calls for more volunteers for the neighborhood watch. A street curfew. None of it was binding—Cindy didn't have legislative power, not yet, anyway—but social pressure can be just as powerful. If the comments on iNeighbor were anything to judge by, and I should've known by then that they were not, most people supported her initiatives. I didn't know anyone other than Susan and John well enough to really understand why that was, and I tried not to take it personally, but that wasn't a strong suit of mine.

John could tell I was down about it. While we were paused on his front driveway to stretch, he'd pulled out his phone and read the entire message in a dead-on impersonation of Cindy, until I couldn't take it anymore because I was laughing so hard.

"Maybe that should be your new business," I said, when I could catch my breath. "Impersonations."

"Oh, yeah, I can see it now. I'll put on a few pounds and wear clothes that are too tight . . . I'll make a killing at barbecues all across the nation."

He shifted the way he was standing and sucked in his stomach. Then he touched his hair the way Cindy did, making sure it was still perfectly smooth at all times, and he really was channeling her.

"Don't be cruel."

"I'm amazed you could say that, given the circumstances."

"I don't like bullying."

A familiar feeling overwhelmed me. Like too many kids, I'd been bullied at school. I wore the wrong clothes, I weighed too much, I lived up in my head. I thought I'd put all that behind me long ago, but moving to this place, being the outsider again after so many years of belonging, brought me right back there. I brushed away a tear. It felt cold on my cheek.

"You okay?" John asked.

"Yeah. I . . . I was that kid. The fat kid. The kid whose clothes were too tight. The girl with the childbearing hips."

"Someone actually called you that?"

"They did. One girl, anyway. Of course, she was anorexic, so . . . I shouldn't joke. I certainly wasn't joking then. I started running track in tenth grade. It helped."

"Well, you look great now."

"It's mostly the running, but . . . thank you."

I gave him an awkward smile. I never knew how to take a compliment. Was I supposed to repay it? We were both sweaty and a bit unkempt, and John's nose was red like he might be recovering from a cold. I did find him attractive, but if I said that out loud, where was it going to lead?

"So," he said, "what should we do?"

"About what?"

"Cindy. And her insane drive to know what everyone's doing all the time."

"I wish I knew why no one stands up to her."

"Speaking from experience, it's usually easier to go along with what she wants. Besides, her heart really is—"

"In the right place. So Susan told me. Maybe. But I really don't like feeling as if I'm being watched."

He looked around. The street felt deserted, like it always did in the middle of the day. But maybe that was an illusion. Maybe there were people peering out of the cracks in their curtains, their tablets in hand, logging in our every movement.

March 8, 1:12 p.m. John Dunbar and Julie Prentice spend much too long talking after their "run" together.

I shivered. "I should get inside."

"Me too. Oh, but I meant to tell you, I've applied for a new job. And I'm pretty sure I'm going to get it."

"That's good," I said, stifling my disappointment. When John went back to work, I'd be all alone again during the day. Even though we didn't usually see each other except for our runs, it was a comfort knowing there was a friend nearby, especially these last few weeks. "What is it?"

"I'm going to start my own IT business. Networks, websites, that sort of thing. I'll be working from home."

He grinned. He'd been reading me like an open book.

"That's fantastic. I need a new website."

"Yeah?"

"Yeah."

"Well, maybe you'll be my first customer, then."

"That'd be great. See you tomorrow morning?"

"Absent another deluge, you got it. Break a leg this afternoon. With your pages."

"That's what people say to actors."

"Same difference, right?"

"Maybe a broken leg would give me something to write about."

I trotted across the road. As I approached my front door, I noticed a white plastic bag hanging from the door handle. As I picked it up, a god-awful smell ran out of it. Rotting feces, possibly of the human variety. Nothing that came out of Sandy—who I could hear on the other side of the door, pissed at me because I'd left her behind—ever smelled this bad.

As I held my breath and went to tie the two halves of the bag together to cut off the nauseating smell, something crinkled inside. Had someone really left a note in there? One they expected me to read?

I reached inside with the tip of my fingers and pulled it out.

I read the block letters once, twice, then once again.

And then I began to scream.

My therapist had all kinds of technical explanations for Heather's obsession with me. Apparently, stalking behavior can be brought on by a combination of loneliness, lack of self-esteem, and an overwhelming feeling of self-importance. How someone who has low self-esteem can feel self-important was never really explained to me. Yet it described Heather Stanhope so well, from the very first time I met her.

Only a couple of weeks into law school, I was already deeply regretting my choice. I'd ended up there like many of my friends who had good grades and no idea of what they wanted to be. I chose McGill because it seemed exotic and foreign, even though my mother was from Montreal and we'd spent numerous holidays there with her family.

Such was my thought process at twenty-two.

It was a bad choice. Everyone in my class actually wanted to be a lawyer, and spending day after day with a group of people who'd never failed at anything was both intimidating and exhausting. So when I found myself standing next to Heather at one of the early first-semester mixers I was still going to because there had to be *someone* in my class worth hanging out with, I made a concerted effort to talk to her.

We were in a dive bar on St-Laurent called something that sounded like "Frat Bay." I'd heard one of the guys say that you could buy cocaine in the bathroom. The music was recycled '80s songs, and the air smelled of dry ice and stale beer.

Heather reminded me of me in high school: pudgy, a bad haircut, and clothes that were more aspirational in size than realistic. She was dead smart—she'd already become our property prof's favorite student, her hand shooting in the air whenever he stopped to take a breath—but she didn't fit into the slick, khakied crowd.

It turned out that she was from Upstate, too, and we talked about ski areas, camping trips, and how bad the economy was. Neither of us was going back there; you didn't go to law school to end up back in Upstate.

I asked her how she liked school so far.

"Harvard is the home of American ideas," she said in an odd tone, like she was quoting from the Bible. I knew McGill was sometimes referred to as the Harvard of the North, but I was still confused.

"What's that?"

"P. J. O'Rourke. He said that."

"Aw," I said, desperately trying to remember who P. J. O'Rourke was and why he might be considered quotable in this context. "This party is lame. I said that."

She laughed, but not as hard as I thought she would. I don't think she got the Dylan reference, either, but then again, she hadn't spent high school in love with a Dylan freak.

We were standing at the bar, holding gin and tonics because it was that or watery beer.

"How do you think they do that?" Heather asked.

"Do what?"

"Just . . . blend in?"

She pointed to our classmates, who were sitting at group tables, playing pool, flirting, arguing. They had, in the two weeks we'd been there, congealed. The Class of 1999. A moniker they'd always carry.

"By sublimating their identity?" I said.

This time I did get the laugh.

"You're funny," she said.

"Thank you."

"How come you're not out there?"

"Sometimes I get shy in social situations."

"Me too, but that's because I look like this."

She swept the hand holding the gin and tonic up and down her torso, splashing some of it onto the flower-patterned shirt she was wearing.

"Don't do that," I said. "Don't be the one who puts yourself down. There are enough people in the world who will do that for you."

"That's good advice. Do you follow it?"

"Are you kidding?"

She barked then, an actual bark that was followed by her clapping her hand over her mouth.

I took a gulp of my drink and pretended nothing odd had happened. Thankfully for her, the music was loud enough that no one seemed to have heard. I wondered if she suffered from a mild form of Tourette's.

"That's never happened before," she said, after she'd taken a few large sips of her drink.

"I sang out loud in class once."

"You did?"

"In high school. Took me two years to live that down."

"I'll bet."

She put her drink on the bar. "This thing is awful."

"I kind of agree with you."

"Why did we order it, then?"

"Because Queen Bee did?"

I was referring to Kathryn Simpson, the undisputed beauty of our class. Tall, blonde, thin, she was the kind of girl who must've been the most popular in high school and yet also seemed nice and smart. The men in our class had all flocked to her, and she was on the dance floor as we spoke, surrounded by a bunch of them. They were trying to show her that despite the fact that they were law nerds, they could dance, too!

"She's really pretty," Heather said.

"She is."

"We totally hate her, right?"

"Yup."

"Seems kind of unfair to be that beautiful *and* be able to get into law school."

"Maybe she slept her way in?" I said.

"Maybe she cuts the inside of her arms at night to remind herself not to eat?"

Now it was my turn to almost bark with laughter. But also: Who says something like that?

"You're a little dark, aren't you?"

She shrugged and kept on watching Kathryn. And eventually, I turned my back to the bar and joined her. A few weeks later, Kathryn and I would be assigned to do a legal research project together. She would introduce me to Booth and Kevin, friends of hers since boarding school, and suddenly, I had a group of friends. School became fun. Heather faded into the background.

Was that what started the worm turning?

How can you ever know?

After finding the bag and the note, I managed, somehow, once John had calmed me down and I'd sent him away, to get through the rest of my day. I didn't write anything—I couldn't—but I went to the grocery store and bought supplies for a week of dinners and lunches and breakfasts. I spent the afternoon cooking meals I could pull out of the freezer: lasagna and baked chicken nuggets and dumplings I could fry up in a pan, which the kids loved dipping in soy sauce. I kept the TV on in the kitchen, my phone in my pocket. When everything was in the oven or tucked away, and my house smelled like a restaurant, I frantically Googled home security systems until my MySanity settings set in. I started when the phone rang, but when I picked it up, there was only the sound of ragged breathing, then a dial tone. A blocked number, probably nothing, but everything felt like something that day.

It was Daniel's day to pick up the kids. I was supposed to be seeing Susan that night, but I texted her to cancel, not offering an explanation.

Something came up, was what I wrote.

Something came out, was what I almost wrote.

When Daniel got home with the twins, I let them haul me to the floor in the living room, turning me into a Mommy sandwich, the strength of their love literally crushing me. I told Daniel I'd cooked because I felt like it, and I opened a good bottle of red to go with our lasagna and garlic bread. We ate as a family in a show of domesticity that felt like a stage play. Polite queries about each other's day, reflexive disciplining of the twins, first one and then another glass of wine. The phone rang twice, then cut off midring before Daniel could get there. "Wrong number, I guess," I said, as if I were reading a line.

When Daniel came down from giving the kids their bath and tucking them in, he sat down next to me on the couch, poured himself what was left of the wine, and asked me what was going on.

"And don't tell me nothing, because I know that's bullshit."

"Heather left me this today," I said, handing him the piece of paper that had been resting on the feces. I'd placed it in a plastic bag like the evidence it was, but also in an attempt to mask the odor that was still wafting off it. Despite the wonderful cooking smells that now soaked the house, I couldn't get the stench out of my nose. I'd almost thrown up twice that afternoon, hovering over the bowl like I had too many times during my pregnancy.

"What is that smell?" Daniel asked.

"Shit."

"What?"

"That note came in a bag of shit."

He dropped it on the table, then left to wash his hands. Daniel had been working hard on his compulsive hand washing, and I should've known better. I was a jerk, really, for even putting that bag anywhere near him.

When he came back, his hands red from the scalding water he used, I explained how I found the note. I made a point of mentioning I'd been with John, knowing my screams had likely drawn the attention—if not the immediate action—of more than one of my neighbors. He'd never said anything about our friendship from that first day, but I knew Daniel. He wasn't a jealous person, but he was watchful, and he knew me better than anyone. By mentioning it like I would've mentioned I was with Leah, I was defusing what might, or might not, have been an issue. Exposing it to sunlight and air in the hope it would evaporate.

"I'm glad someone was with you, but why didn't you call me at the office?"

I'd asked myself that more than once, but calling him wouldn't have changed anything. Calling him would've made it all too real, something I wanted to put off as long as possible.

"You had that big meeting today."

"This is more important."

"No. If we make it more important, then she wins."

He ran his hand through his hair. He'd had a haircut recently, and I hadn't even noticed.

"When did you cut your hair?"

"I . . . a couple of days ago. How do you know it's her?"

"Read it," I said, turning the baggie over so he could see the text.

You can run, but you can't hide.

"Is that written in . . . it's not blood, is it?"

"I think it might be."

"This is what she wrote before."

"Yeah, and she's a cutter. She was anyway, in law school."

Heather's suggestions about other people, I was to learn, always had something to do with herself. Her remark that Kathryn might be cutting herself was because *she* was. A casual mention that she'd heard Kevin stayed up all night on Ritalin meant *she* was stealing pills from her younger brother to make her grades. And so on. Back then, I thought it was an odd quirk of hers. Later, it became a kind of warning system.

Daniel drained his wineglass. Then he went to the liquor cabinet and poured himself a large scotch.

"You want?"

"No."

He added another finger and sat on the ledge in front of the window.

"We have to call the police."

"I know."

"Then why haven't you?"

"I'm not sure I can go through all that again."

It wasn't only the intrusion and the questions and the fear it would leak to the media; it was the scrutiny, the feeling that no matter what I said, they'd be looking for holes in my story. It was one of the reasons I stopped practicing law. I didn't want to be scrutinized, and I didn't want to be the person doing the scrutiny.

"But if this is really her," Daniel said, "if she's really found you, us, started all this again, then we can't take the risk. It's dangerous, Jules, it's—"

"I know, okay? I know." I pulled my knees up and rested my chin on the knobby bones I could feel beneath my jeans. I wasn't eating enough lately, and it was starting to show.

"I keep thinking . . . remember that article?"

"The one you wrote about Heather?"

"Yeah."

"What about it?"

"It said all the stuff she did. The notes she left, the way she got to me. What if this isn't her? What if it's someone in the neighborhood imitating her to get under my skin?"

"You think that because of what they used . . ." He waved his hand around, indicating the smell I feared would never go away. "You really think someone would do that to you?"

"Have you looked at that iNeighbor thing lately? They're calling it the 'dog incident,' and there's a whole update section. Like it's *People. com* or something. People are watching what I do with Sandy: where she is, whether she's on her leash, whether I'm picking up after her. They're logging my activities."

Everything is innocuous until it's written down.

6:00 a.m. to 7:00 a.m. Ran with dog and John Dunbar. Again.

2:20 p.m. Seen entering Kroger's. Not carrying reusable bags.

2:50 p.m. Seen leaving Kroger's. Non-use of reusable bags confirmed.

I'd spoken to my lawyer, Lee, about it, but he'd said that so long as what they were writing were things I'd done in public, there wasn't anything I could do. I was sick of hearing that from him. Maybe I needed another lawyer.

"That's fucked up," Daniel said.

"Completely. Cindy is crazy, and she's got half the street under her spell."

Truth be told, Cindy was the one doing most of the logging, but a woman two doors down had added an entry yesterday, and almost everyone had stayed registered on the site.

And yet: not one person had written anything about the package left on my doorstep.

"You can't think Cindy did this?"

"Probably not. Maybe it was one of the kids?"

"Did you ask John about Chris?"

"How could I do that? After what Sandy did? I feel so bad."

Daniel shrugged. "He shouldn't have been creeping around at night."

"Daniel."

"What? He shouldn't have. And anyway, whoever it is, we have to call the cops."

I motioned for him to come sit by me. He picked up his drink and sank into the couch. I felt better having him next to me, which felt like something I needed to remind myself. The fact that I had to sat like a yoke across my shoulders. I knew this feeling. The creaky neck, the need to cough when there wasn't anything in my throat, the fading appetite. It was the feeling I got before depression set in. Sometimes it was transient, and sometimes it moved in and took me down. I needed to do all I could to make sure that didn't happen.

"I know," I said. "In the morning, okay?"

I leaned back, and he gathered me to him. I took the glass of scotch from his hand and sniffed it.

"This smells almost as bad as that bag does."

"That's heresy, that is."

"Burn me at the stake, then."

"Never, even if you *are* a witch."

"Is there any doubt?"

He smiled into my hair, and we sat like that till the moon rose high and the street settled into silence. We'd spent many similar nights over the course of our relationship, the quiet our companion, our heartbeats keeping time with the clock on the mantel. Sometimes, like that night, I'd even fall asleep, and Daniel would carry me to bed as if I were one of the children.

It was, I think, the first time I'd felt at home, at peace, since we'd moved.

If I'd known I'd never feel that way again, I would've stayed on that couch forever, and barred the dawn from coming in.

Mount Adams Record

Famous Author 'Julie Apple' Claims Harassment

Police: No leads yet

March 10

New Mount Adams resident Julie Apple Prentice recently advised the police that she has been the subject of harassment at her home on Pine Street. Mrs. Prentice, forty-two, is the author, under her maiden name, of the *New York Times* #1 bestselling novel *The Murder Game*.

Although Mrs. Prentice declined to comment for this article, police sources have revealed that she complained of a breach in her home network and her personal e-mail that occurred in the previous months, as well as offensive and threatening material being left on her doorstep on March 8. Mrs. Prentice was previously the victim of a stalker in Washington State named Heather Stanhope, as

Prentice famously wrote about in a *Vogue* article called "Why Me?"

The official statement from the police department is that they are not pursuing any leads at present.

Mrs. Prentice's neighbor, Cindy Sutton, forty-five, said that Mrs. Prentice has had some trouble fitting into the neighborhood.

"She's not much of a joiner," Mrs. Sutton said. "We're real big on community around here, but she hasn't volunteered for anything yet. And then there was the issue of her dog."

Mrs. Sutton was referring to an incident that occurred last month when Mrs. Prentice's dog, a German shepherd, attacked the fifteen-year-old son of Mr. and Mrs. John Dunbar. Neither of them could be reached for comment, but "he's probably going to have a permanent scar," Mrs. Sutton said. "Because of her, we've had to adopt a bunch of new rules around here."

When asked whether she thought Mrs. Prentice deserved to be harassed, Mrs. Sutton replied, "Well, I wouldn't go that far. But we tend to reap what we sow, don't we?"

Other residents feel differently. "Julie has been a good friend to me," Susan Thurgood, forty-seven, said. "And what is happening to her is horrible. I hope the police are taking it seriously."

The Murder Game, about a group of law-school friends who plan the perfect murder, and then— maybe—execute the plan years later, caused an impressive stir when it was published two years ago. With almost three million copies sold, there has been persistent online speculation that the book is at least partially based on Mrs. Prentice's own experiences, in particular, the mysterious death of her law-school classmate, Kathryn Simpson.

"That is complete nonsense," Mrs. Prentice's representative said when reached for comment. "We have serious reasons to believe that Heather Stanhope is behind the bulk of those comments, which is a matter of record."

Learning to Fly
John
Seven months ago

"Did you know about this?" Hanna asked me a few days after Julie found the bag of turds on her front doorstep along with that creepy note.

We were having a lazy Saturday morning. Not our turn, for once, to take our kids to their endless extracurricular activities. Lounging in our kitchen. A patch of sunlight was warming my back. The scent of slightly charred bacon hung heavily in the air. Becky had decided to take charge of breakfast.

Hanna handed me the local paper, her finger tapping a headline. FAMOUS AUTHOR 'JULIE APPLE' CLAIMS HARASSMENT. I read it quickly. It mentioned several things that had happened to Julie in the past few months. It did not mention the details of the note. The one that might have been written in blood. The thought of it made my skin crawl.

What could possess someone to cut some part of their body in a way that would produce enough blood to write a note?

Julie was shaking like a leaf when I reached her and stopped her screaming. I'd wanted to call the cops, call Daniel, do something. But once she'd calmed down, she told me she'd take care of it, and there wasn't anything I could do but leave.

She'd canceled our run the last couple of days, texting as I was lacing up my shoes that maybe the next day would be better.

"Some of it," I said to Hanna. "I was the one who told her that her Internet could be breached. I could see her Wi-Fi network from here. She thought it was one of her kids who changed the password. And that e-mail thing happened in Mexico. Remember? I was helping her put more security on it that first day we ran into them?"

"I remember." Hanna arched an eyebrow. Her hair was tangled and messy from sleep. I always liked her best that way, though she never believed me. "Did anyone call you about Chris, asking for a quote?"

"Not me. You?"

"No. Those guys better watch what they're doing. They may only be a local paper, but still."

"They probably didn't know what to do with themselves," I said. "This story is way more exciting than the usual Cat Stuck in Tree."

I never used to read the local paper. But now that I was home all day, I found myself perusing it cover to cover.

I read the rest of the article. The part about Julie's book being based on her own experiences reminded me of what Daniel had said in Mexico at the bar. I'd thought he was fucking with me. Until I'd seen the glint in Julie's eye as the crazy taxi driver did his best to put our lives at risk. Was it possible Julie had somehow been involved in someone's death? That she'd used it as the foundation for her book? I shook the thought away. I clearly needed to get out more if I was taking the *Mount Adams Record* seriously.

"She has a 'representative,'" Hanna said. "She has people! I need some people."

"You have an assistant."

"Yeah, but I can't call her 'my people.'" She took the paper back and read the article again. "This seems pretty mild. I can't believe she called the police."

I hadn't told Hanna about the package or the note because Julie had asked me not to. And given the lack of details in the story, I didn't feel as if I could betray her trust. Perhaps the police were holding it back in order to catch the culprit.

"It sounds kind of serious to me," I said.

"Come on, John. You just said at least one of those things didn't even happen when she was in Cincinnati."

"The person who tried to break into her e-mail wasn't *in* Mexico. It just happened while we were there. And maybe she was wrong about her kids. It doesn't seem likely, does it, that a six-year-old could change her network password?"

Hanna rose and started loading the dishwasher. There was a ring of maple syrup where her plate had been. Becky's attempt at pancakes was only slightly better than her go at the bacon. I made a mental note to give her some lessons.

"Why are you defending her?" Hanna asked.

"Why aren't you? Can you really blame her for feeling harassed? Particularly given that whole iNeighbor thing?"

"Cindy is a bit out of control, I grant you. But it's hard for me to have too much sympathy for Julie, given the state of Chris's face."

In the end, Chris hadn't needed traditional stitches. The plastic surgeon told us the scar would likely fade to a thin line without surgery. Nothing that would be noticeable in a couple of years. So he'd glued the cut together, and we'd chosen to let him heal naturally. But Hanna winced every time she caught sight of his face. As if she were being cut each time. Chris didn't really seem to care. Or so he said. I'd caught him scowling at himself a few times. I offered to buy him an eye patch to complete his pirate look. He'd laughed, and we'd had a wrestling match, which he won. That made it the last six times in his favor. I might be back in shape, but fifteen could take forty-five. Which was probably a good thing.

It had taken me longer to convince Hanna not to bring a lawsuit. I still wasn't sure I'd succeeded.

"Chris is fine," I said. "And she's apologized for that. Accidents happen."

She closed the dishwasher and wiped her hands on a towel. She was wearing her workout clothes. Hanna hates running outside, preferring the perfectly sealed atmosphere of the gym.

"It wasn't an accident. And something about this feels off."

"What?"

"I just get this vibe from her. She reminds me of that client I had. You know the Munchausen-by-proxy one?"

"That woman who was making her kids sick?"

"That's the one. I knew something was wrong from the first time I met her."

"What are you talking about?"

"People do weird things to call attention to themselves."

"I know that. But Julie doesn't want attention. She didn't even speak to the press."

"Then how did they get the story?"

That was a good question. Hanna was always full of good questions.

"You're the one who's always saying journalists bribe the clerks to let them know if any juicy gossip comes in."

"Sure, that happens. But the local paper? Besides, when something comes out about a celebrity, it's usually because they called it in themselves."

"Julie's not a Kardashian."

"No, but she keeps saying one thing and doing another. Like how she let her real last name 'slip' the first time you talked to her. If she was so into privacy, why do we know who she is?"

I expelled a breath. There wasn't any point in arguing with Hanna when she was like this. And it was more than likely my fault she was thinking this way in the first place. I was spending too much time with Julie. It was time for it to stop. Hanna trusted me. I'd never given her any reason not to. The thought that I might be giving her cause now sickened me.

Because I wasn't that guy.

I really wasn't.

Chris turned fifteen and a half a week later. We'd stopped celebrating his half birthday when he was eight, but this half birthday meant something. He could get his learner's permit. Chris had circled the date on the kitchen calendar the day it was put up. Hanna shuddered and said no way. But he'd worked on her, and now she was resigned.

So on a sweet-aired March day, I built Chris a stack of half-moon pancakes to imitate the half-birthday cake he'd be getting later, and drove him to the DMV. We went to the driver exam station, and I read box scores on my phone while he answered questions like "When is a driver permitted to turn right on a red traffic signal?" He passed the test with flying colors. After I promised he'd always be accompanied by Hanna or me, he was given his temporary permit.

We'd let him take the day off school, thinking we might use the time to start driving lessons. Once his permit was in his wallet, I drove him to the Eastgate Mall, counting on its enormous parking lot to be nearly deserted on a Thursday morning. I parked in one of the spaces and turned off the engine.

"Ready?" I said to Chris.

His scarred cheek was facing me. I felt a pang. Whenever something happened to one of the kids, I couldn't help feeling like I'd failed. Like I was wounded myself. No matter how small the incident. It was the terrible thing about parenthood. Did that ache ever go away?

His voice cracked. "I think so."

"You'll be great."

"You're not going to yell or anything?"

"Of course not."

"That's what Ashley's dad did when he was teaching her to drive."

"Well, he shouldn't have." I unbuckled my seat belt. "Let's switch."

We met at the front bumper. I gave his shoulder a squeeze. "Have I ever yelled at you when I was teaching you something?"

"No."

"My dad used to do that, and it drove me crazy. So don't worry. You can do this."

"Okay."

We climbed back in. I talked him through starting the engine, putting the car in reverse, and depressing the gas. After confusing the gas and the brake a few times while the car was still in park, he eased us out of the space a bit too fast. I was glad the parking lot was empty.

"Follow this road to the stop sign," I said. "Be careful of pedestrians. They tend to leap out between cars."

Chris looked left and right, then slowed down even more.

"This is stressing me out."

"You'll get the hang of it. But it's not a bad thing to be cautious."

He didn't look so sure.

"Why don't we talk about something? Something to distract you."

"I thought I was supposed to concentrate?"

"You are. But you also need to learn to do two things at once."

His hands gripped the wheel tightly. "I think I need to build up to that."

"Why don't you take a right up here?"

He slowed to a stop, the car jerking twice.

"Sorry!"

"It's fine, Chris. Remember, gas is on the right, brake is on the left."

"Why can't I use two feet?"

"Well, if you ever drive stick, you'll need your left foot for the clutch. You'll get used to it. Now, put on your turn indicator and turn the car gently around this corner. Then drive over there and park between those two cars."

Chris leaned forward and followed my instructions. When he stopped crookedly between the two cars and turned off the engine, his hands were shaking.

"You okay there, buddy?"

"It's a lot more difficult than I thought."

"You'll get it, I promise."

"Thanks, Dad."

A phone buzzed, then stopped, then buzzed again. I checked my own phone, but there weren't any new messages.

"Sounds like someone's trying to reach you," I said.

"Yeah."

"Something going on?"

"It's probably Ashley."

"Has her mom relented about you two seeing each other?"

"Sort of?"

"So how come you're not answering?"

"I'm doing this right now."

"She text you a lot?"

"What's a lot?"

I almost laughed. I was glad my first relationships hadn't had to deal with e-mail or texts or any of the things we now took for granted. Though, I'd been so awkward at talking to girls on the phone back then that sometimes whole minutes would pass in silence. I dreaded those phone calls about as much as Chris was dreading this conversation. Maybe texting would've saved me.

"I think a lot is anything that makes you uncomfortable, taking compromise into account."

"What does that mean?"

"Compromise, son. It's what makes relationships work. I'm sure you've noticed that girls talk a lot more than boys?"

"Yeah."

"And they worry more, too. Take your mom, for instance. How she likes you to call her or text her when you get somewhere. You do that, right?"

"Sure, but that's Mom."

"Right, but I do it, too. Because I know otherwise she'd worry. And that's compromise."

"What do you get in return?"

"It's not really about that. It's more like, if there's something I really care about, then she'll let me have my way."

He sighed. "That sounds like a lot of work."

"It can be. It depends if it's worth it."

"How do you know?"

"With you guys, it's obvious. Everything is worth it. But in general, that's hard to say. I think you have to ask yourself whether the good outweighs the bad. No one's perfect. Everyone has their stuff. Things they'll do that you find annoying or don't understand. But if you love someone, or think you might, then you decide what's the most important thing. Them in your life, or not."

His phone buzzed again. His fingers closed around its shape in his jeans.

"Why don't you go ahead and answer that?"

He put his hands back on the wheel. "I think I'd like to try this again."

"You sure?"

"I'm sure."

"Okay. So, you'll need to check your rearview mirror and back out slowly. Don't try turning the wheel until I tell you to."

"Thanks, Dad."

He gave me a shy smile, and I knew he was thanking me for more than the driving lessons.

Months later, I'd asked myself repeatedly whether, if I'd said something different that day, things would've turned out the same.

Life is made up of turning points. Forks in the road.

We make choices every day that take us down one path over another.

The thing I've learned is, there generally aren't any signposts along the way.

Today

John

12:00 p.m.

We're at lunch. Around eleven, the prosecutor came downstairs to tell us we wouldn't testify until the afternoon. We needed to eat, so we decided to go to The Rookwood, the former site of Rookwood Pottery that's been turned into a restaurant. The old kiln still sits in the middle of the building. Renovations have added a stone patio with a view over the river. The threatening sky has cleared, so we accept a table outside in the sun.

Chris used to love this place when he was a kid. He and Becky would order Shirley Temples and French fries. Things they weren't normally allowed to eat. Special treats to bribe good behavior while the grown-ups tried to eat a meal in semi-peace.

Today, he orders a classic burger, which now comes with artisanal lettuce, whatever that is. I know he won't eat much of it. Like the pancakes this morning that congealed in their syrup. And all the meals since the morning of the accident that have been pushed around his plate.

He's shredding his paper place mat into little pieces, leaving a trail of confetti across the metal table. His face is blank, dazed.

"Chris, is there something you haven't told us?" Alicia asks.

"I dunno," Chris says. "Like what?"

"What's going on, Alicia?" Hanna asks.

"I want to hear from Chris first. Is there something about that day, or the months before it, that you haven't told us about? Something important?"

Chris squirms in his seat. Hanna's told me more than once that all witnesses have something at the forefront of their minds. Something they're worried they'll be asked about. It's as likely to be important as innocuous. The challenge is to get them to disclose what they're scared to reveal before they testify.

I wonder if this is what Alicia's doing. Trying to get Chris to release whatever's scaring him before he takes the stand.

We watch Chris struggle. My heart wants to believe there's nothing there. That there aren't any secrets left to tell. I know that's a fantasy. I just don't know how big a fantasy it is.

The waitress arrives with our food. Chris seems to think he's off the hook, and actually takes a large bite from his burger. But Hanna doesn't touch her beet salad. Her eyes shift back and forth between Alicia and Chris like she's watching a tennis match.

"What is it, Alicia? Please, tell us," she says finally.

Alicia gives Chris one last look and relents. "They think Chris was behind some of the harassment Julie was getting."

"Who thinks that?"

"The police. The prosecutor. They've gone back and looked at her complaints more closely. I gather they didn't take them that seriously when it occurred."

Chris puts his hamburger down. There's a splotch of ketchup at the corner of his mouth. Hanna's hand reaches unconsciously to wipe it away. How many times has she done that in the last sixteen years? Cleaned up after Chris. That swirl of chaos he always seemed to leave around him, even as a tiny boy.

"Chris?" I say. "Is this true? Did you have something to do with harassing her?"

I know even before he nods that it is. That it's the explanation for a lot of things. That even though the threat of Heather Stanhope has been, to some extent, real, the boy next door is a more likely explanation.

"Sort of," he says, his voice rising an octave above its new register.

"What kind of answer is that?"

"I'm sorry."

"We're all sorry. But we said. We agreed. We'd tell Alicia everything so we could deal with it up front."

His eyes brim with tears. "You really want me to tell everything?"

There's something in his voice. A threat. A warning.

"If you were involved in what happened to her, then yes," I amend. "You need to tell us. Right now."

He breaks my gaze and pushes his plate away.

"It wasn't my idea."

"What wasn't your idea?" I say at the same time as Hanna says, "Whose idea was it?"

"Ashley," Chris says. "It was Ashley's idea."

It comes out of him in fits and starts. How Ashley's parents had grounded her after Chris was found escaping their basement. That they'd confiscated her phone and forbidden her to talk to him at school. How upset she was at the state of his face. She wanted to get back at Julie for what she'd done. She was, like, *obsessed*.

"She wasn't responsible for you being in Ashley's house that night," I say.

"I know. But she told that dog to attack, Dad. She did."

162

Hanna shoots me a look. *How dare I blame our son for anything right now?*

How dare I.

"So what happened next?" Alicia asks. She takes a yellow legal pad out of her bag and starts taking notes. Another pad to add to the pile. I've always meant to ask her what she does with all of them.

"She kept talking about it and talking about it. How we should do something. Get back at her. Make her feel like I did that night. It sort of became like this game? We could toilet-paper her house. We could key her car. We could—"

"Leave a turd with a scary note at her front door?"

"Yeah."

"It was yours?"

Alicia looks embarrassed for the first time since I met her. I wouldn't have thought it was possible, given what she does for a living.

"Yeah."

"And the note? How did you do that?"

"Ashley pricked her finger. She saw something online about this woman who stalked Mrs. Prentice. She'd done something like that."

Our sunny waitress appears.

"Everything all right here? Burger not to your liking?"

"I'm not hungry," Chris says.

"I'll take that, then," she says, stacking our plates and ushering them away.

"What does this mean?" Hanna asks Alicia. "For the case?"

"Is that everything, Chris?" Alicia asks. "The only thing you did?"

"We called her a couple of times and hung up. Stuff like that. Ashley might've done some other stuff. I didn't really want to know."

"Well, if that's everything, then I think we can contain this," Alicia says.

"How?"

"It's a question of emphasis. It was all Ashley's idea, wasn't it, Chris?"

"Yeah, but—"

"I know you don't want to blame her. I get that. But it *will* make a difference to how the jury perceives you. If you tell it like you told us. Reluctantly. Let the prosecutor drag it out of you, but make it clear you never would've done something like that without her influence."

"To keep their sympathy?" Hanna asks.

"Yes. And you and your husband didn't know, I presume. Didn't even suspect?"

"No."

"No," I echo. "We didn't know. How could we?"

Alicia gives me a fleeting look. "People don't have a tendency to believe that. We assume people must know what's going on in their own house, their own family."

"Nobody knows everything that's going on," Hanna says. "Even in their own house."

"That's true, but that's not a winning strategy. We have to convince them you didn't know."

"I didn't tell anyone," Chris says. "Ashley didn't tell anyone."

"Tell that to the jury and we should be all right."

The waitress brings the bill and we pay up. Hanna walks ahead while I hang back with Alicia.

"Is this really an issue?" I ask. "A stupid prank?"

"It doesn't look good. It might seem like it's a motive."

"A motive for what?"

"If Julie knew who'd been pranking her. If she'd threatened to expose them."

"How would Julie have known?"

"She hired someone to look into everything because of the lawsuit."

"She did?"

"Daniel did, actually."

"So you're saying they knew Chris and Ashley had done those things?"

"I'm not privy to all the details. The testimony is sealed."

"But you knew enough to ask Chris."

"I have my sources, but they're not perfect."

We drive back to the prosecutor's office in silence. Our perfect parking place is gone, so I put the car in the lot across the street. Hanna and Alicia walk ahead, back in their huddle. Chris waits for me by the front doors. He watches the women enter before he speaks.

"You really want me to tell the truth?" Chris says, when we can't see them anymore.

His posture is aggressive, like a caged animal. What has brought about this transformation in my son?

"We've been over this. Like Alicia says: you have to answer the questions that are asked, but you don't have to volunteer information."

"Okay, Dad. Okay. I won't *volunteer* anything. If they don't ask, I won't tell."

My gut twists. I regret having eaten anything for lunch.

"What's going on, Chris?"

"Nothing."

"Clearly there's something."

"It doesn't matter. It doesn't change anything."

"How can you know that if you don't tell me what it is?"

"Because it's the kind of thing where it doesn't matter what the truth is. It only matters what I thought when I saw it."

"Saw what?"

He shoves his hands in his pockets. I doubt he'll ever wear this suit again. Like the suit I wore to my father's funeral. Maybe I'll burn it along with this one in a barrel in the backyard.

If this day ever ends.

"What, Chris?"

"Nothing, okay. Nothing. Who knows what I saw."

"Was it the morning of the accident?"

He shrugs his teenaged shrug.

Hanna's head pops out of the doorway.

"John, Chris, let's go."

Chris shrugs again. Then he turns and follows his mother's instructions.

I stand waiting on the sidewalk, trying to understand his meaning. What was he trying to tell me?

My stomach gives that empty thump again, and I remember.

Another morning where something momentous happened.

But he couldn't have seen that.

Could he?

I'll Be Watching You

Julie

Six months ago

"And the police really aren't doing anything?" Susan asked, on one of our nightly walks in April.

Most nights we talked about our kids, the little aggravations and dramas of the day. Or she'd tell me a bit about her divorce, can-you-believe-what-Brad-did-now stories. Every once in a while, I'd talk to her about where I was in Book Two, getting another perspective to help me solve a corner I'd written myself into as I neared the fifty-thousand-word mark. Leah and I used to do that on our runs, and being away from her made me feel cut off from the kind of gentle support I needed to get from point A to point B.

I'd never really let Susan in before. I didn't know if I could trust her, and something always held me back, even though she didn't feel the same restraint, but there was something about that night. The air was pregnant with rain, and the scent of wood smoke wafted from more than one of the colorful houses that made up our neighborhood. Though the days were warming up, the nights still clung to winter. It all felt alien, otherworldly, and yet comforting. Like the bluebells that poked through the remnants of the snow in Eden Park, something opened up inside me.

I told her everything. Why I'd run out of the coffee shop the first day we met, and the attempt to break into my e-mail while I was in Mexico, and the breach in my network that John had helped plug. I told her all about the "present" left at my door, and the amateurish note left with it, how it was similar to something Heather had done right before we decided to move. I told her all the things Heather did, and why what was happening now felt both foreign and familiar.

It poured out of me like a river breaching its banks. The hang-ups I'd been receiving for the last couple of weeks, so that now I wrote with the phone off the hook. The time I was certain the back-door lock had been picked when I'd left it locked because I always do. And the heart-chilling moment when Melly talked about the new teacher at school named "Header," who turned out to be a friendly woman in her midtwenties.

"What do the police say about all of this?"

"They think I'm being hysterical," I said. "I didn't even bother telling them about the hang-ups."

"Couldn't they trace them?"

"Maybe. If they actually investigated."

"But what about the fact that you had a stalker before? And that this was exactly the sort of stuff she was doing?"

"You'd think that would matter. If I'd had a heart attack before, and I had the same symptoms, wouldn't that bring me to the front of the line?"

"Of course it would. Men."

Susan said this often, as if all men were as faithless and disappointing as her ex.

168

"I haven't told you the craziest thing. I've been thinking about it, and I don't think it's Heather."

It was true. When I'd had time to sit and really think it over, I realized it couldn't be her. Heather was smart, I always had to give her that. And though she'd left a note or two, she never repeated herself, or did something that would leave traces of her DNA behind. She'd won the criminal-law prize, after all. Although I'd succeeded in getting a restraining order against her, it was more fluke than the result of mistakes, a haphazard passerby who saw what she was doing and called 9-1-1 instead of walking away.

"How can you be sure?"

"They did check on her, at least. She's in Seattle, and there's no evidence she's left there recently. She turns up at work, does her community service, no flights booked in her name, et cetera. End of story."

"So, who, then?"

I hesitated. It was one thing to discuss the possibility with Daniel, another to release it out into the open. "Most likely, it's someone who lives here."

We turned onto a new street. We structured our walks like we were doing hill training. One block up, then down the next. Although I'd gotten used to the terrain, my pulse was usually beating in my ears by the time we crested each street.

It had finally started to rain, the fat drops plopping against the pavement and the hoods of our anoraks, but somehow, I didn't mind it the way I usually did. It felt like the proper backdrop to everything that was happening, or going to happen.

"Any idea who it might be?" Susan asked.

I hadn't shared our theories with the police. I'd done enough damage to John's son. If he was getting back at me for the dog bite, perhaps I deserved it. And if it was him, then I didn't have anything to worry about.

But if I wasn't worried about it, why was I spilling my guts to Susan?

"Not really," I said. "God, I hate how paranoid it's making me. It's hard enough getting used to a new place, plus that bloody website of Cindy's isn't helping. And then the newspaper article. Heather didn't know where I was, but maybe now she's found out."

"I never even thought about that."

"It's not your fault. It's Cindy's."

Cindy with her constant checking on me. I was sure she was the one who saw the cops arrive at my door and set the local reporter digging.

"Have you talked to Cindy?" Susan asked. "Maybe if you told her some of what you're telling me, she'd calm down."

"You really think it would make a difference?"

"She's not *that* bad. She has too much time on her hands. You know how it is. Her kids are in school all day, and she's probably bored out of her skull."

I knew what she meant, but I didn't know how it was. I never had enough time to think about things. Whether the twins were home or not, my thoughts were always cluttered, trying to find enough space to stretch themselves out. Was there an opposite of "bored out of your skull"?

"So that makes it okay for her to turn everyone into spies?"

"I doubt she sees it that way."

"I'm sure she doesn't, but it's pretty ridiculous, and it's not making us safer. John said that if someone hacks the website, which would be pretty easy given the security levels on it, then they'd know exactly when people are home or not. That's going to make it easier for someone to break into your house, not harder."

"John said?"

I pulled my head back farther into my hood. "John Dunbar. He does IT."

"I know. I've known him a long time. When did he tell you that?"

"We run together sometimes. I thought you knew." I thought everyone knew. "Why?"

"No reason."

I tried to catch her eye, but her own head was deep within her bright-green hood.

"Say what's on your mind," I said. "I can take it."

"I'm overly sensitive to this kind of stuff."

A streak of lightning flashed in the sky. I counted the seconds till the thunder reached us: at least three. I only get nervous when it strikes within one.

"Brad's a cheater," Susan said. "Was. I guess he can do what he wants, now."

"I'm really sorry about that, but . . . how did we get to cheating?"

"I've . . . heard some things."

I stopped. "Such as?"

"I don't think Hanna likes that you guys hang out, that's all."

"We don't hang out. We run. I hang out with you."

I started moving again, and Susan trotted to keep up with me.

"Are you mad?"

"No. Thank you for telling me."

"But you're something?"

"I wish no one was talking about me. Ever."

"They aren't. Not really."

I wiped the rain away from my face, but rain isn't salty.

"Talk to Cindy, Julie. I think that will really help."

I doubted it, but I said I'd try.

The whole year I was in bar school, I tried to keep Daniel at bay. We'd met during my law-school finals in my fourth year. He'd sneaked into the new law library, and we spent a week studying at adjoining tables.

There wasn't much time for talking, and it wasn't really the place for flirting, what with the law nerds shushing everyone if you said more than ten words. But he asked for my number, and I gave it to him, even though my heart still felt trampled by Booth, the guy I'd dated since first year. When exams were over, Daniel called, and we went for drinks a few times. I liked him, and I wanted to really like him, but we didn't catch fire. I didn't, anyway. Then bar school started—this ridiculous yearlong thing that most people failed—and all my time was allotted to the part-time work I was doing at the prosecutor's office and studying for my exams.

I suppose you could say I put Daniel in the friend zone. Daniel acted as if he was okay with it, but he was only biding his time. He'd come over and cook me a meal before each exam, making sure I didn't forget to eat—something simple and filling like spaghetti with meat sauce, as if I was carbo-loading for a race. As I passed each exam, he'd take me for a drink, just one, and listen while I complained about the arcane questions the exam contained. Then he'd tell me funny stories about the weirdos in his program, and I'd be laughing so hard my sides hurt.

Then one day when my exams were finally over and I had started articling, Daniel asked to get together and surprised me at the bar by telling me he was going to stay through the summer, but then he was pretty sure he was going to leave and go do his PhD somewhere else. As he pulled me to him for a hug, I felt like an idiot. A sad, misguided dummy. Daniel was leaving? No. Daniel couldn't leave. He was the only good thing in my life. I had to tell him. I had to show him.

I kissed his neck.

He backed away, startled, and I felt even worse. That whole year, neither of us had talked about anyone else. I'd assumed he was single, still interested, waiting, but of course he wasn't. Of course some other woman wasn't as dumb as I was.

He stepped toward me, taking my face in his hands, curling his fingers through my hair.

"What are you doing?" I asked.

"Looking at you," he said. "Okay?"

I nodded. I'd left a smudge of cherry-colored ChapStick on his neck. I reached to rub it off. He ducked down and caught my lips midway, and although we were in a bar, and there were whoops coming from the next table, and eventually calls for us to get a room, we stood there like that for hours.

Kissing like we had all the time in the world.

I caught Cindy in line at school pickup. Her son, Tanner, was in fifth or sixth grade—I should probably have known which, but I could barely keep the details of my own life straight—at the same Catholic school where the twins were finishing up first grade.

The private school was about a fifteen-minute drive from Pine Street. They wore adorable little uniforms: white shirts and pleated skirts for the girls; shorts or long, blue pants for the boys. No boy above second grade would wear those shorts, and I knew my days of seeing Sam in them were numbered. My favorite shot of him and Melly was one where they were both in their uniforms, but wearing the other's bottoms. "Look, Momsy," Melly had said, "I'm Sam now."

I arrived at pickup ten minutes earlier than I normally did. "Pickup" being a long line of SUVs and third-row-seating Acuras, each waiting to collect their individual children. What had ever happened to carpooling, I often wondered, that loose organization of mutual trust that had ferried me through my childhood unaffected and secure? It seemed an alien concept here, at least in our neighborhood.

I showed up early because I'd noticed Cindy was usually at the beginning of the line, a badge of organized parenthood that was never something I tried to achieve. My goal, every day, was to get there in time for the twins to see me right when they came out the door. That was my pledge to them: they'd never have to search for me, never have to wonder whether I'd forgotten them. My own mother—a single mother of two—had committed that sin more than once. Most of me forgave her, but I certainly wouldn't forgive myself if I imitated her. So I had two alarms set—one on my watch and one on my computer—to make it impossible for me to miss it, no matter how engrossed I was.

It was raining again; some low-pressure system seemed to have us in its grip. My running shoes were permanently sodden, so much so that I'd gone and bought a second pair at Bob Roncker's. I traded them off every other day, but I'd still developed two bloated blisters on my big toes, ones I wasn't sure if I should pop and bandage, or wait to resolve naturally.

My early arrival paid off. I was the first in line—yeah, me!—and Cindy pulled up behind me shortly thereafter. I gave myself a pep talk, then jumped out of the car and rapped on her window. She lowered it, looking puzzled. The humidity had turned her hair abnormally frizzy, and she smoothed the back of it down with her hand.

"Hi, Cindy. Do you have a minute?"

She checked the clock. The bell would ring in four minutes. The implication was clear.

"Sure, what's up?"

"I want to talk to you about iNeighbor."

"Are you having technical issues? Perhaps John Dunbar could help you with them."

So, it's going to be like that, I thought.

"No, I'm not having technical issues."

"What, then?"

"I was wondering . . . I was hoping, actually, that you might consider removing our street from the site."

"Removing? Oh, no, I don't think so."

"But . . . will you hear me out?"

She checked the clock again. Two minutes to the bell.

I spoke as rapidly as I could. "You know who I am, right? You wrote about it in the newsletter?"

"You wrote that book."

"And you read the article the paper wrote about me, the one that quoted you. So you know I have a stalker, and you know I'm being harassed by someone here."

"Some jilted ex-boyfriend?"

"No, that's not how . . . it's a woman, one I knew years ago. She became obsessed with me after my book came out, and she did all kinds of . . . it was terrible. That's why we moved."

"I'm sorry for that," Cindy said in a way that could've equally been an expression of sympathy, or regret I'd moved onto her street. "But I don't see what that has to do with iNeighbor."

"Can't you?"

She blinked at me. I wondered what kind of antidepressants she was on, and whether there was a sedative thrown into the mix, too.

"That system is making my stalker's job easier, or whoever's harassing me now, and it's pretty sick what they're doing."

"You mean that . . . package that was left on your doorstep?"

"Among other things."

"That was a prank."

"Wait. How do you—"

The bell rang. The sound of it always triggered a Pavlovian response in me that made me want to run through a hallway and into the outdoors. Bells of freedom, another day done. Only I was already outside, and I could go wherever I wanted. The feeling-free part, though? I couldn't remember the last time that was a possibility.

"Cindy, how do you know about the package?"

She was watching the front door. Kids started to trickle out, their uniforms covered by superhero raincoats, some of the girls holding clear, miniature umbrellas. I knew my own kids would be a few minutes late; like me, it was almost impossible for them to show up for anything on time.

"What's that?" Cindy said.

"You said it was a prank. How do you know that? Do you know who did it?"

"You must've misunderstood what I said. There he is!"

She started to open her door. I pressed against it. She pushed at it, but my body's deadweight held her in place.

"You're blocking me."

"Tanner can get to the car all by himself. Please tell me what you know."

"You can't . . . trap me in my car like this. Let me out!"

She sounded panicked. I backed away as another woman came up to us.

"What's going on here? Cindy? Everything okay?"

"Everything's fine," I said. "It's a misunderstanding."

I raised my hands and walked around her car toward the school's front entrance.

"Julie. Julie, stop right there."

Cindy hustled around me, her friend in tow.

"I need to get my kids."

"You can't . . . threaten me like that and walk away."

"I did no such thing."

"You wouldn't let me out of my car. You saw. Right, Leslie?"

Leslie bit her lip. "I'm not sure . . . I didn't hear her say anything."

"I was asking Cindy to help me out with something. I would never threaten anybody."

"What's going on here?"

Now Susan had joined us, and I could sense others watching as well. A circle was forming around me as more kids started schooling out the door, weaving their way to the line of SUVs. They all looked so similar in the rain. Did anyone ever pick up the wrong child? Or was I the only one for whom that seemed like a possibility?

"I told you this was a bad idea," I said to Susan.

"What?" Cindy said. "What's a bad idea?"

The women pressed closer, forming a circle around me. Cindy's face was close enough to mine that I could smell the garlicky hummus she must've had for lunch. I could feel the claustrophobia set in, the kind I felt in crowds or shopping malls.

"I just want it all to stop."

Susan put her arm around me. I leaned against her, feeling faint, my ears ringing.

"Where are the kids?"

"I'm not sure . . ."

I spotted them in their matching raincoats and boots splashing in a puddle near the entrance. That moment of relief I'd never quite overcome coursed through me. Only this time, it made me feel weak in the knees.

"There. They're right there," I said to Susan. My voice sounded strange, like I was speaking underwater.

"I'll go get them. Go back to your car."

"I'm okay. I can handle it."

"I don't think so. Go back to your car, and I'll bring the kids over."

"What's wrong with her?" Leslie asked.

"Ignore her, she's a drama queen."

Susan gave me a nudge. The women parted, and I walked shakily back to my car. I leaned against it, feeling light-headed. One of my therapists told me I had a mild form of PTSD. I wasn't sure that was right, but this wasn't right, either. The world was snapping in and out of focus like a pair of cartoon goggle eyes.

"Momsy!" Melly cried, throwing herself against me. "We were jumping in puddles!"

I willed myself to concentrate. "I saw that, honey. How was school today?"

"Bo-ring," Sam said. "And my painting is melting."

He thrust a watercolor drawing of a house at me. The rain was washing away the black he'd used to mark the outline.

"Let's get this in the car."

"You okay to drive?" Susan asked.

"I think so."

"We could leave your car here and all pile into mine."

"I'm fine. I'll be careful."

· "I'll follow behind you, then."

I started to protest, but I knew it was no use. Besides, we were going to the same place. She'd be behind me, anyway.

I strapped Melly and Sam into their booster seats, making extra sure their seat belts were tight against their precious chests, and sat behind the wheel. I made eye contact with Cindy in the rearview mirror; she was waiting for me to pull out. We were all caravanning back to Pine Street.

Though I knew the way, I hit "Home" on the built-in GPS. It was so easy to get turned around in Cincinnati; no route was ever as the crow flies. And though I'd studied and studied the city map before I moved there, no flat image could capture the pop-up reality.

As the mechanical voice guided me, I drove carefully, making sure I stopped at every stop and signaled every turn. Melly and Sam were chattering in the backseat, peppering me with the usual series of questions. "Why, why, why," Sam always started, stuttering because his brain was processing too many things at once. I answered their questions patiently, and when I pulled into my driveway, I sighed in relief. I'd be safe inside soon, all better.

Sam and Melly unclipped themselves and jumped from the car. There were more puddles in the driveway, and they started jumping up and down in them. I grabbed their things from the backseat, picking up Sam's muddled painting from the floor. I held it up; it really was, for a six-year-old, a good likeness of our house. Stick figures, who I assumed were Daniel and me, stood near the front door with Sam and Melly in front of us. There was another stick figure on the side of the house where we parked the cars, holding out its arm like it was pointed right at me.

A car horn hooted. It was Susan. I waved to her, letting her know all was good, and made a walking symbol with my fingers. She nodded yes and started backing down the street.

When I turned back around, I caught a flash of something yellow just past my car, near the entrance to the back deck. I took a step forward, blinking the rain out of my eyes, but it was gone.

And when I looked down at the painting again, the extra person I'd thought I'd seen there had also disappeared.

Eye of the Tiger

John

Six months ago

I was lacing up my running shoes when my phone dinged with a text.

Come around back, Julie wrote. Will explain when you get here.

K, I wrote back. There in a sec.

I tucked my phone and key into the special pocket in my running shorts and zipped up my rain jacket. The rain was relentless. The wettest April on record already, and there were still nine days left. There was concern about erosion for the houses on the hillside. A house a few blocks over had lost part of its back deck when the footing was swept away after a particularly violent burst. Our street had turned into a river.

I crossed the street and unlocked the gate on the side of Julie's house. I pushed a lilac bush fat with rain out of my way. Water splashed against my bare legs. Pink petals clung to my arms. A few more steps brought me to her backyard, a series of decks and terraced patios built into the slope. A rusting swing took up much of the middle patio, puddles forming in the depressions left by two generations of children's feet. On the deck next to it, a newer picnic table contained two left-behind plastic cups, filled to the brim. Daffodils hugged the ground. An empty bird feeder twisted in the wind.

But there was no sign of Julie.

I said her name softly, not wanting to wake anyone inside. It was just after six in the morning, the bongs of the church clock still lingering in the air.

"Here," I thought I heard, but I still couldn't see her.

I walked onto the upper deck.

"Julie?"

"Here," she said again. A flash of white. A hand waving behind a wooden toy box.

She was cowering behind it. Her knees were pulled up under her raincoat. Her teeth were chattering.

"What's going on?" I asked as I knelt in front of her.

"I thought I heard someone out here."

I looked around. The same sodden landscape, empty of menace.

"I don't see anyone."

"There's no one."

"So why are you . . ."

"Huddled on the ground?"

She unfolded her hands. She held a child's toy, a Barbie doll. A headless Barbie doll.

"This is Melly's."

She bit back a sob. Her hair was pulled back tightly from her face, slick from the rain. She looked young and tired and scared.

"Becky was always doing that," I said gently. "Pulling the heads off her dolls. Cutting their hair so it stuck up in the air. We took it as a sign she was too old for Barbie."

"Melly didn't do this."

"How do you know?"

"It was propped up against the back door. The head was sitting in its lap, like this."

She placed the doll on the deck in a sitting position and put the head in its lap. I swept the pieces up.

"You need to call the police."

"No."

"Why not?"

"They didn't take me seriously last time, and I'm sure they're the ones who told the newspaper about it. What's the point?"

"Was there any kind of note?"

"No. She's too smart for that."

"Who? I thought it *wasn't* Heather?"

"The last thing wasn't. This was."

I dropped the doll as if it might contaminate me.

"My prints will be on that now."

"It doesn't matter." She held out her hands. "Here, help me up."

Her hands were frozen. Her bitten cuticles scratched at my palms. I rocked back. She sprang up and against me. She smelled like sweat, like she might at the end of our run, rather than the beginning. The rain spat down around us.

"I'm scared," she said.

"Everything's going to be okay."

"It isn't, it isn't."

I pressed her face to my chest, worried she'd hear my heart thrumming.

"There has to be something we can do." I stroked her hair, twisting it through my fingers. "Something that will make you feel safe."

"I've been through this. There isn't anything. There's nothing to do but run."

"Don't do that."

She went still against me.

"You don't want me to go?"

"No."

She tipped her head back. Her eyes were rimmed red. It set off the flecks of gold in her brown eyes. Ones I hadn't noticed before.

"Why? All I've been is trouble since I've arrived."

I couldn't put it into words. How she brought color into my life. Color I didn't know was missing. How I woke up with anticipation, instead of a mild sense of dread. How I'd been complacent and happy, and now I was nervous and alive. It was too much to think. Too much to say.

So instead I kissed her.

I expected her to pull back. She didn't. Her lips met mine with so much force our teeth clicked. We drew back for a second, then came together again. All slick tongues and hot breath and God, the thoughts in my head.

My hands were up and under her sodden shirt, my thumbs tucked under the edge of her sports bra, when a sound broke us apart.

"Someone's here," Julie said.

I stepped away. It had sounded like a twig snapping. But the world was so full of sounds that morning, we both could've imagined it.

"Oh, shit, shit, shit. What have we done?" Julie said.

I turned back to her. Tried to take her in my arms again.

"Don't. That was a mistake. A terrible mistake. It can't happen again."

"I know."

"I love Daniel."

"I love my family, too."

"I mean it. He's everything to me. Please don't tell anyone."

"I'm not going to tell anyone."

"People say that, but then the guilt sets in and . . . promise me. Promise me you won't say anything, no matter what. Not to . . . Hanna. Not to anyone."

She held out her hand, the pinkie crooked.

"Seriously?"

"I know it's stupid, but do it, okay?"

I tucked my pinkie into hers.

"This didn't happen," she said. "Now you say it."

"This didn't happen."

She dropped her hand, muttering something under her breath. Like she was making a promise to herself. Or a wish.

"You going to be okay?" I asked.

"How would I know?"

"I mean right now. Right this second."

"Are you leaving?"

"I think that's a good idea, don't you?"

"Yes. Go. I'll be fine. I'll wake Daniel."

Her eyes met mine, and we both thought the same thing.

Why didn't she wake Daniel in the first place?

She looked away.

"This doesn't have to change anything," I said.

"It already has."

I spent the week after the kiss running alone. I'd wait at the window every morning, drinking my coffee, looking for some sign from across the street that things could continue on as they had before. That a minute of thoughtlessness hadn't set our lives spinning off into some wonky orbit. But it had.

On the third morning, I risked a text.

```
Is your injury any better?
```

I'm not sure what I was thinking, exactly. I was fairly certain she hadn't gone running since that morning, though I'd been doing my best not to pay too much attention to her house. But maybe Daniel had noticed? Maybe she'd said she'd hurt herself? So that he didn't ask any questions. Didn't ask what had happened, why the sudden change in routine.

It's what I would have done if Hanna had asked.

But Hanna didn't ask.

I watched my phone. A bubble appeared below my text indicating she was writing. Then it disappeared. Then reappeared. Then disappeared again. I could feel her indecision as if it were my own.

I was about to put my phone away when it buzzed.

Lots of RICE.

?? I wrote.

Rest. Ice. Compression. Elevation.

Got it. Good idea. Take care of yourself.

Thanks. Have a good run.

I got the message. Carry on acting normally. Return to life as it was. Before.

It felt like a betrayal.

It's hard to explain. I'd already betrayed my family, their trust. But I'd promised not to tell. And she was right. All the hurt and anger that would be caused by a moment. I was better off stuffing it down. Tucking it away. Forgetting it had happened.

But still. That she could shut me out so quickly. So completely. It was hard to take in.

So I ran. Harder, longer, faster than I had before. Up and down the hilly sections of Eden Park. Doing the stairs from Mirror Lake to the

Playhouse over and over. That morning, and the next. Then I'd peel the sweat-soaked clothes from my body and wash the salt off as if it had leached something unclean out of me.

Friday morning, Kiss plus four, was cold and rainy, and I decided to skip it. The clouds parted around three in the afternoon, right after I received a depressing e-mail from my old boss at P&G asking if I wanted my job back. I was okay doing some contract work for them, but actually going back there was out of the question. Although we were financially fine with me not working, I felt that man-guilt tugging at me. Be the provider. Suck it up. If I couldn't be right in my heart, at least I could do that.

I grabbed my running stuff and pounded some of the self-loathing out of my body. When I got home, Hanna was standing in my usual place at the window. She was dressed in one of her court suits. The ones that made her look strong and terrifying.

"Did you know about this?" she said.

"What?"

She pointed across the street. There was a utility van parked in front of Julie and Daniel's house. It had been parked there on and off for the last several days, but I hadn't paid much attention to it.

"What am I looking at?"

"That's a security company."

"How do you know?"

"I asked one of the workmen who he worked for." She shoved her phone at me. The home page for Secure It! was showing. Alarms. Outdoor lights. Cameras.

"What's the big deal?"

"They're installing cameras on their house."

"What?"

Her finger stabbed at the air. "There. There. There. And they all point at our house."

"How can you tell?"

"Because I have eyes."

She turned toward me. Her cheeks were mottled with anger. "What the hell is going on?"

"I have no idea."

"Please don't lie to me."

"I'm not."

"You guys haven't been running together this week. And you've been acting weird, and now she's putting cameras up on her house."

My mind whirred. I'd promised. I couldn't tell. I'd promised.

I'd promised Hanna, too. I'd promised her everything.

"When I went over there the other morning for our run, she was a mess. Someone took the head off one of her kid's dolls and left it propped against the back door. It looked really spooky. She was freaking out. I told her to call the police, but she said they hadn't done anything when she'd complained before."

"Because she probably made it up."

"Not this again."

"You always defend her."

"I don't mean to."

"That doesn't explain why she's installing cameras pointing at our house."

"I honestly don't know. But . . ."

"But what?"

"She said something about the other things not being done by Heather . . . her stalker. Maybe she thinks it's someone in the neighborhood?"

"As in *we're* the ones doing the made-up things that she's complaining about?"

"Of course not. And I don't think the cameras are pointed at us. It just looks that way from here."

Hanna shut the drapes.

"I want to sue."

"Wait, what?"

"I want to sue her."

"For what?"

"For what happened to Chris. He's going to have a scar. And now she's got cameras pointed at our front door. Plus, I heard she almost assaulted Cindy at pickup the other day."

"Oh, come on. That's not what happened."

"How do you know?"

"I read Susan Thurgood's post. On that iNeighbor thing. Which is completely ridiculous, by the way."

Susan had written an account of Julie and Cindy's confrontation at the school in a now-let's-everybody-calm-down tone. It had elicited a series of mixed comments before it was taken down. By Cindy, I assumed. Only to be replaced with a semicoherent post about school-pickup etiquette.

"You're reading posts on iNeighbor now?"

"I have to fill my days somehow."

"I thought you were building up a business?"

"I am. You know that. I thought we agreed I could take the time to do it."

"I didn't think it would take this much time."

I bit back that it hadn't even been six months. What if she knew, somehow, what I'd been offered two hours before? My run had clarified one thing: whatever happened, I couldn't go back there.

"What do you want me to do?" I said. "Go back on the job market?"

"I didn't say that."

"What, then?"

"When we agreed to you staying home, I didn't think you'd be spending your days hanging out with another woman and surfing the web."

I counted to three in my head before I answered her. "That's a complete distortion of my days. And my job is *about* surfing the web. What's going on, Hanna? Why are you acting like this?"

"I told you. I want to sue."

"And that's going to make this all better? You're always telling me how awful litigation is for your clients. How much stress it creates. How you take that stress off them. Who's going to take the stress off us?"

"Don't do that. Don't use my own words against me."

"I'm trying to make you see reason. Money isn't going to fix Chris's face."

"It might get her to take those cameras down."

"Why don't we start by asking her?"

"I already did."

"When?"

"Two days ago. When the van first showed up."

"Why didn't you tell me?"

"I was waiting for you to say something."

"Seriously? What did Julie and Daniel say?"

"I didn't speak to Daniel. Only her."

"What did Julie say, then?"

"You swear you don't already know?"

"This is the first I'm hearing about any of this."

"She said the cameras were going to take in the whole street, and all the way around her property, too. That it was the only way she was going to be able to get the evidence she needed. If the harassment stopped, then that proved it was someone who lived here. And if it continued, then she'd have them on tape."

"But that would only work if people knew about the cameras."

"Right. Which is why she's going to tell everyone they're there."

"How's she going to do that? Oh, iNeighbor?"

"You got it."

"That's . . ."

Genius? Diabolical? Stupid?

"It's pretty smart," Hanna said. "I never said she wasn't smart. So are you with me on this or not?"

"She really refused to take them down?"

Hanna looked at me. "Why haven't you been running with her this week?"

I was about to tell her Julie was injured. But she'd spoken to Julie. I didn't know when.

"She's been putting me off. Probably because she's upset about what happened. You really think a lawsuit is the only way to go?"

"We'll start with a letter of demand."

"I think this is a mistake. But I'll back you."

Her lip quivered. "You will?"

I took her in my arms. "I will. I always will."

I looked over her shoulder out the crack in the drapes that didn't quite obscure the view. A man was standing on a ladder, fiddling with something black and oblong attached to the front of Julie's house. A camera. He was holding an iPad. Looking at it. Adjusting the oblong. Looking at the iPad again.

It might have been a trick of the light, but I could swear the camera was staring right at me.

Today

John

1:00 p.m.

When I get through security and ride the slow elevator up to the fourth floor, I'm too late to catch Hanna before she's called in to testify. All I see is the back of her going through the doors to the grand jury room. She's standing erect, her shoulders back as if she's waiting for morning muster.

I wish I'd had a moment to talk to her before her name was called. I wish I knew what was going on in that brain of hers.

I've known Hanna my entire life. We grew up on the same street in similar red brick houses with large trees creating a canopy over the front lawn. We ran through sprinklers in each other's backyards. Went through the same haunted house the neighbor down the street set up at Halloween, complete with a skeleton that sprang from a coffin that scared her every time. Elementary school. Middle school. High school. I can pick literally any moment of my life, and there's Hanna. Sometimes front and center, sometimes a little out of focus. A constant.

There's something about knowing someone like that. We didn't start dating till the second year of college—we both attended Ohio University—but we just got each other. We didn't have to create history, although we did.

We *were* history.

I cherish that. I really do. But I took it for granted. I took us for granted. And so, when an attractive stranger moved across the street and we connected on a different level—not better, not worse, just different—my head was turned. I forgot about history. I made room in my heart for more than Hanna and Becky and Chris. I dwelled on thoughts I should have banished.

And that day in the rain on Julie's back porch, I don't know what I would've done if she hadn't pulled away. How far things would've gone.

I live with that every day.

They say that if a butterfly flaps its wings in the Amazonian rain forest, it can change the weather half a world away. Chaos theory. What it means is that everything that happens in this moment is an accumulation of everything that's come before it. Every breath. Every thought. There is no innocent action. Some actions end up having the force of a tempest. Their impact cannot be missed. Others are the blink of an eye. Passing by unnoticed.

Perhaps only God knows which is which.

All I know today is that you can think that what you've done is only the flap of a butterfly wing, when it's really a thunderclap.

And both can result in a hurricane.

◆ ◆ ◆

Hanna's always told me that lawyers make the worst witnesses. They think they know better. That they won't fall into the traps they warn their clients against. But they can't turn off their lawyer brain. The one trying to figure out why they're being asked a particular question. What's the lawyer's strategy? What are they hoping to achieve? How am I being perceived by the jury? Have I said too much? Not enough?

With all those questions running around, it's no wonder they often fuck up.

And that's what we've all been worried about from the beginning. That one of us will slip. Say too much or not enough. That what we agreed on—our story, if you will—won't be believable or enough. That the jury will sense the missing moments because the rest of them, the ones we do reveal, don't quite cover the others over.

Traces will remain.

I search the waiting room outside the grand jury chamber for Chris. He's sitting in a chair with his back against a wall covered in beige wallpaper. There's a police officer sitting two seats over. A dozen others are scattered around the room. I don't recognize any of them.

Alicia told us that there are always two grand juries sitting at any given time. They usually hear many cases in a day. Our situation is different. Because of Alicia's strategy, our grand jury will take longer. So the rest of these people—that man chewing his fingernails, and the one who looks strung out, and the lawyers reviewing their notes—they must all be involved in someone else's tragedy.

I take a seat next to Chris. The multicolored fabric chair is surprisingly comfortable, though the finish has been rubbed off the curved arms. Worried away. Chris turns his body away from me. I catch a look from Alicia across the aisle. I shrug, *teenagers*. She bends her head back to her legal pad. I think she's trying to write the future there. But it's the past Hanna's talking about now.

That day.

I wait out the minutes, counting to sixty in my head again and again. It's been thirty minutes that Hanna's been in there. I try to do the math on that, how many seconds it's been. My mind feels stiff, an unused muscle.

I cannot take this anymore.

"Chris," I say, keeping my voice low, "what did you mean outside?"

"Leave it, Dad."

"I can't. Whatever it is, I want you to tell me."

He shifts back and forth in his seat. I'm not sure why I'm pushing him for an answer. Why I can't take my son's word for it that I don't want to know.

"I didn't say anything," Chris says.

"I know. You said."

"No, about . . . I didn't tell anyone what I saw."

"What did you see?"

"I saw you, Dad. You and *her*."

My hands start to tingle. I look at Alicia again, but she doesn't seem to have heard us.

I take Chris by the elbow and raise him up. I put a finger to my lips: *Don't talk.* He nods and lets me lead him out of the room and into the hall. We walk past the elevators toward the bathrooms. The hall is narrow and smells antiseptic. But I'm close enough to Chris to smell his nerves. Or maybe that's me. A man walks out of the bathroom and wipes his hands on his pants. I watch him turn the corner.

"What did you see, Chris?" I ask.

"I was coming home the back way. From Ashley's. I wasn't supposed to be out. It was . . . really early in the morning."

There's only one possible morning he means. I plot it out in my mind. There's a path that runs along the edge of the backyards on the river side of our street. It's beautiful, really, with the trees forming an archway above the path.

A lover's lane.

"I started climbing the hill to get up to the lane next to her house, and that's when I saw you." His voice cracks. "You were kissing her!"

"No, Chris, we weren't—"

"Dad, come on. I'm not Becky, okay? I know what I saw."

"That was a mistake," I say. "A mistake."

"How do you kiss someone by mistake?"

Each time he says the word "kiss," it's as if he's kicking me in the gut.

"It's complicated. I . . . I can't explain this to you. It's irrelevant."

"How can you say that? Did you . . . were you going to leave Mom?"

"I would never leave your mother." I put my hand on his shoulder. It's shaking. "Chris. Please. You won't say anything?"

His disappointed look is worse than the guilt that's been gnawing at me for months.

"I thought I was supposed to tell the truth, the whole truth, and nothing but the truth?"

"About what they need to know about, yes. But this . . . so many more people could get hurt by this. More than they already are. And it doesn't have anything to do with what happened. So, will you keep it to yourself? Please?"

He doesn't say anything, just looks me in the eye in a way that makes me feel reversed. Like I am the son, and he is the father.

His name is called over the loudspeaker. It's time for him to go. I drop my hand from his shoulder, though all I want to do is hold him close. A horrible part of me wants to ask him again to keep my secret. But there's nothing more I can say. Nothing more I *should* say. Either he'll tell or he won't. There's so little left in my control. And all the things I've tried to manage—my thoughts, my heart, my actions—none of it made any difference, anyway.

There are so many versions of the truth, I've found. One for each person.

But the whole truth? No one ever tells the whole truth.

Do they?

On the Outside Looking In
Julie

Five months ago

Is there anything worse than the shrill ring of a phone?

I remember how I used to welcome that sound as a teenager, spending hours in idle chatter with my friends. But as May took hold, it became a sound I dreaded, then hated, then feared.

There wasn't any pattern to the calls other than the fact that the number was always blocked, so there wasn't any way to block them in turn other than to take the phone off the hook. We did that for long stretches, but then we'd get panicked e-mails from our un-tech parents, who couldn't absorb the fact that they could call our cell phones if the landline was engaged.

Whoever it was seemed to have a sixth sense about the right moment to call to inflict the greatest impact: at the quietest time of the day, or while we were giving the twins their bath, that moment right before you fall asleep.

On the other hand, the calls were the only thing that had happened since we installed the cameras.

"It must mean it's someone in the neighborhood," I said to Daniel when he came into the living room after dinner one night. Weeks' worth of footage had turned up nothing, according to the report we'd received from the monitoring company.

"It doesn't mean that at all," he said. "Maybe whoever was doing things changed their mind, or went away or were dissuaded by the cameras." His eyes shifted away from mine. "There could be any number of explanations."

"Such as?"

"I don't know, Julie. What do you think?"

"You don't think I had anything to do with it, do you?"

"Why would you ask that?"

"Only because . . . last time . . ."

Guilt clouded his face. He'd accused me of that in Tacoma, when the notes and messages first started, and they couldn't find any trace of Heather, except those that led back to me. Because that was another thing Heather had done—she'd hijacked my IP address and my e-mail account and made it look like I was the one doing the harassing. She was so good at it, she even had me questioning myself. Maybe my medication was to blame? I did seem to have holes in my memory—not blackouts per se, but things I used to have no trouble remembering suddenly became hard. But could I have done something so bizarre? So strange? I don't think I ever really believed it was possible, nor did Daniel. But he'd asked the question, and that had felt like a betrayal of everything we'd meant to each other since he'd scraped my heart back together all those years ago in Montreal.

"Last time," he said. "I didn't understand what was going on. No one did. And you know how badly I feel about that. I thought we'd agreed not to bring it up again."

"You're right. We did. Sorry."

"It's fine, but I'm on your side, Jules. I wish you'd believe that."

"I do." I wrapped my arms around his middle and pressed my face into his neck. "I don't know what to do anymore. It feels like everyone here is against us."

"We can move again, if you want."

My stomach turned over, because I did want to move, but it was as much about what had happened with John as the fact that Heather—or someone like her—might be behind everything else going on. But how could I do that to my family again? To the twins who'd settled well into school? To Daniel, who liked his job and couldn't find a new one every six months because of my crazy life.

Because of my crazy.

"No. We'll stick it out here. Maybe . . ."

"What?"

"Maybe I should stop writing."

I felt, in a way, as if I already had. Despite my positive updates to my agent, my word count had dwindled to a trickle. My book was due in five months, and it was barely half-done. If I could even call the loose collection of scenes and characters I'd written a novel.

"How would that solve anything?" Daniel asked.

"It's what started all this, isn't it? So if I stop, then maybe it will go away."

"I don't think it works like that."

"You're probably right, but one can hope."

"No," Daniel said. "I don't want you to do that. Writing makes you happy. Before . . . remember how lost you felt? How overwhelmed? Which is totally normal. I'd be like that, too, if I was home with those monsters all day. But then you started writing, and it helped."

"That and the medication."

"Who knows what worked. Let's not upset the apple cart."

"Geez, Grandma. I won't go poking around, neither."

"Har, har, har." He kissed me. I tensed up, flashes of the kiss with John flitting through my mind. I pulled back.

"What?"

"Where's Melly?"

"She's upstairs with Sam. I put them to bed half an hour ago."

"Right, sorry. I was distracted, reading the report from the alarm company. Don't you think it's too quiet up there?"

"They're getting older. Let's enjoy it."

"And soon they'll be teenagers and dating and . . . ugh."

"Speaking of teenagers, did you ever end up asking John if Chris had anything to do with the note or any of the other stuff?"

"No, I . . . haven't seen him around much lately."

"Oh? I thought you guys were running together in the mornings."

"We were."

"What changed?"

I let him go and started picking up the kids' things. Was there ever going to be a time when that didn't take at least an hour of my day, every day, if not more?

"I think I felt . . . embarrassed by the way I reacted to all that stuff. I really lost it when I found the note, and then again with the headless Barbie. He was around for both those meltdowns. Not pretty."

"Wait, so, you've been running *alone* since then?"

"Um . . ."

"What the hell, Julie? That's really dangerous."

"I take Sandy, and I have my lanyard."

"That's not enough. Not until we know the harassment has either stopped or they've caught who's doing it."

"You're telling me I can't run alone?"

He paused. We didn't tell each other what to do. That wasn't part of our bargain.

He held out his hands, palms up. Our signal to each other that compliance would be appreciated and reciprocated. "I would really,

really prefer it if you didn't run alone. I don't want to have to worry about you every day."

"So I have to run with John?"

"Maybe you could find a running group in the area. There must be several. Why don't you check iNeighbor?"

"You're hilarious, you are. Fuck. This is such a mess."

"Mommy said a bad word."

I turned around. Sam was hanging over the upstairs railing in a way that always got my heart thumping. If it were up to me, jungle gyms would be removed from every playground.

"What are you doing out of bed?" Daniel asked.

"I'm hungry."

Daniel walked up the stairs and picked him up. "I thought we agreed bedtime snack was it for food until morning?"

"I know, Daddy. But my stomach is real hungry. I think I'm growing again."

"You'll be taller than me soon."

"No, I won't!"

"Oh, yes, you might!"

He swooped Sam upside down and tickled his stomach.

"Stop it, Daddy. Stop it," Sam said, laughing. I would have been worried they'd wake Melly, only she sleeps like the dead.

Daniel deposited him at my feet. "You keep Mommy company while I go rustle up some food to make you grow taller."

Sam leaned into my legs and looked up at me with his big brown eyes. "Daddy was telling a joke, right, Mommy?"

"Daddy was telling a joke."

"I don't want to be *too* tall."

"Why not?"

"Because you read me in the pilot book that fighter pilots can't be tall because they won't fit in airplanes."

"You want to be a fighter pilot?"

"Yes."

"What happened to being a fireman?"

"That was when I was *five*, Mommy."

"Oh, dear. Well, I'll have to update my book, then." I pretended to take a notebook out of my pocket and flip its pages. "Mmm, let's see, where is that page? Melly, Daniel, oh, here we are. Sam. What I want to be when I grow up. I'm putting down fighter pilot?"

He nodded enthusiastically. I pretended to write.

"Okay, then, done."

"That means it will come true now, doesn't it, Mommy?"

"Well, if you study and practice really hard, probably."

"But you wrote it down. And if you write it down, that means it's true."

"Who told you that?"

He shrugged. "Everyone knows that."

"Sam!" Daniel called from the kitchen. "I think there's some peanut-butter toast with your name on it."

Sam skipped away down the hall to his midnight snack. I cleaned up the rest of the living room while Daniel got him fed and back to bed. When he came downstairs, he was checking his e-mail on his phone.

"This is funny."

"What?"

"Guess who's hosting this month's block party?"

"No one?"

"You wish. The Dunbars."

"Maybe we shouldn't go."

"Oh, no. This is the perfect opportunity for you to get over your embarrassment, or whatever it is, so you can run with John again. Or find some other women in the neighborhood to run with. I don't care, so long as—"

"It's not alone, got it."

The May block party was the last I ever attended.

There's a moment before it starts to rain, where the wind is high and the air has announced its certain presence. The calm before the storm, they call it. Only it's not really calm, it's simply a moment of anticipation. As the trees rustle and the leaves blow, nature is taking in one last breath before it expels it.

That's how it felt as Daniel and I stood on the front step of the Dunbars' house.

Although I didn't want to go to the party, I was curious about one thing: would alcohol be served, given John's refusal to accept the no-alcohol policy at other events?

It was proving to be a warm May, and the Dunbars had let it be known (through iNeighbor, but of course) that dinner would be—weather permitting—outside. I sprayed the kids with insect repellent and dressed them in long pants; the last couple of nights the mosquitoes had come out in attack formation around dusk. Melly had several welts on her face where they'd bitten into the downy skin of her cheeks, and my own ankles seemed to be a favorite snacking place.

Hanna greeted us with her smile caught between her teeth. Daniel was carrying his customary bottle of wine. I had a large potato salad in Tupperware, because every good summer event needs a good potato salad, even when it's not summer yet. The sight of the wine seemed to loosen her up a bit, her smile widening to reveal slightly stained teeth. She'd clearly been into the red wine already. I wondered if I should tell her that her transgression was visible, but then, as someone who used to have to hide her drinking, I was probably too attuned to that possibility. I decided to let it be.

The twins spotted some of their classmates and looked at Hanna for permission before sprinting through the house. We followed them out onto their patio. I tried not to be too curious about the house, which I'd never been inside. Like most of the houses on our street, it started out as a modest, narrow Victorian. Subsequent generations had added on a floor over the garage and an extension at the back, so it was multileveled, like the series of decks at the back of our house. It was filled with traditional furniture in blue and beige tones, and twenty years of family photographs. John's running shoes sat on a rack full of sports equipment. The wall above was covered with coats and hats and umbrellas.

I didn't feel at home or uncomfortable. It felt like someone else's life.

The backyard was pretty, though. Round Chinese lights were strung between the trees, and three long picnic tables formed a comfortable place for the grown-ups to sit and eat while the kids sat on plastic benches. It was a backyard that had seen a lot of large parties, and was well equipped.

Half the block was there already, the men circled around the barbecue, the women keeping half an eye on their children. Music flowed at a gentle volume through the outdoor speakers, a mix of light jazz that neither pleased nor offended.

No one else came to greet us, so we stood there, watching, like kids waiting to get picked for a team in gym class. Not that Daniel ever had to worry about that. *I* was the one who was holding us back, literally and figuratively.

"Are we on the schedule?" I asked Daniel. I'd left the potato salad in the dining room, and was holding on to his hand like a kid being left off at the first day of kindergarten. I was rarely so clingy, but with one thing and another, I felt like I had to keep my ally close.

"You mean for car pool?"

"No, for the block parties. Aren't we supposed to host one of these at some point?"

"I think we only get put on the schedule in the second year. Or something like that. Give us a chance to settle in."

"Right. Sure."

"You so anxious to host?"

"No, but I'd like to prove a couple of people wrong about me."

"Stop being so paranoid. You don't have to prove anything."

My jaw clenched. He knew I hated being called paranoid, but I took a deep breath and let it go. It was too early in the evening for conflict.

"There's John," Daniel said, pointing to the grill. "Go on."

He nudged me in the back, and I let go of his hand. John was standing with two other men, ones whose names I hadn't nailed down yet. It reminded me of the first few weeks of law school; there seemed to be a window to learn everyone's name. If you missed it, then you were shit out of luck for the next four years.

All the men were holding beers, but when I looked more closely, they were O'Doul's—nonalcoholic. So the ban was still in force, at least in the backyard.

"Let me guess," I said with some of the old confidence I used to have at college parties after a couple of mixed drinks. "You guys somehow managed to fill those bottles with real beer?"

John laughed. "Don't go spilling our secrets now."

Cindy's husband, Paul, looked at his bottle in surprise.

"Is that why this tastes so good?"

"She was joking, Paulie."

"Ah, right. Well, still, I'd better take it easy on these, just in case."

He wandered off in the vague way I'd noticed about him before. Without Cindy by his side, he seemed to be missing some fundamental parts of his personality. A few seconds later, the other man's wife called him, in an exasperated tone, to come do something with their kids.

And so John and I were alone.

If you can be alone when a party full of people are watching.

"How's it going?" he said, turning over a raft of sausages.

"It's been a weird month, to be honest. You?"

"Same." He took a swig of his beer. "Are those cameras pointed at my house?"

"What? No."

"Where, then?"

"They show the perimeter of my house from every angle, so if someone comes on the property again, we'll know who it is."

"Do you get the video feed live?"

"Only the camera over the front door so we can see who's there. Why?"

"Is there a way you could show Hanna that?"

"How would I do that?"

"Invite her over, show her there aren't any monitors in the house."

"Why? Isn't my word good enough?"

"She's just . . ." He closed the lid on the barbecue and glanced around. Hanna wasn't in view, but Cindy was eyeing us. "She feels like she's being watched. And between that and what happened to Chris . . . if she knew I was telling you this, she'd kill me, but she wants to send a letter, a formal lawyer's letter, telling you to take the cameras down and asking for compensation."

"She what?"

"Keep your voice down. I shouldn't have said anything."

"Is this because of . . . she doesn't know about . . ."

"Do you think I'm crazy?"

"I don't know what to think right now."

John looked over my shoulder.

"Daniel's coming."

I stared down at my shoes, trying to process what he'd said. Was the world really so off-kilter that someone who'd terrorized me could get away scot-free, and people I'd been doing my best to befriend could sue me because their son acted like a thief?

"Are you guys back on?" Daniel asked, placing his hand on the small of my back. I leaned against it for support.

"Back on?" John said.

"He means running. He thought we should start running together again so he doesn't have to worry about me, because I've been doing it alone."

I met John's eyes as I said this, pleading with him to say no.

"I'm actually suffering from shin splints right now," John said. "But do you know Stephanie and Leslie? They run pretty frequently. And I agree with Daniel. You shouldn't run alone."

My shoulders shrank. The shin splints were bullshit. I'd seen him go out for a run at noon every day. But who was I to force the issue?

"Can you introduce me?"

"They're standing over by the swing set," John said, pointing to a redhead and a bottle blonde I recognized as one of the women who'd stood by Cindy during our confrontation in the pickup line at school. Neither of them looked particularly in shape, but beggars can't be choosers.

"Thanks," I said, and walked away, leaving Daniel with John.

I hovered on the edge of the circle Stephanie and Leslie were a part of, wishing I had access to John's flask. I hated asking people for things. Maybe my nightly walks with Susan would be enough? And where the hell was she, anyway? She'd promised to be here tonight for moral support.

"Can I help you?" Stephanie said when she finally noticed me standing there. She had a china-doll complexion, with round, blue eyes.

"Um, hi. I'm Julie. I'm not sure we ever formally met? I live across the street?"

"We know who you are."

"Right. Well, um, John mentioned you guys run together some-times? And, uh, I was wondering if I could join you?"

"I thought *you* ran with John?" Leslie asked. She was shorter than I was and had the stocky thighs of a sprinter.

"He's injured."

"Really?"

"That's what he says. Anyway, if I'm not welcome, it's fine. Just thought I'd ask."

I started backpedaling away. Three steps in, I plowed right into someone, pushing them off balance so she dropped the plate of drinks in her hands. It fell to the ground with a crash, glass and china shattering everywhere.

I turned around to come face-to-face with a shocked Hanna.

"I'm so, so sorry. I'm the world's worst klutz."

I bent down to start picking up the glass shards. Stephanie went over to where the kids were playing to keep them in place.

"Do you have a garbage bag or something? Or maybe a broom?"

"Leave it," Hanna said. "I'll deal with it."

"I really want to help. I'll pay to replace the glasses and . . ."

"Julie. Please. Don't you think you should just go?"

I looked up at her. The red stains had moved from her teeth to her lips, like a berry lip balm that had been applied unevenly.

"What?"

"Just leave. I can't believe you showed up here in the first place."

John approached with Daniel. John looked like he wanted to say something but was holding himself back.

Daniel came to my side and helped me up.

"Is that really called for, Hanna?" he said, his voice full of controlled anger. "It was an accident."

"Everything's an accident with her! Chris, the glasses, the cameras that just happen to be pointed at our house."

"I've apologized for what happened to Chris over and over. What more can I do? What do you want me to do?"

Hanna walked into the kitchen, leaving the debris behind. I looked at Daniel.

"Can you get the kids?"

He nodded and walked to the sandpit where they were building a castle with their friends. The party had gone silent.

I caught John's eye, and he gave the faintest of shrugs. No one was going to come to my aid or my defense. I was alone in a sea of shattered glass.

"Here," Hanna said, returning from the kitchen, her face full of red splotches. She thrust a thick envelope at me. "This is what you can do. It's all in there."

I started to open it mechanically, but Daniel stopped me.

"Read that later. Let's go."

Everyone watched as the four of us walked out of the backyard. We ran into Cindy in the hall, coming out of the powder room. Her eyes looked glassy.

"Leaving so soon?" she asked, her voice listing.

"What's wrong with you?" I said.

"Leave it, Jules."

"No. I'm so sick of this. Ever since I got here, she's been acting like I'm something stuck to the bottom of her shoe. Is it because I wasn't enthusiastic enough about your welcome basket?"

"You didn't even write me a thank-you card."

"Seriously? I didn't thank you for something I never even asked for, and that's license to ruin my life?"

The people from outside crowded into the hall behind us.

"Stop being so melodramatic," Cindy said. "Ruin your life? What about that poor boy? What about Hanna having to feel like everything she does is caught on camera?"

"This all started long before then. You've never welcomed me here. Ever since that first party, we were a bunch of outsiders who weren't good enough for you."

"Can you blame me? With your new money, your misbehaving daughter, and those creepy books you write? They're right. You're as weird in real life as you come across on the page."

"I think you've said enough," Daniel said sharply.

"I quite agree," John said, getting a look from both Daniel and Hanna. "Cindy, why don't you go back outside. And the rest of you, too. Show's over."

Cindy huffed and stormed down the hall. Hanna took her by the arm in a gentle way that promised a forbidden glass of brandy. Everyone else seeped away, and it was just me, John, Daniel, and the kids left in the hallway. John and Hanna's wedding picture tilted precariously behind him.

"I'm sorry about all of this," John said.

"Not your fault, man."

John looked at me. "Take care of yourself. This will all blow over."

He reached out and briefly squeezed my arm as Hanna returned. It was nothing, a second of encouragement, but before his hand had fallen away, Melly said in that clear voice of hers, "No kissing!"

Service

John

Five months ago

The morning after our block party, I found Hanna in the backyard, the small vacuum cleaner in hand, hovering over invisible shards of glass on our back porch. We'd spent an hour the night before making sure every last piece was gone. Everyone had pitched in. It had even sort of become fun. We'd collected the glass into a small pile. Looking at it, on the towel we'd placed on the picnic table, it seemed like there was more glass than needed for six drinking glasses.

Glass is funny that way.

"What are you doing?" I asked. Hanna's hair was tied in a tight ponytail on the crown of her head. She looked like Becky, young and vigorous. And angry.

We'd gone to bed silently. It had taken me a long time to sleep. Though I'd given Hanna the go-ahead with the lawsuit the month before, I hadn't heard anything since then. I didn't know for sure what she'd handed Julie at the party, but I could guess.

"What does it look like I'm doing?"

"I thought we got it all last night?"

She held up a tiny sliver of glass. It glinted in the sun. "I almost stepped on this."

"Accidents—"

"No, I will not listen to that again. I knew there was something off about her the first night we met. Remember I said so after the block party?"

I didn't, but I nodded.

"She's poison. She's poisoning us. We used to be happy, didn't we?"

I bent down and took the vacuum out of Hanna's hand.

"What do you mean, used to be? We're okay, aren't we?"

"It doesn't feel like it."

"Hey, come here." I helped her up and led her to one of the picnic tables. It was a beautiful, crisp morning, a perfect one for running. But that was the last thing I needed to do today, alone or otherwise.

"Talk to me," I said. "What's going on?"

She put her chin on her forearms on the table. "I know this isn't rational, or at least, I hope it isn't, but ever since she moved in, I feel like things are different between us."

"Different how?"

"It's like you're standing right next to me, but you're in a different room."

I would've liked to pretend I didn't know what she meant. But I couldn't. My mind *had* been across the street since October. And I didn't seem to be able to pull it back.

"I'm right here. I'll always be right here."

"What if I asked you never to speak to her again?"

"Do you think that's necessary?"

"It might be."

212

"Then, yes. I can do that. If you want me to."

"There's really nothing going on between you?"

"No. We're friends. *Were* friends, I guess."

Hanna's always told me that, despite what she does for a living, she can't tell when people are lying. She might know they are because she has a document that proves it or they said something different in a deposition. But those signs you see television lawyers picking up? They either don't exist or fly right past her.

I placed my hand on the side of her face and turned her toward me. I looked directly into her eyes.

"I promise you," I said. "There is nothing between us other than friendship. We're both home all the day. You know the transition to being home has been weird for me. It's nice to have a friend, someone who knows what it's like. But I should've realized it might seem like something more to you. I should have talked to you about it."

I kissed her. Our lips were dry against each other's. I didn't push for anything more, but I could sense Hanna relaxing.

"Can I ask about one more thing?" she said when we broke apart.

"Of course."

"It's going to sound stupid."

"Just ask."

"Why do you think her daughter said that last night? As they were leaving?"

"What?" I said, my voice tight despite my best efforts. "The 'no kissing' thing?"

"Yeah. That was weird. Wasn't it?"

"I have no idea why she said that. She's six."

"Sometimes kids say things others are afraid to."

"What are you saying? You think I kissed Julie in front of her daughter?"

She leans away from me. "When you say it like that . . ."

"Is that what you really think of me?"

213

"No."

Feeling like the complete and utter asshole that I am, I got up and walked into the kitchen, leaving Hanna on the porch. For lack of something better to do, I opened the dishwasher and started putting the dishes away.

"You'll wake the kids," Hanna said, closing the patio doors behind her.

"Worse things have happened."

"Are you mad at me?"

"Nope."

"You're something."

I put a plate on the counter. "I'm tired, Hanna. This is hard to understand and take in. I don't know how we ended up here."

"Now you sound like me."

"I guess we're both searching for answers."

She placed her hands on my hips. I turned around. Hanna didn't often look or seem vulnerable, but she did in that moment. And my desire to protect her was as strong as if she were one of my children. She never liked it when I told her that. But I thought that day might be an exception.

"We're in this together," I said.

"Really?"

"We're a family. You are my family."

"I still want to go ahead with the lawsuit."

"Is that what those papers were last night? The ones you gave Julie?"

"It was a formal request that she take down the cameras and compensate us for Chris. But if she doesn't do those things, then . . ."

"Do you really think that's going to accomplish anything?"

She leaned her head back. Her eyes were wet. "I can't tell. But I feel like I don't have any control over anything right now, and that needs to change."

"Would it . . . would you let me try one last time to convince her to take the cameras down?"

"The cameras won't solve Chris's face."

"I know, but maybe there's a way we can put a claim in with their insurance? Let me at least ask, okay?"

"And what about the lawsuit?"

"Don't you think it would be better if I told her? To show her how serious you . . . we are."

"No. If we have to go there, I want the element of surprise. I want to see how she feels if a bailiff comes to her door and serves her papers."

Hanna looked hard, then. The way she did when I'd gone to see in her court. Like reinforced glass.

"Okay," I said, the lie rolling out of me the way too many had already. "I won't tell her about the lawsuit."

I waited until Monday to talk to Julie. I didn't want an audience. I didn't want to have the conversation at all. But I owed it to my wife. And I owed it to Julie, too. I started something with that first conversation in October. A push in a direction that snowballed.

I had the perfect excuse. I'd finally managed to get her webpage looking like I thought it should. We'd had one conversation about it, months before. She'd shown me sites she liked. Told me what she didn't like about her existing site. Then I'd gotten a contract from P&G, and I'd lost track of time. It was unsettling how the days slipped by now that I didn't have a fixed schedule. It wasn't how the years speeded up when you got older. Each year taking less space than the last. It was more like how something that has no shape can be difficult to define. Other than the markers of mealtimes, there wasn't anything specific I needed to do at any given time. Even lunch was fluid. What did it matter if I ate at eleven or one or three? So long as I met my deadlines, none of it mattered.

And somehow, Julie's site didn't feel like a deadline. It felt more like a point of connection I could only keep if I didn't complete it.

But I had to cut all ties. So I'd spent the weekend working feverishly to finish it after Hanna went to bed. It wouldn't have done to have her find me deciding between two of Julie's head shots.

I spent much of that morning at the window. There were scuff marks in the floor now where I usually stood. Or perhaps that was my imagination. Maybe they'd always been there, a remnant of another generation of owners I'd never noticed before.

Regardless, I stood on my mark and pushed the curtain aside. I watched as Julie helped get Daniel and the kids into the car, then return inside. I was still watching when she emerged half an hour later in her running clothes. I resisted the urge to run after her, and occupied my time until I knew she'd be back. I was at my post when she returned an hour later.

Then I counted out the minutes her stretch and shower would take.

I didn't leave quite enough time.

I stood on her front porch, searching for a doorbell. Instead, there was a key panel and an intercom, but there wasn't any button to press.

I raised my hand to knock. I heard the whir of a camera swiveling.

"What is it?" A disembodied voice asked before I touched wood.

"Julie? It's John. Can I come in?"

"I just got out of the shower."

"I can wait."

"Hold on."

I sat down on the front stoop. I looked across the street at my own house. Unremarkable as always. A garbage truck worked its way up the street. Its gears ground loudly. Other than that, the street felt deserted. But yet, I felt watched. Felt certain that if I pulled out my phone and checked iNeighbor, someone would've checked me in.

John Dunbar is sitting on Julie's front porch. Looks like trouble.

The door beeped behind me and opened. Julie's hair was wrapped in a towel, but she was otherwise dressed.

Julie lets John into her house in a state of undress.

"Did you know about this?" she asked once I was inside, fluttering a piece of paper at me.

I felt a surge of anger. Had Hanna gone ahead and served the papers, even though I'd asked her to hold off?

"What the fuck is wrong with that woman?" Julie said.

"Hold on a minute now. You can't speak about my wife like that."

"Your wife? What? I meant Cindy. Is Hanna behind this?"

"Behind what?"

She handed me the paper. It was a note from Cindy telling her she was no longer welcome at the monthly block parties.

"Did you guys take a vote or something? I tried to check iNeighbor, but I've been blocked there, too. Ha!" There was a note of hysteria in her voice.

"I had no idea about this."

"Of all the petty things, to actually disinvite me from the block parties! As if I ever wanted to go to them in the first place." She smiled, but her bottom lip quivered. "What the hell is wrong with me?"

"Nothing."

"You know, you and Susan are the only people who've been at all welcoming to me."

"That's not true."

"But it is. I feel like the fat girl in high school all over again."

"Hey, now, come on."

She brought her hands up to her face. She was crying hard. I didn't know what to do. So I did the wrong thing.

I wrapped my arms around her and let her cry into my shoulder. My hands went reflexively to her hair.

Julie and John were observed in an embrace.

She took a deep shuddering breath, and we both pulled away.

"Oh, God," she said. "I need to call Daniel."

"Daniel?"

She wiped her tears away. "I promised myself that this would never happen again."

"Nothing's happened."

"Something was about to happen."

"Okay, maybe, but it didn't. We didn't."

"I need to stop this. I need to take responsibility for my life. Everything is so screwed up right now."

"This can't all be about Cindy."

"It isn't. But . . . why are you here?"

"Oh. Um, I finished your website."

"You did?"

"Yeah, remember? You asked me to work on it for you."

"But I didn't pay you."

"It's fine."

"I'll write you a check."

"Why don't you take a look at the site and see if you like it first. Then you can pay me if you want."

"Okay."

"I'll e-mail you the link."

"Thank you."

"There is one more thing."

"Yes?"

"I feel like a shit asking you this now, but do you think there's any way you could take down the cameras? Or see if your insurance company would pay something toward plastic surgery for Chris?"

"That's what Hanna asked for in that letter she gave me." She frowned. "What you're suing me for."

"We haven't sued you."

"But you're going to, right? You said so on Friday. So you're here to make one last effort to get me to take the cameras down or else."

"It's probably something like that," I admitted.

"I can't."

"Why not?"

"Because ever since the cameras went up, everything but the phone calls has stopped."

"Couldn't that be a coincidence?"

"Sure. Or maybe, it's someone in the neighborhood who's been doing everything."

"Do you think it's someone in my house? Is that why the cameras are pointed our way?"

She unwound the towel from her head. Her hair was half-dry and tangled. "I already told Hanna, the cameras aren't pointed at your house."

"I feel like we're going around in circles."

"So do I."

"What's the solution?"

"You go your way, and I go mine. You came to tell me that too, right? That we couldn't speak anymore?"

"Yes."

"That makes me sad."

"Me too."

Our eyes locked. I knew this was the right decision, but that didn't make it any easier.

"Are you going to drop the lawsuit?" she asked.

"Are you going to take the cameras down?"

"No," she said. "I can't."

"There's no way I'm going to be able to convince Hanna otherwise."

"I can . . . write you a check for Chris."

"No."

"I want to."

"Maybe you should talk to Hanna about that."

"Hanna and I talking doesn't turn out well."

"She's . . . she's really nice, you know. I love her. I always have."

A slight wince. "You can tell. It's nice to see."

"Daniel loves you, too."

"He does."

"I should go. But . . . why don't you try and make friends with Hanna? All of this . . . I feel like we all got off on the wrong foot."

"Those damn matching Asics," she said, and we stood there for a minute longer, looking at our feet.

Pine Street Neighborhood Association

Monthly Newsletter

June edition

Hello Neighbors!

Wow, it's summer! How did that happen? Time FLIES by.

My almanac says it's going to be a hot one! I know we all love our lush backyards, but let's take it easy on the watering!**

Exciting update on the speed-bump campaign. We, okay, me, ahem, were able to get a meeting with our city councilor and I'm pleased to report that she is SERIOUSLY considering the idea. The fact that I was able to show her the *many* complaints logged on iNeighbor about cars speeding on our street seemed to tip the scales in our favor. So, keep up the good work data collectors! No word yet on when they'll be installed, but fingers crossed it's soon!

A big shout-out to all of you who took the time to vote for Ashley's Eden Park series in the Cincinnati Junior Photo Contest. While runner-up is fantastic, I've launched an official investigation into whether the winner's parents were using a form of robocalling to tip the scales in their daughter's favor. I think we can all agree that her photographs had nothing on Ashley's. If you have any skills in that area— John Dunbar, I'm looking at you!—please give me a ring.

For those of you in the book club, this month's read will be *Wreckage* by Emily Bleeker. I hear it's much better than some books that will remain nameless!

Stay cool (but not too cool**).

Cindy Sutton,

PSNA Chair and Founder, 2009–present

**In accordance with bylaw 201.45, sprinklers may only run for thirty minutes, twice a week.

Today

John

2:00 p.m.

When Hanna comes out of the grand jury room, she won't look me in the eye. Though she was put together when she went in there, now she's a mess. She's pulled her hair from its pins, something she does when she frets. It's hanging in her eyes, half hiding her face. Her suit looks slept in, the skirt rumpled from where her hands have been clutching at it. Her expression reminds me of the time we were on a plane that landed in a lightning storm. We lost significant altitude several times. A woman behind us threw up. One of the flight attendants briefly floated toward the ceiling, then slammed to the floor. We had to assume the crash position. When we were finally safe on the ground, we'd stumbled off as if we'd flown through a war zone.

That's what Hanna looks like. As if she's been at war. Perhaps with herself.

I gesture for her to come to me, my arms half-open. Instead, she walks up to Chris and pulls him into a hug. She whispers something in his ear. The "I love you," I hear. The rest is lost. Then the clerk calls his name. Hanna clutches Chris's arm, not wanting to let him go. He loosens her fingers gently, one by one. Says, "It's okay, Mom." I give his shoulder a squeeze. He doesn't look at me. Maybe he thinks I'm still trying to get him to keep my secrets. But that's the furthest thing from my mind. My son is about to walk into a place where we can't help him anymore. Perhaps that's been true before. But it's never felt like this.

Then he's away from us. Through the doors. The doors are closed. We're left behind in a roomful of strangers who are trying not to act as if they're watching our every move.

"Why did they call Chris now?" I ask Alicia, keeping my voice low.

Her brow is furrowed. "I'm not sure. They'll have their own logic to what they're doing, wanting to put together the puzzle in a particular way. As I've said, this isn't going to be X said this, what do you have to say about that? They'll ask their questions, and then make their argument to the grand jury. The questions themselves will be a type of argument. Building blocks. That's why it's important we stick to the strategy individually."

Building blocks. Shovels of dirt. Building a wall. I've heard her use all of these analogies and more. Instead of saying straight out what they want to do: bury us.

"How did it go?" Alicia asks a still-silent Hanna.

"I thought I wasn't supposed to say."

"Not the substance, but are you okay?"

"I've been through worse."

Alicia puts her arm around Hanna's shoulders. She tenses, then relaxes. I can't help feeling jealous. I should be the one she leans on. The one she relaxes against.

I was that person in the car this morning. Was it simply because there was no one else to fit the bill?

"He'll do fine in there, you know," Alicia says. "He's a bright kid, and he knows what he needs to do."

Hanna gives a deep shudder. Her bottom lip's quivering. She and Alicia sit in adjoining waiting chairs in a coordinated movement.

"It was awful," Hanna says. "I didn't expect . . . I really didn't expect it to be like that. Do I make people feel like that?" She looks at me.

"It's not the same, honey," I say. "What you do is about money."

She shakes her head. Is Hanna's career going to be another casualty of the day of the accident? That horrible day.

"But they asked everything we thought they would?" Alicia persists. "Everything we talked about?"

A look passes between them. One that excludes me. Have they had meetings I didn't know about? Or am I so full of secrets myself I assume everyone else must be similarly situated?

Hanna looks at me. Looks through me. I turn to see if there's someone behind me, but there's only the dingy oatmeal wallpaper, and strangers looking uncomfortable.

"What, Hanna?" I say.

"I can't tell you. You know that. I can't repeat my testimony."

My anger boils over. I speak through my teeth.

"This is ridiculous," I say to Alicia. "I can't talk to my own wife about—this is my family. Our family. How can they make us testify against each other?"

"Do you really think I'd testify against you?" Hanna says. "How can you think that?"

"I feel like there are all these things you're keeping from me. Like you and Alicia have some secret strategy I'm not allowed in on."

"Ha! That's rich."

"What are you talking about?"

Hanna looks as if all of the energy has drained from her body. And I'm the one who pulled the plug.

"If you'd done what I'd asked, if you'd stayed away from her, none of this would have happened."

"I did. I did stay away. And what happened that morning . . . that's only what anyone would've done."

"That's always been the problem, hasn't it?" she says. "It wasn't *anyone*. It was you. And now look where we are." She points to the doors Chris disappeared behind. "Look where your son is right now."

I Love New York in June

Julie

Four months ago

"And then," I said as I huffed up to the top of another hill, wishing I'd worn my sleeveless running shirt, "my lawyer said that if she actually goes through with this, it could cost me $50,000 in his fees alone."

Susan and I were on one of our night walks. I'd been speaking to my lawyer, Lee, that afternoon. He'd finally gotten around to giving me a full report on what he thought my options were. He'd been in trial, but still, given all the dollars I'd already sent his way, I would've thought I'd be more of a priority. Which I told him, and which I was certain he didn't appreciate.

"That's a lot of money," Susan said.

There was something in her tone I didn't quite like, or understand.

"It is."

She pulled her shirt away from her skin. "I can't believe it's still this hot at nine thirty at night."

"$50,000 *is* a lot of money for me."

"Is it?"

"Of course it is."

She pulled her shirt over her head and tied it around her waist. She was wearing a large black sports bra underneath, something that provided more cover than most swimsuits. I copied her maneuver, though my own sports bra was more revealing. The air felt momentarily cool against my slick skin. Still, I looked around to see if anyone was watching. If we were on Pine Street, you could be certain Cindy would be finding/inventing a new bylaw about proper workout attire. I'd had enough interventions in what I did and said in the last few months to last a lifetime.

Susan had lost some weight in the last couple of months. All of the trudging up hills and down dales had helped bring some definition back to her body. I, on the other hand, felt lumpy and unfit. Two months ago, I could've taken this hill without a second thought. Now I was huffing right along with Susan.

Damn John and that stupid kiss.

"Didn't you sell, like, three million copies of your book?"

"It's . . . something like that."

"And you get, what? Two, three dollars a book?"

God, how I hated that question. I'd never ask Susan, or anyone else, what she made for a living, working as a bookkeeper for several local businesses, or what she received in support payments from Brad. But every Tom, Dick, and Susan thought they had a right to know what an author's income was, how many books we've sold and whether we're successful. Even though my book had done well, I felt as put off by the questions as I would have if I'd sold the five hundred copies I expected to when The Book came out.

"It's not that linear. There are a lot of e-books in there, and price drops, and my agent gets fifteen percent, and there are taxes . . ."

I trailed off, because what was the use? She was right. On paper, $50,000 shouldn't mean anything to me. The fact that it did was a form of denial. The money was still coming in like it was being sprayed out of a fire hose, but I didn't want to think about it. I didn't even talk about it with Daniel, who tended not to read the stories that came out every six months or so when I crossed another significant sales threshold. I'd hung the framed copy of my book they'd sent me when it reached a million copies, but had put the other two in a drawer.

"It's not only the money," I said. "It's the whole principle of the thing."

"I'm sure Hanna feels that way, too."

"Have you talked to her?"

"Not in detail, but I've known them for a long time."

"I know that, and I appreciate you taking my side, I really do."

"I'm not taking sides," Susan said. "I'm just not going to stop being your friend because of this."

"Thank you. That means a lot to me."

We walked to the next street and started down the hill.

"Any word from Brad lately?"

"I think he's trying to win me back."

I glanced at her. Her cheeks were red, and her hair was puffed up from the humidity. She looked puzzled and vulnerable.

"Why didn't you say anything before?"

"I'm not sure what to think about it."

"What's he been doing?"

"I told you he's going to AA? Well, he seems to be taking it seriously. He says he's been sober for three months now, and he's doing that whole making-amends thing."

"That's good, isn't it?"

"Maybe for him, but what does it mean for me? Am I supposed to forgive him for all the times he chose alcohol over his family?"

"You don't have to."

"But I *feel* as if I do, you see? Alcoholics are so selfish. It's always about them, even in recovery. This is what *I* need. Blah, blah, blah. I'm sick of it, you know?"

"I get it. How are the kids handling it?"

"The *kids*," she said, a sob escaping her. "That's what makes this all so impossible."

"Because you're worried what he might do?"

"Because he's got them in on his act. Suddenly I'm the bad guy if I don't back down and take him back."

"That doesn't seem right."

"It isn't."

"Can you talk to Brad? Tell him how you're feeling?"

"That's the thing. If I talk to him, I might give him hope, but I can't totally destroy his hope, either, because then he might start drinking again. It's a no-win situation, either way."

"I'm so sorry, Susan."

"Fucking Brad."

We walked for a few minutes in silence, reaching the bottom of one hill and starting up another toward one of the lookouts over the Ohio River. Despite everything that had happened, I still loved the neighborhood. The colorful houses hugging the sidewalks, the views of the river and its different moods. A runner passed us, breathing heavily, doing what we were doing but at running speed. Hill work. I used to do that. It was unpleasant, but it made me feel so strong when I could get all the way to the top of the "awful hill," as Leah and I called it, without feeling like I needed to puke at the end.

"How long," I said eventually, "do you have to keep walking on eggshells around him?"

"I went to one of those Al-Anon websites. I think he needs to be sober for a year."

"What does that mean for you?"

"I'm keeping my contact to a minimum, but I can't tell him that there's no hope for us. I can't tell him the truth."

"Is it the truth?"

"I think so."

"I'm sorry."

"It's fine. I've kind of accepted it."

"Maybe the website is wrong? There's all kinds of misleading stuff on the Internet."

"You're right . . . anything going on there, for you?"

With everything else happening, Heather had receded into the background, where I wished she could stay forever. "I'm almost scared to say it, but all seems quiet on the Heather front."

"That's good. Did you see Ashley won an award for that picture she took? When you ran out after her at the Bow Tie?"

"Where did you see it?"

"Facebook, I think."

"Are we . . . are we in it?"

"Not recognizably. It's all blurred and foggy . . . I was pretty impressed, actually."

"You must have thought I was insane, running out like that."

"It was a normal reaction after everything that's happened."

I agreed, but then went silent. I scrolled through everything that had happened since I'd arrived in Ohio. The lack of video evidence on my camera feed. The way the police had dismissed me. The fact that none of the events, in and of themselves, actually proved anything.

Was it possible that it was *all* innocent?

Was it possible it was all in my head?

The first time I really knew there was something wrong with Heather was the summer we spent working in New York.

As far as I'm concerned, the summer associates program is the main reason to attend law school. At these well-paid jobs, your only responsibility is going for expensive lunches with the senior associates and making sure you don't nod off at your desk in the afternoon as the pasta dish you ate spreads its carbohydrates through your bloodstream.

I got one of those jobs at Kerr, Byrne & Grant after my second year at McGill. I knew it was a Faustian pact: one well-paid and lazy summer in return for seven brutal associate years that would start after I passed the bar. But I had the grades, and I needed the money, and: New York!

It was Kathryn's idea, and Booth and Kevin came along because they went along with whatever Kathryn decided. Kathryn and I shared an apartment a few blocks from them in the Village. The guys worked at a different firm, but we had enough hours to ourselves to become familiar to the bouncers at Fiddlesticks, our local Irish bar.

Heather was there that summer, too. Not in our apartment, but nearby, and working at the same firm as Kathryn and me. She seemed to be the only student who hadn't gotten the take-it-easy memo, getting stuck on some deposition document prep that took up every waking minute. She lost weight and developed deep circles under her eyes, and when I'd occasionally try to pry her from her cubicle, she'd give me this weary look and tell me what she was doing was too important to step away from.

I felt different that summer. I ran along the East River every morning. I was going to parties and wearing clothes I couldn't afford because Kathryn insisted what was hers was mine. I felt like time was winding backward, the years peeling away. How did I already feel *old* at twenty-four? I couldn't even say. Only I'd been so focused on getting somewhere, anywhere but where I came from, I'd never sat in one place long enough to just be.

I did manage to "just be" that summer with Kathryn and the others. Though I was with Booth and she was with Kevin, we were a seamless unit.

I believed that almost all of the time.

But every once in a while, when Kathryn would come by my cubicle, laughing at some inside joke from the night before, I'd catch Heather watching us out of the corner of her eye, a small smile playing on her lips. Something about the way she looked at me made me feel small, like she was in on a joke that was on me, and was waiting for me to figure it out. Then I'd tell myself I was imagining things and go back to pretending to work.

Then one day, deep in August, Heather brushed past me on the way to the bathroom, and I watched a piece a paper flutter behind her to the ground. I was about to call after her when I saw my name scrawled across it.

I picked it up and turned it over.

You'll never be one of them, it read, and I felt its truth in every fiber of my being.

It was the first of many notes I'd receive.

On a Saturday in mid-June, I was standing in the entrance of Joseph-Beth, feeling awkward. There were two massive posters made up of my book cover and my face hanging in the front windows, which always made me feel like an impostor. Were people really going to show up—and okay, there was kind of a line, I could see, inside the store—just for me?

How had that happened?

I hadn't wanted to do this public appearance, but my publicist insisted. The movie was coming out in a couple of months, and it would be good to spur more sales, she said. I wondered if she'd ever been to a bookstore signing. Even if it went well, I'd sell maybe a hundred books; no way that would move the movie dial. But she'd pressed, and my editor got into the act, and in the end it was easier to agree. Besides, I was starting to believe that Heather really had forgotten about me. Even the creepy phone calls had died down and then stopped.

I used to love bookstores. On the rare afternoon when I'd have a sitter and could escape the twins for a few hours, that's where I'd go. Not to run the errands that were supposed to justify the expense, but to the big leather chair in the fiction section where I could browse the newest releases and read in peace for an hour or two. Now I'm ashamed of myself, reading whole books without paying for them. But then, it never occurred to me that I was getting something for free. I was escaping; that was the important thing.

Those stolen afternoons are the whole reason I started writing. I'd stumbled across a book written by another one of our McGill classmates, a woman named Moira, whom I hadn't known very well. Her book was sitting in the bargain bin, ALL BOOKS ON SALE FOR $1.99! It had a lurid cover, its title written in a script that seemed to be dripping blood. *Mens rea*, it was called—the guilty mind.

I knew it was about Kathryn as soon as I saw Moira's name, my pulse quickening as I plucked it out of the bin and took it to my hiding place. It had been published during the foggy first year of the twins' birth, when it would've taken police at my door to arrest me to register anything outside of my own personal bubble.

There was nothing new in the book, I found as I raced through it. All the same theories and speculation about how Kathryn died, and who might've done it, were there. The "suspects"—me and the twenty other people who'd been at the party who knew her—picked up and examined, then discarded. She even considered herself, because she and Kathryn had a fight once when Moira kissed Kevin at a party and claimed she didn't know he and Kathryn were dating, and she'd been there that night, too. Her verdict: it was a tragic drinking accident. No one could know that she'd never wake up from the nap she went to take while the party raged on around her. The idea that someone pressed her face into the pillow was too unreasonable to believe. She might have died a rock-star death, but that wasn't any reason to create conspiracies.

The book was badly written and vaguely libelous, and the title didn't even make sense. If there was no *mens rea* that still might mean there was an *actus reus*—a guilty act. Both were missing from her book.

And yet, that's what stuck in my head. *Mens rea*, the guilty mind. It was an old debate Kathryn and Booth and Kevin and I had dozens of times over beers at McKibbin's and cheap bottles of wine at one another's apartments. At what point did thinking about something, even planning for something, become criminal? Where does the switch occur? At what precise moment? At the beginning of the plan? The End?

And how?

Those discussions were the genesis of The Murder Game—our name for the drunken conversations that became long planning sessions of how to pull off the perfect murder.

"Ms. Apple?"

A store clerk wearing a green apron with a Joseph-Beth logo on it stood in front of me with an inquiring expression. I didn't look much like my publicity shot, I knew, mostly on purpose, but also because I couldn't be bothered most days with the effort that would take.

"That's me."

"Oh, I thought so! This is so exciting." She took my elbow and nudged me into the store. "Look, there are already a *huge* number of people here."

She pointed to the line I'd seen earlier. There were rows of empty seats scattered around a lectern. I wasn't sure why they were making them line up to sit down, and I said so.

"It's all psychological! You know? Like if they see a line, then it's something important."

"Ah," I said. "Should I go over there now?"

"That would be fantastic! So, you'll read first? And then you'll take questions? And then sign books?"

I already felt exhausted.

"That sounds great."

"They had to buy the book first! Look, they're all holding their copies!"

They were. Perhaps a hundred women—and only a few men—were clutching their books to their chests. I was happy to see so few men because, despite Heather, the men were usually the weirder fans. I had a wistful moment thinking back to the beginning. How I'd snap a picture of the meager crowds who'd come out to hear me speak holding their books in the air, and post it online. *I'm in Seattle! Ottawa! Frankfurt!*

The exclamation point on my keyboard was worn down, faded.

I felt the same.

The chipper bookseller introduced me while I shifted uncomfortably, trying to pretend she was speaking about someone else. I slapped on a smile and started reading:

It's hard to pinpoint the exact moment when your life becomes unmanageable . . .

Six months ago I had a successful career in Montreal, and now I was nearly a fugitive, living anonymously in a beach town on the other side of the world.

I wasn't really happy before. My job was stressful. I slept badly. I weighed less than I should. I pushed away those who tried to get close to me.

But at least I was living.

Now, I'm in stasis. I sleep, but I wake early. I eat, but it's out of habit. I run along the shore at dawn, but I can't see the beauty that surrounds me.

I need to go back. To my life. But also to the beginning. So I can know. So I can understand.

How I got here. What we did. Why we did it.

But really, what I most need to know is: Were we innocent?

Were we guilty?

You tell me . . .

◆ ◆ ◆

"I loved your book," a woman said to me, handing me her copy.

"Thanks so much!" My exclamation marks were back. "Who can I make this out to?"

I asked, and wrote, and signed for an hour. The bookstore was thrilled, my guide told me, thrilled. I told her how much independent bookstores meant to me. How they'd been my salvation, the first to embrace The Book and lead it to what it had become.

"Oh, here's a latecomer," she said.

Hanna was standing there. She was wearing a blue tank top that accented her shoulder blades, and jeans that fit her just right. Her blonde hair was wavy and relaxed, but her face told a different story.

I pushed my seat back, my arms rigid.

"Don't worry," Hanna said. "I come in peace."

"Okay."

"Will you sign this for me?"

She thrust a book at me. It looked read. Reread, even.

I took it from her and opened it to the signature page. John's name was written neatly in the corner with the date next to it. Two years earlier.

I looked up at Hanna.

"John's a big fan, didn't you know?"

"I knew he'd read it."

That seemed like the safest answer.

"Well, he is."

"Should I make it out to you?"

"How about you make it out to both of us?"

Was there a pointed note to her voice? Perhaps.

I uncapped my pen and wrote: *To Hannah and John,*

"There's no *h* in Hanna."

"Oh, goodness, I'm so sorry. I usually ask! I've never seen it written down."

But that wasn't true. It was on the letter she'd given me at the block party. *We are the attorneys for John and Hanna Dunbar. We have been mandated to advise you that our client has reason to bring the following legal complaint against you . . .* Someone in the firm she worked for had signed it, but that didn't make it any less real, or any less of a threat.

"You can scratch the *h* out," she said.

"But I wouldn't want to ruin it. I can grab another copy . . ."

"No, it's fine." She took the book and pen from me and put a line through the *h*. "See? All better now."

She put it back on the table. I pulled it toward me as I wondered what else to write. *Thanks for being so welcoming! So great to know you! Thanks for coming out; it means so much to me!* All the usual phrases seemed impossible, so I wrote: *Hope you enjoy(ed) this*, and signed my name.

I handed it back to her.

"You must get sick of being asked whether you're Meredith."

Meredith. The narrator of *The Murder Game*. The person I wish I'd worked harder at differentiating from me. But would that have changed anything? I was conscious every day, now, as I tried to write, that no matter what I did, anything that seemed to resemble my life remotely would be thought a product of anything other than my imagination.

"Did it show?" I said.

I'd been asked that question in the talk, and I gave my stock answer: *If I planned a murder, I'd never get away with it.*

It usually gets a laugh. It did that day, too.

"Not obviously. So . . . someone in your law-school class died?"

"Kathryn. She got pretty drunk at a law-school party and went to lie down. We found her dead a few hours later."

"How awful."

"It was."

"A close friend?"

"Fairly close. I met her in law school. You know how it is. I hardly speak to anyone from my class anymore. But during school, we were close."

"Same. So, she wasn't murdered?"

My hands clenched under the table. "The autopsy said she'd stopped breathing. There were a lot of pillows on the bed, and she'd been drinking pretty heavily . . ."

"They say you write what you know," Hanna said.

"That's what they say."

"You don't agree?"

"I think people confuse that with writing about yourself. I took a real thing I went through and used the emotions I had from that to make the things I imagined feel real."

"They felt pretty real."

"Thank you."

If she was expecting me to say more, she was going to be disappointed. Others had tried and failed, and I was on my guard. Was she this obvious in court?

"What made you stop by?" I asked.

"I'm not sure, to be honest. I saw something about it in the paper, and I grabbed the book and came."

"I haven't answered the letter. The lawyer's letter."

"I know. Why is that?"

It felt weird talking like this. With me sitting, and her holding my book to her chest like someone might steal it from her.

I spoke impulsively. "Why don't you guys come for dinner? Say, next Friday? Maybe we can talk this out and come to a solution?"

"I . . ."

"Or the two of us could go for a drink? Whatever's easiest."

"Dinner's fine."

"Great!" I said, using my last exclamation mark. "See you at seven?"

The Dinner
John
Four months ago

When Hanna told me that she'd agreed to go to dinner at Daniel and Julie's, I thought she was joking. Even though it wasn't like Hanna to joke. But, no. It was true. She'd inexplicably gone to Julie's book signing. She had the inscribed book to prove it.

"I don't understand," I said as we worked through our Sunday list of chores together. Laundry. Changing the sheets on our bed. Getting a week's worth of clothes ready. I had a couple interviews for contract work. I couldn't show up to them in the old Ohio University sweatpants I'd taken to wearing most days. I was adding shirts to the pile to get pressed. "You said you were going to do the grocery shopping."

"I did. But I also went to Joseph-Beth."

"Did you know she was going to be there?"

"Yes. How else would I have known to take your book?"

"So you deliberately took my book to get her to sign it?"

"I did."

"Why?"

"I wanted to."

"That doesn't make any sense, Hanna. You're not making any sense."

She finished stripping the sheets and tossed them into the laundry basket. She pulled fresh ones from our closet.

"Will you help me with this?"

I took the other end of the fitted sheet and walked to my side of the bed. I snapped a corner in place.

"I'm having second thoughts, okay? I woke up this morning thinking: What if I misread this situation? What if there's an explanation for everything? And I thought . . . that if I went to see her, maybe I'd be able to figure that out."

"And did you?"

"I listened to her speak about how she came up with the idea for her book. Did you know about that?"

"Not really," I said. "No."

"This woman in her law-school class died in this kind of horrible way, and then she wrote a book about it."

"Is that what she said? That's not even the plot of the book."

"She didn't write about it literally. It's what gave her the idea."

"What's wrong with that?"

She tossed the top sheet to me. I spread it out, making a hospital corner the way my mother taught me.

"Nothing, I guess. It just seems parasitic."

I crushed my instinct to stand up for Julie. "How did that end up with us going over there for dinner?"

"I felt kind of sorry for her when she was speaking. She was very polished, very good, but she seemed . . . vulnerable. And she's talented."

"She is."

She stuffed a pillow into a case and tossed it at the headboard.

"That must be a lot of pressure, having to write a book after a massive success like that."

"Do you feel that way after a big win in court?"

"I've never really thought about it," Hanna said. "I guess so. I feel pressure with every case; you know that."

"You told me once that was because you cared."

"I do."

"Maybe it's like that for her? Imagine spending all that time on one thing. And then it goes out into the world, and people write all kinds of horrible things about you. Plus, the stalker."

"Yeah, that occurred to me. It's part of why I felt for her. Plus, then, all the stuff with us . . . anyway, I said we'd do dinner on Friday."

I watched her, trying to figure out what she was really thinking. "Because you felt sorry for her?"

"Because she asked me. And because it's always better to settle than to sue. You in?"

"I'm game if you are."

She finished the pillows. We adjusted the blanket together. I thought about how, when we climbed into bed later, the sheets would feel cool against my skin. A feeling that wouldn't survive the night. By the time dinner rolled around on Friday, the sheets would be a tangled mess.

But for that moment, the bed looked so pristine and inviting.

If only a few nips and tucks could make life feel like that.

We stood in the entranceway to Julie and Daniel's house, shrugging off the raincoats we'd worn for the ten-second walk across the street in the heat-relieving rain. I didn't know if Hanna had been in the house since Julie and Daniel had moved in. She was certainly acting as if she hadn't. Absorbing every detail, her eyes roving around like the cameras that made her so mad.

What did she see? A cool palette of paint on the walls. Family photographs. The same scatter of toys and small shoes that used to litter our house.

Daniel greeted us warmly and beckoned us to follow him. We took a seat in the living room. Two dark-brown leather couches faced each other. A blue-and-gray oriental rug covered the floor. The mantel was cluttered with more photos in mismatched frames. Daniel offered us each a drink from the old-fashioned bar cart that took up the corner near the front windows. I had a fleeting thought that maybe this should be a sober evening, but Hanna asked for white wine, and the beer Daniel offered sounded good.

It tasted good, too. Cold and clean after a long day locked in front of my computer.

"Where are the kids?" Hanna asked when Daniel took a seat on the couch across from us.

"You've noticed the quiet?" he said.

Hanna smiled. "I did, actually."

"They have a sleepover tonight. At the Hendersons'? Brave people. Eight six-year-olds!" He shuddered. "Do you know them? Nice couple."

"Their oldest is in Becky's class."

"Great, great."

He played with the label on his beer. His hands were rough. Chapped. They'd been that way in Mexico, too. I made some crack about our crazy car ride back from the bar, which broke the tension. We talked about our favorite restaurants on the resort, and whether we'd go back. Then Hanna asked after Julie. She was in the kitchen, seeing to the dinner preparations. That surprised me, for some reason. Although I knew she and Daniel traded off meals—one of the many subjects covered on our runs—there was something undomestic about her. Hanna would probably beat me about the head if I said that out loud.

"Whatever's cooking smells delicious," Hanna said.

"It's nine-minute pasta," Julie said, coming into the room. She was holding a glass of red wine and wearing a pair of cream-colored pants. She was wearing an apron, too, which made my previous thought ridiculous. She looked entirely domestic. At ease. At home in a way I hadn't seen before.

"Oh," Hanna said, "I read about that! You put everything in the same pot, right? Water and pasta and everything?"

"That's right. It sounds completely wrong, but it's fantastic."

"Changed our life, really," Daniel said.

"Stop teasing me," Julie said, swatting at his arm. "*He* forgot to set the timer one night, and it ended up as a great gloppy thing. That wasn't the recipe's fault."

"You can make other things that way, too, can't you?" Hanna asked. "Other pastas, and ramen soup, I think."

"Yes, that's right. Our kids love pasta, so it's great. With both of them usually running around like banshees . . ." She trailed off and looked around, as if she'd just realized the children weren't there. "Should we call the Hendersons and check on them, you think?" she asked Daniel.

"Absolutely not. They have our numbers."

"But they can be a handful . . ."

"You were so worried when Chris had his first sleepover. Remember, honey?" I said, giving Hanna an affectionate pat on the knee.

"Yet, *you* were the one who drove over there to make sure everything was okay, if I remember correctly."

"Did I do that?"

"Don't blame you, man," Daniel said. "I think it's worse for us because we're supposed to be all nonchalant, but really all we want to do is check on them," Daniel said. "Can I get you another beer?"

I looked down at my empty bottle. How had that happened so fast?

"Sure. That'd be great."

He took my bottle along with his into the kitchen.

"Four minutes!" he called.

Julie took a sip of her wine. "Do you like it?" she asked Hanna, who hadn't made much of a dent in her glass. "We have something else if it's not to your taste."

"It's fine, thank you."

We fell into silence. I racked my brain for something to say, but every subject felt like a minefield.

"How's the next book going?" Hanna asked. "Do you have a deadline?"

Daniel returned with two beers swinging from his fingers.

"That's two minutes."

"Yes, it's due in a couple of months. I'm at about sixty thousand words."

"That sounds like a lot."

"It's not enough, unfortunately."

"What's this one about, if you can say? Another murder?"

"Something like that."

"Julie's cagey about her writing," Daniel said. "I didn't even know she'd finished writing *The Murder Game* until she'd gotten an agent."

"Really?" Hanna said. "You weren't even a bit suspicious? She must've been spending a lot of time on the computer."

A beeper sounded.

"That'll be the pasta," Julie said, draining her glass. "Why don't you all go sit down and I'll bring it out?"

We followed her instructions, bringing our drinks with us to the dining room. Hanna's glass was suddenly empty. She had a hard glint in her eye: a look she sometimes got when she'd been drinking.

"She wrote in coffee shops," Daniel said. "We'd hired a babysitter for the afternoons to give Julie a break."

We sat down at the dark wood table. There were four chairs around it covered in white suede fabric. The room was lit by a glass chandelier. Several candles glimmered on the table.

"How old were the twins?" I asked.

"Two, two and a half. She survived two years home alone with them all day. Enough to drive anyone mad, I say." A look of guilt shot across his face. "Not that Julie didn't love being home with the kids . . ."

"Don't worry about that," Hanna said. "I would've needed to be heavily medicated if I'd had to stay home any longer than I did."

"I was heavily medicated," Julie said, walking in with a large bowl full of steaming pasta. "I highly recommend it."

I laughed. It seemed like the only appropriate response.

"I wasn't joking," Julie said, taking a seat at the head of the table. "Pass your plates up."

We obeyed her while Daniel filled fresh glasses with red wine. A generous pour.

"I had a bit of the baby blahs," Hanna said. "After Becky was born."

That was news to me.

"This was a bit more than that," Julie said. "But it's fine. I'm not ashamed. Besides, who knows why things happen. Maybe, if I hadn't been depressed, I never would have written The Book."

"That's Julie's name for it," I said, instantly regretting it. "I mean . . ."

"It's this silly affectation I have," Julie said as she passed plates along the table. The pasta, in some kind of red sauce with sausage and fresh basil, really did smell wonderful. "Capitalizing the things that seem outsized in my life. The Book. The Deadline. The Lawsuit."

I nearly choked on my drink.

"I thought we were here to bury the hatchet?" Hanna said carefully.

"We are," Daniel said. "Please don't take that the wrong way."

"Yes, please," Julie said. "I blurt things out sometimes. No filter. It's my greatest fault. Right, Daniel?"

Daniel tilted his wineglass at her. "It's what keeps you interesting."

"I have a horror of not being interesting."

Hanna was watching Julie carefully, her pasta steaming on her plate. If Hanna was flinty, Julie had a kind of manic quality about her. I'd never seen her like this. Was she mixing pills with alcohol? Or did Hanna bring it out in her?

"I think we all feel that way," I said.

"Please dig in."

I twirled some pasta onto my fork and took a bite. It was crunchy.

"Dammit," Julie said. "This isn't cooked."

"It's fine," I said. "Delicious."

"No, no." She stood up, grabbing her plate and the bowl. "I'm so embarrassed. Let me put it back on for a few minutes."

"That's really not . . ."

"I'll help," Hanna said, getting up as Julie approached her seat. Her shoulder caught the plate, which clattered to the floor. Julie lost her grip on the bowl, and its contents spilled over Hanna's shoulder and down the front of her sweater. Her favorite sweater. Given to her by the kids last Christmas.

Hanna let out a yelp of pain.

"Oh my God, I'm so sorry. Is it burning you?"

I rushed to Hanna's side. She was pulling her sweater over her head.

"It's hot!"

I helped her lift it off. There was an angry red mark blooming on her shoulder. Her bra was soaked in pasta sauce.

"Come upstairs with me," Julie said. "You should step into a cold shower. Quickly."

She pulled Hanna away from me and out of the room.

"That looks bad," Daniel said. "I'm so sorry. Maybe we should call 9-1-1?"

"Let's see what the cold water does. I don't think the burns were that serious. At least, I hope not. Maybe I should go up there?"

He put his hand on my shoulder. "I'm sure she'll call if she needs you."

"Yeah. Dammit. This is *not* how this evening was supposed to go."

"That could apply to a lot of things lately."

"Ain't that the truth."

"We should clean this up before it seeps into the rug."

I looked down. The rug matched the one in the living room, in a slightly darker blue. The red sauce was spreading out in a rough circle. The seat of Hanna's chair was also covered in it.

"Might be too late for that," I said.

Daniel walked into the kitchen, returning with a bunch of towels, a bowl of soapy water, and a garbage can.

We both got down on our hands and knees. He scooped up the broken plate and bowl with a towel and put it in the garbage can. I soaked another towel and started blotting at the rug.

"I think you're going to have to call in the professionals," I said.

"I was afraid of that. This rug was a wedding present from my folks."

"It's worth saving, then."

Daniel handed me a new soaked towel and we traded, the old one going into the trash.

"One more mess to clean up," Daniel said.

"I tried to talk Hanna out of giving her that letter."

"It's fine. Maybe if I lived where you do, in the path of the cameras, I'd feel the same way. Hanna and Julie do seem to mix like . . ."

"Pasta and this carpet?"

"Precisely." He sighed. "I tried to talk her out of it, too. The cameras, I mean. I even hired a PI."

"A PI?"

"A private detective."

"I know what a PI is. Why did you hire one?"

"To look into . . . everything."

Daniel gave me a hard look, like he wanted to probe me for information. Was he expecting me to flinch? Confess?

"Did you find out who's been harassing her?"

"Clearly not. He had a theory, though. One that might make sense. He thought that Julie was the one—"

"Do you have any soda water?" I blurted.

"What?"

"Soda water. I remember my mother always saying it got stains out."

He shook his head. "I don't—did you hear what I said?"

"I heard you. But should you really be telling me this?" I sat back on my heels, giving up on the rug.

"Probably not. I never even told Julie I'd hired him. It was going to be a surprise. Am I a total dick?"

Daniel looked ashamed.

"I've thought she might be behind it, too, to be honest," I said. "Has she . . . done anything like that before?"

"I don't . . . Heather was real. *Is* real."

"I'm not saying she isn't."

"She's just been so . . . lost since she got here."

Daniel fell back on his rear and put his hands over his face. His breath had that smell beer makes when it's fermenting inside someone. Like it's almost turned to hard alcohol.

"Did he have any evidence?" I asked.

"There's a few things . . . he's still digging. What made you think . . . ?"

"She told me that's what the police believed. I guess it planted a seed."

"Is it possible to live with someone every day and not know them? At their core?"

The kiss flitted through my mind.

"I think that happens all the time."

"What should I—"

"I told you to stop!" Hanna's voice. Angry. Distressed.

I stood up quickly. The room tilted. I pushed against the wall and ran toward the stairs.

"Hanna?"

She was standing on the landing, a towel wrapped around her. Her clothes were clutched in her hand.

"Keep her away from me."

She almost ran down the stairs and into me. Her hair was damp. Both her shoulders were red, the one where the pasta had fallen, especially. A small blister was forming on her collarbone.

"What happened?" Daniel and I spoke together.

Julie was standing at the top of the stairs. Her hair was down, disheveled. She looked like she'd been in a fight.

"Forget it; we're leaving."

Hanna marched out the front door. I looked at Julie for a moment, waiting for some explanation, then turned and hurried after Hanna, grabbing our raincoats off their hooks.

She crossed the street in her bare feet, walking through several puddles.

"Hanna, wait. Should we go to the hospital?"

She rang our doorbell as I reached her. Chris opened the door a moment later.

"Mom! What happened to you?"

She fell against Chris, resting her head on his shoulder.

"She did," she said.

And I knew we were broken.

Today

John

3:00 p.m.

Chris is in the grand jury room for almost an hour. The witnesses for the other grand jury shuttle in and out of the waiting room with quiet efficiency. I ask Alicia again why our case is so different. She repeats the words I already know by heart: we chose to testify, which the accused almost never does. By doing so, we forced the prosecution to present a fuller case. To respond to what we're going to say. And that's how we're going to win, Alicia says. Because when they hear the whole story, rather than only the prosecutor's side, they won't be able to indict.

I think about what I'm going to say as I watch the doors for any sign of Chris. A few minutes after three, they open, and there he is again. He looks thin and pale. There are marks on his face that show he's been crying. But something has shifted. He went in there still mostly a boy. Now I can see the man he is. The man he will become regardless of the outcome.

The clerk announces a fifteen-minute break as Chris walks to us in a daze. Hanna gathers him close, leading him away from me. I want to ask him how things went. But he's not allowed to tell me anything. Besides, it's written on his face. The moments he was forced to remember, reconstruct. The emotions he's been tamping down for two months bubbling up and over. The hurt, the horror, the heartbreak. Our eyes meet. He nods once, quickly. Our secrets are safe, I think. I'm not sure whether to be sick or relieved. Perhaps I am both.

Then the force of what I've done hits me. I feel as if my knees might buckle. Alicia puts her hand on my elbow.

"You look pale."

"I'm not feeling very well."

"Why don't we go outside and get some air?"

"Aren't I up next?"

"I think there's someone before you."

"Who?"

She shakes her head. After a moment, I nod and follow her to the elevators.

"Let's walk around the block," she says when we get outside. "I find that helps."

I follow her lead. The sky has cleared. It feels like it's going to warm up overnight. I breathe in and out slowly. The city air. The familiar combination of exhaust and people. I feel some of my self-control returning. The edge of my panic blurred by being removed from the imminent sense of danger the room upstairs holds.

"Have you ever testified at one of these things?" I say to Alicia.

"I have, actually."

"How come?"

"Soon after I started working at the firm, one of our clients shot one of the associates. Right there in the office."

"My God, that's terrible."

"It was. Especially since I think he was looking for me. We'd switched offices."

"Why would he be looking for you?"

"He lost his case. I was the junior on the file, but he blamed me, I guess."

"That must be hard to get over."

She gives me a weak smile. "I don't think you ever really recover from something like that, do you? But we moved offices, a whole different building, and I had counseling. It was a long time ago."

"I'd shut down, I think."

"But you haven't . . . oh, goodness."

She's looking across the street. There's a heavyset woman standing near the parking lot where my car is parked. She looks like one of the many lawyers who've waltzed in and out of the waiting room this afternoon. Her dark-brown hair's cut short, almost boyishly. She's talking emphatically to a man who's standing in front of her.

I guess it's the hair and the suit, but it takes me a second to place her. The first time I saw Heather Stanhope, she was wearing a tracksuit, and her hair was long and shaggy.

"You can't speak to her," Alicia says.

"I wasn't planning on it."

"They didn't call her this morning."

"What does that mean?"

"I'm not sure. She's with her lawyer. You stay here, I'm going to find out."

I watch Alicia cross the street, trying to slow my heart.

Heather Stanhope. In the flesh.

For so long she felt like a made-up person. Snuffleupagus.

I looked her up online months ago. Julie had shown me some of her posts when we were still talking. I used those as a starting point. It was easy, really, when you knew where to look.

I knew, for instance, that she was in Julie's law-school class at McGill. A few searches showed me she made law review, something I understood was prestigious without understanding why. Then I tracked down their yearbook. The only pictures of Heather were the formal shots everyone took, and one of the law-review group. Julie was in that photo, too, dressed in clothes that looked like they came from the men's department. There was another picture of Julie, a few pages later, her arms slung over the shoulders of a very pretty girl and a nondescript guy. Another guy had his arms around Julie's waist, his face half-hidden.

At the back, there was a big in-memoriam spread for Kathryn Simpson—the pretty girl from the earlier picture. She died from drinking too much at a party. Julie and the guys from the earlier picture were scattered throughout the collage. In one photo, I thought I saw the corner of Heather's face, scowling as she watched them laugh.

I did other things, too. Not all at once, but over the following weeks. I read through the condolence book for Kathryn that was still online. Everyone in the class had left a heartfelt message, as had the faculty. Julie wrote: *You took me in when I was friendless and helped me find my way. You were the most generous person I knew. There will be a hole in my heart—my life—forever. Life is not fair, but nothing has taught me that more than your passing. I love you always.* Booth and Kevin—the boys in their group photos, I figured out through more digging—wrote similar things. Everyone becomes perfect when they die, I've noticed. But these sentiments seemed genuine.

Heather also left a message. It sent a chill down my spine. *You were my only friend in the world. What will I do without you?* I'm not sure what it was about, precisely, but in a long line of earnest messages, it felt false.

I kept reading and came across a series of more recent posts from Heather. She wrote something every year on the anniversary of Kathryn's death. How she missed her, still thought of her, wished she was there to confide in. It was as if she knew no one was reading them anymore, five, ten years later. A couple of years ago, the entries picked up the pace.

Did you know that Julie wrote a book? I think it's about you.
Julie says she made it up, but I don't think that's true.

Those guys were always hanging out, playing that stupid game. They thought I didn't know because no one really pays attention to me, but you did. And I heard them. Planning. Plotting. Deciding who the perfect victim would be. You were always better than them.

The entries went on for several pages. As Heather's theories got wilder, she stopped using names. But she kept on asking Kathryn questions, as if she could answer. Asking her to tell Heather how she'd died, what had really happened.

It took me more than an hour to read them all. I felt dirty at the end. Sullied. I closed the browser and tried to pretend they didn't exist.

But after the disastrous dinner party, after what Daniel had told me about the private investigator, I went back to the site. Then I started matching up Heather's entries with the suggestions in blog posts that Julie's book wasn't entirely fiction. The first couple were made by different screen names commenting on high-profile reviews of her book. But then a more serious blogger picked up on the story and wrote a "What if" kind of piece. Not accusing Julie of anything, simply piecing together snippets here and there that made it seem as if *The Murder Game* were more *In Cold Blood* than *Gone Girl*.

I don't know if anyone ever took the time to look properly before, but it became pretty clear to me that Heather was the source of those rumors. Heather posing as several different people online, including the blogger who'd put it all together.

But why would she accuse Julie of doing such a thing? Why would she claim she and Kathryn were close friends when there didn't seem to be any evidence of it? What was her end game? Was she simply off balance, mentally ill, or was there a kernel of truth she'd stumbled across? A thousand monkeys at a thousand typewriters . . .

Alicia crosses the street and comes back to me. Heather and I make eye contact. She recognizes me. Grimaces. Turns away.

"What's going on?" I ask.

"They asked her to be on call this afternoon. Just in case."

"In case what?"

"In case they need her as a rebuttal witness, I think."

"You mean, to contradict something we might say?"

"Yes."

"But that, that . . . she . . ."

"I need you to tell me what happened that morning again. From the beginning."

"What would you consider the beginning?"

"It's your story, John. You decide."

Reinforcements

Julie

Three months ago

Leah arrived in the middle of a heat wave.

The Monday after the disastrous dinner party, I was served with legal papers. Hanna and John were suing me for the dog bite and the cameras and the "possibly permanent burns incurred at the dinner party." The potential liability written down in those papers would wipe us out financially.

Even the money generated by The Book wasn't enough to overcome the price of Hanna's anger.

When I'd recovered from the shock, I called Leah, and asked if she and her family could come visit as soon as possible. I would pay for everything, and we could do . . . whatever.

Leah consulted with her husband, Rick, and called me back within the hour. Everything was all set. They'd arrive in two weeks, she'd rented a cabin near Lake Cumberland, a "lakeside delight," she said, a twenty-five-hundred-square-foot rental property with a view, a pool table in the basement, and a perfect deck for stargazing. The kids would have fun swimming and riding the WaveRunners that came with the rental. *We* could drink wine all day and slosh around the deck. It sounded perfect.

When Daniel calmed down from wanting to cross the road and knock some sense into John and Hanna, he was game. Anything to distract us from the upcoming months of stress and expense and hostility.

So, when we met Leah, Rick, and their two kids—Liam, five, and Owen, seven—at the airport, we piled them into a rented Suburban and drove directly there.

The two weeks between that call and their arrival had been, frankly, awful. I couldn't sleep. I felt like I spent all day on the phone with my lawyer. I couldn't write, literally could not put a word down on the page. The worst of it was when I caught Daniel, who was doing his best to be supportive, looking at me when he thought I was doing something else with a puzzled expression on his face. I'd seen that look before, but I couldn't ask him about it. I had enough doubt to deal with on my own.

The last two days, I was back to putting vodka in my morning orange juice.

Not good, as Sam would say, not good.

"So, wait," Leah said, when we finally got onto the I-75. "We were never in Ohio?"

We were seated on the middle bench. The three boys were in the back row, their heads bowed over the two iPads we had to share between them. Melly sat next to me, watching something on my phone.

"Look out the window, kids!" Daniel cried. "You're going to see horses."

I don't think they even heard him.

"The airport is in Kentucky," Rick said from the front seat. He had a large map spread out over his lap, even though the car was equipped with GPS, because GPS—and all technology, really—was for losers, apparently. "I told you that a zillion times already."

Daniel caught my eye in the review mirror, a large grin on his face. It was impossible to feel anything other than happy around Leah and Rick. They radiated fun the way some people sucked it away.

"That's so weird," Leah said. "Isn't it weird?"

"It's not *that* weird," I said.

Leah pushed my hair out of my face. "You need a haircut."

"Probably."

"I'm thinking of shaving my head."

Leah had thick brown hair that she'd worn short for as long as I'd known her. She had the face for it, gamine, with large brown eyes. It was a face that invited men to help her, even though she was more than capable of taking care of herself, and everyone else for that matter. We'd met in the birthing class I signed up for when I was pregnant with the twins. She'd been pregnant, too, but not for long. She'd had a second-trimester miscarriage, the only time I'd ever seen her and Rick laid low. While some people would've pulled away from a woman in my hugely pregnant condition after going through that kind of loss, Leah did the opposite. She threw herself into my pregnancy as if it were her own, bringing little Owen around frequently to help me put together furniture, or stack meals in the freezer for us to eat once the babies came.

"You are not."

"Don't goad her," Rick said. "Then she'll do it just so she can prove she can."

"That sounds like me, doesn't it?" Leah said, laughing.

"It sounds exactly like you."

"Oh, look! A horse."

Melly looked up from her screen.

"Are you joking, Aunt Leah?"

"Who would joke about a horse? Look!"

She pointed to a grassy meadow. A horse stood in the middle of it, its brown coat glossy under the hot sun.

"What's he doing there?" Melly asked. "Where are his parents?"

"I think he belongs to that barn over there, honey," I said. "But he looks like a grown-up horse. So he's okay on his own."

She gave me a skeptical look. "I would like a horse, I think."

"You would?"

"Yes. We read a story at school about a girl with a horse. She mu . . . mu . . ."

"Mucked out?"

"Yeah. She did that every day."

"Do you know what that means?"

"I think I do."

"It means cleaning up all the horse poop. Like we have to do for Sandy, but way bigger."

"Oh," she said, her head falling back toward the screen. "Every day?"

"Twice a day."

"Oh," she said again, and I knew there'd be no more talk of horses. Melly knew that starting in the fall, she and Sam would be responsible for one of Sandy's walks, the one on our street, and that they'd have to pick up after him. She was already trying to get out of it, coming up with increasingly elaborate plans to get her brother to do it for her, or Daniel. "I'll tickle your back," I'd heard her tell Daniel the other morning. Since this was her favorite thing, she thought it had currency with everyone.

"So," Leah said, "what's our first stop?"

"McDonald's!" Sam answered her.

"Yes," Owen said. "Good idea. I want French fries."

"Oh, yes, please, Mommy?" Liam chimed in.

"Their grandparents take them to McDonald's," Leah said, rolling her eyes. Not that she had a problem with an occasional Happy

Meal—only that Rick's parents were adamant about being involved with the kids but then never seemed to know what to do with them. Leah and Rick lived near both of their parents. Mine were scattered in two different directions, and Daniel preferred visits on the High Wasp Holidays *only*, as he put it. Easter, Thanksgiving, and Christmas. We hadn't seen them for any of those since we'd moved. They'd been replaced with monthly Skype conversations.

"We'll see," I said.

"Oh, navigator," Leah said. "What says the giant map?"

"It says we're about two hours away, and that there's lots of stuff to see once we get there."

Leah pouted. She always wants to stop at every ridiculous World's Biggest Whatever along the way to anywhere we've traveled together.

"Looks like we might be going to McDonald's, kids!" she said.

"Yeah!" came the chorus from the back.

"World's Biggest Hamburger?" I said.

"Now you're talking."

A few days before Leah and Rick arrived, I'd been searching for some beach towels in one of the closets when I knocked over an old box of mine I hadn't opened since law school. It was full of memorabilia, most of which I didn't even know the provenance of anymore. Why, for instance, had I held on to a place mat from a diner, one of those paper ones you throw away after every meal? Or what was the significance of the baseball hat with no logo? Was it Booth's, or some random piece of clothing that got cast into the box? Part of me was disturbed I didn't remember, but part of me was glad, too. There was a time when those three people seemed to take up all the space in my life; it was good to see I'd moved on.

I spent an hour sifting through the contents. Laughing at photographs, crying at a few of Kathryn, taken on our last weekend together. At the bottom was a black book with a spiral binding. It was the diary I'd tried to keep back then, a habit I was never good at and abandoned not long after Kathryn died.

It was full of things I didn't remember: fights, ideas, flights of fancy. Near the end was an entry that made me pause.

February 3, 1998

It's late and I've been drinking but I said I'd write every day and so I'm writing.

Was out with Booth and Kevin and Kathryn again. That same corner booth at McKibbin's, the one we've scratched our name into. Booth and Kevin were particularly drunk, gulping down pints like they'd spent months in the desert. I ran into Heather in the bathroom. I invited her to join us, hoping she'd say no. I was feeling mean, a hollow feeling, but one she seems to bring out in me. She thanked me and left, but later I saw her watching us through the mirror behind the bar.

What is her problem?

Around ten, Kevin pulled out his notebook, the one we've been playing the game in, and turned to his "magnum opus," as he called it. He was talking quickly, like I imagine someone on coke might, sped up, almost unintelligible as he threw out ideas, potential problems, but only a few solutions.

"You're so drunk," Kathryn said.

"Me? What about you?"

She held her head carefully. "I am perfectly fine."

"Ha," Kevin said. "You should see what she's like when she gets home."

Kathryn punched him in the side of his arm.

"What? It's true. Last time she passed out so hard I wasn't even sure she was breathing."

"Fucker," Kathryn said. "Don't talk about me like that."

"I'm worried about you, babe. I mean—Oh. Oh, oh, oh."

"What now?" Booth asked. He'd been tracing circles on my thigh under the table, making me squirm.

"That's perfect, that is."

"Out with it."

"I could kill Kathryn."

She shook her head. "Right. No motive there."

"But that's the beauty of it, see?"

"I don't," I said. "I really don't. You'd be the prime suspect."

"Exactly, but they'd never be able to prove I'd done it. That is truly the perfect murder."

"So tell, us, genius," Kathryn said. "How are you going to do it?"

"You'll have to wait and see."

I took the book downstairs to the kitchen, turned the burner on the gas stove on, and held it there until it caught hold. Then I took it out onto the back porch and tossed it into an empty metal wheelbarrow that belonged to the kids.

I watched the flames lick away the words until all that was left was ash. And then I went back inside, packed the box away, and went about the rest of my day.

We pulled up to our cabin with our bellies full of fat and nitrates.

Uncharacteristically, the kids were happy to walk to their new bedrooms and collapse on their beds for a nap. Leah's kids had been traveling for more than a day; I wasn't sure what our kids' excuses were—maybe they were putting sleep waves in iPads now?—but we were all too happy for the quiet in which to unpack and get familiar with our four-bedroom house.

I'd imagined a quaint cottage by the lake with a nautical motif. Instead, we'd ended up in an ultramodern house that had been renovated the year before. It might have been made of old logs on the outside, but on the inside it was all maple cabinets and stone floors and fresh white paint. I was fairly certain the owners were going to regret renting the place to us when we were done.

We woke the kids after a couple of hours, and they ran around on the lawn with Sandy while we made them an early dinner and got our own meal ready. The next several hours were occupied with our raucous families—eating, drinking, and catching up. When they were done with their pasta, the kids ran laps around the dining room while Leah and Rick filled us in on our old neighborhood. The little dramas and victories we'd missed since we moved away. Listening to them, I felt nostalgic, as if our move had been a mistake. For a moment, the fear that drove me to run away seemed distant, minimal.

When the kids were down for the night, Leah and I decided to take a walk down to the lake. We found a picnic table near a sandy beach. The air smelled like conifers and lake water. Leah pulled the backpack she was wearing off her back and took out a bottle of white wine.

"You naughty girl."

"Living on the edge, as always," Leah says. "You're drinking again."

"Clearly."

I took the bottle and poured myself a glass into one of the plastic wineglasses she'd brought along.

"No, I mean, really drinking. Like morning drinking."

There wasn't any point in denying it. Leah always knew what I was thinking and doing before I told her. Why should this be any different?

"Just the last couple of days."

"Vodka?"

"Yes."

"You can't, Julie. It's too dangerous."

"I know."

"Do you?"

I held a sip of wine in my mouth. It was cool and tart. The night was still hot, almost as if we were sitting under an air dryer. I thought there'd be a break from the heat out here in the wilderness, but no such luck.

"It's been a tough year."

"It has, Jules. But you know what happens when you mix your meds and hard alcohol."

The thing was, I didn't, exactly. To me, it had been a few hazy days on the couch, but to Leah, who'd found me and had to slap me awake, it had been a deeply scary experience. One she'd promised to keep from Daniel after I promised I'd never do it again.

"Please don't tell Daniel."

"Don't make me tell him, then."

I rested my back against the picnic table. The rough wood dug into the space between my collarbones. The realtors weren't exaggerating about the sky. It was as if someone had spilled out a box of glitter.

"Everything's falling apart."

I said the words in my head. Then I said them out loud. Then I fell apart.

Leah let me break down for a moment, then gathered me to her. There was something in that act, something so familiar, that it made it worse, not better.

I never used to be someone who cracked. I was resilient, I'd always said. Even the postpartum depression hadn't changed that view of myself. That was something chemical, like cancer. I wasn't going to blame myself for a chemical imbalance, and I wasn't going to change because of it. The medication would fix things, and it did. That I hadn't gone off it since then, well, that wasn't something I thought about . . . much.

But this felt different. This felt like failure.

"What's really going on?" Leah asked.

I wiped my tears away. "What do you mean?"

"This isn't only about a lawsuit or a fight. There's something else."

"It's Cincinnati, I think. I can't explain it."

"So why stay here?"

"We can't just pick up and leave again."

"Can't you?"

She gave me a deep look, one that told me it wasn't any use pretending with her, or trying to cover over what I hid from everyone else. I needed to tell her . . . something.

"I got close to the wrong person."

"Close? You mean an affair?"

"No." The Kiss, the Kiss, the Kiss. "I would never do that."

"How many people have said that over time, you think?"

"I know, I know. But it's true. Please believe me."

"So what happened, then?"

"I got emotionally close to someone. We became friends, but he's a man and I'm a woman, and he's attractive, and I guess he finds me attractive. So. Well, it felt different."

"Exciting?"

"Yes."

"And this is who? The guy who lives across the street?"

I nodded.

"That's why they're suing you?"

"I don't think so. I guess it's possible his wife picked up on something, but . . ."

"Oh, honey. If I picked up on something from across the country, I'm pretty sure she did."

"But I told you, we're just friends."

"Friends with inappropriate feelings. Do you really think she doesn't know that? That Daniel doesn't?"

"Oh, God, Daniel. He's been so . . ."

"Daniel?"

"Yes, exactly. I don't deserve him."

"No one deserves Daniel."

That's what everyone always said, back in Tacoma, and it was true in so many ways. He was this generous, beautiful man who'd done so much for me in my life, more than I could ever repay. But he was, still, a man. He had flaws; he was better at hiding them than most. But this wasn't about Daniel, this was about me. Me.

"And yet, here we are," I said. "Still together."

"What does he think about all of this?"

"He's angry. Probably angrier than I've ever seen him."

"Angry how?"

"You know Daniel. He'd never really show it, but he's definitely feeling it. Right now, it's directed at the enemy."

"Heather?"

"In a way that would be so much simpler. Hanna and John. He's acting like a character in some conspiracy movie. He's got an evidence wall up in the study. He's taken every allegation in the proceedings and blown it up and pasted it on there, and he's got all these note cards underneath them, how to refute this and how to refute that."

"That sounds like it could be helpful."

"Maybe. So long as he doesn't think the radio is talking to him, or his fillings."

Leah refilled our glasses. Only Leah would give alcohol to someone she'd just lectured about drinking.

"And what are you doing about it?"

"Pretending it isn't happening?"

"I'm guessing that's not a winning strategy."

"There's not really anything for us to do. Every time I try to do something, it ends up making it worse."

I told her about the dinner party, and how my clumsiness had reared its head once again with disastrous results.

"What did you do to her in the bathroom?"

"I was trying to adjust the water temperature. I made it too hot."

"On purpose?"

"Of course not!"

She took a long sip. "I might have."

"You would not."

"Well, it's fun pretending, anyway."

"The thing is: she's actually a really nice person."

"You don't truly believe that."

"Well, okay, she hasn't been nice to me. But somehow, I can't blame her."

I tilted my head back and watched the sky. The Big Dipper was bright against the background of stars. A blinking object—a satellite? The space station? Perhaps a plane—moved lazily through the night.

"So, what happens next?" Leah asked.

"I wish I knew. Finish the book I'm writing. Go to court. Move, maybe."

"Would you come back to Tacoma?"

"There's a whole other set of problems there."

"There are problems everywhere, Julie. It's called life."

A couple of days later, sunburned and feeling fat from too much vacation food, we drove the kids to Mammoth Cave National Park. In her quest to find the Greatest Whatever, Leah had declared that Mammoth Cave was something we had to see, so off we went.

An early guide had called it a "grand, gloomy, and peculiar place," and so it proved to be. With more than four hundred miles of it already explored, we would only see a tiny part, even though the tour was two hours long. Because of the kids, we decided to take a properly lighted tour, rather than the ones lit by paraffin lamps. Melly and Sam still slept with a night-light on, and sometimes even that wasn't enough. Darkness meltdowns were to be avoided.

As the tour guide explained what we were going to see, I flipped through a brochure, half listening. The caves had names like Grand Avenue, Frozen Niagara, and Fat Man's Misery. That last feature had clearly been named long ago.

If Cindy ever came here, its name would be changed within hours.

As we entered Mammoth Cave, our guide told us that, despite its name, there had never been any woolly mammoth remains found within.

"See, I told you," I said to Daniel, who shrugged his shoulders sheepishly. "I hope the kids aren't too disappointed."

"Are you kidding? Look at this place. When I was their age, you wouldn't have been able to drag me out of here."

I caught his hand, imagining a six-year-old Daniel as we followed the group through the cave. The kids were awed into silence, pointing to one rock formation after another. The caves had been occupied by humans for six thousand years. I thought about the people whose remains were found there. All those families who sought shelter, gave birth, laughed, and died. They lived on the brink all the time: starvation, sickness, injury, but were their lives that different from ours?

One misstep could create chaos in both timelines.

One misstep already had.

Leah came up to me while we were standing in the rotunda room.

"Isn't it funny," she said, "how we feel like we need to name these places after things that are familiar to us?"

"I'd never thought of that before."

"Like we wouldn't be able to understand it if we didn't relate it to something from now."

"Like names are a frame story."

"Exactly."

"I hate frame stories."

"Why?"

"I think it's lazy. Tell your story. Give the audience some credit. Plunk them down in the middle of it and they'll figure it out."

"You know *The Murder Game* is a frame story, right?"

I grimaced. "I wrote the thing."

"And?"

"And it was my first novel. I didn't know how to begin."

It was true. I'd been struck by the idea for The Book, but when I sat down to try to make sense of it all, I couldn't find the words. Then I remembered how we all were at Kathryn's funeral. I saw it like I was on a crane, not outside myself exactly, but as if I could see inside the three of us as we stood there. I thought about how I'd run away from it all. Not immediately, but when Daniel asked me to leave with him and go to Tacoma, I'd jumped at the chance. And then I wondered what would happen if something called me back. If *someone* called me back. That was the frame I used, the window through which to look through and begin.

"What about what you're writing now?"

"I'm doing my best," I said, "to learn from my mistakes."

Long, Hot Days of Summer

John

Three months ago

"Chris is being mean to me," Becky said, hanging on to the door to my study.

It was the middle of July. The kids were out of school. I was out of work, both literally and figuratively. My contracts had dried up like the lawn in our backyard. I would sit at my computer every day, anyway. Trying to keep approximate office hours. Applying for everything in sight. Except for the P&G posting of my former job.

Other summers, taking care of the kids was always a complicated hassle of vacation days and summer camps and imposing on our neighbors' generosity. But this year, Hanna had helpfully suggested, the kids were old enough to decide what they wanted to do for themselves. I was home. Neither of them seemed enthusiastic about organized group activities. It would all work out perfectly.

How it had worked out, in fact, was that I felt like I was running a day camp. Becky and her girlfriends flooded through the house at all hours of the day. Turns out there were lots of teenage girls who would rather lie on yoga mats in the sun in our backyard than get herded from the pool to the tennis court. I was regularly making lunch for six to eight of them a day.

A few days ago, I'd noticed a new list had appeared on our fridge. Someone—someone's mother, I assumed—left a list of the suggested caloric intake for "growing girls," and potential menu items such as quinoa salad and homemade veggie burgers. What they were getting was mostly hot dogs and hamburgers. Judging by the happy pitch of their chatter, they were satisfied.

But Hanna and I had a fight about the cost of it all. The way I had to cater to the constant needs of kids I thought should be able to find their own bottles of water in the fridge. How it was one thing to be looking after our own kids—I'd almost said babysitting, which would have sent Hanna into the stratosphere—it was quite another to be offering that service for free to half the neighborhood.

A fight. That's what I called it. But really, it was us scraping at each other in the way that had become routine since the dinner party. It was tiring and upsetting. But neither of us seemed able to stop. Even though it set the whole family on edge. Even though we were violating our number one rule, agreed to years ago, to never fight in front of the kids.

And now the kids were fighting.

"What's going on?" I asked Becky. "I thought Chris was out with Ashley?"

"They broke up."

"They did?" I said. *Again?* This was too much.

"Yeah," she said, pulling the end of her ponytail into her mouth and biting it. She was wearing a one-piece swimsuit and a wide-brimmed hat. I knew she wanted to wear two pieces like her friends and ditch the hat in favor of the tennis visors the other girls were wearing. But we weren't ready for her to be that grown up. And part of Becky seemed relieved when Hanna had given her a firm *no*.

"When did that happen?"

"They break up, like, every day."

"So what's he doing?"

"He's flirting with Cassie."

Cassie was one of the gaggle of girls frolicking in our backyard. A giggle.

"Okay. But why does that mean he's being mean to you?"

"Da-ad."

"What?"

"She's my friend. So inappropriate."

I tried not to laugh. Was I really supposed to tell my son to stop flirting with girls?

I stood. My knees felt creaky. I'd been increasing my mileage all summer, ostensibly to run a half marathon in September. Pounding my body into the pavement. Shaping it. Hoping my mind would follow suit. So far, no such luck.

"Where is he?"

"He's got her out in your *car*."

"What do you girls want for lunch today?"

"Hot dogs?"

"You got it."

We walked downstairs and separated in the hall. Instead of heading right outside, I went to my spot at the window. Becky was right. Chris was sitting in the driver's seat of my car. Cassie was in the passenger seat. Chris seemed animated, his hands moving around as he spoke. Cassie looked shyly pleased, getting attention from an older guy.

Ashley came huffing up the street, her arms pumping at her sides. Then she was yanking on the door handle of the passenger door.

"Get the hell out of there!" Ashley shrieked at Cassie, loud enough so I could hear her clearly through the window.

Chris got out of the car. His face flushed with anger and embarrassment.

I wasn't sure what to do.

Would he want me to intervene? Or should I let him handle this by himself?

The eternal struggle of parenthood.

Chris spoke. He was harder to hear.

"My life . . . friend . . . why do . . . stop . . ."

What finally pulled me outside was the expression on Cassie's face. She looked scared that tiny Ashley might harm her.

I strode through the front door, my father-knows-best voice already coming on.

But Julie got there before me, marching across the street from her house.

"Leave her alone," she said, holding on to Ashley's arms as she struggled against her.

"Don't touch me, you crazy bitch."

Julie's hands dropped, and Ashley stepped away from her.

"What's going on here?" I asked, trying to be calm.

I hadn't spoken to Julie since the dinner party.

"Don't, Dad," Chris said.

"Don't what?"

"You don't need to be here. I got this."

Cassie used the distraction to leave the car. She sprinted to my side.

"Mr. Dunbar! I didn't do anything. Don't tell my mom."

"It's okay, Cassie. I'm sure this was all some misunderstanding. Right, Chris? Right, Ashley?"

Chris nodded, but he still clearly wanted me to leave.

Ashley stood glaring alternately at Julie and Cassie. Julie seemed frozen.

"Cassie," I said, "why don't you go out back with the other girls? Lunch will be ready soon."

"Hot dogs?" she said hopefully, on the edge of sniffling.

"You bet."

She turned and ran into the house.

"Chris, why don't you and Ashley go and talk this out?"

"Yeah, okay."

He slammed the car door and slouched over to Ashley. She raised her chin, pride taking over. Chris said something I couldn't hear, and they turned and walked down the street.

Which left me and Julie.

"Sorry for interfering," she said. She was wearing a pair of short pajama bottoms and a ratty T-shirt, no bra in sight. I guess she'd been writing.

"You were trying to help. You did help."

"I doubt it."

"Why do you say that?"

"I think the evidence is pretty substantial, don't you? Everything I touch turns to shit."

"You sound bitter."

"Do you blame me? This will probably become another allegation in the lawsuit."

She looked at her shoes. The same pair of Asics I met her in, worn down now, dusty.

"I don't want that," I said.

"Everybody else does."

"I guess that's right," I said. "Why do you think that is?"

"I have a theory."

"Lay it on me."

"It struck me when we were in Mammoth Caves. You been there?"

"Sure. I love that place."

It was, in fact, one of my favorite places on earth. All that geological history made me feel like the hopeful eight-year-old boy I'd been the first time I visited it.

"We were in one of the smaller sections, I can't remember the name, and I had this thought: *Someone's about to lose it.* And then someone did. This woman had this terrible attack of claustrophobia, and they had to hustle her out of there through some emergency exit."

"What does that have to do with what's going on here?"

"It was the thought; don't you see?"

"I don't. I honestly don't."

"I thought it, and then it happened. That happens sometimes."

"That sounds . . ."

"Totally crazy. I know, but it's the only explanation I have. I expect bad things to happen, now. And then they do."

"Lots of people expect bad things to happen. That doesn't mean they make them happen."

"Forget it. I shouldn't have said anything."

"No, it's fine, I—"

"I should go before the gestapo log us in as talking to each other." She bounced on her heels, like she was getting ready to start a race.

"Wait, Julie . . ."

"What?"

"I . . . I'm sorry things are so hard for you."

She lifted her shoulders. "I'm kind of getting used to it."

"I'm sorry."

"You said," she replied, and turned and ran away.

I made lunch for the girls, then waited on the front steps for Chris to come back. I was reading a programming manual. It was dead boring and the sun was strong. I drifted into a half-awake state. Birds and cicadas and flies mingled to create a steady thrum. There was the occasional giggle coming from the backyard as the girls turned over every quarter of an hour. I couldn't say how long I sat there. But I was startled by the unwelcome hiss of a garden hose, followed by a blast of lukewarm water in the face.

"What the hell?"

Chris stood there holding a green garden hose in his hand, a child-like grin on his face.

"Chris!"

"Sorry, Dad. I couldn't resist. You were asleep."

"I was?"

"Totally."

"Why don't you put that down."

"What? This?"

He lifted the nozzle to his waist like he was going to quick-draw on me.

"You wouldn't dare."

"Wouldn't I?"

"Not if you know what's good for you."

His finger itched on the trigger. I found myself bouncing on my heels like Julie had earlier.

Ready for flight.

"I'm a teenager. Why would I know what's good for me?"

"Listen to your father, then."

He seemed to be considering it. Which gave me enough time to lean forward and sprint toward him.

A blast of water hit me when I was halfway there, but I kept going.

I tried to grab the hose, but I couldn't get a good grip. We fell to the ground, the hose spraying upward, showering us both.

"You're getting me all wet!" Chris cried.

"You must be joking."

I stood up and walked to the spigot, turning it off.

I turned back to Chris. "What was that all about?"

He shook himself like a dog. "I told you. I couldn't resist."

"No, earlier. With Ashley?"

"Oh, that."

"Yeah, that. What's going on?"

"I don't want to talk about it."

"I'm sure. But I think I'm going to have to insist."

I went back to the front steps and sat down. I patted the concrete next to me. Chris sat reluctantly.

"Have you guys broken up again?"

"Maybe?"

"It seems like that's a thing you would know."

He gave me a look that made me feel very old. As did how long his legs were, splayed out next to mine. His shoes looked like they could fit me.

"Well, then, why were you flirting with Cassie?"

"I wasn't."

"Chris, come on. You need to be more careful. People's hearts are fragile."

He muttered something. *You should talk,* maybe.

"What's that?"

"Nothing. Is that all?"

"I guess. I . . . I want you to be happy."

"I'm all right."

"Maybe we could go for another driving lesson today? You want to make sure to pass that test."

Chris was still getting the accelerator and the brake confused every once in a while. Plus, he needed to work on his parallel parking.

"Sure. Say, are there any hot dogs left?"

That night I told Hanna an edited version of the incident between Ashley and Chris. I reduced the level of conflict. Julie was removed entirely. Hanna said she'd talk to him. This thing with Ashley had gone on long enough. It wasn't good for either of them. Trying not to fight, I bit back the impulse to say that giving him rules would produce the opposite result. She knew that. And maybe he would see sense if it came from her. He didn't seem to want to listen to anything I had to say lately.

Afterward, in bed, I couldn't seem to shake what Julie had said. How she felt that if she thought something, it came true. What she'd said wasn't rational. I placed it in the pile of things that didn't seem to add up. Chief among them being that she'd generated suspicion even in Daniel. After tossing and turning for an hour, I got up and went into my office. I did a search and found an e-mail address.

And then I wrote to Heather Stanhope.

Today
John
4:00 p.m.

I get called in to the grand jury room at 4:02 p.m.

I've been watching the clock on the wall for the last thirty minutes. Each and every second as it ticks around the dial. I don't know who's been in there testifying. If they did call Heather, they brought her in the back way.

I stand on uneven legs when my name is called. Hanna says something I don't hear. I walk through the same doors everyone has. A wood-paneled room. Nine men and women sitting on black desk chairs. The wooden witness box. The prosecutor's podium. It's all so much smaller than I imagined. Closer. To the extent that I look at them, the jury seems tired. I wonder what they think of me.

After that, it's mostly a blur. Everything except the prosecutor's voice. Alicia told me to listen to his questions carefully. So that's what

I'm doing. But I'm not supposed to answer to *him*. I need to tell my answers to the jury. To speak to them because, ultimately, these are the people I need to convince.

He wants me to tell them about that morning.

I've done this before. Told the police, Detective Grey, and his side-kick, more than once. I've read over my statement enough times to memorize it, but now I have to put it away. I have to forget that this is a repeat and tell it like it's an original broadcast.

Or it will sound rehearsed.

It will sound like a tale I'm telling.

That day, two months ago, started with Hanna and me fighting.

It had been building for a while. Her insistence on bringing the lawsuit. Her suspicions about why I caved. The fact that I wasn't making a success of my new business. The longer hours she felt she needed to work in return. All that piled on top of the usual mess of life like so much fuel.

We were supposed to go to court that day, too. But our fight wasn't about that.

It started when Hanna found me at the window at my usual hour. I'd put on my running clothes, thinking I'd go out, just for a short one.

"Mugging for the cameras?" Hanna asked. Her voice had a biting tone I'd heard too often.

I let the curtain fall from my hand.

"Checking the weather." I tried to keep my voice bland. "Looks like it'll be a nice day. Less hot, hopefully."

August had been one sweltering day after another, leeching all the rain that had fallen in the spring until the leaves were yellowed, and the grass crunched beneath our feet.

I faced Hanna. She was wearing a tank top and soft cotton shorts, what she'd slept in the night before. Our air-conditioning was on the fritz. We'd both slept badly, lying on our backs, quietly sweating. Not a breeze stirring. Once, we would've turned to each other. Distracted ourselves with sex. Or talked about something funny. Some silly story to get us laughing. Instead, we watched the shadows on the wall until one of us fell asleep, then the other.

"Chris is missing," she said that morning.

"What?"

"He's not in his bed. He's not answering his phone."

"Are you sure he's not out with his paper route?"

"I don't think so," Hanna said. "I don't think he slept here."

I pulled the curtain back again. "Shit. Your car's missing."

I walked to the front door and onto the sidewalk. Pebbles bit my feet. Our driveway was half-empty. My Prius was there, but not Hanna's Acura.

"Why would he take your car?" I asked. "He's barely ever driven it. And he knows he's not allowed to drive without an adult present. We made that perfectly clear."

She held out her phone and hit "Redial." She got his voice mail.

"Chris, please call us back. Where are you? We're worried."

"Maybe he fell asleep at Ashley's?"

"I think they broke up again," Hanna said.

"Did he say something?"

"Haven't you noticed how moody he's been?"

"Hasn't he been moody since he turned fourteen?"

She put her hands on her hips. "Can you please take this seriously?"

"I am taking this seriously. What do you want to do?"

"Maybe we should call Ashley."

"Good idea."

We both started at the sound of a dog barking. Julie was standing on her front porch with Sandy. She held her leash tightly.

We must've looked strange: me without shoes, Hanna in her pajamas. Arguing on the sidewalk at six in the morning.

Julie gave us a wave. A nervous gesture that seemed to set something off in Hanna.

"You stay out of this," she said, almost growling. Sandy barked in reply.

"Stay out of what?" Julie said.

I put my hand on Hanna's shoulder. "Let's go back inside. We can call from there."

Hanna shrugged me off. Julie took hold of Sandy's collar as Hanna strode toward her.

"Why are you always around?"

"What? I . . . I came out my front door to walk my dog."

"Always playing the victim. Leaning on my husband. Where's your own husband, Julie? Why isn't he enough?"

"Hanna, please," I said. "Stop this."

"Why, John? You want me to keep my voice down? You don't want the neighbors to see? She's going to capture all this on video. What do you do with all that footage, anyway? Do you watch us? Does it give you pleasure?"

"I've told you again and again, it's for security purposes. I don't even have access to the feed."

"And yet you denied our discovery request to verify that information."

"I don't need to let strangers into my home."

"Strangers. Ha. Yes, you and I *are* strangers."

Julie's eyes meet mine in a plea.

"Hanna," I said again, "you're going to wake Becky. And the twins."

"They're away," Julie said. "Daniel took the twins away."

"Am I supposed to feel sorry for you?" Hanna said.

"You can do what you want."

"What I want is for you to disappear."

I took Hanna's elbow. "Okay, that's enough. This isn't going to help us find Chris."

Hanna seemed to come back to herself. "You're right. Let's go."

"Chris . . . ," Julie said.

"Do you know something about my son?"

"I saw him leave in the middle of the night."

"I *knew* you were spying."

"I wasn't spying—"

"What did you see, Julie?" I said, tightening my grip on Hanna.

"I was going to the bathroom. I heard a car door slam and looked out the window. I saw him driving your car down the street."

"Was he alone?"

"I think so."

"Did he stop anywhere?"

"I think he stopped in front of Ashley's house."

"I knew it," Hanna murmured.

"Leave it, Hanna, okay?"

I tugged her arm and almost pulled her toward the house.

"Thanks, Julie," I said over my shoulder.

"See you later," she said. "I hope you find him soon."

"See you later?" Hanna said as we got inside. "Is she kidding me? Like we're all going to the same party instead of the courthouse?"

"It's just an expression." I grabbed my running shoes and knelt to tie them up. "I'm sure she wasn't thinking."

"What are you doing?"

"Going to talk to Cindy and Paul. Are you coming?"

She threw her raincoat on over her pajamas and shoved on her rain boots. We didn't talk during the short walk down the street. Oddly, Brad Thurgood was sitting on his old front stoop, his head in his hands. I couldn't imagine what he was doing there, but I had bigger worries on my mind.

Hanna stopped me as I reached for the bell.

"Maybe we should call Ashley first. Do you know her number?"

"Why? You heard what Julie said."

"Exactly. And if they've only gone off on a drive . . . I don't want to get her in trouble."

"What are you talking about? They're both in big trouble."

Hanna didn't say anything.

"What is it? What do you know?"

"Nothing for sure, but . . . I overheard him on the phone the other day. I didn't understand what he was saying then, but now it makes more sense."

"What did he say?"

"I didn't hear the whole conversation, but something about how they could do it at her house. Or our house. And then I missed part of it, and then I heard the word 'Acura.'"

"Are you telling me that Chris and Ashley are off somewhere having sex in the back of our car?"

"I think it's possible, yes."

"Fuck."

"Shh. You're the one who told me to assume they were having sex."

"Not in our car," I said. "In the middle of the night."

"I could be wrong."

"So what do we do?"

"Maybe we should wait an hour and see if he turns up in time for school?"

"Okay, maybe we are overreacting. It's not like he's run away or anything, right? He wouldn't have run away."

"Chris is a good kid."

"He is. He's a good kid. So, we go home?"

She seemed unsure. "What if Cindy notices Ashley's missing? She'll freak out."

"I hadn't thought of that."

"We have to let her know that she's probably okay. That she's with Chris."

"You're right."

I reached for the bell again, pressing it long enough to wake those within.

We waited. A light turned and the front door sprung open. Paul was in his robe. Cindy tumbled down the hall behind him.

"Do you know where Ashley is?"

Sent: August 1st, at 9:30 a.m.

From: Cindy Sutton

To: PSNA mailing list <undisclosed recipients>

Re: Speed Bumps!

Pine Street Friends!

I just got off the phone with our city councilor.
The speed bumps have been approved! They'll
be installed next week! I'm certain you're all as
excited as I am that our street will soon be consid-
erably safer.

Feel free to e-mail me for further details. Updates
will be posted to iNeighbor.

Cindy Sutton

PSNA Chair and Founder, 2009–present

Another Day, Another Conflict

Julie

Two months ago

Memory isn't a provable thing. We see what we want, hear what pleases us, and remember what grieves us. That is the human condition.

But I swear I remember every detail of the day Kathryn died, like a movie camera was recording it.

It happened at law games. I'm not sure when the law-games tradition started, but when I was in school it involved matching coveralls, almost like prison uniforms, school buses, and drinking games. All the law schools would get together at one school or another every winter, and mayhem would ensue. Drinking, recreational drugs, hookups; *Fuck it* was the motto. Maybe you shouldn't play that game of quarters? Fuck it. Maybe you shouldn't go up to that guy's room? Fuck it. Maybe you shouldn't take that pill that guy gave you without really knowing what's in it?

Fuck it.

I said and did all those things. And so, even though I remember every detail of that weekend, it's off-kilter. Filtered through a fog of drugs and sex and Ace of Base.

Here's what I know for certain.

The Saturday-night party was at what can only be described as a frat house, even though there wasn't a frat at that particular university. It was a large Victorian building, complete with turrets and multicolored shingles. I arrived with Kathryn around ten. We were already pie-eyed from the drinks we'd had that afternoon in the dorm room we were staying in. I think we were trying to one-up the boys, but that might be my adult take on what we were doing. The boys weren't there that afternoon; they'd gone off to play flag football in the snow. It was just the two of us and our host, a girl whose name I never learned, and whose face I feel like I'll remember forever. She had a lollipop head on an anorexic body, with large brown eyes framed by too much mascara, and pale, almost-invisible lips.

The minute we got inside, the house felt claustrophobic. It was already so full I was thinking about fire codes despite how drunk I was. I asked Kathryn what she thought. "Maybe we should leave," I said. "Fuck it," was her reply.

We pressed in.

Even though it was February, and so cold the ground crunched as if it was made of gravel, and my hair felt frozen even though I hadn't gone outside with it wet, the house was so hot people were stripping down. The fashion trend for the night was unzipped coveralls with the arms tied around the waist to keep them from falling off completely. Many men were shirtless. Many women wore only bras. One or two, dared into it or because, you know, *fuck it*, weren't wearing bras at all.

The music was so loud you had to yell to be heard. I started losing my voice a half hour after we got there. Drink after drink was pressed into my hand in a candy-colored stream of Solo cups. Kathryn was usually the life of the party, but she seemed a bit subdued that night, happy to hang out by my side and gently nod the constant stream of men away. I'd suggest every half hour or so that we leave, but she shook her head. She seemed to be waiting for someone to show up. She'd broken up with one of the bland Dockers-wearers she dated during the perpetual off-periods with Kevin a few weeks before, and he hadn't come to law games.

When Booth and Kevin showed up, I realized how stupid I'd been. Of course she was waiting for Kevin. I could never quite follow or understand the ups and downs of their relationship. (Which I admit, I used in *The Murder Game*, only I transferred it to Meredith—the character supposedly based on me—and another character, Jonathan.) Kevin was a puzzle. Some days he hung on Kathryn like he didn't want to let her out of his sight. Others, he'd barely look at her. I wouldn't have put up with it, and I couldn't understand why Kathryn, who could get whatever she wanted, did. But it wasn't the sort of thing you brought up.

So, like, why do you let that guy treat you like a doormat? I don't think so.

It was Kevin who suggested we smoke some stuff he'd bought on campus. I'd love to be able to say I resisted, had some trace of a thought, even, that maybe it wasn't a good idea. But that didn't happen. *Fuck it*, you know. Instead, we all tramped out into the night and inhaled the warm smoke and the cold night air. Maybe the stuff was bad or was laced with something. Maybe Kathryn had too much of everything that day. She turned gray and felt woozy, and I led her back inside and to the bathroom. She hovered over the toilet, waiting to throw up, but it didn't come. So I found a bed for her in one of the rooms upstairs. I made sure she had a glass of water. I told her I'd come back for her when I left.

And then I went downstairs.

Two hours later, a shout pierced the party noise. There was a stampede upstairs. When I saw where everyone was headed—the room where I'd left Kathryn—I got down on my knees and crawled through the legs and feet like they were an obstacle course.

When I finally got into the room, Kevin was standing over her, half hugging her to him. She flopped like a rag doll. I flung myself through the last human barriers and told Kevin to let her go. I yelled at someone to call 9-1-1, and then I began administering CPR.

I worked on her until the paramedics came, pumping her chest and blowing air into her lungs. I knew it was useless. I knew she was gone, but I did it anyway, and I remember every breath I gave her until the paramedics pulled me away.

An investigation followed. A young girl dies at a party, there's going to be an investigation. The autopsy results were inconclusive. She'd been smothered, or smothered herself, in one of the pillows on the bed. All the alcohol and drugs had depressed her breathing, and it might only have taken a matter of seconds for it to be too late. Since they couldn't tell if it was a homicide, no one was charged. Rumors swirled. Information passed behind cupped hands, over e-mail, in dark corners at parties. The police did their best, trying to sort out who was where and when, but there were more than two hundred people in and out of the house that night, at least twenty of whom knew Kathryn. Today, there might've been multiple cell-phone camera videos, but back then there were only our impaired memories. After a month or so, they closed the case and moved on.

They never found out that Kevin liked plotting perfect murders, or that he roped me and Kathryn and Booth into his game, or that Booth had seen them have a humdinger of a fight the night before in the room he was sharing with Kevin. And no one asked to see my diary, where I'd documented so much of it.

I could fill a page with the things they never found out.

Some of them made their way into my book, and some of them did not.

Write what you know, they say.

And where was Heather that whole time? That night at law games in the bitter cold?

I don't know.

She's said she was there. She's said she saw things, but Heather says she saw a lot of things. Most of them have been proven false, but there are some things that are not verifiable.

With so many people with things to hide, separating out the fact from the fiction was impossible.

Even if you managed to piece some of it together, the result would be fractured.

The night before the accident, Susan and I had a blowout.

At first I wasn't sure what set it off. One minute we were on a night walk, and the next we were yelling at each other in the street. Or she was yelling and I was listening, baffled. At one point I thought about putting up my hands in surrender, of saying, *Okay, stop. Whatever it is you want. Whatever you think I've done. Just stop.*

But I didn't. Instead I sat on the ground, a physical protest against what I felt was an unfairness. I come in peace, shoot me if you will.

Susan stopped yelling.

"What are you doing?"

I looked across the street at a crooked house. Its foundation had slipped on the downhill side. It looked like it had been printed out of register.

"I don't know what to do, Susan. What did I say?"

"Nothing. Sorry. It's not you, really."

I looked up at her. She'd been sweating so much her hair looked like she'd taken a shower. The back of my T-shirt was soaked through.

"Then what?"

"Brad wants to get back together."

"Oh?"

"Yeah, he . . . he's been e-mailing me and calling me a lot. Apologizing."

"I thought he did that before?"

"That was his AA apology. That didn't count."

"What's different now?"

She pulled her hair free from her elastic, smoothed it back, and retied it. "I'm not sure. Something in his voice, and what he's saying. He's recognizing stuff from way back. Years ago. Stuff I didn't even think he remembered."

"Are you thinking of taking him back?"

She sat down next to me. We were both sitting cross-legged on the sidewalk, two blocks away from Pine Street. I didn't know how to react to her change of mood. Was I supposed to forget the way she'd been talking to me a minute ago? Let it drift away on the blown-dry wind that was making me sweat, even as I sat there?

"Do you think that would make you happy?" I asked.

"I'm so far from happy, I don't even know what it looks like anymore."

"Is that true, or just something to say?"

"Not sure. It felt true when I said it."

"And what does your life look like if you let Brad back in? Happy?"

"If he's sober."

"That's a big if. It hasn't even been six months. They told you a year, right?"

"Six months can be a long time."

"Look who you're talking to."

"Right. Maybe I'm just tired?"

293

"Of doing it alone?"

"Of being alone. You've never really had that, have you?"

How could I answer that? Tell her that I was always alone? Say that she didn't know anything about me, really, other than what she could see? That our moments of confidences didn't mean she knew me?

"I've been alone. Before Daniel—"

"Not like this. Not every moment of every day, always needing to be available for the kids or making a plan that involves them . . . you have Daniel to rely on."

"I do. I'm not complaining."

"Ha."

"Okay, so I was complaining." I had been. I'd been talking about the lawsuit, and iNeighbor, and Cindy, and the shit in general I'd had to put up with since we moved to Pine Street. "I have to go to court tomorrow. I'm being sued because I tried to defend someone's house and protect my family. Is that not something to complain about?"

"Rich people's problems."

"We live on the same street."

"But we don't live in the same world. I'm about to lose my house. Did you know that?"

"No, I didn't."

"Because you never asked. You never ask me about anything."

"I don't think that's true."

"If that's the way I feel, then it is."

I clicked my teeth together. I'd said the same thing myself many times. If I felt something, then it made it true. It was the other person's problem if they didn't agree. But sitting on the other end of it, I saw my mistake. Just because I felt something didn't mean the person who had caused the feeling had done anything wrong.

It could, literally, be all about me.

I stood up. "I think I'm going to go home."

"That's it? That's all you have to say to me?"

"I don't think there's anything I can say that's going to fix what's going on in your life. If you want me to listen, I'm here. But because things are shit, or I have something you don't, doesn't mean I can't be having a shitty time, too. I don't want to be in some misery competition with you."

"I'm not competing with you."

"Right. So, there's no point in discussing this. Not now."

Susan's mouth hung open. I knew I wasn't being fair, in a way, but Jesus: Hadn't I been through enough lately? I couldn't even find my own happiness. Did I have to feel guilty for someone else's loss, too?

She stood next to me. I thought for a minute, trying to decide what the quickest way back was. I looked up the hill. Chris Dunbar was standing at the top of the street with his arm slung across Ashley's shoulder. We made eye contact for a moment, then he spun her around and back up the way they'd come.

I checked my watch. It was late—after ten—and a school night. I knew neither of them had permission to be out this late, even if Cindy's ridiculous curfew wasn't being respected. And yet, if I marched after them, or told on them to their parents, would I get thanked?

Not bloody likely.

"What is it?" Susan asked.

"Nothing. Let's go."

I started walking downhill and Susan followed after me. We didn't say another word till we got to the front of her house.

"I'm sorry," I said. "Let me make it up to you tomorrow. Tomorrow night, bring the kids over and we'll have dinner. Daniel's taken the kids to his parents."

"He's not going to be in court with you tomorrow?"

"His mom's not doing well."

"You didn't say."

You see? I wanted to say. I don't say everything. I haven't placed all of my burdens on you.

"I didn't."

"I'm really sorry to hear that."

"Thank you. I'll see you tomorrow, okay?"

"Can I think about it?"

"Of course."

"Good luck."

"I don't believe in luck."

"Break a leg, then."

"That, I think I can do."

The next morning started like any other. I rose, I dressed, I moved soundlessly through the house, even though I had it to myself. With Daniel away, I decided to risk a run, so I put on my running shoes and gathered Sandy's leash.

I could tell it was hot. Though our air-conditioning kept the house at an even seventy degrees, the air felt wet. There hadn't been a break in the heat for weeks. Every day contained the same heavy blue sky, and sweat broke out the moment you stepped outside. The trees looked limp, and water-usage restrictions had been put in place, and then restricted again. Cindy was having a field day making sure they were being enforced.

Though I felt hungover from the fight with Susan, and nervous about the day in court coming up (our lawyer had decided to bring a motion to dismiss, based on the fact that the action wasn't driven by facts, but emotion), I had no premonition about the scene waiting for me outside.

But there John and Hanna stood, he in his running clothes and she in her short pajamas, having an argument. I thought about going back into the house, but decided, against my better judgment, to tell them what I'd seen when I got up to go to the bathroom a couple of hours earlier, after I realized they were talking about Chris. I'd seen him moving stealthily to get into Hanna's car, driving up the street and picking Ashley up. What had happened between when I'd seen them together at ten and again at three? Had they never gone home? And why didn't he use John's car, the silent-running Prius?

I'd decided to stay out of it. Not my family, not my problems, not my rules to enforce. Besides, they were probably going off to have sex somewhere, and I didn't need to interfere with that. I hoped Sam would find a more comfortable place to sleep with his girlfriends in the future. Then I laughed, because this thought was so ordinary I couldn't help it. When I climbed back into bed, I wished Daniel was there so I could cuddle into his back, hungry for the warmth of him despite the heat pushing at the windows. I hadn't wanted him to take the kids with him to Tacoma, but he wanted them to say good-bye to his mother, if it came to that, and how could I refuse?

But that morning, seeing the anguish on Hanna's face, I knew I had to speak up, whether she wanted to hear what I had to say or not. Whatever they might've thought of me, surely they knew I wouldn't make something like that up. Besides, the car was gone, as was Chris, apparently. The proof was there.

After I told them what I knew, I waited for them to walk down the street, then began my run. If our street wasn't basically a dead end, I would've run in another direction.

But it was basically a dead end.

How dead, I didn't even know yet.

Gut Punch
John
Two months ago

Cindy did not react well to the news that we didn't know where Chris and Ashley were. Or that they'd driven off in Hanna's car. When she heard the source of that piece of information, her face puckered like she'd swallowed something sour.

"Why didn't she stop them?" Cindy said. "Or call you to tell you?"

"It was the middle of the night," I said, feeling guilty, not wanting to even look at Hanna. There I was again, defending *her*. "She's not their parents."

"That is so typical. Anyone else would tell the parents *immediately* if they saw two teenagers running off in the night . . . oh, goodness."

Cindy broke down. Paul put his arm around her shoulder.

"They're being kids," he said bravely, patting her neck. "It'll be okay."

"You don't know that. You can't know that."

"Well, we certainly don't know that anything's wrong," Hanna said, shifting into her lawyer mode. Problem solver. "So let's work with the facts we have." She looked at her watch. It was ten after six. "They've been gone for about three hours. Where could they have gone?"

"They could be anywhere," Cindy said. "We should call the police."

"I'm not sure that's necessary yet. Have you called Ashley?" I asked.

"She's not picking up."

"Chris, either."

Cindy sobbed again.

"They're not picking up because it's us calling," I said. "They know they're in trouble."

"Oh, they're in trouble all right," Hanna said.

"This isn't getting us anywhere," I said. "Let's think, where have they gone in the past? Where do kids go these days?"

I thought about my own boyhood. All those nights at Alms Park and Ault Park, depending on where the wind took us. Alms was mostly for hanging out. The woods at Ault were where you'd lay out a blanket to get laid or get high—sometimes both.

"Maybe they're in Ault Park?" I ventured.

Thankfully, Cindy hadn't grown up in Cincinnati, so she didn't quite grasp what I was referring to. But both Paul and Hanna gave me a look.

"Why would they go there?"

"Now, honey," Paul said.

"No, no, no. Ashley's a good girl."

"And Chris is a good boy," I said. "But they're almost sixteen . . ."

Cindy's hand rose to her mouth. I thought she might be sick.

"Mom, Dad!"

Becky was running down the street waving something above her head. She had a slight hitch in her step, left over from when she'd broken her leg on my birthday.

"What is it, sweetheart? What are you doing out of the house?"

"I heard you guys outside my window. You woke me up."

"Why did you run down here?" Hanna asked. "Do you know something?"

She thrust her phone at me. "Ashley posted a picture."

I took it. Ashley had indeed posted a picture a few minutes before. She was sitting on a red brick wall, her face half in the early light. A dark shadow sat next to her. *Chris.*

"It doesn't say where they are," Hanna said.

"I know where that is," I said.

"Where are they?" Cindy asked. "Where's my daughter?"

"In the Authors Grove."

It was Julie who first mentioned the Authors Grove to me. She'd seen it on a map before she moved here. It appealed to her. She hadn't been able to find it the first few times she ran in Eden Park, and soon stopped looking. Did I know where it was?

Despite living near the park for more than ten years, I hadn't even heard of it. I said I'd ask around, then I forgot about it until one bored day at home. I typed the words into Google. The third hit was a blog post by a woman who was chronicling her newly single days in Cincinnati. She, too, had been curious about the Authors Grove, and went to the trouble to unearth its history. The post was written a couple of days before I went looking. Serendipity.

The monument was a ruin now, but probably still worth taking a look at. I was excited to tell Julie about it. Figured I'd surprise her on our next run. Then I kissed her.

I checked it out myself, anyway. One day I followed the signposts the blogger wrote about and found the dilapidated structure. I hung out there for a bit, contemplating life, checking out of my problems. So when I saw the photo, I knew where Ashley had taken it.

I took off running. I'm not sure what drove me. The fact that Chris and Ashley were in the park, a ten-minute jog away, should've calmed us all down. But instead my heart was racing. Not from the pace I was pushing myself to. Something else.

I realized what it was when I got to Parkside and saw the back of her head, her ponytail bobbing. The efficient way her arms pumped at her side. Sandy trotting next to her. She'd gotten faster since we'd stopped running together, but I could still catch up.

Idiot, I thought. With everything you know about her now, you're still excited for a moment alone with her.

She turned on Martin Drive, then stopped suddenly and whirled around, her hand clutching something around her neck. Sandy barked twice.

"John!"

"Yes, it's okay. It's me."

I reached out my hand to Sandy. She gave it a tentative sniff, as if she too couldn't quite believe her senses.

"What are you doing here?"

"Chris and Ashley are in the Authors Grove."

"How do you know?"

"Ashley posted a picture. I recognized it."

She looked away. "I thought you didn't—forget it. So, that means . . . they're okay?"

"I think so. At least physically."

"I guess they'll be in a lot of trouble."

"Chris will be. I've got to get going."

I ran past her and she joined up with me, Sandy on her other side. Our rhythms matched. An easy fit.

"How did Cindy and Paul react?" she asked.

"About how you'd expect."

"I wouldn't want to be Ashley. For many reasons."

"Ashley's all right," I said.

"Hasn't she been breaking Chris's heart all over the place? And what was that the other day with the car?"

"Teenaged drama."

"Maybe I should send Melly and Sam to military school. I'd miss them like crazy, but maybe they'd avoid all of this."

She swept her hand in front of her. Her nails were bitten down to the quick, her cuticles chewed at.

"That seems like a drastic solution."

"Sometimes that's what's needed."

We fell into silence. Our feet struck the pavement. Sweat ran down my back.

We ran into the park and on to the conservatory. I kept thinking she might peel away, but Julie stayed with me.

"Why do you think they went here so early?" Julie asked.

"Could be lots of reasons. They seem to have a lot of stuff to work out."

"Remember that? Love like that. So intense it made you sick."

I wasn't sure I'd ever been in love like that. I loved my family. The thought of anything happening to Hanna or the kids made me feel ill. But sick on love alone? No. Not me.

"When I got my heart broken for the first time, I threw up for six months," she said.

"You were bulimic?"

"Not on purpose. My body couldn't take it. Whatever I tried to put in, it rejected. I was literally lovesick."

"What happened?"

"I got over it before I had to be hospitalized."

She said this with a laugh, which seemed to fit her mood. Everything about her seemed off that day, like she was half a step out of tune with herself. Like Becky's gait as she ran toward us with the phone.

I stopped at the stairs up to the water tower. I ran up them, taking them two at a time. When I got to the top, I cupped my hand over my eyes and scanned the flat plain.

"It's right over there." I pointed. I couldn't see anyone on the structure, but they might be hunkered down behind it. Or moved on to some other point.

I started to walk toward it. Red brick and cement with a blank, chiseled book opened across the top. It was surrounded by the remnants of what used to be a thicker grove of trees, each planted in memoriam to a great author. Emerson. Longfellow. Alcott. According to the blogger, the area was "renovated" after the monument became a favorite spot for drug dealers. At the request of those who lived in the area. Cindy's predecessor, perhaps.

"Some mighty fine weather we're having today!" Julie said loudly. I jumped. She held my arm and pointed to the side of the monument. There was a tennis shoe half visible.

"Probably a bad idea to sneak up on them, right?" she said quietly.

"Right."

She picked up a stick and threw it as far as she could. She let go of the leash. Sandy bounded after.

"This weather really is delightful," she said with the volume up.

I chuckled. If Chris was listening, he'd think we'd taken leave of our senses.

We rounded the corner. There was a loose tennis shoe, but it was empty.

"Ah, shit. Chris? Chris!"

I spun around in a circle, but I couldn't see him or Ashley anywhere. There was a stand of trees a hundred yards away. Sandy brought the stick back and dropped it at my feet.

"I found something," Julie said. She was holding a pink elastic in her hand. "I think this is Ashley's."

"How do you know?"

"She wears that color all the time."

"Chris!" I yelled again. "Christopher Dunbar! If you can hear me, come out right this minute. You're not in trouble!"

Julie pointed to the trees. "I saw something moving in there."

I ran across the grass. Julie was right. Chris and Ashley were there. Sitting on a blanket leaning up against the base of one of the big trees, just out of view.

"Chris, what the hell?"

"Hi, Dad," he said almost calmly. He looked disheveled, as if he'd slept in the open.

A sound turned my attention to Ashley. Her face was streaked with tears. She was holding her knees and rocking gently. She was wearing shorts, and her shins had grass stains on them.

"Are you okay, Ashley?"

"It's fine, Dad. Why are you here?"

"Do you have any idea what time it is? Your mom couldn't find you this morning. You're not answering your cell. When we heard you'd driven off with Ashley in the middle of the night . . . where is the car?"

"The car's fine, I—what's she doing here?"

Julie came up behind me. She waved awkwardly.

"I ran into her trying to find you."

"I can't believe this."

He stood angrily. He looked between Ashley and me.

"What's going on, Chris?"

"Is everything all right, Ashley?" Julie asked, squatting down beside her.

"Get away from her!" Chris yelled.

Julie jerked her hand back.

"You'd better tell me what the hell is going on," I said. "Right now."

"Jeez, Dad. I cannot handle this right now."

I took a step in his direction.

"Leave us alone, okay? Can't you do that?"

"Only if you tell me why."

"I can't . . . I . . ."

He looked at Ashley again. She wouldn't meet his eye. He gave me a fleeting look. Then he bolted.

"Chris!"

I ran after him. He was fast. Faster than I knew he could be, youth and adrenaline pushing him past his usual limits.

He ran directly into the denser woods. I followed him in. A tree branch caught me in the leg, tearing at my skin. Blood ran down my calf, but I couldn't stop. I was losing on Chris, the energy I'd expended getting to the park making it that much harder for me to catch up. He cut left suddenly. I tripped over my feet and fell to the ground. When I got up, I'd lost sight of him. Then I heard a car door. I ran toward the sound, coming out of the woods and onto the road. Chris was behind the wheel of Hanna's car. I waved at him to stop, but he drove like he couldn't see me. I jumped out of the way, yelling after him. He didn't stop. The car careened around a bend.

There was nothing I could do.

I watched the car drive away, lost in my own life.

Today

John

5:00 p.m.

"What happened next?" the prosecutor asks.

I reach for the water the clerk placed on the edge of the witness box. I catch the eye of one of the members of the jury. A woman about my age. She looks tired. I'm exhausted.

But I am not done.

"I went to find Ashley and Julie."

When I got back to the tree, neither of them were there. I walked back into the field. Julie was standing at the broken memorial. Sandy was running laps around her.

Julie made no sign that she heard me approaching, but when I got closer, she said: *"To be yourself in a world that is constantly trying to make you something else is the greatest accomplishment."*

"What's that?"

"Emerson."

"That's lovely."

"It is. Where's Chris?"

"He drove off."

"Oh, no. I'm so sorry, John."

I sighed heavily. "Hopefully, he'll turn up at home soon. Where's Ashley?"

"She took off, too."

"Did she say anything to you?"

"Just to fuck off."

I reached for her. Her hand rose reflexively to the disk hanging from her neck.

"What is that?" I asked. "I've always wondered."

"My panic button. If I press it, the police come running. Theoretically."

"Because of Heather?"

"Yeah."

"Are you going to push it?"

"Should I be panicking?"

I dropped my hand. "You have nothing to fear from me."

"And yet, a couple of hours from now, we're supposed to be in court."

"We should settle."

Her eyes lit up with hope. "Really? You mean it?"

"I'll talk to Hanna. This has all gone way too far."

"Thank you, John." She leaned into me quickly, letting her lips brush against my cheek. I breathed her in. She smelled sweet that morning, like clover. Like the woods Chris and Ashley had been doing God knows what in. She pulled back. "Whatever she wants. I mean it. I'll pay. I need all of this to stop."

"Me too."

"We really messed everything up, didn't we?"

"I think we did."

"You should go. Maybe Chris is home by now. And Cindy will be worried about Ashley."

"Thank you." I touched her shoulder briefly, then turned and left.

Though my legs felt weak, I ran home as fast as I'd come. Cindy and Paul were standing outside their house with Becky.

"Did you find them?" Cindy asked in a panicky voice.

"Yes. They were in the park."

"Why aren't they with you, then?"

"They ran away."

"What?" Paul asked. "Why didn't you stop them?"

I explained briefly about finding Chris and Ashley in the woods. How Chris had bolted. How Ashley was gone when I got back.

Cindy was crying into Paul's shoulder by the time I finished.

"They were in the woods?" she said in a muffled voice.

"They're okay," I said. "In a lot of trouble, but okay. I think they were having a rough patch and—"

She lifted her chin off Paul's shoulder. "My daughter never got into trouble before she started hanging out with your son."

"Come on now, Cindy. I know they've done a couple of stupid things in the last year, but they're teenagers. Teenagers do stupid shit."

"Da-ad!"

"Sorry, Becks." I glanced at my watch. It was a quarter to seven. "You should get home and ready for school. Where's your mother, anyway?"

"She ran after you."

"What? Why?"

Becky shrugged. "She ran off. In her rain boots."

"Not funny, Becks."

"Sorry, Dad."

I hugged her to me. There was a loud clatter as one of the garbage bins in front of Susan Thurgood's house clattered to the ground.

"What's he doing here?" Cindy asked, pulling away from Paul.

Brad Thurgood was trying to lift a large black bin into place.

I jogged across the street, nearly tripping over the newly installed speed bump.

"What's going on?" I said to Brad.

He jumped, knocking the bin over again. Alcohol was coming off him in waves.

"I got it," he slurred, reaching down.

I bent quickly and raised it up. "What are you doing here, Brad?"

"I want to talk to my wife."

His eyes were unfocused. I'd heard that he was in AA, trying to clean up his act. Perhaps I'd heard wrong.

"Then why are you outside?"

"She won't let me in."

I looked at the house. Susan was standing in the window, a phone in her hand. She waved it at me. Mouthed *9-1-1?* I shook my head.

"It's not even seven in the morning, Brad."

"I knows thats," he slurred. "What's your point?"

"Maybe you should go home and sleep this off?"

"What I was trying to do."

"This isn't your house anymore."

Brad's lip quivered. "Why you think I've been drinking?"

I looked around. There didn't seem to be any cars I couldn't account for.

"How did you get here?"

He shrugged. "Walked, I think."

"Why don't you come to my house? You can sleep on the couch, and I'll drive you home later."

"That's awful nice of you."

I called across the street. "Becky, walk home on that side of the street."

"Okay."

I motioned to Susan, trying to mimic what I was going to do with Brad. She seemed to understand, lowering the phone and nodding her approval. I put my hand on the small of Brad's back and directed him up the hill. He looked up at the church that sat overlooking our street. He raised his hand to his eyes.

"Too bright," he said.

The sun was always bright at that time of day, shining like a spotlight at the church.

"Let's go."

It only took a minute to get to our house. Becky walked inside, leaving the front door open. I maneuvered Brad into the living room. He sat on the couch and belched. The stink of him was awful, the room already stale. I walked to the window and cracked it open. Brad shoved off his shoes and turned to lie down, tucking one of the end cushions under his head. Hanna was going to be pissed.

Where the hell was she, anyway?

"Becky?"

"Yeah?" she called from upstairs.

"Stay up there, okay? In your room."

"Not dangerous," Brad said.

"Go to sleep, Brad."

He snorted and pulled the corner of his shirt up over his eyes. He was snoring in less than a minute. I watched him for a second. When I met Brad, he was a vice president at First Financial. Now, he looked almost homeless. Which I guess he was, in a sense.

"What happened then, Mr. Dunbar?"

I reach for the water again. My mouth feels like it does after I've drunk half a bottle of wine. Like my tongue has extra layers.

"This . . . this next part is hard for me."

"I understand that, Mr. Dunbar. But it's getting late. Let's finish this, shall we?"

I make eye contact with the woman juror again. She nods, briefly.

I take a deep breath. "I found a blanket for Brad. And then I heard a scream."

Let's Call the Whole Thing Off

Julie

One month ago

Before they made the arrest, the police came to see me again. The same two who'd been haunting our street for weeks, mismatched in terms of looks, and probably fulfilling some good-cop/bad-cop protocol.

The older one, Detective Grey, tall and fit-looking under his dark-blue suit, did most of the talking. He tended to pinch the tip of his nose, as if he was rubbing a spot where his nonexistent glasses were bugging him. The younger one, Detective Fowler, just into his thirties, was already on his way to accumulating a TV cop's body—too much flesh around the middle, and a slackening along his jaw. He was the note-taker, his left hand wrapped around a pen in a way that conveniently hid what he was writing.

They sat on one couch in our living room; Daniel and I sat on another. The summer heat had stretched into September—the air looked wavy out our front windows. But the air-conditioning kept the inside of the house at a pleasant temperature, the cycling hum of the compressor filling our silence. The twins were in school. Susan had taken pity on us and was driving them in the morning and picking them up at the end of the day. They were mostly oblivious to what was going on, only asking, sometimes, why they couldn't play outside when they wanted to.

Daniel and the twins had flown home the day after the accident. I'd called him, hysterical, as soon as I was able. Words tumbled out of me, mostly nonsense. It took me days to be able to tell him the entire story, despite the fact that I'd increased the meds I was taking. I felt like I was jumping out of my skin, a constant tinge of panic that started in my chest and radiated to the tips of my fingers and toes. I couldn't run. I couldn't eat. I couldn't think. But I'd tried to convince Daniel to stay where he was, anyway.

"I'm coming," he'd said. "There's no question."

"But your mom. She shouldn't be alone with only your dad to take care of her."

"Martha's here." I was surprised. His sister lived in New York and visited infrequently. "She was going to stay for a while, anyway. And Mom's . . . Mom's okay."

I didn't think to ask, then, how that was possible when he'd told me only the day before that he wasn't sure how long he was going to have to stay. At least a week, he thought, maybe longer. I just cried with relief. Barring canceled flights, in twenty hours I'd have my family back. And then we could get the hell out of here.

Only, we couldn't leave. No one had asked us, formally, to stay, but we were trapped anyway. By the police and their questions. By the fact that no one else was going anywhere, so how could we? By the journalists camped outside the church, their cameras trained down the street, blinded every morning by the same sun that had blinded me as I turned the corner onto Pine Street the morning of the accident.

"Yes," said Detective Grey. "The sun. Everyone keeps mentioning that."

He said it with an accusing tone, as if I might be conspiring to describe the weather.

"What's that supposed to mean?" Daniel asked. He was almost as on edge as I was, feeling guilty that he'd left me to deal with the court case alone, and everything else that had happened instead. I'd told him again and again that he couldn't have known, that he had to go, but he'd just shake his head and pour himself two fingers of scotch. We might both have to check into rehab if anything more happened.

"Nothing, sir," Detective Grey said. "Just an observation. You turned onto Pine from Church Street?"

That was the unimaginative name for the short street the church sat on.

"That's right."

"That's not the most direct route."

I squeezed Daniel's hand. A few nights after he'd come home, I'd told Daniel everything, including about The Kiss, even though I was the one who made John promise not to tell. And in telling him, it had simply become a kiss, nothing worth capitalizing. "I know. I did a couple of street laps. I was trying to leave a bit of distance between me and John."

"Why is that?"

"You know why."

"Do I?"

I met his brown eyes. "Detective Grey, I promise I won't underestimate you if you don't underestimate me."

He waited a beat, then nodded his head.

"That iNeighbor program is quite something."

"You could say that."

"Provides an interesting timeline."

"That, too, but don't believe everything you read."

Daniel had taken it surprisingly well. In the grand scheme of things, a moment's indiscretion, one that hadn't even been initiated by me, and that I'd shut down almost immediately, didn't seem so life changing, so in need of capitalizing. Not compared to me almost dying, the likely result if the car had tilted left instead of right when it hit the speed bump.

"So," Detective Fowler asked, "when you turned down Pine, what did you see?"

"Besides the sun?"

A ghost of a smile crossed his lips. "Yes, ma'am."

"Cindy was outside of her house, yelling at Ashley. I could hear her all the way up the block."

"Did you see Chris? Or Mrs. Dunbar?"

"No. Were they there? I mean before?"

Detective Grey shrugged. "I can't say."

"Fair enough."

"You were supposed to be in court that morning, weren't you? You and the Dunbars?"

"That's right."

"Interesting lawsuit."

"Isn't it?"

"What's happening with that?"

"I . . . I honestly don't know. I haven't thought about it since that morning. I guess . . . well, I hope we can resolve it."

"Was Mrs. Dunbar the one who wanted to sue?"

"Why would you think that?"

He raised his eyebrows at me. Now I was the one violating our pact.

"Yeah, okay. I guess it was more her than John, but they both agreed to it."

"Was that a source of tension? Between you and Mr. Dunbar, I mean."

"Obviously. That morning was the first time we'd spoken since this disastrous dinner party we had several months ago."

Which was almost true. After the altercation with Ashley, we'd nodded at each other once or twice when we'd both been outside our respective houses, when it couldn't be avoided, and once he'd sent a text asking how I was doing. But we hadn't spoken. Not a word.

"And what about Mrs. Dunbar? Do you think she hates you?"

"It certainly felt like it when I read the lawsuit. But when we were together, it was more like we were constantly on the wrong foot with each other. Like we never connected. I never felt hatred. Anger, maybe, but not hatred."

Detective Grey cocked his head to the side. "That's an interesting way of thinking about it. I'll keep that in mind. Now, you're a writer. You notice things. Set the scene for me, will you?"

"From when I heard Ashley scream?"

"Yes, please."

So, I set the scene.

It was a few minutes before seven. I stood on the corner of Church and Pine and looked directly into the rising sun. I knew it was a bad idea, something stupid I used to do in childhood when I needed to escape for a minute. I'd look long enough for a gray spot to appear over my eyes, then away, leaving my eyes closed, watching the sparkling show. I looked away earlier than I did when I was twelve. I was out of practice. But my vision was blurry just the same.

A car drove by me. A nondescript sedan. I never notice the make of cars. Perhaps I wasn't so observant. I rubbed my eyes as I heard what I thought was a scream. I turned the corner. Three figures stood outside of Cindy's house. Ashley was yelling at her mother, her voice a high pitch. John bolted from his house and ran down the street. I jogged after him.

Cindy's voice carried. "You get inside right this minute, young woman."

"No!" Ashley said. Her arms were crossed, and her feet were planted far apart. She looked like Melly, about to throw a fit. "I *won't*."

"You will. You will, or else."

John arrived at the group.

"Or else what, Mom? You gonna report me to your public? Your perfect little Ashley. You're such a hypocrite." Ashley looked at John. "Do you know what? *She* was the one who brought those cookies to school. The ones that nearly killed Chris all those years ago? I bet you didn't know that, right?"

"Stop it," Cindy said. "Stop talking like that."

She shook her head. "No. You're going to listen to me for once. Because I'm not perfect, okay? I break your stupid rules and you don't even notice because you're too busy spying on everyone else. Trying to make your pathetic life more interesting. Trying to control everything! But you can't control me, Mother. You can't."

Cindy raised her hands over her ears. "Stop it. Stop it."

"Don't talk to your mother like that, Ashley," Paul said as I arrived. I hadn't noticed him there before, but that wasn't so unusual. No one noticed Paul, almost never.

"Stay out of this, Dad. Besides, I know you think she's as crazy as I do."

I felt as if I should look away then, but I couldn't.

"I'm not crazy. How could you say such a thing?"

"Right," Ashley said, "because it's okay to make everyone else's life miserable? To control everyone? That's totally normal? Well, guess what? I'm not a baby anymore. I'm not about to die. And you want to know what I was doing out all night? What Chris and I were doing in the woods? We were f—"

Crack!

Cindy's right hand slapped the side of Ashley's head so hard I saw it turn in my direction.

"What the fuck is wrong with you?" someone said.

Not me.

Heather.

When the police got up to leave an hour later, I felt wrung out, as if someone had taken me by both ends and twisted as hard as they could.

I'd answered every one of their questions, but that didn't mean I hadn't left anything in reserve. I'd caused enough trouble—I could see that now—and there wasn't any point in making things worse.

"This was all a terrible accident," I said, not for the first time. "I know you have to take everything seriously given what happened, but this was a tragedy. Nothing else."

"That's very magnanimous of you."

"It's what I think."

Detective Fowler walked out of the house, but Detective Grey lingered.

"Was there something else?" I asked.

"You should be careful. You may still be in danger."

"I can't believe Heather would be stupid enough to try something now. Not with all the police and cameras around."

Heather was arrested at the airport for violating the terms of the restraining order. But she'd been released on the promise she'd return to Seattle or face jail time. She never explained what she was doing on my street, but I was, amazingly, okay with that. I saw something break in Heather as she helped me with my useless CPR attempts while we waited for the ambulance to come. Whatever bubble of madness Heather had been living in, whatever thoughts she'd been harboring in her head about me, about what she thought I'd done, seemed to seep away with every breath I blew into the limp mouth of the person I was trying to save. When the ambulance arrived and the EMTs pushed me out of the way, I'd tumbled into Heather. We made eye contact, and then I pulled back from her, feeling sick at the thought that she'd touched me.

"Get out of here!" I said.

"Julie, I . . ."

I squeezed the button on my lanyard. "The police are coming."

Her mouth formed an "O," and she seemed to come back to herself.

"I wasn't here to—"

"Just go!"

She tried to speak again, but the wail of an approaching police siren cut her off. She looked left, then right, looking for an exit.

"I'm sorry," she said, then ran away straight up the hill.

"I didn't mean . . ." Detective Grey looked flustered. "Forget it. I shouldn't have said anything."

"You don't think . . . it was an accident. It was."

"Perhaps. Thanks again for your time."

I watched him walk to his car, then shut the door.

"What was all that about?" Daniel asked.

"I'm not sure."

"Maybe there's something we don't know?"

"For a change," I said, and Daniel grimaced.

I found him at the kitchen table a couple of days later at dawn.

I'd woken to find him missing from our bed. I was the restless sleeper, and I could count the number of times I'd woken with him gone on one hand. I listened to the quiet dark. No noise from the kids' rooms, only birds chirping outside, greeting the day. I rose, feeling that sense of precognition I get sometimes, imagining him sitting exactly where I found him, a cold cup of coffee in front of him, his hands flat on the table because he'd tried to push himself back but couldn't quite make it. His hair was a halo of red spikes, his beard two weeks past a trim. I wanted to slip my hand into the frayed collar of his T-shirt and feel the warmth of his skin. Instead, I sat at the table.

"What's going on?" I said, placing my hand over his as I sat next to him. "Can't sleep?"

"Nope."

"Is this my fault?"

"Nope."

"Is your mother okay?"

He shuddered. "It's not that."

"What then, Daniel? This isn't like you."

He pulled his hand away. "I did something bad."

That's the problem with precognition. It's not like a radio station you can tune in to whenever you want. Sometimes you get the feeling something's off without any warning about what it will be. So I had no idea what he was going to say, only that I wasn't going to like it.

"What do you mean?"

"In Tacoma."

"You . . ." I was choking on the words. "You slept with someone?"

"No!" His retort echoed around the room. "Sorry, I didn't mean to be so loud."

"It's okay. Just tell me."

"I'm not sure where to begin."

"What's the first thing that comes to mind?"

"I hired a private detective."

"What?"

"A private detective."

"To do what?"

"To investigate the things that were happening here. To you."

I sat back. The chair rungs dug into my back. "When? When did you do this?"

"A few months ago."

"Why didn't you tell me?"

"At first, it was because I didn't want to get your hopes up. If he didn't find anything . . . I didn't want you counting on him to find a solution."

"And then?"

He tucked his thumbs into his fingers, forming two fists. His hands were chapped, fraying almost. He'd been washing them more than usual lately, trying to wipe the accident away, I thought.

"And then I didn't want you to see the results."

I knew what that meant. "He thought I was doing it?"

"Yes."

"And you believed him?"

"I didn't know what to think. He said that when he checked the electronic stuff, it looked like you'd been the one posting online as Heather."

"What? That's ridiculous."

"Everything tied back to an e-mail address that was created from our IP address."

"But that's exactly what happened last time! She knows how to do that. Or knows someone who will help her. What the hell, Daniel?"

"There was other stuff."

"Such as?"

"He found a bank account. One I didn't know about."

My face burned. "Okay, that's true, but that was only because I was starting to feel uncomfortable about all the money I was making. It doesn't have anything to do with Heather."

"There were payments going to her out of it."

"What?"

"You're paying her money every month."

"I am *not*."

"I've seen the transfers."

I stood up, my heart hammering, adrenaline coursing through me. I grabbed my laptop off the kitchen counter and slammed it down on the table. I pulled up my online bank and entered my password, making sure to let Daniel see me do it, that it was the same password I've used since we've banked online, that he's always known.

The balance was higher than I remembered. I rarely looked at this account. My agent deposited most of what I earned in there directly, and I only transferred money out when I needed it for our joint expenses.

I opened the account and looked through the details for that month. There was nothing I didn't know. I went back a month. Still nothing. But three months earlier, in July, I found a transfer of $5,000 I didn't remember making. And the month before that, another. Going all the way back until January when we were in Mexico and someone was trying to access my e-mail.

"I never made these transfers," I said to Daniel, but I had no idea how I was going to convince him of that.

"I know," he said. "Heather did."

I flopped down in my chair. "Now, I'm completely confused."

"I went a bit crazy when I got that information from the PI. I didn't want to believe it. I felt so guilty, but it seemed like there couldn't be any other explanation."

"Because you didn't know about the bank account."

"That was part of it."

"So what happened? Why do you believe me now? Assuming you do."

He hung his head. "That's why I was in Tacoma. To find out."

"Wait, what? Your mother isn't sick?"

"Not really. She isn't well, but . . . I had to know. I had to find out. I felt like I was going crazy."

"But what would being in Tacoma—oh, no. You didn't?"

"I did. I went to see her. Heather."

"You brought the kids with you when you knew you were going to do that?"

"They were never in danger. I made sure of that."

I told myself to calm down. The kids were fine, and the last thing I needed was another fight in my life.

"What was the point of going to see Heather?" I asked. "Did you think she'd tell you the truth?"

"I didn't know. I thought I could . . . get it out of her."

I felt as if I was talking to a stranger. This wasn't the Daniel I knew. The gentle man who kissed our children's bruises better and was everyone's friend within moments of meeting them. But yet, I also felt grateful he was willing to step so far outside of himself for me. For us.

"And did you?"

"Eventually."

"But how?"

"I can be very persuasive when I want to be."

"What does that mean?"

"I didn't hurt her."

"I know you wouldn't."

"I wanted to."

I reached out for him and he took my hand. I rubbed his raw skin gently.

"I'm not proud of what I did do, though."

"You don't have to tell me."

But he did. How he waited outside her apartment and then followed her inside, rushing her in, scaring the hell out of her. How he'd threatened to harm her if she didn't tell him everything. And it worked. Heather curled into a ball on the floor and cowed like a child about to be beaten, which I gather she had been, more than once. I felt sick for both of them, listening to Daniel, and sicker still about the part I'd played, making him feel as if those kinds of tactics were necessary, the risks he'd taken for me.

"What did she tell you?"

"That she'd broken into our home system. That she managed to get your banking info after she accessed your e-mail. That she'd staged those online profiles to make it look like you were the one writing about yourself."

"What about the crap that was left? The note?"

"She didn't know anything about that. Or the doll, or the calls. She hadn't been here."

"Are you sure she was telling the truth?"

"It doesn't make sense for her to admit to all those other things and not that. Taking that money—that's illegal, right? And I was recording everything. She agreed to that."

"So who was doing those other things?"

"Probably some kids in the neighborhood, like we thought." He looked pained. "Do you forgive me? For not believing you."

"Of course I do."

"Really?"

"It's nothing, Daniel. In the grand scheme of things, it's really nothing."

A sob broke from him. "It's not. It's not nothing."

"You forgave me for John. I forgive you."

"But it's my fault. It's my fault she's dead. If I hadn't gone to see Heather, she never would have come here. And if Heather wasn't there that morning, the accident wouldn't have happened."

The Truth

John

One month ago

The truth is, Heather was there that morning because of me.

I don't know what I thought I was doing when I contacted her. Why I felt like I needed answers to the mystery of Julie. Why it seemed like there was a mystery in the first place.

Julie was a woman. A woman I spent too much time with. A woman I spent too much time thinking about. An unhappy person, mostly. A writer. Someone who lived in her head most of the time. She'd lost a close friend in law school. Maybe she had something to do with that, but I doubt it. More likely, rumors followed her—and others—because people like sensational explanations. A beautiful girl with a bright future drinks too much and smothers herself with a pillow at a party and no one notices? No. A group of clever law students see an opportunity to get away with the perfect crime by killing her right under the noses of two hundred partyers? Perhaps.

Heather had been more than willing to tell me her theories. All I had to do was tell her that Julie had moved across the street from me and had been acting oddly. That I'd read some of Heather's blogs and thought she was on to something.

I think, now, conspiracies appeal to something base in human nature. That was the only explanation I could come up with as I spoke to Heather. But they've never appealed to me. And as she unfurled her conspiracy about Julie and her friends, I felt my body resist. I was wound up at my desk like a tight spring. I kept thinking, *That's ridiculous*. So there were similarities between Julie and her main character, Meredith. So what? So Julie and her friends played something like The Murder Game. What did that prove? So Julie worked for a year as a prosecutor and then quit abruptly. Who could blame her? These weren't clues to a conspiracy. They were, perhaps, signposts of her creative path. She used what she knew to breathe life into her characters. There wasn't anything wrong with that.

And if you treated books like horoscopes, you were sure to see similarities where none existed.

So I told Heather I thought she was wrong, and I hung up, vowing to forget I'd ever spoken to her. Erase her insidious voice from my head.

I should've known she wouldn't let me get off so easily.

It started with an e-mail an hour after I'd hung up on her. And then another. Then texts. Then she called my cell phone until I blocked her number because I'd made the mistake of calling her without hiding it. I couldn't keep her from e-mailing me as easily. I'd block one e-mail address only to have another pop up a few minutes later. She was relentless. After a week of it, I thought about abandoning my e-mail address altogether, though I'd had it for most of my adult life. After two weeks, I did, advising only those closest to me that I'd been attacked by spam. Asking them to keep the new address to themselves. Then she found the e-mail address I'd set up for my company and flooded that. And so on.

Her e-mails began by talking about Julie, her theories, all the things she'd told me on our call spun out and out until they were in outer space. But then they switched to me. Photos she'd found of me online. Photos she'd found of my *family*. How she'd heard something in my voice. She knew I understood her. She thought we were meant to be.

Against my better judgment, I replied to that e-mail.

> You are delusional. There is nothing between us and there never will be. Please leave me alone or I will call the police.

She wrote me a long diatribe in return. I'd used her, she said. Used her to get the information I wanted about Julie, whom I was clearly having an affair with. She had the proof. She attached e-mails between us. Ones she'd intercepted. Flirty exchanges mixed in with perfectly innocent inquiries. Rereading them made my face burn. Not because there was anything explicit. More that reading them all together, the few words that seemed innocent, separated by days, told a different picture. How they'd been leading to something. Increasing in frequency up to the morning Julie and I kissed, then stopped.

I didn't answer that e-mail or any of the others Heather sent. I only hoped she didn't start writing Hanna. Wondering if, *what*, I could tell her to make sense of it all, if Heather did.

Then the e-mails stopped. An hour. Two. A whole day stretched out in silence. I breathed a sigh of relief. Perhaps she'd come to her senses. Or exhausted herself. Or . . . I really didn't care what had happened to her. I was just glad she was gone.

She wasn't.

The day before the accident I received an e-mail that simply said:

> I'll see you soon.

So I was the reason Heather was there that day. She was there to see *me*.

And none of this would have happened if I hadn't been such a fool.

Every night after the accident, those last moments leading up to it replayed as if I was watching a movie projected in my mind. Whether I was asleep or awake made no difference. It was always the same.

It began with me in my house. Becky upstairs. Brad snoring on the couch. Then that scream.

I yelled at Becky to stay where she was, then bolted outside. I saw a jumble of people down the street outside Cindy and Paul's. I ran down the street. Julie was right behind me. Ashley yelled accusations at Cindy, goading her until Cindy snapped and slapped her.

Heather appeared from nowhere and wrapped her arms around Cindy, pinning them against her side. She was shrieking at Cindy. Telling her she shouldn't hurt a child like that. No one should ever hit a child. Ashley was backing up. Away, trying to get out of the tangle Heather and Cindy made. Julie circled them. Our eyes met and she nodded. I took a step forward and put my hands on Heather's shoulders.

"Let her go," I said. "Let her go right now."

Heather thrashed against me, but her grip on Cindy relaxed. Cindy struggled free and fell to the ground. Julie started toward her, then stopped. She looked to Ashley, who was standing in the street, her arms by her side, rigid in shock, a red handprint visible on her face.

"Help her," I said to Julie.

Heather started emitting a noise I can only describe as a growl. Animal. I wrapped my arms around her chest, holding her tighter. She was doughy and smelled sour. Her greasy hair washed over my face.

"Stop it," I said. "Stop it. What's wrong with you?"

Julie ran to Ashley. She stood beside her, wrapping her arm around her shoulders. I blew Heather's hair away. It struck me, as it had the first time I saw them together, how much Julie and Ashley looked alike. They were both in shorts and tank tops—Julie in her running clothes, Ashley in cotton. Each had their brown hair tied up in a ponytail.

Julie said something I couldn't hear over Heather's sounds.

Ashley shook her head, shrugging Julie off.

Heather started thrashing again. Cindy tried to stand.

Julie moved forward. Ashley stepped back, her hands up in front of her as if she was warding off danger.

As the church bells started to gong, I heard the sound of a car engine. Someone driving down the street too fast. It hit the first speed bump with a *whump*.

I couldn't see who was driving.

"Watch it," I yelled over the crescendo of bells. "Get out of the way!"

Julie turned and took a step backward, onto the safety of the sidewalk.

"Ashley!" she cried.

The car hit the second speed bump. It lurched to the side, first right, then left. I dropped my arms and waved frantically.

"Ashley!" Julie said again.

Another bump. An awful *crunch*. Tires squealed.

The car shuddered to a stop. The bells stopped. The car door flung open. The *ding, ding, ding* warning that the keys were still in the ignition filled the awful silence.

The air smelled of burned rubber. And something worse. Something metallic.

We all ran to Ashley, who lay crumpled on the ground.

Heather. Me. Julie.

And Chris.

Today

Julie

6:00 p.m.

I haven't been able to sit still all day.

I was up at my usual running time, earlier even, but all I ended up doing was watching John and Hanna's house, waiting for them to exit. I'd spent many hours doing that in the last two months, particularly during the hours when the twins were at school and Daniel was at work. It's my reward for writing. Perversely, a few days after Daniel's confession, something opened up in me. I cast my old draft aside and started anew. For the last month and a half, I've churned out pages like in the glory days of The Book, 2,500 words a day, most days, sometimes more. My fingers flew over the keyboard and, almost to my surprise, I wrote "The End" yesterday. I even printed the whole thing up to start reading it on paper, my final step before turning it in to my editor.

I couldn't read it this morning. All I could do was watch, anxious, biting my nonexistent fingernails past the quick, checking my watch every five minutes because I had to get to the grand jury. But I'd spent the last two months doing everything I could to avoid being seen by any of them, particularly after Chris was arrested. Today, of all days, I didn't want to break that streak.

It wasn't easy to avoid being seen, living across a narrow street with kids who needed to be taken to school, and groceries that needed to be purchased, and the outside that needed to be visited so I didn't lose my mind. The journalists made it easier. Their constant presence gave me the excuse I needed to lay low, depending on Daniel and Susan and delivery services. I'd leave to run with Sandy under the cover of darkness, once they'd gone home for the night. Daniel didn't want me to run alone, so I hired a trainer who met me two blocks away and ran with me up the path along the embankment.

When I got back from my nightly runs, I read everything I could about the case. I had to remove my MySanity settings to do it, but I felt compelled to understand everything I could about how the penal system worked in Cincinnati.

I learned a lot of things in those hours between ten and midnight, when I'd finally drag myself to bed and into Daniel's waiting arms. For instance, it was the detectives who decided to charge Chris, kindly Detective Grey and his sidekick. They thought Chris ran Ashley down deliberately, upset over the fact that they'd broken up again and that Ashley was keeping time with an older kid, one who'd been a few years ahead of them at school. Their text history told quite a tale, apparently, of manipulation and hurt and some veiled threats from Chris about what he'd do to her one day if she kept pushing his buttons.

Because he wasn't yet sixteen when the accident happened, he was originally put through juvenile court, but the judge, a newly appointed law-and-order type, decided Chris should be tried as an adult. He was released under the care of his parents, with strict instructions regarding where he could go and when.

The grand jury should've been a simple affair. It usually took only an hour or two, a few witnesses and a quick yes or no. When I'd received the summons to testify, I was surprised. I expected to testify at the trial if there was one, but what did they need with me now? I called the prosecutor's office, and the chief was nice enough to answer my questions.

Because Heather was one of the potential witnesses, they agreed to let me arrive at a specific time and come in the back way. My gut might be telling me that Heather had let me go, but my brain—and Daniel's—didn't want to take a risk. An assistant met me at the side door, her hair twisted on top of her head with a pencil through it, and we went up in the elevator with a man in a striped jumpsuit who had the craziest look in his eyes. I squeezed over to the farthest corner and tried not to smell the prison odor that was filling up the small space.

I went into the grand jury room the back way, too, through the employee entrance. I did the best I could recounting the jumble of that day. I'm not entirely sure what I said, whether it made sense, whether it matched up with the others or was its own bizarre tale.

But I was clear about one thing: there was no way this was anything but an accident.

I was unwavering in that belief, even after I was asked, like Detective Grey had asked a few weeks ago, whether I'd seen Chris that day as I ran along Church Street and turned onto Pine. The prosecutor explained why he was asking: they thought Chris had parked his mother's car at the top of the street and waited. Someone had seen him there, but they wouldn't tell me who. So, he hadn't rounded the corner and been blinded by the sun and come unexpectedly up against Ashley; he'd been waiting for her, and then put the car into drive when he saw her in the street.

That was their theory, anyway.

I had another one I didn't share with the grand jury.

Chris hadn't been aiming for Ashley.

He'd been aiming for me.

I'd scarred his face and gotten too close to his father and brought out the worst in Chris, and in Ashley. They were the only candidates for the shit left on my doorstep, and the headless doll and the hang-ups. Perhaps he'd seen some of the e-mails or texts between John and me and assumed the worst. That would explain why he was so upset in the park when he saw us together. Why he'd chosen to run away from Ashley—whom he certainly hadn't been broken up with, not that day—rather than be anywhere near me.

I don't think he thought about what he was doing. I don't think he intended for me to die. I think he was sitting in that car, a half block from his house, because he didn't know what to do. But when he saw me there, trying to comfort Ashley, with his father again, without his mother around, I can understand why he might have slipped the car into gear, wanting it all to stop. And then, an inexperienced driver, he lost control as he struck first one speed bump and then another, hitting the gas instead of the brake, as John had told me, once, that he was prone to do.

That I could believe.

But those detectives, they'd seen so much grief. They'd seen so much hurt inflicted by ones who claimed to love their victims. It was their job to imagine all the possibilities, and to put together a picture from what people admitted and what they did not.

I'm sure Chris hadn't helped himself. That kid was a bundle of secrets, keeping in almost more than he could hold. And while everyone has something to hide, he was driving the car, and a girl was dead, and Cindy, when she came out of a medication fog I had nothing but sympathy for, was out for blood.

I couldn't say all of that to the grand jury, but I did what I could. I told them I'd seen love between Ashley and Chris in the park that day, that he'd run away because he was in trouble, not because they were fighting, that he was a good kid who'd suffered enough. That I hadn't seen him waiting in his car at the top of the street, though I'd been right there, and I would've noticed him. That if they'd been there, if they knew the players involved, they couldn't think anything other than that it was all a horrible mistake. So, please, I said, don't make him suffer any more.

I put all the skill I learned in my year doing jury trials into those last statements, my closing argument, if you will. There's a tie that binds a speaker to the listeners, a thread you can tug if you want to. I turned my head a fraction with every phrase, making eye contact with each member of the jury, and felt that old pull of conviction.

My words might've been simple, but the message underneath was clear: when you're left alone later today to decide the fate of a sixteen-year-old kid, remember my voice, remember my certainty, make it your own.

It was the most I could do, and then I was whisked out the back way and brought to my car. I turned on the GPS and let the robotic voice direct me home. Daniel was there with the twins when I got back, a welcome distraction. And then he gave me one more thing to think about, a proposal of how to change things, a choice he wanted me to make.

I resisted for a moment, but then I agreed. What Daniel was saying made sense, and we have enough money so that it can all be taken care of easily, painlessly even, by others.

At least on the outside.

Now I sit on the window seat while Daniel makes calls. Soon I'll have to get up and help him, which I'll be able to do, wholly and completely, when I know that everything is right. That everything is as it should be.

Headlights cut up the street.

I come up on my knees, watching the scene as if I'm a child seeing Santa appear with his reindeer-driven sleigh.

John's Prius slows and turns into their driveway. He cuts the engine, but there's no sound anyway. They don't immediately exit the car, but their front door bursts open and Becky runs out, tripping down the stairs and ripping open the back door. She's bouncing up and down with excitement, so I know the news must be good. My heart fills with gladness as my hands touch the glass. It's cold, although the room is warm. I shiver.

Becky pulls Chris from the car and hugs him. John and Hanna get out, and they're all hugging. Hanna's crying, Becky's crying, Chris looks bewildered and terribly sad. John looks relieved, and something else I think I recognize because I feel the same way.

Ashamed.

We did this, him and me. From a conversation that went on too long on our cracked street a year ago, all the way up to that horrible morning. If we'd pulled back, kept a neighborly distance, none of this would have come to pass.

None of these lives would have been fractured.

I will have to try to make up for that for the rest of my life.

But at least there's this: Chris is free. The grand jury saw sense and decided to let him go and move on with his life, if he can after what's happened. Across the street, the Dunbars are having, as far as circumstances can allow, a beautiful moment as a family.

And yet, a small part of me is waiting until they all go inside and then trying to find some excuse, some way, to speak to John. To let him know I did my part. To be, perhaps, forgiven.

I want to do this, but I will not.

Instead, I will peel my hands away from the glass and let the curtain fall back into place.

I will turn back to my family and help Daniel start to pack the things we'll need in our new life, far away from here.

I resolve that things will be different next time. Wherever we end up, I'll be more careful, more cautious, about whom I place my faith in. Or I will open my arms to those around me, but I'll make sure my welcoming self is open to those who cannot tear my life apart, who do not pose a threat to my peace, and whose peace I cannot threaten.

Tomorrow, I'll leave John an explanation for all of this. I'll leave him a printout of the novel I'm finishing even now. And he'll read it and understand, or he'll ignore it and forget.

And that will be okay. That will be fine, because he has his family back, and I have mine.

In the end, we were a hurricane wind in each other's lives. But a year from now, we'll already have forgotten each other, life rubbing away at our memories until they fit whatever narrative we need them to.

Only you will be left to judge.

Were we innocent?

Were we guilty?

You tell me . . .

ACKNOWLEDGMENTS

Each novel is its own journey. Some take a long time to come to life; others happen more quickly. I cannot truthfully say that, even after six novels, I know when I start writing a book that it will all turn out okay, or how long it will take. Each day is an adventure, and that keeps things interesting.

One thing that is constant, though, is the circle of support around me. My friends—with a special shout-out to Tasha, Tanya, and particularly Sara, who both supported and taught me much this last year—my family, the wonderful writing community I've become a part of, and you, dear reader.

For the baking of this cake, special thanks go out to:

My sister, Cam, for reading it as I wrote it, and for the last-minute trip to Cincinnati to help make sure I had as many details right as possible. Any errors as to geography, or anything else, are mine alone, a product of my imagination, or I meant to get it wrong. Ahem.

Kathleen McLeary, Lisa Blackmann, Jamie Mason, and Mary Kubica for reading early drafts and providing encouragement. Therese Walsh for constant moral support, and texts that make me laugh.

Shawn Klomparens, Wilma Ring, and my brother-in-law, Scott, for their Ohio knowledge. The members of the Fiction Writers Co-Op for being my watercooler. My mother for checking for typos. And all the writers who've been kind enough to blurb this book—your generosity is humbling.

My agent, Abigail Koons, to whom this book is dedicated, for making it possible for me to have this amazing career. Thank you.

Tara Parsons for acquiring this book, and her general enthusiasm about my writing. Jodi Warshaw for her excellent editorial guidance. The amazing team at Lake Union for continuing to put my books front and center and help me find new readers, including Dennelle Catlette in publicity, and the Lake Union author team. And a special shout-out to Jeff Umbro and Kathleen Zrelack at Goldberg McDuffie for helping get the word out.

My assistant, Carolyn, who clears the decks so I have time to write.

To my amazing grandmother, Dorothy Lillian Delay, who turned one hundred this past January, and who, in the year since my grandfather's death (at age ninety-six, and after almost seventy-five years of marriage), has shown me—again—what real courage and strength of character are. I hope you keep kicking ass for as long as possible.

To Steven Tolbert at the Cincinnati Prosecutor's Office, who was kind enough to take my questions and show me a real grand jury room. Any deviance from real grand jury procedure is either my mistake or a victim of the requirements of plot.

And to my husband, David, who has stuck by me through thick and thin.

I'm writing this note on January 1, 2016. Ten years ago today—on January 1, 2006—I opened a Word file and started writing . . . I didn't know what. Six months later, I had a book, of sorts, something I'd never set out to write, but I'd had a tremendous time doing. That book wasn't good enough to publish, but it opened a door to one that was. Ten years—and six novels later—I'm grateful I listened to myself that day and wrote down what was in my head. Because I did, I've met many people who've become close friends, traveled to places I never would've been, and learned things about myself that might otherwise have been locked away forever.

I can't imagine what the next ten years will bring, and for that I am immensely grateful.

BOOK CLUB QUESTIONS

1. *Fractured* begins with John at his front window, spying on the house across the street. What is it about living in close proximity to someone else that gives people the need to know what is going on in their lives? Have you ever been "caught looking"?

2. Julie and her family initially tried to fit in to their new neighborhood in Cincinnati but were not very successful. Why do you think that is? Was there really something about Julie that was just "off"?

3. What did you think of Cindy? Why does everyone in the neighborhood seem to kowtow to her? What power does she hold over them?

4. When famous people have stalkers, the public sometimes lacks compassion or treats it as a normal side effect of celebrity. Did you feel bad for Julie? Did she "deserve" all that unwanted attention just because she wrote a bestselling novel?

5. Julie began to experience more "stalking" behaviors once she moved to Cincinnati, including prank phone calls, and the mutilation of her daughter's doll. At one point, Daniel thought that Julie was doing these things herself—a sort of Munchausen syndrome with phone pranks instead of faked physical ailments. Did you think Julie was faking it? What do you think of Daniel hiring a private investigator to look into his wife's behavior?

6. What did you think of John's character? He calls himself an "asshole" for having feelings for Julie, and does some questionable things throughout the novel, including coming on to Julie and giving alcohol to a recovering alcoholic. Yet we also see him as a caring father and husband. Is it rare to find characters in novels who are similar to how we are in real life—not all good, but not all bad, either?

7. Throughout the novel we know something tragic has happened, but not to whom or how. What did you think happened prior to the final reveal? What tricks did the author use to make you think that?

8. When Julie's book became successful, she started a secret bank account so that her husband wouldn't feel emasculated by how much money she was making. He was clearly uncomfortable on the vacation they took to Mexico, knowing that he couldn't

have afforded to bring his family there on his own income. Why do you think this double standard persists?

9. Do you think Chris intended to run over Julie that morning? Ashley? Or was it truly an accident? If he had intended to run over Julie, should he still be punished for killing Ashley?

10. People assumed that the main character in Julie's book was based on her, and/or that she had some involvement in Kathryn's death because she wrote a book about something similar. While the old admonition to "write what you know" often holds true, why do we jump to the conclusion that what an author writes about is autobiographical? Is there anything in *Fractured* that you think might have really happened in Catherine McKenzie's life?

Q&A WITH MARY KUBICA

Mary Kubica is the *New York Times* and *USA Today* bestselling author of *The Good Girl* and *Pretty Baby*. She holds a bachelor of arts degree in history and American literature from Miami University in Oxford, Ohio, and lives outside Chicago with her husband and two children.

1. **Julie and John are both the perfect characters to spearhead the novel *Fractured*, though many others play a prominent role. Why did you choose Julie and John to narrate this tale?**

    I liked the idea of showing the same events from two different perspectives, one an insider and one a new-comer. John's voice came to me quickly—the first chapter is the first thing I wrote basically intact, but I always knew that Julie would be the central figure in the book.

2. **Julie is an author, and your inclusion of the fine points of an author's life (meeting daily word counts or stumbling upon a stranger with her book in hand, for example) is spot-on. Is Julie purely a fictional character, or do you find any of your own tendencies in her?**

Julie is purely fictional, but I definitely understand some of the things she's going through. It's always tricky to write about a profession you know well—oddly harder than one you don't, I find—because it's so easy to include too many extraneous details. I wanted to give a glimpse of what it's really like without it being overwhelming.

3. **The plot of *Fractured* is quite complex, with a deep layering of secrets and a nonlinear time frame. How do you go about crafting such an intricate novel? Do you outline your novels in advance?**

I don't generally outline the whole thing in advance. I think of the premise, the end of the book and the twist, the main characters, and then start writing. Plot comes to me in chunks, usually a couple of chapters at a time. For this book, unlike any other I've written, I had to write a short outline because I sold it with the first third and an outline. Then I wrote the book without looking at the outline again. I read it recently—after I finished the book—and was like . . . oh, right, that's what I was going to do!

4. **You do a terrific job of withholding much pertinent information from the reader, thereby piquing our curi-**

osity even more. Did you know all along how the story would end, or did this come as a surprise to even you?

The precise ending is always a bit of a surprise, but no, I always knew what the central ending would be. I think—in this kind of book, in particular—that's necessary. But, then again, I always need to know the end before I start writing.

5. **Knowing you're a native of Montreal, I'm curious as to why you chose Cincinnati as the setting for *Fractured*? Along the same lines, Julie and her family stem from Tacoma, Washington. Have you ever been to the Seattle/Tacoma area? Why did you choose it as the place she's come from?**

My first three novels were all set in an unnamed city. The next two in fictional towns. I like to set myself a challenge with each book, and so, for this one, I decided to set it in a real place. I've spent some time in Cincinnati—my sister's husband is from there, and I attend the wonderful Books by the Banks festival every year—and I like the feel of the city, so that's why I chose it. As for Tacoma, my sister-in-law lives in Dupont, Washington, which is near it and Seattle, so I've spent some time in the area. I wanted a place that had a different feel from the East Coast, so that's why I chose it.

6. **Though you do a phenomenal job of keeping the specifics under wraps, we know early on that a crime has been committed and legal matters ensue.**

How much of your own lawyering background did you rely on to bring the legal elements to life in *Fractured*?

Almost nothing! I practice civil litigation and know next to nothing about the criminal law system in Canada, let alone the one in Cincinnati. However, with the initial help of the Internet, and then a very generous prosecutor, I got to visit the grand jury room and ask a zillion questions. My first research trip!

7. **Children play a prominent role in *Fractured*, from preschool to high school–age. Though you have no children of your own, you do a meticulous job of crafting these characters. Are there children in your life who were the inspiration for Julie and John's kids?**

I have four nephews, aged seven to one (Owen, William, Liam, and Anders), and they are constantly saying and doing things that are both hilarious and insightful. Certainly some of the things the smaller kids say come from hanging out with them. As for the teenagers, I fear I have not quite forgotten what it was like to be one, which is at least useful for writing, if nothing else.

8. **There are characters in *Fractured* I loved, and some I loved to hate. Do you have a favorite? If so, who?**

I have a soft spot for Julie. She means well, but the harder she tries, the more mistakes she seems to make.

9. **You're a full-time attorney and manage to publish a book every year or two. You also run an online book club, generously help promote your fellow authors, and more. I'm so impressed. How do manage your time?**

When it's written out like that, I don't know! Seriously, though, I'm a pretty organized person, and I also don't have kids, so . . . that's my story and I'm sticking to it, though robots might also be involved.

10. **I know you're an avid reader. What types of books are your favorite to read, and are there any novels or authors who inspire your work?**

I read eclectically. I grew up reading detective fiction because there was a lot of it in my house. I read about a book a week: contemporary fiction and some nonfiction, mostly. I try to read all the "big" books; I think it's important, as a novelist, to know what else is out there. I wouldn't say there is any one author who inspires what I write, but I am inspired by great writing in general, whether it be in a book, a song, a TV show, or a movie.

11. **What's next for Catherine McKenzie?**

The Murder Game—the book Julie Apple wrote—is based on a book I wrote almost ten years ago that I keep coming back to. So I decided to release it under her name . . . keep an eye out for it!

ABOUT THE AUTHOR

Photo © 2016 Jason Trott

Catherine McKenzie, a graduate of McGill University, practices law in Montreal, where she was born and raised. An avid skier and runner, Catherine's novels *Spin, Arranged, Forgotten, Hidden,* and *Smoke* are all international bestsellers and have been translated into numerous languages. *Hidden* was an Amazon #1 bestseller and a Digital Book World bestseller. *Smoke* was an Amazon bestseller, a Goodreads Best Book for October 2015, and an Amazon Top 100 Book of 2015.

Visit Catherine online at www.catherinemckenzie.com, on Facebook at www.facebook.com/catherinemckenzieauthor, and on Twitter or Instagram at @CEMcKenzie1.